THE GATEWATCH

THE GATEWATCH

A NOVEL

JOSHUA GILLINGHAM

CROWSNEST BOOKS

Crowsnest Books
www.crowsnestbooks.com

Distributed by the University of Toronto Press

Library and Archives Canada Cataloguing in Publication

ISBN:

Cover design and illustration by Helena Rosova.

Map illustrations by Tiffany Munro.

Typeset in Norse, designed by Joël Carrouché, and Adobe Caslon, designed by Carol Twombly.

Printed and bound in Canada

For Min, who keeps asking for more stories.

◇ CONTENTS ◇

◇ PREFACE ◇

The myths endure.

After countless retellings across continents, despite the translation gaps between languages and cultures, and even against efforts to warp them for nefarious political purposes, the Norse Myths have sailed their way through the centuries. This journey, nearly as incredible as the voyages of Viking explorers like Leif Erikson, is something to celebrate. I find myself distinctly drawn to these stories of the northern gods and goddesses, of their grave power and their great pettiness. Beneath the vivid narrative is a poignant critique of our insatiable desire and our mortal struggle. And myths are not dead things! Every generation reaches back in history to dredge them up and revitalize them in their own way. That is exactly what I hope to achieve with this story.

The Gatewatch began as a simple retelling of a few of my favorite myths, including Thor's journey to Útgarð, Odin's encounter with the giant Vafþrúðnir, and the forging of the treasures of the gods thanks to Loki's meddlesome cunning. In fact, the three central characters in this book are inspired by the three dominant figures in Norse Mythology: Odin, Thor, and Loki. In Gavring the gatekeeper are hints of Heimdal, watchman of Asgard and guardian of the shimmering rainbow bridge between worlds. Keymaster

Signy embodies the archetypally maternal Frigg while the passion and fury of Wyla echoes wrathful Freya, goddess of beauty and war. The dwarves, or *nidavel* as they are called in this book, reflect the portrait painted by Viking skalds and perhaps challenge a few of the tropes associated with dwarves in modern fantasy. The Troll King, an ancient giant from far in the north, is the type of figure Odin or Thor might encounter while wandering across the nine realms. Finally, the trolls cling close to their portrayal in northern folktales: dim-witted and horrible. Leavened with bits of Viking culture gleaned from the Icelandic sagas and sprinkled with hints of Scandinavian folklore, The Gatewatch quickly grew beyond a simple retelling into its final form as an epic fantasy adventure.

Those who have had the fortune of travelling to Norway or Iceland will find certain parts of Torin Ten-Trees' journey familiar. In 2015 my wife and I took a trip to Norway which strongly influenced my vision for the imagined realm of Noros. From the towering rafters of Håkonshallen in Bergen to the gut-wrenching heights of Preikestolen and Trolltunga, Norway is a place that, once visited, remains forever carved into the mind. Sore and sunburnt from our hike across the snow shelves around Trolltunga (if you think a sunburn on the beach is bad then double it – that's what nine hours of hiking across the snow in a t-shirt and shorts will do!) we returned to Canada via Iceland. There we had the distinct pleasure of recovering in Iceland's famous and admittedly touristy Blue Lagoon which, if you've been there, will also be a recognizable influence.

To you, the reader, *tusen takk* (a thousand thanks). Your purchase of this book has spurred the constant cycle of regeneration that the Norse Myths must undergo to stay vital and relevant. And know that the adventures of Torin Ten-Trees are not over! I am well into writing the sequel to The Gatewatch and hope to share it with you in the near future. However, reviews are the lifeblood of book series and so if you enjoy this story I humbly ask that you invest a few minutes of your time to leave a review online. I sincerely hope that the story of Torin Ten-Trees stokes your adventurous spirit, inspires you to be brave, and kindles your imagination.

Sincerely,

Joshua Gillingham

October 9th, 2019 (Leif Erikson Day)

◇ PRONUNCIATION GUIDE ◇

Certain words in this book are based on Norwegian and Icelandic, both descendants of Old Norse in which the myths were originally told. These words are not always direct translations but are meant to give the text a phonetic flavor that is distinctly Scandinavian. However, certain consonant combinations that roll smoothly off the tongue in these languages are phonetic tripping hazards by the rules of English. In words like *fjell/fjall* (Norwegian/Icelandic – 'mountain') the 'j' makes a 'y' sound. Instances of 'skj', 'sk', or 'sj' should be pronounced 'sh' as in *skjold/skjöldur* (Norwegian/Icelandic – 'shield'). The combination 'kj' is pronounced 'ch' as in *kjekk* (Norwegian – 'handsome'). For ease of reading I have altogether avoided the use of 'æ', 'þ', 'ð', and any letters with diacritics (e.g. 'ø' or 'å').

◇ A NOTE ON VERSE FORMS ◇

No consideration of Viking Age culture is complete without a mention of their favorite pastime: poetry. Viking poets, or *skalds*, used specific poetic forms to craft epic tales which were told in the fire-lit halls of ancient Scandinavian and later recorded in writing. I have adapted some of the rules of skaldic verse in an attempt to capture the force and rhythm of the original forms. This adaptation, not as viciously rigid as *dróttkvætt* (court meter), bears similarities to more forgiving forms such as *málaháttr* or *fornyrðislag* where the emphasis is on internal rhyme and alliteration rather than end rhyme. The adapted verse form used in this book is based on three rules:

1. Every line must have exactly six syllables.

2. Every odd line must contain *full rhyme* (e.g. sail/whale) while every even line must contain *half rhyme* (e.g. wind/land).

3. Every pair of lines must contain three cases of **alliteration**, twice in the odd line and once in the even line (e.g. '**wr**ong' and '**r**ing').

As a demonstration of the form and as an incantation for the telling of tales, I offer these verses:

Flee the frigid *sea*storm
Foul and deadly *howl*ing
Here *a* while *lay* **a**nchor
All *your* troubles leave *there*

Come shed your *cloak soak*ed through
Cast frosty helm aside
Keep sharp *swords* **s**afely *stored*
Guests here *scarce* need a blade

Now *light* logs to *bright*en
Longhouse d*im* and gl*oo*my
Let *long* flames grow *strong*er
Like *red* wolves *wood* licking

Fetch *more* **f**urs *for* comfort
O'er cedar benches **f**old
Wr**a**p *thick* hides 'r**o**und you *quick*
Be **r**id *of* this *grave* chi**ll**

Bring *here* **b**eer in barrels
Fill every horn **b**rim-*full*
Also *fine wine* **a**nd mead
Till throats *are* dry no *more*

Foul **w**inds of **w**inter *howl*
Harsh seas *slosh* icy **w**aves
Yet let them yonder rage
Now **y**ou m*ust* but l*ist*en

GATEWATCH

TUNNELS

1

◇ AS⟨ENT ◇

THE MIST ON THE MOUNTAIN settled low as the damp morning chill turned to drizzling rain. Three figures made their way through the fog and up a narrow mountain pass on horseback. From under the hood of his dew-drenched, coal-grey cloak, each one watched his white breath swirl and rise before it joined the surrounding mist.

One of the dim grey figures coughed violently and yanked his horse to a halt. With frozen fingers he fumbled for a sip of firemead. Finding his flask empty, he tore it off the strap and hurled it far into the mist. "Damn this cold."

"Damn this fog," said another. He stopped close behind, drew out a flask, and tossed it to his companion. "And damn these stinking horses."

The leading figure, now thirty paces ahead, tugged gently the reins. As his horse turned to face the others, a swirl of fog danced around its ankles. He lifted his hood and squinted. Even from such a short distance they were hardly visible. However, despite the foul weather, he could hear the click of every buckle, clasp, and hoof beat echo between the flat rock faces.

"As for the cold and the fog, I'm afraid there isn't much I can do about that. However, as far as horses go, you are certainly welcome to walk."

The trailing figure gargled the last of the firemead and gulped it down. "And damn you, Torin Ten-Trees!" The other two laughed and soon all were on their weary way once again.

The airy cliffs of Norhaven were far behind them now. The soft rush of wind over the fields around Jarl Einar Ten-Tree's wood-fired hall had long since given way to the towering trees of Stagwood Forest. Then came the River Noros which cut through the hills, its rushing waters as quick and strong as a rugged stallion. For a few days they had followed the river, often stopping to rest at shanty inns and thatched-roof villages. Now it had been two days since they had left those rushing waters to start the slow, steady ascent up Shadowstone Pass. Every hour since the air had grown colder, the rocks rougher, and the trees scarcer.

Torin passed both reins to his right hand so that he could draw his cloak together with his left. As he did a trickle of water rushed down the front of his hood and splashed onto his exposed hand. The back of his cloak had long since soaked through and now weighed on his shoulders, icy cold and as heavy as chain mail. His woven pants stuck to his skin and both his boots were beginning to fill up with frigid mountain rain.

He and his two companions had spent the previous night in a shallow cave at the bottom of Shadowstone Pass. Now he fondly recalled the roar of the fire, the last great chunk of salted pork, and the bitter malted ale. These were all luxuries whose weight they could not afford on the steep ascent. In just a few short hours, those comforts had come to seem as far off as his father's hall.

As the path levelled off, Torin hoped they had reached the crest, but soon it began to climb again, this time much steeper than before, up and up into the mist. The jagged stones grew sharper and at times the path became so narrow that Torin's boots would scrape against rocks along the edge. Even the horses, sure-footed as any, started to slip and stumble.

The companion who trailed farthest behind now coughed again then cleared his throat. "It's a wonder any survive the journey up Shadowstone Pass to defend Gatewatch. Who would have the strength to fight trolls after this ascent?"

The second companion laughed. "Grimsa, it seems we should have asked your mother to pack along some warm milk and sugar to soothe you. Though, lacking her, perhaps you could play the part, Torin?"

"Honestly Bryn, I don't envy his mother," Torin said, "nor do I envy his horse. If that steed's spine isn't crooked from his weight its ears must soon be deaf from his whining."

"By Orr and all the gods, Torin Ten-Trees, I'll knock your brains out if we ever make it over these damn mountains!"

"Though wit has long abandoned you, your brawn is never in short supply Grimsa. I'll give you that," said Bryn.

"Bryn, you twig-legged, spindly, sparrow-minded twat, remember that I'll have to bash my way through you to get to Torin on this narrow path."

"I give you the last of my firemead and this is what I get in return? I suppose to lend to a bear and expect honey in return is a fool's mistake."

Grimsa sighed and growled as he often did whenever he had exhausted his best insults. "Aye, fools you are. Both of you. Soaked from head to toe and still giggling like a pair of tavern maids. How I have offended the gods to deserve friends like you I can't say." Bryn and Torin laughed as they continued up the winding trail.

At midday the air was thinner and the glittering frost that glazed the dark rock faces started to melt. Though the fog was heavy they could faintly see the sun, now at its pinnacle in the sky above. Patches of snow beside the path shone when the dim light broke through while the rest of the light fell into the empty spaces between the black boulders. Off the side of the trail, Torin thought he saw shapes like snakes sliding through the stones. He shook his head and kept his eyes fixed on the path ahead.

Then Torin heard a strange noise close behind him. He turned in his saddle and saw Bryn's long slender nose sticking out from under a soaking hood as his teeth chattered in the cold. It seemed they all needed some distraction from the miserable trail.

Torin called back to his companions. "Which of us do you think will be the first to slay a troll?"

"I'll be the first, no doubt," Grimsa said, "though that should hardly be a surprise. We Jarnskalds are born troll hunters. My father slew eight during his time in The Gatewatch and my older brother five."

Torin chuckled and shouted through the mist. "You need more than strength to kill a troll. You need a keen eye and a quick wit."

Bryn whistled and pretended to pull a bowstring. "A keen eye have I and a sharper arrow. While you two are being smashed to bits I'll be up in a tree raining fire from above."

Grimsa snorted and shook his head. "Arrows won't pierce a troll's hide. It is as thick as mail. Nothing but a long, sturdy, goose-necked axe will do. I doubt you can even lift one!"

"Ha! We'll see about that," Bryn said. "What I know is that accuracy is more important than force. My grandfather used to say that every troll had a weak spot. If you can find it, and you're quick, you need only a knife."

"Well my uncle, who, mind you, has killed no less than ten trolls single-handedly, has told me plenty of stories and none of them involved killing a troll with the prick of a pin."

Torin looked back at Grimsa and grinned. "Ten trolls? When you talked about your uncle last night it was eight trolls, same as your father. He must have been busy to have slain two more in that time."

Grimsa's face flushed red and he threw up his hands. "Eight, ten, what does it matter? The point is that trolls are thick-skinned, stone-headed, bloodthirsty beasts."

Bryn twisted around in his saddle and smirked at Grimsa. "Now that you say that it occurs to me that perhaps you are descended from a troll. That would explain a lot!"

Torin laughed. "None of us have even seen a troll! But enough banter, let's put some weight on this. I propose that we three agree to a pact: whoever kills a troll first the other two shall keep him *two drinks in hand til he can no longer stand.* Agreed?"

Grimsa perked up for the first time that morning. The thought of mead, ale, or wine always cheered him up. "Agreed!"

"Of course!" Bryn said, "If you two are really feeling so generous toward me, how can I refuse?"

Another gust of wind brought with it soaking sheets of mountain rain and the mood soured again. With this turn came memories of relatives and friends who had been killed fighting trolls and morbid thoughts of how they too could soon be troll fodder. For a long while they continued to climb in miserable silence.

"Stop," Bryn said. He yanked on his reins and held up his hand. "Listen."

Grimsa's horse sputtered and clicked its hooves against the stone for a moment more before there was silence. All three companions felt a swell of tension in their shoulders and each strained his ears for any sound. Dancing across the icy rocks came a melody, quick and haunting, which chilled their already icy bones. A gang of voices, low and terse, filled the empty air.

> *Ruby rare with blood-red gleam*
> *Amethyst and emerald green*
> *Ammolite with rainbow swirl*
> *Obsidian the night-black pearl*

Gold all fair with sun-bright hue
Silver just like drops of dew
Copper filled with fiery glow
And iron to dig deep below

Bleed the earth as dry as bone
Til we've broken every stone
Til the secret depths are known
And every treasure's safe at home

Fifty paces ahead the singing band stopped abruptly. A low rumble followed by a sudden silence signaled that they had been spotted. Bryn and Grimsa looked to Torin and he nodded sternly.

Torin called out into the mist. "Hail dwarves, *nidavel* of the mountain! We bring greetings from the House of Einar Ten-Trees, Jarl of Norhaven and kin to King Araldof Greyraven."

For a moment Torin's words hung unanswered in the cloud of fog. Then a low grunting voice replied. "Hail *madur*, kinfolk of the mighty king! We are servants of Mastersmith Ognir. Approach!"

Grimsa growled. "Cave-dwellers. Just our luck."

Bryn motioned him to hush. "Quiet, Grimsa! Let's not offend needlessly." He raised his hand over his brow and squinted at the figures far out in the mist. "How many times have I dreamed of meeting the *nidavel* of the mountain?"

Torin shook his head at both of them, then flicked his reins and moved forward. Bryn and Grimsa followed, the latter with a hand over the hilt of his axe.

Soon the troupe came into view: six dwarves, or *nidavel* as they called themselves. In pairs they bore long wooden chests which were each supported by two wooden poles that rested on their shoulders. Each of the *nidavel* smoked a long pipe through his bristled grey or black beard and wore a dark blue cloak coated in wax to shield against the rain. None spoke, but each one eyed the three companions intently.

"Greetings," Torin said. "My name is Torin, son of Jarl Einar Ten-Trees. This is Grimsa, son of Gungnir Jarnskald, and this Bryn of Clan Foxfoot. We are on our way to Gatewatch."

The *nidavel* that led the troupe chuckled, his voice thick with a rich baritone timbre. "We know your business, young Ten-Trees. Why else would young *madur* wander these forsaken paths?" The rest of the troupe laughed among themselves, which sent puffs of pipe-smoke swirling into the air.

"Very well. By what name should I call you?"

"Call me Drombir, young Ten-Trees."

"And your business?"

"Does our business concern you, young Ten-Trees?"

Grimsa's red beard bristled and his nostrils flared. "We are men of The Gatewatch! The business of all who travel through Shadowstone Pass is ours, cave-dweller!"

Torin feared that Grimsa had caused offence but once again the troupe snickered. Grimsa's face flushed nearly as flame red as his beard when Drombir continued. "Not a member of The Gatewatch yet, young bear-cub. But you may be soon and there is no harm where there is no secret. We are merchants travelling to the city of your cunning king, Araldof Greyraven."

Bryn's eyes widened and he took a step toward the *nidavel*. "Chests full of jewels?"

Now uproarious laughter rose from the troupe and one *nidavel* almost dropped his pipe. "No, young *madur*, jewels and precious stones are the pursuits of idle men. What use would Araldof the Greyraven have for these? No, these are all fine weapons and artifacts forged by Mastersmith Ognir himself."

"Very well," Torin said, "we are weary of the road. How far to the top of the pass?"

"Not far at all, young Ten-Trees, not if you walk." Drombir furrowed his brow and shook his head. "But those horses might never make it." The other *nidavel* said nothing but nodded with enthusiastic agreement.

Bryn frowned and narrowed his eyes. "What do you mean by that, Master Drombir?"

"It is well known to all those in Gatewatch that rockslides often make the way impassable for horses. Why, just this morning we traversed a fall which no horse could navigate. Even we, *nidavel* of the mountain, found it a nuisance to cross." Again the *nidavel* nodded to each other with vigour.

Torin shifted uneasily in his saddle. "Speak your mind, Drombir."

"It seems to me that your horses will soon be nothing but a hindrance. We, on the other hand, could make use of such strong beasts to haul our heavy chests down the mountain."

Grimsa laughed. "Ha! A *nidavel* trick. I'd expect as much from these jewel-hoarding mushroom munchers."

Bryn scratched his chin and tilted his head. "Perhaps. Or perhaps not."

Torin sighed. Since they stopped moving, his joints had stiffened and now a monstrous hunger clawed at his stomach. A fog like that around the horse's hooves began to fill his mind. Worse still, the sun was now clearly past its highest point and would soon descend toward the horizon. According to his father's description, they should be very close to the top of Shadowstone Pass. Besides, he knew full well what a hinderance the horses would be if there really was a fall.

"Very well, Drombir, but I should expect you mean to trade."

"Of course, Master Ten-Trees," Drombir said, "and fairly no less. The Gatewatch protects all who live east of the mountains, not just *madur*."

Grimsa leaned toward Torin. "You don't mean to strike a deal with these *nidavel*?"

Bryn shook his head and threw up his arms. "Grimsa, you blustering oaf! What use will our horses be if the trail is blocked? We'll have to leave them behind and then they are completely useless to us."

Torin eyed each of his companions for a moment, narrowed his eyes, and then leapt off his horse. Bryn and Grimsa also dismounted. He walked up to the *nidavel* whose long nose came up only to his elbows. "What sort of trade do you propose, Drombir?"

Drombir stroked his beard slowly then glanced up. He fingered an old leather coin purse as he inspected each horse. His eyes moved back and forth as he made his calculation. At last the *nidavel* shook his head and threw up his hands. "No, no, that would never do." Then he paused and held up a single finger. "Wait, what about our wares?"

At this, Drombir's whole company erupted in a flurry of strange words, *nidavellish* as far as Torin could tell. Some nodded with such eagerness that their hoods fell back exposing long braids of coal-black hair. Others shook their heads with utter indignation, wet beards waggling with fury. Torin, Grimsa, and Bryn all took a large step back as the *nidavel* squabbled.

"Quiet! Quiet!" Drombir said, "I have made my decision." Immediately the troupe stood silent. "We will give to you and your companions one item each from our chests so that they stay evenly weighted."

"A slimy mold-ridden trinket for a horse? I'd have to be three days into the firemead to act such a fool," Grimsa said. "Besides, the sun is not getting any lower in the sky. Torin, enough of this. Let's go!"

Torin saw Bryn's wide eyes fixed on the chests. "*Nidavel* crafted wares forged by a mastersmith? That is a kingly prize." He turned toward Grimsa and punched the hulking man in the arm. "You could buy a stable full of horses for even one of these treasures you barrel-headed boar!" Grimsa, neither moved nor afflicted by the blow, simply growled.

Torin looked at Bryn and Grimsa then shrugged. "Well, it's the old way then."

"You know my vote," said Grimsa.

Bryn nodded. "Mine as well."

Torin eyed the chests then scanned the eyes of each *nidavel*. Drombir and those in favour looked him squarely in the eye with an unblinking gaze as hollow as a cavern. Those opposed pulled their hoods down over their noses and smoked their long wooden pipes with angry puffs. Torin's looked back to the chests, intricately decorated with inlaid silver and ornately carved.

"Drombir, we accept your offer."

Bryn grinned, sighed, and shook out his arms. Beside him Grimsa groaned and sneered then stomped back toward the horses. With quick, angry movements he began to untie his gear.

Drombir motioned to his companions and they promptly brought the three chests forward. "Very well, young Ten-Trees, very well. Which of you shall choose first?"

Bryn stepped forward and inspected each chest thoroughly. "I had a book once on *nidavelish* inscription. I wore the pages thin until I had memorized each word. I believe the word on the lock here is 'River'."

Drombir chuckled and his thick eyebrows shot up in surprise. "Very good! Few are the *madur* that can read our language."

"And this one," Bryn said, "this inscription either says 'Mountain' or 'Sky'."

"In our language they are the same word young *madur*. The jeweled heights of our caverns are the sky and stars above us."

Grimsa rolled his eyes.

"And this last chest, I do not recognize the inscription on the lock."

"This is the inscription for 'Peak' or for 'Spear'," Drombir said, "It is told that long-ago giants in a realm beneath the earth, below even the *nidavel*, threw spears at the sky for sport. Where their spear-heads stuck is where we see mountains today."

"Peak or Spear." Bryn mouthed the word silently and committed it to memory.

Grimsa heaved his belongings over his back with a grunt. "Are you done drooling over those moldy old chests? Choose one already and let's be off."

"Assuming no one else has a preference I'll choose Mountain," said Bryn, "which is also Sky." He tilted his head toward Drombir who smiled and nodded back.

Torin turned to his disgruntled companion. "Which one do you want Grimsa?" Grimsa spat over his shoulder. Torin shook his head and sighed. "Alright, then I'll choose River."

"And that leaves you with Peak or Spear, Grimsa," Bryn said, "Enough waiting. Let's open the chests!"

From deep within the folds of his cloak Drombir drew out a chain with three keys, each as ornately decorated as the chests and with matching inscriptions. One by one he opened the chests. Each one glowed with an eerie golden light in the wisps of fog.

Any hesitation that Torin felt earlier melted away when he approached the gleaming treasure. Inside the carved wooden walls lay all manner of weapons and finery. A gold-hilted dagger, a curved sword, a thin axe-head, a silver arrow, a jeweled pendant on a chain, a glistening ring, an eagle-crested armband, a shining helm, a coat of thin chain-mail, and a long, jagged spearhead.

"You would trade one of these items for a horse? Each of these looks like a king's treasure. Surely you are not telling the whole truth."

Drombir laughed from deep in his belly. "These? Ha! They are as common to us as moldy boots. Mastersmith Ognir's forge never cools. In a constant churn of burning coals, swirls of grit-black greasy smoke, he crafts such tools and weapons as no *madur* ever could. He knows the secrets of the fire, how to stoke the embers and how to make the metal sing. He knows ancient runes and spells by heart, he even sings them in his sleep! Choose wisely young *madur*, for you will find no such things made in your humble smithies."

Torin's eyes wandered from the sword to the helm to the spearhead. His gaze moved along the ornate lines of inlaid gold and silver which formed *nidavellish* inscriptions or other-worldly figures.

From his chest, Bryn drew out a knife with a braided leather grip inlaid with swirls of silver. He tested it in his hand. "It is as light as a blade of grass."

"That blade is called *Isnif*, or Ice-Blade in your tongue," Drombir said. "A peculiar item this one. It must be bound by blood, a few drops on the base of the blade should do. Once bound it can never be turned on you in battle or harm you in any way. If the blade is thrust into you or slashed at your skin it will simply melt leaving nothing but a splash of water. However, to your foes it is as sharp and as deadly as the keenest blade."

"And that's why it is called Ice-Blade? Because it melts?"

Drombir seemed pleased at Bryn's enthusiasm. "Precisely. Is this your choice then, Master Bryn?"

"Yes, Master Drombir, I will take *Isnif*."

"A very good selection. May it strike faster than a serpent!"

Torin continued to gaze at all the items in the chest before him. He did not usually take an interest in trinkets of gold and silver but these were distinctly beautiful pieces. He had heard of the entrancing goldlust, or *gulthra*, in songs and tales but it did not come to his mind just then. With vivid detail he imagined cutting swaths through the troll-horde with the curved sword, or wearing the golden helm as he entered his father's hall, or launching the spearhead into a frenzied battle. Each object seemed to inspire another fantasy in his mind, each more spectacular than the one before.

"Tell me Drombir, what is the name of this spearhead?"

Drombir peered into the chest. "That spearhead is called *Skrar*, or Screamer. Like a hawk it soars over the sea of swords and screams a war cry that shakes the stoutest foes. Its jagged tooth strikes like the sharp talons of an eagle."

Grimsa laughed. "Ha! Such fools. He must be making this all up."

Bryn was too enamoured with his blade to take any notice of Grimsa's scoffing and Torin was entranced. "Then I will take *Skrar*."

"It is yours. May it strike a troll-king dead." Drombir bowed ceremoniously as Torin picked up *Skrar*. Torin tucked it away in his cloak.

Grimsa pounded his head with his fists. "What fools! Have neither of you ever heard of *gulthra*, the gold lust? It has you both sick as star-struck lovers!" Both Torin and Bryn ignored his ranting and inspected their treasures. "Bah! Your eyes ogle and you are practically drooling. But I am not as feeble-minded as that. I will take this! For if I have fools for friends then what comfort can I have but drink?" He reached for Drombir's sash and ripped off a plain looking cup of dull metal.

Before the shattered metal links which had held Drombir's cup hit the rocky path, five small but sturdy bows had been cocked and drawn. Each one, held in stone-still silence, was aimed directly at Grimsa's head.

Torin started out of his stupor then jumped in between Grimsa and the cocked arrows. He could see from Grimsa's broad stance that he would not surrender the cup. "Everyone stay calm! Master Drombir, please forgive our friend. He is a stubborn fool."

Drombir crossed his arms. His eyes were wide and his lips tight. For brief moment, Torin thought the *nidavel* might give the order to fire. However, Drombir looked once again at the horses and shook out his shoulders. "Very well you brazen bear, if you are such a fool to take a common cup over a kingly prize so be it." The *nidavel* lowered their bows then muttered and grumbled among themselves as they rushed to grab the horses. Drombir hushed them and soon each of the mounts was loaded with one of the chests.

"To you, Torin Ten-Trees and Bryn Foxfoot, may many caverns rich with wonder open wide before you. To you, bear cub, may many rocks fall down upon your stubborn head!"

With that, Drombir was off and the *nidavel* began their song again, the tempo increased as they were no longer laden with the chests.

> *Drops of honeyed amber find*
> *And diamonds of the rarest kind*
> *To Ognir then the treasure bring*
> *And watch him forge a magic ring*
>
> *Coats of mail and axes broad*
> *Steel plate and iron rod*
> *Helms in forms of dragons cast*
> *Spears and arrows sharp as glass*
>
> *Bleed the earth as dry as bone*
> *Til we've broken every stone*
> *Til the secret depths are known*
> *And every treasure's safe at home*

As soon as the *nidavel* were out of sight Bryn heaved a sigh of relief. "Well Grimsa, thanks to you we were nearly slain before we even reached the top of Shadowstone Pass! What a story that would have made." Grimsa stuffed the cup inside his cloak and grinned.

For some time, each companion was content with silence, having become weary of the others. Then once again, though it seemed impossible, the path steepened. As they walked, Torin watched for any sign of the rockslide Drombir had mentioned but saw none. He fingered *Skrar*, concealed in the folds of his cloak. If he could ever bring himself to sell it, he might get twenty good horses for the price it would fetch. Over and over in his mind he imagined casting it into a horde of trolls, striking one dead and scattering the others. Grimsa's words about *gulthra*, the goldlust, came to his mind but he dismissed them. Surely such glory was worth trading a few old horses for. So, on they climbed for what seemed to be a very long time as the shouldered packs weighed heavy upon their aching backs.

2

◇ ARRIVAL ◇

OUT OF THE MIST, two pale peaks emerged, sharp and jagged like gigantic teeth. Between them lay a field of ash-black rubble full of awful stone faces, troll faces, which emerged then disappeared under each wave of sweeping fog. Grimaces and sneers framed by broken sets of uneven teeth littered the yawning gap between the mountains. And bones, a terrible number of bones. Many of these were scattered among the rubble and few were not either splintered or snapped clean in half. It was hardly safe to step, Torin thought, except on the narrow path that snaked around the larger mounds of rock and bone. Soon the shivering companions could see nothing of what lay ahead or behind, just the mountain peaks above the haunting debris.

In the eerie light of dusk, Torin stopped and, with a reverent shudder, recited a verse. On hearing the first line both Bryn and Grimsa joined in with the steady pulsing rhythm of much-practiced recitation.

> *Over rivers raging*
> *Through rugged forest trod*
> *Mighty host most valiant*
> *All, for war, made ready*

To Gatewatch through the pass
There in between pale peaks
Arrived to drive at last
All threat of trolls from home

Sunset done, dusk settled
Dark shapes stirred, rocks shifted
In gloom loomed figures great
Long grey silence breaking

Horrid Troll-King howling
All his dread host calling
Trolls like thunder rolling
Grim-faced rushed to maul them

Beoric he stood bravely
Gathering scattered brothers
Shield sisters yielding
Soon all round him rallied

Slashing, Bashing, Breaking
Battered white bone shattered
Screaming, red blood streaming
All night sharp steel edge sang

Dawn drew near to breaking
Troll-King desperate fighting
Saw first light bright shining
All trolls turned to hard stone

Eyes by red rays blinded
Troll-King reeling stumbled
Quick leapt Beoric boldly
Bearing wrathful death strokes

This he then swore sternly
No troll shall thereafter
Between pale peaks be seen
If kin of his prove brave

Long sang they mourning songs
Vict'ry, sweet yet bitter
Still longer did that throng
Linger as their dead burned

The last word hung in the air as it echoed off the rocks then faded to nothing. The tale of the origins of the Gatewatch lifted their dampened spirits and the sight of Shadowstone Pass left their eyes open wide in awe.

"How many men and women have walked through Shadowstone Pass never to return?" said Bryn.

Torin swallowed, his throat dry. "Too many. It is a great and terrible thing to behold."

Grimsa itched his arms at a nervous pace. "The presence of the dead is strong here."

"To think, no troll has passed through here in over one hundred years."

"And by my life that won't change on my watch," Torin said.

"And mine."

"And on mine."

Bryn reached into his cloak. "I saved a little something for when we reached the top of Shadowstone." He produced a small flask of firemead and uncorked the top. "Gods willing we'll all pass by here again someday. But if not, here's to you, Torin Ten-Trees, my finest friend. And to you, Grimsa, the most loyal and stubborn man I've ever known."

Grimsa was pleased, in part because of the flattering toast but more because of the firemead. "Aha! And to you, Bryn. You're the slyest Foxfoot I've ever met."

Torin nodded. "I think of you two as brothers. Let's keep watch for each other and never let any one of us fall in battle against the trolls if by life we can help it."

"If by life we can help it," Bryn and Grimsa said together.

Just as Bryn raised the flask to take a draught, Grimsa stopped him. "Wait, Bryn, let's have this toast in a more appropriate vessel." From his pack, he pulled out Drombir's goblet. It was plain except for a few crude etchings but was large enough to feel weighty as any cup used to toast health and brotherhood should be. Bryn nodded and poured the firemead into the flask.

With the goblet raised Bryn hailed them. "Brothers!" With that he took a sip and passed it on to Grimsa.

"Brothers!" Grimsa said. He took a somewhat larger gulp. Torin did the same.

As the goblet was still not empty, they passed it around and toasted again. Still, it held more firemead. They toasted a third time.

Torin wiped his lips and felt a bit of lightness in his head. "I am impressed that you hauled all this firemead up the mountain."

Bryn took another gulp, much larger than the last one. "It did not seem this heavy. As I think of it now, the flask did not seem so big."

Grimsa, cup in hand, stopped before taking another sip. He looked inside with squinted eyes then opened them wide. "By the gods, it doesn't look like we've had even a sip!"

Torin and Bryn both leaned over to see. It was as Grimsa had said. A devilish grin lit up Grimsa's face before he gulped down as much firemead as his belly could hold. His companions watched him, their jaws open wide, as he took gulp after gulp. When he finally stopped to catch his breath, all three of them looked in the cup. The firemead had barely gone down at all.

Grimsa's laugh rumbled over the field. "Ha! Treasure of treasures! Who would have known? It is just like the legends! An
ocean of firemead held here in my hands."

Bryn shook his head in disbelief. "A bottomless vessel? Then
there really is magic in the *nidavel* crafts. The gods keep Mastersmith Ognir and dutiful Drombir!"

Torin chuckled and took another sip. "No wonder Drombir
was so foul-faced at losing this crude cup. My father used to say
that the *nidavel* hid their rarest magic in their plainest wares. It
seems you were the sharp stick and we were the blunt ends, Grimsa!" By that time, Bryn had taken another healthy swig and Grimsa once again guzzled the firemead as fast as he could.

Grimsa's words slurred together and a little tear welled up in
his eye. "This has been both the most miserable and the most joy-
ous day of my life! Now I wish I had snatched Drombir's food
satchel as well. Ha!"

All three companions stood there some time laughing and
passing the goblet. The carved stone faces they found so haunting
before now became almost comical, caricatures of people they had
known.

"That fat, howling face! It's just like my cousin, Leif!" Grimsa said, "He was always whining at the slightest bump or bruise.
And there! That scolding grimace of my grandmother. Mighty Fyr
keep her. If she were here, she would beat me black and blue with
her old tree-root cane."

Torin pointed a ways up the field. "That one with the ears! Yes,
those big flapping ears. Do you see it?"

Bryn shrieked when he saw it. "Erik the night watchman! It
is a perfect portrait! How many times did we try to sneak out at
night only to be heard by those bat-like ears?"

"A hundred times, my friend, a hundred times."

Torin and Bryn toppled over in laughter while Grimsa swayed
precariously. The great man took the final sip in several large gulps

before he himself crashed down beside them. It was some time before their laughter faded and they fell silent.

Now the sky had cleared and the sun had almost set. On the horizon, stars appeared, and below them were all the forested hills they had so arduously crossed. The River Noros snaked all the way back to the glistening ocean which could just be seen on the edge of the orange horizon. A warm breeze from down in the valley wafted over the companions and for a moment the trials of their ascent were forgotten. One by one, Torin identified the constellations, just as his father had taught him. The heady firemead, the soft breeze, and the comforting splay of colours on the horizon as the sun set, filled his senses to the brim.

"Just a moment's rest," Torin said, "I'll just close my eyes for a minute then we'll be off." And with that, they all fell fast asleep with no roof but the stars overhead.

◊ ◊ ◊

Torin woke to the sound of a scream.

He sat up with a gasp and felt his heart beat hard in his throat. The piercing sound still rang in his ears. He leapt to his feet but fell over, still too intoxicated to stand. A terrible dry rasp clung to his throat and his vision swirled. He stood again and then tumbled over, this time onto a shard of bone which scraped his hand. He rolled over, away from the jagged bone, only to bash his ribs on a sharp rock beside him.

He muffled a groan, then quit his scrambling and lay perfectly still. With long, careful breaths Torin slowed the white swirls of vapour that rose up from his parched lips and listened. He heard nothing.

After a few quiet moments he rose, careful to steady himself on one knee. He still felt dizzy from the mead, but by then the world had stopped spinning and he could make out the field of bones and rubble before him. Bryn and Grimsa were still asleep nearby.

The shrill noise, that awful shriek, had sounded very close. By the ringing in his ears, Torin thought some awful creature might have actually screamed right into them but he could not hear or see anything close by. He thought of *Skrar*, the spearhead, which lay tucked inside his cloak. It was unnaturally warm against his chest.

"Grimsa. Bryn. Wake up." Neither stirred. Torin scrambled over the rocks. He shook Bryn who woke with a start.

"What?"

"Quiet! Did you hear a scream?"

"A scream? When? Where?"

"Just a moment ago."

Bryn rubbed his eyes. "By the gods, asleep in Shadowstone Pass. No, I didn't hear anything. But what a foul place to be sleeping, this field of bones. Dread spirits haunt this place, no doubt."

Torin's stomach turned. He wondered if he had dreamed the scream, if it had come from *Skrar*, or if it had come from something worse. Grimsa gave a violent twitch and shouted some incoherent phrase in sleepy, slurred syllables.

"Wake up, wake up!"

Torin grabbed one of the great man's legs as it flailed. Grimsa sat up with a jolt, eyes wide and face flushed red.

"Torin! Thank the gods it is you. I was in a terrible dream."

"Spirits," Bryn said, "there must be spirits about. What fools we are. We're lucky not to have been strangled in our sleep or dragged into some moldy barrow. Let's get out of here." Just as Torin had done a moment ago, Bryn rose to his feet then toppled over onto the rocks.

Grimsa bellowed with laughter, but Torin elbowed him quiet. "I heard a scream a moment ago, muffled, but not too far off. It may have been a creature, or worse."

Bryn pointed at the fold in Torin's cloak where *Skrar* lay. "Or perhaps it was *Skrar*? Didn't Drombir say it meant 'Screamer'? If there was magic in that plain cup, how much more must be in a finely crafted weapon?"

Grimsa's face went pale and his eyes widened. Silence fell over the company, and they waited. Though they strained their ears, they caught no sound except the lonely whistle of wind between the peaks.

"Let's get moving," Torin said, "before anything in this foul place finds us." Grimsa and Bryn each gave a single nod. They slung their heavy packs over their shoulders and wasted no time as they hastened down the shadowed path.

The moon was out and all the constellations they had counted earlier shone clear and bright. Every bone in the field around them glowed an eerie bluish white in the moonlight. Gnarled stone faces, which at sunset had been menacing, now appeared entirely malicious. The sharp midnight shadows cast over the path by the moonlight seemed to cut empty voids in the trail, cracks of utter darkness. The three companions hurried along the snaking path through the field of bones and monstrous stone trolls.

As they rushed along, a bitterly cold wind came up, and with it another hazy fog. Torin tried to keep his eyes on the path ahead but noticed that the rippling mist along the ground was unusually thick. It did not flow or disperse with the rising gusts and it crept up his leg to the knees. As he looked down at the strange fog, the sound of his companion's footsteps ceased. Then Torin turned around and saw them. All of them.

One hundred pairs of eyes glared at him, eerie red embers sunk in hulking, wispy forms. Their translucent bodies swayed slowly from side to side, stiff and rhythmic like dead men hanging. In subtle swirls, contours of massive arms and legs faded in and out of the misty forms revealing grossly misshapen limbs. Across the forsaken valley, more figures rose from the mist, more ember eyes lit in the grey gloom. The grisly host was great in number, but none made any move toward them.

Torin ducked down behind a rock nearby. Still the red eyes stared. He rushed back a few paces to where his dumbstruck companions stood. Torin grabbed one with each hand and gave them a vigourous shake. "Run! Run!"

With all the strength they could muster, they sprinted down the path, though each stumbled and tottered violently from left to right. Near the edge of the field of bones and stone, Torin saw the path descend steeply. The terrible stare of those creatures bored into his back, pushing him forward, so he leapt down into the darkness with Bryn and Grimsa close behind.

The host of red eyes flickered as each empty smoldering stare trailed off into the darkness where the three intruders had disappeared. It was a scream that had roused them, sharp and cold and laced with magic. Now all was still again. One by one each smoky form dissolved into the howling wind. Each pair of dying embers, black with ash, dropped down between the jagged, broken bones.

The fall was shorter than Torin had expected and so he fouled his landing and tripped. Bryn, sure-footed as always, nearly landed straight on top of him and would have steadied himself if Grimsa hadn't come barreling down the path behind them at full speed. In a contorted mass of legs and arms and packs they tumbled off the path and down a steep hill. The loose scree crumbled and carried them down at an alarming speed. It was, they would later recount, quite fortunate not only because it cushioned their fall but because they were also spared a grueling set of switchbacks down the other side of Shadowstone Pass. As it was, they tumbled down the hill into the dim green valley below.

Partway down the scree slope, though still sliding, Torin managed to turn himself around so his pack cushioned his back from the rush of gravel beneath him. The slope leveled out at the bottom of the hill which was far below the place they had started. In a manner that could almost be called graceful, Torin slid to a stop, covered in dust and knee-deep in loose rock.

Bryn had already reached the bottom by that time. He lay there for a moment as he wheezed and coughed, then he pulled himself up to his feet. A short distance away they saw a pair of legs that were wriggling furiously out of the side of the hill. Torin and Bryn ran to grab a leg each and pulled Grimsa out from the side of the hill. The dusty figure shook his head and gasped, then coughed up a lungful of loose dirt. As he rubbed the rest from his eyes, he looked up to the sight of his two companions. For a moment, no one said a word. Then, all at once, they burst out into such laughter that each was almost in tears. Torin and Bryn fell down beside Grimsa and each fought to catch a breath.

Bryn wiped a tear from his eye. "Surely wise old Odd and all the gods are smiling or else we should all be dead. And not even for the first time today!"

Grimsa licked his parched lips. "Can I ask one more favour of the gods tonight? A drink to wet my parched throat? Unless they are saving us for some other grisly fate."

Torin narrowed his eyes and cupped his hand to his ear. "It seems you can. Listen."

Through the nearby trees they heard the unmistakable twinkle of a trickling creek. They waded through the thick, dark brush, then fell flat on their stomachs beside the stream and slurped up the cold, fresh water as fast as they could.

In time, the ache of Torin's parched throat stopped and the hammer pounding inside his head ceased to strike his temples. Though his arms and legs were bruised and stiff, he forced himself to his feet.

Bryn sat back on his heels and looked over at Torin. "You don't think that *Skrar* woke those awful things, do you?"

Torin shivered. "I think it might have."

"I told you," said Grimsa, "dealing with the *nidavel* is nothing but trouble."

Torin nodded. "I'm afraid I have to agree." He drew *Skrar* out of his cloak and fingered the swirling patterns etched into the blade. "I think we should hide the *nidavellish* treasures here and retrieve them once we find a way to sell them. Otherwise I think they may turn out to be more trouble than they are worth."

Bryn's face soured as he fingered *Isnif* on his belt. "I am hard pressed to part with this fine blade."

Grimsa searched his bag but could not find Drombir's cup. "By the gods, I think I dropped it!"

"In Shadowstone Pass?"

Grimsa nodded, his eyebrows furled and the corners of his mouth turned downward.

None of them had any mind to climb back up to Shadowstone Pass to retrieve that precious cup, at least not at night. Torin found a hollow crook in an old oak tree and marked it with his axe before placing *Skrar* inside.

"Drombir said that *Isnif* must be bound with blood," Bryn said, "At least let me bind the weapon before we hide it away." He took out his axe and drew his finger along the blade with a quick motion. A few drops of crimson blood dripped down, first on to the ground and then onto the base of the blade as Drombir had instructed.

As soon as the first drop hit the blade the metal evaporated with a hiss. Bryn let out a yelp and tossed away the hilt which, from his reaction, was as red-hot as an iron rod in the fire. He cursed and stamped his foot on the hilt as he shook out his hand.

Grimsa slapped his knees and wheezed. "The trickster has been tricked! Swindled by a crafty old *nidavel*."

Bryn sighed and shook his head. "If I ever run into that Drombir again, he'll be sorry." He kicked a bit of loose scree over the red-hot, bladeless hilt and spat on it.

Torin pointed downstream. "This stream should lead us down the valley and, if not to the road, then to Gatewatch itself." Each companion, though sore, was no longer thirsty and had no mind to sleep any more that night. The creek was small and the water near frozen, but they trekked on despite the low hanging branches, the slippery wet stones, and the haunting image of that red-eyed legion of phantoms.

The sun broke over the crest of the mountain range just as the three companions stumbled out of the forest. They looked like vagabonds, each with muddied boots, a tattered cloak, and a mess of leaves, moss, and broken twigs in his hair and beard. Grimsa didn't seem to care much. Bryn, on the other hand, could not help himself as he meticulously plucked out every leaf and bit of twig. Torin brushed out his hair and beard as best he could, then straightened the tree-ring crest pinned at the corner of his cloak. As the warmth of the sun hit their backs, they continued to follow the winding mountain creek out into the meadow with high hopes of reaching Gatewatch soon.

In the open meadow, tufts of long grass danced beside the trickling creeks with every rush of wind. All around them, wildflowers bloomed in brilliant reds, soft purples, deep-sea blues, and egg-yolk yellows which contrasted sharply with the streaks of copper and grey in the mountains behind them. Their destination lay close ahead.

Eventually the valley narrowed, and they rediscovered the well-worn path. Around the next bend in the trail, they spotted the town of Gatewatch, minute in the distance, but visible now with green banners that fluttered from crooked, crumbling towers. The town stretched wide across the valley's narrowest point so that neither man nor beast could pass. To Torin's knowledge, and to any other than perhaps the mysterious *nidavel*, this was the only way over the mountains.

Grimsa clapped. "At last, a meal in sight!"

Bryn shook his head. "Is there a brain in your skull or a second stomach?" Grimsa, too hungry and tired to care, simply continued to trudge along.

"Those towers look decrepit." Torin said. His grin sagged. "The walls are barely more than rubble from what I can see."

"What did you expect, Torin Ten-Trees?" said Grimsa, "The Great Tower of Noros? The fortress of Stagwood Vale? Or perhaps a homely wood-fired hall surrounded by lush green fields like that of your kindly father?"

Torin shook his head and raised his hand over his eyes to block the morning sun. "I heard it was ancient, but I thought it would at least be formidable. This place looks unprepared for even a raid by roadside bandits. And we are supposed to fight trolls from behind those rubble heaps?"

Bryn stopped, squinted, and frowned. "I'm afraid I have to agree with Torin on this."

Grimsa laughed. "Ha! How little do you know of The Gatewatch? Weren't we told the same stories around the fire in your father's hall? Did we not grow up dreaming of the same heroes and singing the same songs? This is no place for men and women who hide behind walls. Stones have not kept this pass clear, steel and blood have."

Bryn winced and tilted his head. "Let's hope more steel and less blood, at least on our account."

Grimsa chuckled as the three companions continued toward the small town in the distance. The thought of a bowl of steaming stew and a cup of brown ale spurred them forward.

Around noon they came to a rough stone wall about ten feet tall. At its center stood a gate of hefty timbers bound with straps of iron. A gatehouse tower rose up another fifteen feet beside the gate itself and a frayed green banner embroidered with a silver-grey raven hung down loosely from the top.

Torin looked up. "Hail, watchman! Open the gate!"

A hulking man with a wild beard of blazing red appeared atop the tower. He rested two enormous hairy arms on the wooden rail and stared down at the ragged company. A coat of rusted mail lay beneath his heavy grey cloak and he had a huge bow slung across his shoulder. The watchman's two dark eyes were hardly visible between his beard and his eyebrows, which twitched and bristled a moment before he replied.

"Are you recruits or bandits? You look like men of the bush."

"I am Torin Ten-Trees, son of Jarl Einar Ten-Trees."

"Ten-Trees. Hmm," the giant man said, "and I'd bet my beard that's a Jarnskald."

"Yes," said Grimsa, "Grimsa, son of Gungnir Jarnskald!"

"Who's the third?"

"Hail watchman, I am Bryn!" He stopped to draw a breath and shout over a sudden gust of wind. "Bryn of Clan Foxfoot."

"Foxfoot?" said the watchman. Torin thought he caught him utter something obscene below his breath, but it did not appear to reach Bryn's ear. The watchman stared and squinted a moment more before he disappeared from view. Then, from inside the tower, there came great grinds and creaks as the oak beams rose.

When the rugged door had opened, they saw the watchman himself turning the giant gate winch. Taller than Grimsa by half a head and a good deal wider, his burly form nearly filled the entire frame of the gate. The thick, wiry strands of his beard bristled straight out in streaks of red and orange, and his eyebrows were thick as briar bushes. As the gatekeeper turned from the winch to face them, Torin thought that it was as if a tree, and not a man, was standing before them.

The watchman cleared his throat and crossed his arms. "I am Gavring, master of the East Gate. Now let's have a look at you."

He swung his arms out and grabbed Torin and Bryn by the hair, one hand for each, and pulled them so close that his beard brushed their noses. Before either of them knew what was happening, Gavring let go of them and inspected Grimsa the same way. Then the giant man released Grimsa and took a step back.

Gavring cleared his throat and frowned. "My sight may not be all that it used to be but I can't see any yellow in your eyes so you are free to enter."

Torin was still dazed and more than disgruntled. "Yellow in the eyes? By thunderous Orr and all the gods, what are you talking about?"

"Yes, yes, yellow in the eyes. Rat fever. Some get it on their way over Shadowstone Pass. Rodents stowaway in the packs, you know? Not deadly, no, but miserable business. And contagious. Anyhow, come on in so I can shut up the gate."

The three companions needed no encouragement. Gavring lowered the gate behind them and each took in the view. A cozy cluster of stone houses with tall wood-framed roofs crowded the crooked street that ran away from the gate entrance through the town. At the end of the road was a rough sort of barracks or keep, short, sturdy, and made entirely of stone. Along the wall to either side ran a winding path that led up to the cliffs that walled either side of the valley.

"I assume you'll be needing a bed and a hot meal," Gavring said, "and by the way you smell, a bath as well. You'll find all three at Fjellhall, just down the road here and to the left. Signy is the Keymaster, and the best there is if you ask me. If you come upon Stonering Keep, you've gone too far."

Grimsa's eyes widened. "Fjellhall? Just like the tales!"

"Is that Stonering Keep there at the end of the road?" Bryn asked, pointing at the pile of stones down the street.

Gavring's eyebrows twitched and then scrunched together in a frown. "Yes, young Foxfoot, that is it. Were you expecting the Great Tower of Noros?"

Grimsa laughed out loud. "That's exactly what I said!" He grinned like a devil and Bryn's face flushed red.

Torin stepped in between his companions. "Thank you for your warm welcome, Gatemaster Gavring. Please forgive my companions. I think we all need something to eat." The thought of a warm meal was distraction enough to diffuse the quarrel.

"Gatemaster," said Grimsa, "is Keymaster Signy a maker of brews?"

Gavring sighed. "You lot are brim-full of questions. Yes, young Jarnskald, she is. In fact, not only is she a maker of brews, but she is a master brewer! She collects all her honey, herbs, and flowers from this side of the mountains. Didn't you see the wildflowers on your way through the valley? What wondrous blooms. And the bees? Far larger than any on the other side of the mountains I reckon."

Torin did recall seeing a buzzing bee floating over the sea of wildflowers earlier that morning, a rather large one, he thought. In his mind he again saw the fields, felt the breeze, and smelled the nectar on the wind.

Gavring continued, "The nectar is sweeter here and the flavours sharper. No doubt your first sip of Signy's honey mead will melt away all memory of the weary road over Shadowstone Pass. And after that you must sample the collection from her cellar: floral ciders and spiced wines, earthy stouts and well-oaked ales, fruit brandy and pine-scented spirits."

Gavring's eyes lit with a touch of fire. "And that is not nearly the whole of it! I have not yet mentioned the food!" He paused for effect, then lowered his voice to a whisper. "Do you know where Signy gets her meats? Those on patrol return with all kinds of game, wild stags and boars and pheasants and hares, then bring them straight to her. On this side of the mountain wild game grows to such a size as you would not believe until you've seen it with your own eyes. On Fjellhall's hearthfire there is always a mighty roast rubbed with herbs and salt. In her cellars, all manner of dried meats cure the whole year round. Her tavern hands collect nuts and fruit and honey from the valley for her youngest daughter, Signa, who bakes the bread and cakes each morning. They also work the rows of carrots and onions and potatoes that are kept by her son, Siggam, here outside the East Gate. Most legendary of all is Signy's mighty cauldron *Thaegindi*, a gift from King Araldof Greyraven. Some say it was forged by *nidavellish* Mastersmith Ognir himself. In it there is a stew boiling day and night."

Before Gavring had finished speaking, Grimsa had already started down the winding street. The gate master laughed, his voice a deep rolling rumble. "If ever I met a Jarnskald, that is one. Fate willing, perhaps I will come down to Fjellhall to share a pint of ale with you tonight, master Ten-Trees and young Foxfoot."

Torin's spirit swelled as he and Bryn rushed to follow Grimsa who was nearly sprinting. The misery of their ascent, the horrors seen in the night, and the hunger clawing at their ribs would soon all be far behind them. The weight of Torin's cloak and pack seemed to blow away like smoke as he felt the cool mountain air rush by his face and ears.

Grimsa breathed heavily with his hands on his knees as Torin and Bryn caught up with him. One hundred paces more would have brought them to the iron gate of Stonering Keep, whose rounded wall of uncut stone rose up high behind them.

But not one of them had much more than a thought for the keep. Before Torin stood a wide stone hall with a high-vaulted roof, a hundred carvings of trolls and stags and warriors hewn into the aged rooftop timbers. Out from the rugged stone-framed door wafted odours, both savoury and sweet, such as Torin had never smelled before. Not to say that the scents weren't familiar, indeed for a second Torin thought of his father's hall, but somehow the aroma was keener, sharper, and altogether fuller in richness than anything he had experienced before.

Grimsa wheezed. "Fjellhall! By the gods, we've made it." Torin thought he could see the glint of a tear welling up in the big man's eyes.

"Torin, I think our dear Grimsa is in love. You'd think he trekked up here to eat instead of fight trolls."

"Ha," said Grimsa, "I will be killing plenty of trolls once I have had my fill!"

Torin stepped forward and breathed deep through his nose, his eyes closed and his sore shoulders loose. The savoury smell of roasting meat, the heady aroma of ale, and the sweet scent of honey washed over his body like warm sunshine.

With a lurch, he grabbed Bryn and Grimsa around the neck and pulled them together. "Come on then, the first round is on me!" Then they walked, shoulder to shoulder, through the wide-open door of that ancient hall.

3

◇ A FEAST IN FJELLHALL ◇

TORIN, BRYN AND GRIMSA gazed up at the vaulted ceiling of framed timbers which sat perched high above them on thick walls of stone. Torin thought a dozen spears stacked end on end might not reach the top. Rough-hewn timber tables stretched all the way along either side of the hall and a raised stone hearth ran down the middle. In the hearth here were embers which crackled as they glowed orange and red. Above the fire stood an enormous steaming cauldron and four giant spits with meat roasting on them.

A scant gathering of rugged men and women, a dozen or so, sat at the benches idly eating cakes or bread with honey and drinking ale. Torin wondered how many the hall could hold and estimated that it must be well over a hundred.

"Look," Bryn said, "*Thaegindi*, the enchanted stew-pot."

A tavern hand stood high up on a chair so he could stir the giant cauldron. Two others carried in copper trays full of chopped carrots and onions from the scullery and emptied them into the stew. Each of the iron roasting spits required two people to turn. Between them a young man scurried about with a bucket of gold-brown sauce that he painted onto each roast with a large brush. At the far end of the hall, a dozen loaves sat steaming with golden brown crusts. Other hall hands were wiping tables, sweeping floors, and stoking the long bed of embers.

Grimsa licked his lips and took a step forward, but as soon as he did a voice shouted at him and his companions. "Stop there!"

All three turned toward the shrill sound. To their right stood an old woman with twin braids of silver-white hair that hung down over her shoulders. Her dress was dark blue and embroidered with yellow thread in swirling knotwork patterns. From her waist hung a fine silver chain with a collection of keys both large and small, some simple and some ornate. Though she was short and round in stature, she had a fierce look in her stone-grey eyes and held her spine as straight and stiff as an arrow.

"Now you can't be trudging through my hall in that condition," she said, "but we'll remedy that soon enough. I am Signy, daughter of Sigrilinn, keeper of the key of Fjellhall and Master of Brews."

"At your service," said the three companions. Each took a step back toward the threshold, suddenly aware of their tattered cloaks and muddy boots, and gave a slight bow.

Signy's tense shoulders relaxed when she saw her guests were well-mannered after all. Her tight-lipped stare melted into a radiant smile. "Well, don't I have a group of fine young men here, surely not the rabble I usually must put up with. Let me have a look at you." As she stepped up to Grimsa she wrinkled her nose then chuckled. "Ha, I did not even need to look! I can tell by the smell, this is a Jarnskald. But which one?"

Grimsa smiled wide and puffed out his chest. "I am Grimsa, son of Gungnir Jarnskald and brother to Gunnar."

"Well, Grimsa, you are welcome in my hall. I know more than anyone, save perhaps your mother, that a Jarnskald is hard to keep fed. However, you are all practically bred for troll-slaying. And you," she said as she turned toward Bryn, "you are a Foxfoot if I ever saw one. You have your father's mischievous eyes."

"Greetings Keymaster Signy," Bryn said, bowing low. "He spoke often of your warm halls, your radiant smile, and, of course, your excellent brews."

"And a charmer as well? What a spitting image of your father. A troublesome fellow but damn good with a bow. I roasted many a catch of his on my hearth. He would be proud to see you here."

"And you, young Ten-Trees," said Signy. A soft glow of sadness encircled her steel-grey eyes. "My, I am getting old." For a moment, Torin had in mind to say something but before he could gather a thought she cut in, shaking her head and waving her arms. "But enough of an old woman's rambling. Let's get you clean and then we'll get you fed. Gunnhild! Asleif!" The pair, who had been wiping tables, dropped their rags and ran up to Signy. "A splash of mead for each of these fine young men. And a honey cake each to tide them over until dinner." She looked again at Grimsa. "Make that two for him. Then find a place for their belongings and see them off to the baths." She spun back toward the ragged company. "I will see you all again at dinner, much refreshed I think." And with that she was off to inspect the sizzling roasts.

Before they knew it each one was sitting on a wooden bench with a glass of floral mead in one hand and honey cake in the other. Gunnhild directed a few of the young men from the kitchens to haul the packs up to the lofts then returned to her duties.

Asleif was a nervous young man, long-limbed and fair featured. With one hand he held tightly to a thick cloak of black wool wrapped around his neck, and in the other arm he held a stack of fresh tunics for the rugged trio. He barely let them finish their meal before rushing them out of Fjellhall toward the baths. Asleif knew the city well and the tired companions, especially Grimsa, were hard-pressed to keep up with his quick, light steps.

The cloistered stone streets of Gatewatch had been worn smooth from one hundred years of heavy feet. Down a hidden alley and left around a sharp corner, they came to the base of

Frostridge, the mountain that ran along the entire southern edge of the city. A small set of steps carved into the stone led down a tunnel into the mountain. From it rose a steady stream of billowing steam, silver against the orange lichens and green moss which covered rocks around the entrance like a mantle.

Asleif stopped abruptly. "Master Ten-Trees, Master Foxfoot, and Master Jarnskald, leave your clothes here at the bath entrance and we'll see to it that they are cleaned and dried for tomorrow. Here are some dry tunics and woolen pants for tonight. Enjoy the baths in the meantime. Keymaster Signy expects you for the evening meal." He turned to leave.

"You're a free man aren't you, Asleif?" Grimsa said, "Why not join us? It seems you too could use a moment of rest."

Asleif twirled back toward the company, smiled, and lifted a waving finger, "None of us are free now, Master Jarnskald. We are all in the service of King Araldof Greyraven. While we at Fjellhall may not slay trolls ourselves, we do feed troll slayers and that is busy work." He let his shoulders down for a brief moment and chuckled. "But your offer is kind, Master Jarnskald, and I am sad to refuse it. Another time perhaps. Farewell." And just as quickly as he had rushed them to the baths, Asleif hurried away.

"Just as well," Grimsa said, "besides, as my uncle always said: *Busy men poor company make.*"

Bryn smirked as he pulled off his sweat-stained tunic. "But do they not also say that *Idle men court fortune ill?*"

"A bath, a meal, and a good night's rest," said Torin, "is fortune enough for me."

Grimsa laughed. "Well said! Now let's get down to these baths so we won't miss dinner."

Each muscle along Torin's spine seemed to groan with a weary ache as he peeled the damp shirt off his back. Sparks of pain shot up through his ankles as his bare feet felt the hard stone beneath them. As he kicked off his pants, he noticed a rip in the knee that would have to be mended. For a moment he let the cool breeze flow like salve over his bruised body, then turned to follow Bryn and Grimsa down the steps toward the hot baths. He noticed that their stink, previously muted by clothing, now rose severely in rankness.

The stone stairway that tunneled deep down into the mountain was lit by flickering torches which cast shadows that danced on the walls. The constant flow of steam warmed the steps but also made them slippery, especially where patches of yellow moss or orange lichens grew. At times the passage was uncomfortably narrow; at times three or four men could stand shoulder to shoulder. Still down and down they went.

Then, like a giant giving a great, wide yawn, the tunnel opened into an underground cavern which arched up higher than even the timbers of Fjellhall. A mist filled the upper reaches of the cavern like dark storm clouds hanging overhead. Along all the crevasses in the walls, mosses and lichens and mushrooms grew, some which glowed just enough to light the room dimly.

In the center of the cavern was a large pool of steaming crystal-blue water which bubbled up from the center and swirled around the edges. Encircling the pool was a layer of hardened silt, silk smooth and white as marble. Similar deposits smoothed the pool floor. Clusters of luminescent mushrooms grew thick around the edge and lit the bubbling water with an eerie blue light. As Torin's eyes adjusted he could see dark shadows, two or three dozen, all men and women either wading deeper in or sitting near the shallow edge. The water gurgling up from the natural spring and the waterfalls deeper within the cavern created a soft wash of sound that made the whole place seem very peaceful.

Bryn sighed as he stretched out his stiff limbs. "By the gods, I've never felt anything so glorious. Torin, Grimsa, you can take care of the trolls. I am never leaving this sacred place."

Torin closed his eyes and breathed in deep through his nose, the hum of the deep cavern waterfalls filling his ears as they dipped below the water. "I'd be inclined to keep you company, but I couldn't stand the thought of Grimsa having all that mead in Fjellhall to himself."

Grimsa sputtered with his head half-submerged in the bath. "Ha! I would gladly take all the mead and meat and breads and cakes and pies. Not to mention all the glory of slaying the trolls myself while you two turn into old prunes here in the baths."

Torin sat up and found a groove in the hardened silt to it in. "I would not deny that you could, in fact, drink all the mead and eat all the food with room to spare. However, I would be worried about your safety without Bryn and I there to defend you."

Grimsa nearly choked on a gulp of water as he gasped, his eyes wide in disbelief. "Against the trolls? Don't forget that I am a Jarnskald, a born troll slayer! It comes to me most naturally."

"Not against the trolls," Torin said, "but against the troll slayers. If Bryn and I are hidden away down in the baths, who will tell the good folk of Gatewatch that this monstrous being eating all their food and drinking all their mead is a man and not a troll himself?"

Grimsa swung his arm and soaked Torin with a great splash of steaming water. Then he laughed and his booming voice echoed through the cavern. This drew the attention of some of the others in the pool. Three young women in an adjacent pool peered over the rocks and whispered to each other. When Bryn smiled at them, they ducked back behind the rocks and giggled.

"And then we have you to worry about," Torin said. "What if some monstrous creature, a witch or a giantess, falls under your charm and tries to whisk you off? Then Grimsa and I will have to crash your own wedding to rescue you."

Grimsa nodded. "After we plunder the banquet table, of course."

Bryn winked. "I can go unnoticed when I want to. Remind me again who snuck into your father's cellar years ago and secured a full cask of ale for us to drink at the fall festival?"

"I remember my father finding the cask half empty in his cellar the next week and giving us all a sound beating with a willow branch."

"And I remember when you tried to steal those pork bits from the larder when we were children," said Grimsa, "and old Thorgrid chased you round and round Ten-Tree Hall with a ladle!"

"Hold on now, I was stealing those for you, Grimsa."

"In exchange for the name of my fair cousin."

"Which you never did tell me."

Grimsa grunted. "You got caught. What's worse, I didn't get any pork bits." A rumble came from Grimsa's stomach. A few small waves rippled out from his hairy, half-submerged belly.

Torin sighed and stretched out his bruised arms. "Speaking of pork bits, it must nearly be time for the evening meal." Bryn and Grimsa agreed, and so they were all soon on their way back to Fjellhall.

The sun had dropped behind the mountains while they were in the baths, and now the chill they had felt the night before swept over the clustered town. The green linen tunics and brown wool pants that Asleif had given them were soft on the skin, but too thin to keep out the alpine cold. Twice they took a wrong turn and met a dead end, but when the wind changed direction the smell of meat and spiced ale on the breeze helped guide them back to Fjellhall.

Torin felt as if he had been reborn when he entered the hall for the second time that day. No pack sagged on his shoulders, no damp clothes clung to his skin, and no stench of sweat and mud and horses choked him. Now, the earthy aroma of the mineral baths had soaked into his hair and beard and his limbs felt as light and as limber as rabbits in spring. Just as the tunic had let in the cold outside, now the heat that radiated from the long stone hearth flowed right to the center of his chest.

Torin's impression of the hall was not at all diminished. In fact, now he could fully take it in. With loosened shoulders, he could tilt his head back to see the topmost rafters stretched out like eagles soaring on gusts of wind. Where the walls met the roof, long green banners hung down which depicted all manner of lore: ravens and wolves and trolls. A border of intricately embroidered silver-thread knotwork ran around each one, and the colours of the figures depicted were as striking as those of the alpine flowers he had seen that morning. A few feet below the banners was a crowd of men and women that filled the rough wooden benches.

It was not the largest gathering Torin had ever seen, but it was by far the most ragged and hardy. His father hosted perhaps a dozen retainers of such caliber, but here warrior women and gruff men packed the benches end to end. Some women had wild hair tied back with a leather strap, others had twisted braids, and still others sported shaved heads with swirling designs tattooed in dull black ink. Beards were common among the men and most wore their hair long, though some also had shaved heads and had similar black-ink patterns. Few wore cloaks because of the radiating hearth, but many wore rusted chainmail shirts under light tunics or sleeveless leather tops. Though they did not look friendly, each one certainly seemed pleased to be sitting there among hardy comrades.

Most potent was the aroma of well spiced meat, smoky and savoury, which wafted through the air. It was this smell and a grumble in his stomach that shook Torin from his awe-filled stupor. As he looked along the tables, he saw Keymaster Signy shuffling toward them.

Keymaster Signy approached them with brisk steps. "Well, good evening, Master Ten-Trees, Master Jarnskald, and Master Foxfoot. I was beginning to think you had all drowned in the baths. Let's have a look at you." A quick inspection and a hesitant sniff assured her that they had been cleansed of the road. "Come with me, quickly now because we've already started serving the ale."

They followed her around the crowded hall. At the other side, they saw two women step up onto the end of the table. Each woman had a cask of ale under her left arm and, in her right hand, a tool that looked like a hammer except that it was pointed instead of flat. With a well-practiced swing, each cracked the cask open with the tool and walked down the boards of the broad timber table. Those seated along the bench cleared the table as the two cask-bearers approached. Then those on either side took turns catching the stream of ale in their mead-horns. Each hailed the cask-bearer with a toast to good health as she passed. The companions reached their place at the far end, just ahead of the flowing casks.

As Keymaster Signy pointed to their seats, a booming voice rang out from across the table. "The young cubs arrive at last! I thought perhaps you'd left me to finish off the cask by myself. Now it seems I'll have to share!"

"Gatemaster Gavring!" said Torin, "By the gods, it is good to see a friendly face among such fierce company." Each sat down just in time to pick up the horn laid out for them and fill it with ale from the passing casks.

"I'll leave you here with Gatemaster Gavring for now," Signy said, "but don't believe too much of what this red giant says once he finishes off the rest of that cask."

Gavring smirked. "But that's when I tell my best stories!"

Signy raised an eyebrow. "The best stories," she said, "are rarely true. Now, enjoy the meal and I shall see to it that you are set up with lodging at the end of the night." With that she was off shouting orders to the young men from the kitchen who bore the roast platter down the table, the keys around her waist jingling wherever she went.

The four of them seated at the end of the table had the distinct pleasure of finishing off the last of the cask. It was a dark brown ale, rich and foamy, with hints of honey and cedar. Torin remarked that it was far stronger than the dry yellow ale brewed by old Thorgrid in his father's hall and, as Grimsa pointed out, far less cloudy. Torin himself swallowed three full horns before the last drip signaled that the cask was dry. After that, the barrel was whisked away and each man, horn brim-full, could drink at his leisure.

By then the steaming roast platters had been hauled down along the table and a generous chunk of hard white cheese had been given to everyone seated on the bench. Small loaves of dark rye bread were split between pairs up and down both tables, though somehow Grimsa and Gavring each managed to get a whole loaf to themselves. Last to come down the middle of the table was a steaming bowl of thick stew; its savoury scent made Torin's eyes water. In short order, each companion had stuffed himself full.

Grimsa had certainly not been so contented since their departure feast at Ten-Tree Hall and he now recounted each stage of their journey to Gavring with vigour. He told of the fair fields and towering trees along the mighty rushing Noros. He praised the bacon and the goat-stew and the roasted chicken offered at the shanty inns along the road. Then he told of a particularly foul batch of *skog* they had purchased from a vagrant brewer. Bryn fondly recalled two sisters from the small town of Askedalen who had swooned over a few of his recently composed verses and Torin showed Gavring a silver serpent ring he had won from a tavern-keep in a game of Kings Table. At last, Grimsa described the roaring fire they had made at the bottom of Shadowstone Pass the night before.

"And then began the ascent," Grimsa said, "What miserable business! First the fog, then icy rain, and at last frosty flakes of snow. Up and up and up we went, ever steeper, ever colder. Even worse, we had finished the last of our firemead before noontime so there was not even any drink to brighten our spirits."

"Then," Bryn said, "through the fog we heard voices."

At this Gavring perked up, leaned forward, and furled his wiry orange eyebrows. "Voices?"

"Yes, deep and haunting voices all chanting a melody. I can recall the verse: *Bleed the earth dry as bone, till we've broken every stone, Til the secret depths are known, and every treasure's safe at home.*"

"Ah, the *nidavel!*" Gavring said, perhaps a bit louder than necessary because of the ale. He leaned even further toward the companions then narrowed his eyes and tilted his head. "Nothing good can come from dealing with those mushroom-munching merchants."

Grimsa pounded both fists on the table and spilled a bit of ale into his lap. "That's what I said!"

"Nevertheless, we won great treasures from them."

"Bryn, you oaf," said Grimsa, "you won nothing. You were swindled!"

"What do you mean? Did they attack?"

Torin shook his head. "No. They offered to trade horses for *nidavel* wares."

Grimsa snickered. "And these two ogled the treasures, sick with the *gulthra* and blind to all reason. They told us of a rock fall ahead that our horses could never cross. These two believed him. I knew it was a *nidavel* trick all along."

Gavring sighed, dropped his shoulders, and lifted a gigantic hand to scratch his thick beard. "This is a tale too common lately. Tell me, was it a troop of six *nidavel?*"

The three companions exchanged a glance before any of them answered.

"Yes," Torin said, "the leader called himself Drombir."

"Did they pretend to squabble like a rabble of bandits?"

Torin felt his heart sink inside his chest. "Yes."

"I'll need to speak with Captain Calder about this. This Drombir fellow, along with his company, has been swindling travelers out of their goods and livestock for a few months now."

"What use would cave dwelling *nidavel* have for horses if not to haul their wares?"

A morbid expression came over Gavring's face and he leaned in toward the companions. With bared teeth he whispered. "They cook them and eat them! Some grow tired of mushrooms and glowfish, and I can't say I blame them for that." He shook his head and shivered, "But eating a horse! I reckon it brings the worst of luck."

All three companions got a bit pale in the face and Torin felt a twinge of nausea. He would have to explain all this to his father when he returned home. At the sight of their worried faces, Gavring laughed, his huge belly shaking the table and rattling the plates. "Don't be too hard on yourself. You three are surely not the first to fall victim to their tricks." With a wicked grin he raised his horn. "Welcome to Gatewatch!"

At this they could not do much else but join in the toast and let the ale soothe their bruised pride. The huge red-bearded man could see their spirits were dampened at this discovery, but he soon had them laughing again with stories of other unfortunates who had been swindled by the crafty *nidavel*.

"A girl here in town once traded a chicken for a magic egg which, she was promised, contained a hen who would lay golden eggs! It turned out to be nothing but polished stone, but by sweet Fyr and all the gods she sat on it for a full week before she realized the trick. Her rump must have been bruised purple and blue!"

A few others down the bench began to listen and laugh at Gavring's tales which got louder and more elaborate with each successive story. "Another time I met a smith who traded a donkey for a fine golden hammer. I saw him strike it at the forge and it bent in half like a twig, nothing but gilded copper. A fine hammer indeed!"

These and many other *nidavel* deceptions he divulged, each drawing more laughter and more listeners. Soon the whole company at the end of the bench was laughing, toasting, and chanting for more tales. By then Gavring swaggered about even as he sat. Around the table the roasted meat, the hardened cheese, and the steaming bread had all been eaten up and now a final cup of ale was being poured.

"The best of all," Gavring said, "was the son of a jarl named Hamar who rode a fine steed named Faxi. He met the *nidavel* in the pass late one foggy night and they asked him if he had seen their lost companion. He declared that he had seen no soul upon the road all the way up, but just as he spoke a chilling cry came from up ahead. Faxi was spooked and would not go forward, so Hamar went on ahead with the *nidavel* to investigate the harrowing sound. All they found there was a splash of blood on the rocks. At this all the *nidavel* put on a show of consternation such as Hamar had never seen. *Trolls, trolls,* they bellowed, *the trolls have eaten our dear companion.* Hamar was quite unnerved by the commotion and the thought of trolls had him running back toward Faxi. *Wait,* cried the *nidavel* as they ran after him, *don't leave us alone with the trolls about!*"

Gavring gulped down the last of his ale, wiped the froth from his beard, and continued. "When Hamar returned to the place where his horse had been, he found it was gone and in its place was a tiny horse carved out of stone, small enough to be kept in his pocket. At the sight of this, the *nidavel* screamed with renewed vigour and ran about crying, *Troll magic! Troll magic! It has turned the steed to stone!* Hamar, horrified at this, snatched up the stone figure and grabbed one of the *nidavel* by the cloak. He shook him harshly and demanded to know how to unwork the magic that had been done to his steed. The *nidavel* just cried, *Let me go! Let me go!* Finally, one of the older *nidavel*, quite short of breath, ran up to Hamar and began to shout. *The sun! The fiery sun! At dawn trolls' magic all undone!* At this, Hamar dropped the squirming *nidavel* and began to run up Shadowstone Pass as fast as his quivering legs would take him in hopes of catching the first rays of daylight." Then Gavring was laughing so hard that he could not speak, and all three companions were doubled over on the benches.

Gavring wiped tears from his eyes. "What a sight he was! I remember he arrived at the East Gate at dawn and wouldn't stop babbling about troll magic for three whole days. *The sun,* he would say, *the fiery sun!* Ha!"

The company that had gathered at the end of the table emptied their horns in one last toast to Gavring and then dispersed in twos and threes back to the barracks or to their stone-wall homes. Soon no one was left in the hall but a few hall hands and the four of them at the end of the table. Torin remembered his offer to buy the first round and purchased a bottle of spiced wine.

Torin lowered his voice and leaned in toward Gavring. "The *nidavel* were not our last encounter."

Gavring narrowed his glossy eyes. "Not the last encounter?"

"We arrived at Shadowstone Pass at dusk. Weary from the ascent and without horses, we stopped to rest and fell asleep." He thought about mentioning Drombir's cup, the bottomless vessel, but then thought it better not to.

Gavring's face grew dark at the thought of Shadowstone Pass at night and the three companions could only guess what he was thinking. Torin shuddered as he wondered what horrors Gavring had seen during his time on the wild side of the mountains.

"Then I woke to the sound of a shrill scream, though only I heard it. I woke Bryn and Grimsa and we made haste through the field of bones by moonlight."

Gavring's jolly manner had been extinguished. Now he leaned his enormous face in toward them, grim and flushed red. "And?"

"Soon a swirling fog gathered in the field. It moved unnatural-ly and seemed to cling to our boots. Then we saw them."

"Ten-Trees, what did you see?"

"Before us there was a host of white phantoms rising out of the fog. Each had a pair of burning red embers for eyes. There were at first perhaps a few dozen, then well over one hundred. They made no move toward us; they all just stared. We ran and they did not pursue us."

Gavring's eyes were wide and his jaw hung slack. "By great Orr and the gods! The Watchers."

"The Watchers?" said Bryn, "What are they?"

Gavring slurped his spiced wine and shook his head. "No one can say for sure. I myself have never seen them, and thank the gods for that. Some say they are the stranded spirits of warriors who fell fighting the trolls, others say that they are evil apparitions which feed on the scent of death. It has been many years since they have been sighted and, for my part, I had hoped they had moved on or disappeared." He stroked his beard then sighed. "I'll need to inform Captain Calder about this as well."

At that moment, Keymaster Signy walked up to the table and addressed them all. "I hope you've all had your fill, and by the look in each of your eyes it seems you've sampled quite enough of my stock." She smiled and all the companions thanked her for her hospitality. "Now, from what I've overheard it seems you three have earned your rest. There are three beds set up for you in the loft. Will you be needing a bed as well Master Gavring? You've had quite a lot of ale and wine tonight."

Gavring protested. "No, no, no. I am just down the road." He stood up quickly but then had to brace himself against the bench. He wobbled again and placed both hands on the table in front of him.

Gavring nodded to the three companions and burped. "Good night, young masters. And Keymaster Signy, always a pleasure."

He dipped at the hips in what appeared to be a bow of sorts, then swaggered out of the hall humming a lively tune.

Torin climbed up to the loft and looked out over Fjellhall with its long empty tables and glowing hearth. The banners had been taken down and the torches doused. All was quiet and the loft was warm in the dim red light. He had hardly laid down in his bed before he fell into a deep, deep sleep.

4

◇ MEAD & MAYHEM ◇

THE NEXT DAY did not start early for the companions and was, for the most part, uneventful. Torin slept late and both Bryn and Grimsa slept later. The noon meal was just being served as they came down from the lofts and the afternoon was again spent in the baths. Bruises that went unnoticed the day before now swelled and each limb ached from their tumble down the mountain side, but by the end of the afternoon all three were in high spirits.

As he wandered the streets of Gatewatch, Torin gained his bearings. Stonering Keep stood at the center of the westernmost part of town, and the East Gate, where they had met Gavring, was on the far east side. The main street of cobblestone which connected these two had a large carpenter's hall, two smithies, a leather works, an apothecary, a butchery, a mason's shop, a mill, and an assortment of traders with trinkets of all kinds. Above them all towered Fjellhall, at the west end of the street near Stonering Keep. At the southern edge of town stood Frostridge, a precarious rock face into which the baths were sunk along with many small caves for provisional stores and animals. On the steep north slope of the settlement lay Ironspine Mountain. The rugged barracks near there, which was built of wood, appeared to extend into Ironspine itself. The rest of the town was a knot of small crooked alleys between thatch-roofed houses and small shops. No matter where the companions stood, they could see straight up to the bleak ridges of Ironspine to the north and Frostridge to the south. Like two enormous stone claws, these ran all the way up the valley to their peaks above Shadowstone Pass.

That night, Fjellhall was full of young faces, newcomers that had been rounded up from towns and villages across Noros by a band of Gatewatch recruiters. By order of King Araldof Greyraven, all folk, high or low born, owed two years of service. They were an assorted bunch: sons and daughters of farmers and fisherman, of smiths and carpenters, of sailors and merchants. The custom for commoners who might not survive the journey alone, or who might otherwise skip the journey all together, was to escort them with a small detachment from Gatewatch. That way, all recruits arrived intact and on time. This group that had arrived late that afternoon looked famished and exhausted.

Gavring was on watch that evening and so the companions kept to themselves near the end of the table full of newcomers. The gruff veterans of the Gatewatch they had seen the night before kept to themselves across the crackling hearth at the other table.

Keymaster Signy handed out a flurry of directives to her staff in preparation for the meal. A sweet cloudberry mead was served alongside venison stew and a heavy sweet bread filled with nuts and berries. All the while savoury vapors rose off the evening stew from *Thaegindi* in the middle of the hall. Throughout the meal, the newcomers became livelier and soon the festive atmosphere of the previous evening again filled the hall with stories and songs and laughter.

As the evening meal drew to an end, a grisly man appeared in the lofts above the tables and addressed the present company. He cleared his throat and pounded on the banister. "Members of the Gatewatch! May trolls fall before you." The veteran members of the Gatewatch, Greycloaks as they were called, pounded the tables and gave a mighty roar before falling silent. The man up in the loft chuckled and nodded. Torin noticed the man's face was badly scarred and his left eye was white and milky. His hair and beard, ash grey, fell down over his chest and shoulders in thick braids. His cloak, a bear pelt, hung loose off his hunched shoulders.

"And to the untested recruits, greetings. I am Captain Calder, appointed commander of the Gatewatch by decree of King Aradolf Greyraven. Tomorrow at noon you will gather in Stonering Keep and I will judge each one's spirit, courage, and strength." He raised a hand, the smallest finger missing, and clenched it into a fist. "Long may Beoric's kin defend the pass! Long live the Greyraven!" This time both the rugged company of Greycloaks across the hearth and the newcomers cheered together. Captain Calder left as abruptly as he had appeared.

The scrawny young man beside Grimsa was clearly affected by the mead. "Long live the Greyraven! Death to trolls! Glory to us, the future defenders of Gatewatch!"

Grimsa leaned in toward Torin and Bryn among the racket. "I'm not sure this rabble has ever wielded more than a spade or a fishing rod, but I must admit they are in no short supply of spirit."

Bryn nodded. "Or of spirits, it seems."

Torin chuckled and took another swig of mead from his horn. "Well, we'll see what they are made of in the morning when they are all sober."

The scrawny lad heard Torin's comment and looked over at them with glazed eyes. "Wait, I know you! You are Torin Ten-Trees, son of Jarl Einar Ten-Trees." He turned to the woman beside him who had just guzzled down the last of her mead. "Look Gudrun, Torin Ten-Trees!" He swayed in his seat momentarily then scratched his head and shouted. "You down there! I've been sitting with Torin Ten-Trees, son of the Jarl Einar Ten-Trees, this whole time!" He giggled like a fool then paused as a thought slowly formed in his mind. "I heard a verse about him once. It was, I recall, rather peculiar."

Those nearby glanced down the tables and murmured among themselves. A stout youth called out down the table in a deep voice. "I fear you are about to say something foolish, Erik."

Erik swung his head toward the attentive crowd of eyes and spread his lips in a wild grin. Though he struggled to stand and nearly fell over while swinging his legs across the bench he managed to steady himself against the table. After banging one fist on the table and waving the other arm in the air he cleared his throat. "Ah yes, I remember it now." In slightly slurred syllables he began his recitation.

> *An egg was hatched in Ten-Tree hall*
> *A little chick so soft and small*
> *Who ate much grain and slept on hay*
> *A cock or hen I cannot say*

An uneasy quiet fell over that side the hall and at the last syllable nervous chuckles rippled through the crowd. Erik, slapped his knee, sloshed his drink, and wheezed for air as he laughed. Every set of eyes shifted from the scrawny figure to Torin and his companions at the end of the table.

Erik, still fully enraptured in his own joke, found that his feet had lost track of the floor. Grimsa had leapt up on the table and, in one swift swing of his arm, hoisted him by the collar of his tunic high over the seated crowd. Erik shrieked and dropped his horn of mead which spilled down the front of his shirt and all over his breeches. Then Grimsa tossed him some way down the table. As he slid, Erik scattered bowls and unattended horns off either side of the table onto the laps of those along the way.

Torin finished the last of his horn and calmly swung his legs around the bench seat. In the slow confident manner that he had learned from his father, he stepped up onto the table and walked around Grimsa who, red-faced, had planted himself in the center of the broad planks. Torin scanned the sea of eager eyes and smirked. Erik, drunk as a squirrel, quit trying to stand and fell silent. Torin cleared his throat and spoke.

> *Into Fjellhall flew a bird*
> *Who squawked a verse he once had heard*
> *But when a bear had gripped his neck*
> *This bird found that his pants were wet*

Laughter burst from every corner and the table rumbled as fists pounded it. Many toasted Torin's verse and even some of the kitchen staff dared to stop and listen. Two people on either side of Erik hoisted him to his feet atop the table and steadied him. As was custom in a challenge of verse, Torin gave Erik a full minute to craft his reply. After a few fumbled starts, Erik quit and Torin continued.

> *Tell us bird, why don't you squawk?*
> *Are all your verses now forgot?*
> *Or is your skull too small to fit*
> *More than one foolish verse in it?*

At this the rafters rang with a chorus of mirth. Those at Erik's end of the table began throwing scraps of food at the drunken fool who tried, without success, to dodge each whizzing morsel. Bryn, caught up in the spectacle, hopped up on the table and continued Torin's verse.

> *Speak bird, speak! You gangly kook*
> *You poked your head inside the coop*
> *But found a wolf, a fox, a bear*
> *Who eye you now with hungry stare*
>
> *So fly bird, fly! Now flit your wings*
> *You've caused offence to kin of kings*

Flee back to your stinking nest
And hide beneath a chicken's breast

Erik managed to roll off the table but knocked over two of the other newcomers in the process. It seemed that a brawl might ensue between the three sprawled on the floor. However, the mead had done its work and, tempers doused, all three began to laugh hysterically. Torin, Bryn, and Grimsa, still standing atop the table, had their horns refilled and they toasted the crowd.

Even Keymaster Signy, while not usually fond of these sorts of exchanges, let a laugh escape her lips. Given the nature of Erik's unprovoked insult, it was a matter of justice by way of the long respected old customs. However, it was not this incident but what happened next that would be the talk all around Gatewatch that night and the next morning.

From the far end of the hall, a young woman stepped up onto the table and walked toward the companions. She moved with an effortless grace, calm and calculated, at a pace which seemed both unhurried and deliberate. At first Torin did not notice her because of the crowd of revelers around him. Then she planted herself about ten paces down the table and the crowd fell silent in anticipation of the next round of entertainment which, given her stance, seemed imminent. Torin turned to see what had brought about the sudden change in mood and found her facing toward him square on.

The sharp features of her moon-white face, particularly her slim nose and sharp cheekbones, were framed by thick bead-laden braids of coal-black hair. Her eyes, pale and grey like steel or storm-clouds, seemed to harbour some brewing mischief. A rugged top made of boiled leather, sleeveless and well fit, left her lean muscled arms exposed. The leather straps of her boots were wound in an intricate pattern up to her knee and she wore loose cotton pants tied up at the waist with a green sash.

She called out so that the whole hall could hear her voice. "So, Ten-Trees, you can compose a fine verse." Cheers came from around the hall and the fists that pounded the table made it rumble under Torin's feet. "And it is good sport to best a fool, but there is little glory in it."

"I'm sure we will all have a chance at glory soon enough," said Torin. "I've heard that there is a bit of a troll problem here in Gatewatch." Another round of laughter rattled down the benches. It was clear at that point that she was not one of the newcomers, yet she sat among them so she must be a recruit. Torin felt himself at a disadvantage. "Tell me, what is your name?"

As she addressed both Torin and the present company she opened her arms wide and shouted. "I am Wyla, soon to be the scourge of all trolls." She turned full round so that everyone at the table could see her face then gave Torin a short bow.

Torin scratched his beard and tilted his head but could not place either her face or her name. She certainly bore herself like the daughter of a noble clan. Could it be possible that the hospitable hall of his father, Einar Ten-Trees, had never hosted her kin? Certainly not, Torin thought, for his father had close relations with chiefs and clans from all over Noros.

"It seems," she said, "that you have not heard of me. And if you have not heard of me, then certainly no one else at this table has. Perhaps then I am free to spin the threads of my own tale."

Bryn could not stand to be left out and so leaned over and frowned. "And how does your tale begin?"

"By challenging you three."

At this, howls of laughter spread throughout the hall so that even the veteran members of the Gatewatch took notice of the spectacle. The three companions chuckled as well, but Wyla's smirk stayed dark and confident.

After a moment the laughter died down. "Wyla," Torin said, "no one should doubt your courage, but forgive me if I doubt your strength. Do you mean to take us all on at once?"

"This is what I propose," Wyla said, "that I challenge each of you to whatever you claim to be best at. Then, if I have bested each man, I'll have bested you all."

Grimsa roared at this. "Ha! Then I know exactly where my strength lies—in drinking! Will you out-drink a Jarnskald?"

"I accept your challenge Grimsa Jarnskald," said Wyla, "What is your skill, Bryn of Clan Foxfoot?"

By this time everyone could see that Wyla was serious in her challenge and that, more importantly, the night's entertainment had truly just begun. Newcomers and veterans both called for more barrels of ale and mead. Every eye was on the elevated figures standing on the table.

Bryn, who rarely enjoyed the pleasure of recognition without introduction, was quite pleased. In his regular dramatic fashion, he let the moment linger and scratched his chin thoughtfully. "I certainly can't boast of verse like Torin, and I don't think anyone has a lust for drink as strong as my friend Grimsa. But I do reckon that I could beat anyone at this table in a race."

Wyla nodded. "A race it is then. And you, Torin-Ten Trees, what is your skill? Will it be a test of strength between us?"

Torin did not like the feeling he had about this woman. There was a faint nudge from the back of his mind, a host of whispers echoing, all bits of advice from his father which lingered ever in the corners of his thoughts. She seemed too confident to be fooling and yet also too keen to be a fool. There was something about her that he had yet to learn.

"You are a mystery to us," Torin said, "because we have not heard of you, and yet you seem well acquainted with us though we have been here only two days. So I find it fitting to challenge you to a game of riddles, for if it is to be mysteries from one, let it be mysteries from both." Torin thought he caught a flash of disappointment in her eyes, but he could not be certain.

The great company assembled there happily abandoned the benches, refilled their mead horns, and cleared the middle of the hall for the race. Some of the veteran members took to the loft to watch while the untested recruits lined the walls on the stone floor of the hall. Each shuffled places and nudged past each other until they had a decent view.

Bryn threw his cloak and shirt off onto the table and began to trot up and down the hall. He winked at each of the young women along the bench of recruits and even blew a kiss to one of the Greycloaks as she looked down from up in the lofts. Those up above laughed as she shrugged. "A bit too young for my bed," the Greycloak woman said, "but a fair fill for the eyes nonetheless!" Bryn gleamed and bowed ceremoniously then trotted around the hall again.

Wyla stretched her arms up high then twisted her torso side-to-side, foregoing a spectacle like Bryn. Torin watched her closely and then leaned in close to Grimsa, who could barely hear him shout over all the noise.

"I have a strange feeling about her."

Grimsa frowned and nodded. "Yes, I guess she is quite beautiful."

"No, not that kind of feeling. A dark feeling, like there is something we don't know about her that is going to bring us a great deal of trouble."

"Ah, perhaps. But she is not the only one with secrets." The great man shook his cloak sleeve and revealed the rim of Drombir's cup.

Torin's eyes opened wide and he had to shout over the din. "I thought you lost it at Shadowstone Pass!"

Grimsa grinned his widest crooked-toothed smile. "I did. But Bryn saw it hanging from a bag among the belongings of the untested recruits when they came into the hall. Certainly, whoever had it must have found it beside the path. Just before the evening meal, Bryn stole a cup from the kitchen, similar in make and weight, and placed it where Drombir's cup had been. He slipped this treasure to me under the table right after the last of the empty trays were being taken away!" Both chuckled and thanked the gods for their crafty friend.

The race was set to begin. Each runner would dash down the hall to the other end and back, about one hundred paces each way. The first to touch the starting wall would be declared the winner. As Keymaster, Signy was in charge of conducting the formalities of each challenge and so summoned one of her tavern hands to bring a drum. On the ninth beat of the drum the race would begin and then the swiftest of the two would be determined. Both Bryn and Wyla tied back their hair and readied themselves against the wall.

Erik, who had not slowed his drinking, stood a few feet away from Bryn and shouted in slurred syllables. "Wyla! Wyla! Swift of leg! Fair of face! Fierce of gaze! Winner of race!" Bryn shot one sour look at him and Erik leapt back into the crowd with a squeak.

A stout tavern hand beat a large goatskin drumhead with a rounded club. Both runners drew each muscle and tendon taught as a bowstring ready to let loose a sharpened arrow. Deafening cheers filled the hall from stone floor to vaulted ceiling and people stomped and clapped along to the rhythm of the deep resonant drumbeat. With every beat, Torin could feel a pulse rattle the center of his chest.

At the last beat the runners were off, the whistling noise of their flying forms lost in the roar of the present company. Torin felt a rush of wind as Bryn blew by and marveled at his speed. However, he noticed also that Wyla, like a shadow or a reflection in still water, was matching Bryn step for step in the frenzied sprint. The embers burning in the hearth that ran down the middle of the hall flared up in the wake of rushing air. In perfect synchronicity they bounced off the wall at the far end and dashed back. They barreled forward with such reckless force that Torin thought they might both smash, headfirst, into the wall. Each crashed into the finishing wall and fell to the floor gasping for air.

Shouts came from both sides of the hall, some claiming that Wyla had won and others claiming that Bryn had bested her. Keymaster Signy had to work for several minutes to calm the crowd enough to make her decision. At last the company fell silent to hear her verdict. "Greycloaks of the Gatewatch! Untested recruits! Hear my ruling. These two raced with great speed and furious determination, there is no doubt of that. However, the finish was so close that no difference was found in my eye between Bryn and Wyla touching the wall. I declare the race a draw."

Such an uproar broke out from each side of the hall, curses and jeers, that Signy had to wait a moment more before she continued. Her cool gaze soon doused the tempers of the spectators and she spoke again. "Therefore, we must have another trial. This time there must be no doubt of the winner." Cheers again filled the hall, and everyone toasted her suggestion.

Bryn and Wyla, each still gasping for breath, rolled over and stood up. Both smiled at each other devilishly but Wyla was more convincing. Torin saw Bryn's face sour as he turned away and all he could do was to return his gaze with a blank stare.

Grimsa frowned and scratched his beard. "Who has ever come close to beating Bryn in a race?"

Torin shook his head. "No one. Like I said, a dark feeling."

Keymaster Signy had the drummer beat to draw the crowd's attention once again. "To break the draw these two shall race again. Each must run to the far end of the hall, touch the wall, and return to fetch this key from my hand." She brandished a silver key inset with icy-blue amethysts. "The key to Fjellhall itself. The one who holds this key at the end of the race will be the undis-

puted winner." Applause greeted her suggestion and the race was
set to begin again.

Both Bryn and Wyla looked ragged but determined. Keymaster Signy held up the silver key which glinted in the firelight of
the hall. The drum beat. The crowd shouted. Drinks sloshed and
elbows shoved to secure a better view. Again, the drummer struck
the ninth beat and the race was on.

All Torin saw were two flashes of feet and legs and arms, blurs
of motion. No sooner had they started than it seemed that the two
had reached the far end of the hall and were on their way back.

As Bryn turned around, Torin could see his face, which was
crazed as that of a wild stallion. At that moment it occurred to
Torin, as well as to the runners it seemed, that the fastest way back
to the silver key was to dash along the red-hot rim of the hearth
rather than around it. Both runners leapt up onto the hearth
stones, with fiery embers on one side and a drop down to the hard
floor on the other.

Bryn and Wyla tottered along this edge while balancing as best
they could with their arms, a sizzling sound accompanying each
footstep. Halfway down the hall both lost footing for a second and
it seemed they might crash into each other, or worse, into the fire.
Wyla lost her balance and fell off toward the floor then broke her
fall with a tumbling roll.

Bryn did not relent and caught his footing as he fell toward the
blistering embers. The whole company gasped as he ran right on
top of the embers themselves, his feet kicking up a storm of smoke
and flying ash. As he scrambled over the sweltering heat, he let out
a yelp which turned into a roar. At last, one of his feet found the
end of the hearth and he leapt through the air toward Keymaster
Signy, snatching the key as he flew.

The floors rumbled and the rafters quaked as the hall erupted
into cheers. A dozen recruits rushed over to Bryn and hoisted
him up. Bryn, still wheezing from exhaustion, coughed from the

smoke. He frantically flailed his smoking feet in an effort to cool them off, but accidently kicked one of the revelers in the head. Torin and Grimsa laughed and rushed to join the crowd around their victorious companion. They steadied him on their shoulders and hoisted him up and down as they cheered.

The celebration was short-lived. From across the room a crowd had also gathered around Wyla and someone called out in a gruff voice. "Cheat! Cheat! He pushed her off the hearth!"

One of the recruits near Bryn shouted back. "Hardly! She tried to pull him into the fire!" Jeers and sneers were exchanged on both sides of the hall and Torin feared that an ugly brawl might ensue. He let Bryn down, then stepped up onto the table to address the whole crowd.

"Friends, calm yourselves! Did Keymaster Signy not set the challenge wisely? The one with the key is the undisputed victor. Look for yourself! Who holds the key to Fjellhall?" Bryn, wincing slightly as he stood on his roasted feet, held the key up high with a pained grin. Both cheers and hisses rose from the crowd.

"Let them race again!"

"No cheating this time!"

"Stop whining, you milk-drinking sop!"

Keymaster Signy, who by this time had ascended to the loft, addressed the company again. "Douse your tempers or else I will refuse to host the next two challenges." This soon had the crowd quiet again, as no one wanted the entertainment to end.

"Much better," she said, "As Master Ten-Trees said, the matter is decided. Firm nods came from Bryn's supporters and groans came from Wyla's. "Besides, there are still two more contests to be held, so let's proceed."

Wyla stepped forward with a sour look on her face. "On account of the circumstances of the race I do not consider this matter decided." Her throng of supporters cheered. "However, I do respect the Keymaster of this ancient hall and so I concede for this evening only. But know this—I will challenge you again, Bryn of Clan Foxfoot, then we shall see who is fleetest of foot." Of course, everyone was amiable to a rematch and so all toasted her response.

Keymaster Signy nodded. "Next, the contest of riddles!"

Wyla and Torin stepped up onto the table, and the crowd of onlookers packed tight around its edges. Both were handed a horn full of mead as was the custom. Torin took a healthy swig of his drink and Wyla gulped hers down all at once.

"Perhaps you should not begin your drinking too soon before you face off against Grimsa," Torin said, "It seems you've underestimated one of us already."

Wyla sneered. "Hardly. I would have beat him in a third race and you know it. Enough talk. Speak your riddle, Ten-Trees."

Torin's father had been fond of riddles and had taught him many. More he had heard from the many wanderers who found their way to Ten-Tree Hall. In fact, Torin had even composed a few himself. Now over one hundred eyes were on him and he needed to make his next move very carefully.

"According to custom, you should present first, as I was the one to challenge you to a game of riddles." All around the table heads nodded in agreement. She was bold, Torin thought, but ignorant of the old customs.

"Fine," Wyla said. She waited until the whole hall was quiet then began her verse.

> *Upon the wind a shadow quick*
> *Ancient memory, lightning wit*
> *Mocking calls to king and thrall*
> *Hoarding shining trinkets small*

Torin felt the weight of one hundred sets of eyes fall upon him. It came to his mind how his father often said that it was not just the quality of the steel but the force of the smith's hammer that forges a fine sword. He smiled. Wyla's face was hard to read but her riddle was not hard to guess. "I know the answer to your riddle. It is the raven who is as quick as a shadow, who remembers all it sees, who mocks all with its eerie cry, and who hoards bits of shiny silver." Wyla nodded and the crowd toasted Torin's response with a cheer.

Wyla took another horn full of mead, which she tossed back in a single swig. Torin let suspense quell the chatter before he responded. "This is a verse of my own making," he said, "See if you are able to unlock its meaning."

> *Stags and rabbits both it catches*
> *Chews on roots from garden patches*
> *Every night it has its fill*
> *Yet in its place stands ever still*

Wyla's nostrils flared and her stormy eyes shifted. She crossed her arms and moved her weight onto one foot then the other. She shouted suddenly. "Aha! The trapper's snare, for it catches beasts and does not move."

Torin shook his head. "No, a snare chews no roots."

For the first time that night, she looked miserably uncomfortable. Torin could feel the weight of the crowd's staring eyes press hard on her from all sides. She growled another guess. "A hunter. A hunter may eat both roots and stags and a good one will eat his fill every night."

"A hunter does not stand still in one place. You have one more guess."

"And I believe," she said, "that by the old customs I have until sunrise tomorrow to give my answer."

Torin nodded in agreement. It was a particularly grueling aspect of these duels of the mind, and many a mighty jarl had spent a sleepless night wrestling with a confounding riddle. "Certainly. But we shall be sitting here a long time if you mean to lean back on your heels and think until then."

Wyla smirked and shrugged. "Then perhaps the mead will loosen my mind and give me the answer. Grimsa Jarnskald, let us drink!"

Grimsa, sitting at the bench near Torin, roared with delight and hopped up onto the table. Keymaster Signy had two hall hands bring up a pair of casks, each filled with fine ale. She declared that both Wyla and Grimsa would stand on the table and match each other horn for horn until one could no longer stand. Little explanation was needed because everyone present was familiar with the customs of such contests which were common among village folk and soldiers.

Each was given a mead horn and an ale attendant to refill it. The golden froth of the ale ran down the side of each brim-full horn, and the two toasted the crowd before downing them briskly. A second, a third, and a fourth horn were finished before Grimsa spoke up.

"This is fine ale! May the gods keep brewmaster Signy!"

"Fine ale indeed," Wyla said, "I mean to finish my cask and perhaps finish off yours if you are not up to it."

"Oh, I plan on finishing my cask, do not doubt that. However, with these horns it may take all night. Is there any larger vessel we could use to speed up the contest? Otherwise the crowd may get bored and fall asleep."

Wyla agreed and so from the kitchen two dull grey goblets were brought forth, each which held a little less than two horns worth. A fourth, fifth, sixth, and seventh cup were drunk.

Upon finishing the eighth, Grimsa fumbled his cup and it fell off the table. Bryn was quick to bend down to retrieve it for him and Grimsa thanked him kindly. Grimsa looked at the cup that Bryn had handed him. "Perhaps it is the ale, or perhaps it is my poor sight, but I cannot help but think that my cup is bigger than yours Wyla. Not that I mind having the bigger cup, in fact I prefer it! But if we come to a draw at the end of the night some may say I bested you for drinking from a larger vessel."

"The ale must be getting to your head Grimsa," Wyla said. Her syllables slurred slightly as she spoke. "They seem quite similar to me. But let it not be said that I had the smaller vessel. Give me that cup and I will give you mine. Then, when I have bested you with the larger vessel, no one will doubt the victor." And so they exchanged cups.

Bryn smiled wickedly as he looked over to Torin, who chuckled and shook his head. People all around the table cheered, as these contests rarely lasted past the fifth or sixth horn. Each cup was refilled and, as before, Wyla and Grimsa toasted each other.

Grimsa once again swiftly gulped down the cup as he had done before but Wyla was a long time drinking before she let the cup down with a gasp. A bit of ale sloshed out of her cup and she looked bewildered.

"See?" Grimsa said, "I thought it was larger. Or perhaps you are slowing down?"

Wyla growled at him then took a deep breath and then chugged down the frothy ale again. She drank and drank, so long that most others would have choked or fainted. At last she let the cup down and doubled over, gasping for air. Still ale sloshed up over the rim of the plain grey goblet.

"I'm not saying that you cannot finish this round," Grimsa said, "but forgive me for saying this—if you cannot finish a cup in two swigs, three at most, it would be quite an embarrassment."

This time she roared and drew such a breath as none had seen before and drank with a fury like that of the gods. Again a silence fell over the crowd as she gulped, both hands clutching the vessel, until it seemed her face was blue. Then she let the vessel down. With disbelief she looked down to see that it was still not empty.

Wyla roared. "What sort of trolls' magic is this? All here are my witnesses. I drank no small amount and yet look!" She lowered the cup so those around her could see. "It has gone down just a finger's width!" Grimsa could restrain himself no longer and began to laugh mightily, wheezing in between breaths.

What happened next was hotly contested the next morning, but all agreed on this: the chaos began when Wyla hurled the cup at Grimsa and struck him square in the middle of the forehead. He fell off the table dazed, taking a few of the spectators with him, and knocked the bench over which sent another dozen people sprawling. Horns flew and ale splashed in every direction and then all manner of mayhem ensued.

Brawls broke out between the onlookers and soon the whole hall was in an uproar, arms locked in wrestling matches, drunken fists flying furiously, spilled ale and mead flowing across the table and the floor. Bryn, who was enjoying the company of a young woman tending to his burnt feet, was nearly trampled, and Grimsa had several of the recruits piled on top of him in a wriggling, wrestling mass. As Torin rushed to aid his friends, he heard a voice shout out to him over the racket.

"Torin Ten-Trees, damn your riddles. Keep your secrets! I have answered your challenges, now answer mine! Fight me if you dare!"

Torin leapt up on the table and rushed at Wyla. She fought like Torin had never seen anyone fight before, twirling and twisting in a flurry of fists and feet. Her braided hair spun wildly, whipping Torin's forearms, and her limbs and back seemed to be made of rubber, bending at nearly impossible angles. They exchanged a few misplaced blows, because the slippery table made it hard to keep a solid footing.

At last Torin saw his chance as her back foot slipped and she tipped backwards. He rushed forward, but as he did, she bent her spine backwards and planted her hands on the table behind her. The last thing Torin remembered of that night was the graceful arc of her foot sweeping up to hit his jaw as she flipped herself over backward, then his vision went black.

5

◊ UNTESTED ◊

TORIN WOKE UP in the same place he had the day before, on a
stack of hay wrapped with twine in the lofts of Fjellhall. For rea-
sons that were slow to come to his mind, he also had a splitting
headache and a stiff neck. Foggy recollections of a race, a few riddles, and a drinking contest filtered through from his aching head.
He remembered Erik, the fool, who had sung a fool's verse about
him. Something else, something more important, had happened
after that.

Torin groaned as he sat up. He felt throbbing in his cheek and
blood rushed to his head. There was probably a good bruise. In the
next bed over he saw Bryn, feet wrapped in bandages. The contested race. Grimsa, in the next bed down, snored and grinned as he
slept. In his hands he clutched a plain grey vessel: Drombir's cup.

Torin poked the bruise on his right cheek and winced. He
closed his eyes and remembered Wyla challenging him from
where she stood on the table. Through the murk of half-remem-
bered thoughts, he saw her twirling form, twisting left and right,
a flurry of fists and feet. At last he recalled the graceful arc of her
foot racing up toward his face and the thick black curtain that had
fallen down over the stage of his consciousness.

Keymaster Signy stomped up the stairs with three hall hands chasing after her. "Well, then I will go and tell him myself. That girl is out of control and I won't have a peace-breaking in my hall go unanswered. Now, clean out this loft and set it with fresh hay. There will be another group of recruits arriving in a few days and we've little enough time to refill our store of mead and ale."

Her eyes caught Torin's bruised face and she stopped abruptly. "Master Ten-Trees, what are you still doing here? The untested recruits are gathering in Stonering Keep as we speak. You three must get over there immediately or you'll be stuck sweeping this hall for the next two years!"

Torin leapt out of bed and hauled Bryn onto the floor in one swift movement. He then jumped over Bryn's bed and shook Grimsa furiously. "Wake up, you grisly boar! We've got to get to Stonering Keep!"

Grimsa rubbed his eyes. "By the gods, what time is it? What's going on?"

"We are going to miss the sorting! Get your boots on and let's go!"

All three had barely slipped on their boots and tunics before they tumbled down the stairs. Bryn hopped awkwardly on his raw soles and Grimsa, still a bit drunk, tottered back and forth. Keymaster Signy ordered a cup of fruit wine and a loaf of steaming bread be brought up for the each of them. "Drink this quick and eat these on the way. And do be careful around that girl!"

Torin's mouth was half-full of steaming bread. "That Wyla. Who is she?"

Keymaster Signy opened her eyes wide and gaped. "Who is she? I thought you knew. She is Captain Calder's daughter. Didn't you see her come in with him?"

Torin nearly choked on his fruit wine. All three companions went pale. Each remembered the man in bearskin who had addressed the crowd last night, his wiry grey hair and his pale skin, commander over all Gatewatch.

Signy shook her head. "She's as reckless as a wild wolf. I hold her responsible for breaking the peace last night but do take more care around her. Now be off, before it's too late!"

Torin felt sick in his stomach and worried that he might see the wine and bread that he had scarfed down again sooner than he would like. The sun hit his eyes like the clash of a cymbal when he threw open the door. Each of the companions held up an arm to block the sun as they raced down the rocky road to Stonering Keep.

The gates into the rough stone fortress were wide open. Through the arched passage, they entered a circular courtyard about two hundred paces wide. At the far end, a gathering of recruits looked up at a fur-clad figure who addressed them from the top of the wall. Torin, Bryn, and Grimsa rushed across the uneven stones toward crowd.

"And today we shall decide just how you will serve The Greyraven," the speaker said, "with an axe or with a broomstick, it matters not to me." It was Captain Calder. Torin's face flushed red and he cursed under his breath. A few of the recruits nearby eyed the three but Calder ignored them.

"So consider now whether you have the heart of a hero with the strength and courage to face the dreaded trolls. If, in your consideration, you find fear where there should be boldness, then take your leave of this place and report to Keymaster Signy in Fjellhall for assignment."

A moment passed before four or five recruits began to shuffle back toward the hall. Most of the three dozen or so gathered stood their ground.

Captain Calder grinned. "Now we will see what you are truly made of." Two Greycloaks passed out long wooden sparing poles. From across the crowd, Torin saw Wyla. She flexed her grip on the rough wooden shaft, spun it nimbly, then smiled wickedly at him. Torin narrowed his eyes and clenched his jaw.

Calder surveyed the crowd and hardened his gaze. "You've all heard the stories, fireside tales of troll-hunters and heroes. Gate-watch is where those legends were forged. Now it is time for the smith of fate to strike with his hammer. Will you be broken into pieces or will you be molded into warriors worthy of taking up Beoric's flaming torch?"

Some of the new recruits shouted in unison. "Long live the Greyraven!"

"Will you hide under your beds while trolls threaten to devour your families and burn your homes, or will you take up the axe and stand beside your brothers and sisters to vanquish the horde?"

Energy shot through the crowd like a flash of lightning. "Long live the Greyraven!"

"Will you flee into the depths of despair when doom hangs in the air, or will you follow the blazing flame of your ancestors' call out of that darkness to win glory and victory?"

"Long live the Greyraven! Long live the Greyraven!"

Torin was startled by a loud slam behind him. He turned to see that the gate which led back into town had been shut tight. When he looked back up to where Captain Calder had been, there was no one there. The two Greycloaks had also disappeared and now the group of wide-eyed recruits were left clutching their wooden sparing poles in the middle of an otherwise empty courtyard.

Half a minute passed without a stir. To shake the uneasy tension, Torin bounced on his heels. He exchanged glances with Bryn and with Grimsa but said nothing. Wyla seemed no less confused than he was, her stance cautious, sparing pole ready.

Torin broke the silence. "Gather together, back to back in a tight ring!"

Grimsa and Bryn immediately went to work shoving dazed recruits into place. "Poles outward, fighting stance," Torin said, "Now brace yourselves!"

The haze of confusion had evaporated now, and everyone rushed to join the formation. Wyla shouted similar orders on the far side of the group and soon the whole company had formed a two layered ring. Those on the outside crouched on one knee and those on the inside stood upright making a tight, defensive knot.

In the still quiet, the sparing poles bristled outwards like the thorns on a briar bush. Then, from the West Gate that led to the wilds, a dull thud rattled heavy iron hinges. Torin's shoulders tensed and he felt his heartbeat quicken in his throat. Another thud, louder this time, caused the rusted hinges to creak as the door opened slightly. The West Gate to the wilds was not locked and something from beyond had just pushed it open.

"Brace!" said Torin, "Hold your positions! Watch every side!"

Wyla pushed through the ring toward the gate. "No, break the ring and form a line! Face the West Gate!"

There was an awful commotion as some followed Torin's orders and some followed Wyla's. The ring broke at several points and soon there was a confused knot of recruits all tripping over each other and shoving to get into place.

A third bang against the door flung it wide open. In the frame of the West Gate stood a great hulking bear. It shook its head, stood on its hind legs, then roared with such ferocity that Torin felt the stones rattle beneath his feet.

Screams and shouts came from every direction as the recruits trampled each other or stumbled over abandoned sparing poles in their retreat. Those that made it to town gate found it securely locked. Despite their pleas and their pounding, it did not budge. Wyla and the three companions rushed to rally their peers but only succeeded in pulling a few back into formation.

Torin roared out over the chaos. "Hold your ground! Defend Gatewatch! This is what you came here for, to protect your families, to gain honor, to win glory!" A few recruits took courage from Torin's words and picked up their sparing poles again. Well over half continued to wail and pound on the town gate.

"Do not run like cowards," said Wyla, "Make a stand, you yellow-livered eels!" She caught Erik, the fool from the night before, as he tried to flee and threw him to the ground. "Grab your sparring pole and stand your ground!" She picked him up by the collar of his tunic and shoved a pole into his hands. Erik did not dare to run again, in part because his knees were shaking so violently.

Torin gave up on the mob at the town gate and rallied those who had found their courage. This company was significantly smaller than the first, but they formed a small semi-circle, staffs extended, and moved toward the shaggy beast.

The bear saw them approach and fell back down onto all fours with force. It growled; a sound so low that the rumble it seemed to come from the earth itself. Then let out a roar which nearly deafened Torin's ears. Two more recruits dropped their poles and ran. As they drew closer, Torin realized the dreadful size of the bear. Its shoulders stood just above Torin's eye level and was at least three times as wide as Grimsa. Even at one hundred paces he could smell the beast's rancid stench. The bear lowered its head and bared its teeth, shoulders flexing and claws extended.

The small company stopped advancing and stood their ground. Torin's stomach lurched inside his ribcage and he gritted his teeth. "Hold!"

"Break off the end of your sparing pole," said Wyla. She snapped the tip off with her foot. "Create a sharp end!"

Everyone in the company did the same except for Erik who could not get the end of his stick to break. Wyla grabbed it, snapped it clean in half, and threw it back at him.

Torin raised his pole. "Charge on my count!"

"No," Wyla said, "Split into two groups and flank the bear!"

Torin glared at her, his eyes ablaze. "We barely have enough strength as it is. Do not split up!"

"What if the charge fails? Then we are finished!"

It was too late. The bear charged at them full speed, teeth bared and claws flashing. Its massive muscles rippled under its greasy brown fur and fury burned in its hollow black eyes. Each footstep could be felt as a tremble in the stones beneath them, and panic struck the recruits again. Torin, Grimsa, Bryn, Wyla, and a handful of hearty recruits gritted their teeth, stood their ground, and braced themselves against the charge.

Suddenly a host of Greycloaks rose up from behind the jagged stones around the top of the courtyard wall, two or three dozen in all. Hoods obscured their faces, like thieves or phantoms. Each one lifted a thick-shafted longbow in one hand and drew an arrow from their leather quiver with the other. A chorus of creaks echoed all around as they pulled their arrows tight on the bowstring. From the top of one of the crumbling towers Captain Calder reappeared. "Loose arrows!"

Like a whirring swarm of raging insects, the arrows flew over Torin's head. Almost every whizzing shaft stuck fast. The bear reeled as the steel arrowheads bit into its flesh like crooked teeth. Torin, Grimsa, Bryn, Wyla and those few who had stood against the bear leapt out of its path as it staggered forward. It stumbled straight past them toward the crowd of recruits quivering at the city gate.

Captain Calder used his long-necked axe as a climbing pick as he leapt down from the crumbling tower, then scaled the rocky inner wall to the courtyard floor. He stepped in front of the unarmed mob at the town gate and, just in time, sunk his axe blade deep into the bear's head with a resonant crack. The mass of fur and arrows and blood collapsed on the courtyard stones and for a moment all was still.

Captain Calder braced his foot against the bear's head and yanked his axe free. "Anyone with a sparing pole still in hand stays. The rest of you report to Fjellhall."

The gate back into town opened up again. On the other side stood two Greycloaks with disapproving looks on their grizzled faces who directed those who had failed the test back toward town. Most who had fled seemed all too happy to spend the coming months sweeping floors if it meant not seeing another bear up close. Nevertheless, a few cursed their cowardice as their dreams of glory faded like the last red rays of light at sunset.

Captain Calder growled as they passed by. "Move quickly!"

Torin, Grimsa, Bryn, Wyla, and about a dozen other dazed recruits stood silent in the courtyard, splintered sparing poles in hand. The host of hooded archers eyed them from the top of the courtyard wall.

Captain Calder grinned as he walked toward the recruits, his teeth wolfish and yellowed. He wiped the last of the gore off his axe onto the sole of his boot. "So, there is still courage to be found in Noros. You few have passed the first trial. But do not think that you are worthy to become Greycloaks of Gatewatch just because you did not flee at the first sign of danger. The wild lands beyond the West Gate are full of dangers far greater than mere beasts. The wilds themselves, the tangled woods and the rushing rivers, have taken just as many men and women as wolves or boars or bears."

Torin met the captain's iron gaze and his stomach twitched. Calder narrowed his eyes and continued. "And then there are trolls! Dim witted and ill-tempered, they have legs as thick and as hard as tree trunks and skulls like iron buckets. I've seen trolls swallow men and women whole, stomp them flat, or cook them into stew like mutton. Once my horse was tossed one hundred paces by a troll as big as a house before I could hack the head from its mountainous shoulders." He lowered his voice and leaned on the handle of his axe. "I've even encountered a few that dabble in magic. One had learned a charm that could douse any flame. It kept our camp frozen and fireless for over a week. Half my party was frozen to death before we hunted the fiend down."

Every word pricked Torin like a needle, each syllable a twist inspiring increased horror. Erik's face was pale as an egg white and Bryn's eyes were wide. Even Grimsa looked a bit queasy. Torin shivered when he saw that while Captain Calder had been speaking, the host of Greycloaks on the wall had disappeared unnoticed, like smoke on the wind. He wondered where they had gone and when.

Calder stepped back and pointed with his long-handled axe at the West Gate that led out to the wilds. "Tomorrow you will go out into the wilds and prove yourselves worthy of walking beside those who live and die under the Greyraven's banner as Greycloaks."

The town gate swung open once again and through it came a huge woman. She had blonde braids of bead-laden hair that bounced off her shoulders and a stern look on her flushed face. Rough chainmail hung down to her knees and she had a rough grey cape draped over her shoulders. Her burly arms were covered from wrist to elbow in intricate designs, swirling knots of black and green, depicting trees and birds and beasts. After greeting Calder ceremoniously, she planted her feet firmly on the stones, crossed her arms, and stood with her shoulders square to the recruits. Her face was as still as stone.

"This is Almveig, veteran troll-hunter of the Gatewatch. Four trolls have fallen by her axe. She is the head of your company now." Calder's narrow eyes swept across the untested recruits and settled on Wyla for a brief moment. "May the gods keep you. May Orr fill your arm with strength, Odd fill your head with quick wits, and Fyr fill your heart with courage. Long live the Greyraven!"

The company shouted together in response. "Long live the Greyraven!"

As Calder departed, Torin searched Wyla's face. Her eyes followed him as he walked away with a look that could have been either spite or deep affection. Perhaps it was both.

Almveig grinned like a devil. "Listen up, untested whelps! It seems you each need to replace the sparing pole you broke during the testing today. The best trees are in the wilds and tomorrow we will go hunting for saplings, one to replace your sparing pole and one for a bow shaft that you will craft yourself." Almveig's heavy legs remained planted like tree trunks as her gaze drifted back and forth across the company. "We leave from this very spot at dawn. Anyone who fails to arrive by the time the sun has left the horizon will be sweeping floors until the next two winters have passed." With that she turned back toward Gatewatch and left the gathering of wide-eyed recruits alone in the middle of Stonering Keep with the stinking bear carcass.

"Well," Wyla said, "it seems our company has been greatly reduced." She walked through the crowd toward Torin, Bryn, and Grimsa. "Though I believe those left here are much more worthy of my company than the rest of that rabble. Not everyone is born with courage."

"Though some find it," said Torin, "when circumstance demands it."

Wyla ignored Torin and turned away. "Any of you here with courage to spare are welcome to join me at Frostridge Falls this evening. There is a natural steam spring near the top of that peak." She pointed the tip of her broken sparring pole to the top of the mountain ridge that hung over the south edge of Gatewatch. "Anyone with heart enough to join me will look over the wild lands at sunset and drink a toast with me. We will swear loyalty to each other and take the kin-oath of shield brothers and sisters."

She turned to Torin and faced him nose to nose. "Though if you would rather spend your last night here in Gatewatch tucked into a cozy bed at Fjellhall, drinking milk and nibbling honey biscuits, you are welcome to do that as well."

Torin narrowed his eyes as he weighed his response. Climbing the ridge at night seemed unwise but he could not stomach backing down. He had the patience to let the tense silence linger a moment longer before carefully crafting his response. Grimsa, it seemed, did not.

"What do you take us for?" Grimsa said, "A bunch of spineless eels?"

Wyla spun toward him and laughed. "Your words, not mine. Are you afraid to join me, Grimsa Jarnskald?"

"Not in the least! What is more, we will beat you to Frostridge! We have already bested you in one race so why not a second?"

Wyla's face darkened and she sneered. "I do not consider that matter closed."

Bryn smirked and crossed his arms smugly.

"What I remember is that you fell off the table before I did. What a surprise that was! Me outlasting a Jarnskald in a drinking contest."

Grimsa's cheeks boiled beneath his bristling beard. "You lobbed a goblet at my head! I was unaware that this was allowed. But if you want to challenge me again, this time to a stone throwing, I will gladly crush you with a boulder twice the size of your head!"

Torin cut in front of the huge huffing man. "Grimsa, I think we are forgetting who our real enemy is." Torin shot a tight-lipped glance at Wyla, then addressed the crowd of recruits. "We are here to fight trolls, not each other. Am I right?"

"Aye," said one of the recruits. A few others nodded.

Torin let his shoulders down and smiled. "Then let us act together. If we should stay and feast in Fjellhall tonight, then let us stay together. If we go to revel in the day's success at Frostridge Falls, then let us go together."

Wyla's eyes blazed and her nostrils flared. "Who elected you leader Ten-Trees? Just because your father has a gilded hall does not make you prince over us." At this the recruits stood uneasily, their eyes shifting back and forth between the two.

Torin drew slow steady breaths to calm his twitching nerves. "Every leader must prove his or her worthiness to lead. That is the old way."

"And you, Torin Ten-Trees, have not proven yourself to me, so quit acting like a noble lord and embrace your new position: a soldier, a ranger, a gritty, greasy troll hunter." She shoved him so hard that he lost his footing and stumbled backwards.

Torin's patience broke like the crack of thunder. He flew at her, his fist whistling through the air at her mocking scowl. When he anticipated making contact there was nothing but air.

Wyla clapped and laughed. "That's more like it!"

Wyla and Torin circled each other as the recruits formed a ring around the pair. As he lunged forward, she swung her torso back at a nearly impossible angle, spine like rubber, and planted her hands against the stone like she had done the night before. Wyla shot her foot up toward Torin's bruised chin as she flipped over. He heard her foot whir past his ear just as he craned his neck to the side. He had at least learned that much from the night before.

"That bruise on your cheek is not flattering," said Wyla, "but perhaps another will even things out." In a twirl of fists and feet she pelted him left and right with blows. He braced, his arms shielding his face and upper body, not so much to deflect but to absorb her flurry of blows. He swung his fist like a hammer, but she leapt back nimbly, landing in a crouch a few feet back.

Torin drew a heavy breath. "Who taught you to fight like that?"

"Aspens in the wind," Wyla said. Torin thought it sounded as if she had been waiting for that question and had rehearsed the answer to herself one hundred times. "Where other trees snap, aspens simply bend. When the storm is over and other trees are stripped naked, the aspen still has her branches." Torin was not certain that this was true but nodded anyways.

"Well, I did not learn to bend either my back or my knee." He let the insult sting for a moment. "We Ten-Trees are taught to stay rooted and hold our ground."

Wyla sprinted at him and twisted at the last minute, slamming her knee into his ribs. Quick as she was, Torin was able to catch her by the forearms mid-kick. They grappled arm-to-arm, twisting and thrashing like mighty river salmon until they tumbled over onto the rough, unforgiving stone.

Torin could not pin Wyla. Whenever he saw an opportunity, she twisted out of range or butted him with her forehead. She tried to strangle him or yank his arm into a contorted position, but he muscled his way out of each hold. After a minute or two of struggle, Torin threw his whole weight over her hoping to end the match with a crash but she rolled away just in time. He collapsed with a groan as he slammed against the stones. Wyla, half a dozen paces away, drew raspy breaths and laid sprawled out on the rough rocks.

Each rolled up onto one knee and eyed the other, exhausted but still cautious. A trickle of blood ran down Wyla's forehead and Torin tasted some of his own in his mouth.

Bryn stepped in between them. "Alright, enough already. Slaying each other won't prove anything. But slaying a troll certainly would."

"Is there any doubt that I will be the first?" said Wyla.

"There is until you've done the deed."

Each stayed crouched, tense but tired. Their glaring eyes met like steel blades grinding against each other. However, like the hottest embers that fall out of the fire, their tempers began to cool.

Wyla coughed and spat out a bit of blood. "Then let us agree to this: whoever first slays a troll the other must concede by means of a poem of praise." She drew another hoarse breath. "A poem to be recited in full view of all the company of Fjellhall."

Torin nodded. In his chest, beside raw lungs, bruised ribs, and a pounding heart, he felt the very first sliver of good will toward her. "Agreed."

Each one, shaking as they stood, spit in their right palm. With smoldering gazes, they squeezed each other's hand in the way of oath making. The recruits clapped and Bryn and Grimsa laughed.

Bryn slapped his hands on Torin and Wyla's backs as they released their white-knuckled handshake. "So, are you going to show us the way to Frostridge Falls or what?"

With that, the whole company headed back toward the town gate and the stone street that led through Gatewatch.

6

◇ FROSTRIDGE FALLS ◇

GATEMASTER GAVRING filled the arch of the East Gate, his arms crossed and his eyebrows drawn together into a frown. Before him stood Wyla, Torin, Bryn, Grimsa, and a few of the other recruits, cloaks on and bags packed full of festive provisions.

"What foolishness is this? To Frostridge? What for?"

"To celebrate!" Bryn said. "We passed the first trial."

Gavring muttered something obscene and then pointed one of his giant fingers at Bryn. "You will get a taste of the wilds outside of Gatewatch soon enough." He shook his head and stared at the small band with a stern eye. "Better to spend one last night in comfort at Fjellhall than to scramble up a frozen mountain. There may not be trolls on this side of Gatewatch but there are plenty of other hazards. And what if a storm blows in? You could be stuck on that mountain for days!"

Wyla stepped forward. She looked ridiculous next to the gigantic watchman, but she placed her hands firmly on her hips and thrust her jaw out. "I know a quick way up Gavring. I've been there before. We will be back just after sunset. You have my assurance."

"Forgive me for doubting your assurances Wyla. Did you not tell me once that the pet rat you had found in Siggam's field did not have the fever? Or that you could scale the East Gate tower without falling down and breaking a limb?"

Her face flushed red with hot blood. "That was years ago. Besides, if you won't let us pass, I know another way over the wall. So, unless you plan on tying us all up, you had better let us through."

The huge man rolled his eyes and sighed, then dropped his shoulders to a sloop. "I have a feeling that no good will come of this." He gripped the gate winch wheel and began to turn it slowly. Torin grinned at Gavring, but the big man just shook his head.

A gust of wind off the field blew in through the opening gate and filled Torin's nose with the scent of green grass, wet earth and sweet mountain flowers. The valley before them was a feast for the eyes: swaths of rippled grass, clusters of flowers in rich reds, yellows, purples, and blues, and wandering streams of icy mountain water. The air above was intensely clear so that every detail of the mountain ridges on either side of the valley was crisp against the pale blue sky.

The gate closed behind them. Gavring scrambled up to his post at the tower and called out again. "I hear that Signy has a roast on, wild boar, I think. And I saw the bread being baked this morning, honey-glazed fruit biscuits stuffed with wild-berry preserve. I bet she would pair such a feast with a dark fruit wine or perhaps a thick, frothy stout. A pity to miss all that. Are you sure you still want to leave?"

Grimsa frowned and leaned over to Torin. "Perhaps we should reconsider. After all, Frostridge will still be there until after dinner, won't it?"

"Too late, Grimsa. The feast will have to wait."

Grimsa sighed and shrugged, then joined the rest of the company as they hiked up the lush green slope toward the towering ridge.

Of the dozen or so recruits that passed the morning trial, only a few of them could be convinced to journey up to Frostridge.

The others had stayed for fear of ill weather or, more likely, of Almveig's wrath. Wyla led the way, her long braids of coal-black hair swaying in the breeze. Torin followed closely behind, along with Bryn and Grimsa who were debating the virtues of firemead over ale.

Erik, the fool, had thrown his lot in with them, though he tended to straggle. There were also the twins Inga and Asa, daughters of a famous huntsman named Grettir Longstride. These seven trekked up the valley, splashing through creeks and wading through waist high grass, under the radiant gaze of the afternoon sun.

Torin stepped up beside Wyla, leaving Bryn and Grimsa to their debate.

"So why did you not introduce yourself as Calders-daughter last night at Fjellhall?"

She screwed up her face and sneered. "Calders-daughter. I hardly know him. Besides, I plan on casting my own shadow on the world, not living in his."

Torin frowned at the disregard she showed for her father. It was especially shameful given her father's high position. He pondered this quietly. After a moment, he sighed. More than anyone else, Torin knew the burden of expectations, the heavy dreams his own father had laid on him, and the yoke of obligation which had constantly weighed on him while he lived under the thick rafters of Ten-Tree Hall.

"I know what it is like to grow up in the shadow of a great man."

Wyla smiled with her lips but her eyes remained dull and stony. "Then you know nothing about me." She took a few quick steps ahead and left Torin behind.

Grimsa and Bryn agreed to disagree on the matter of firemead versus ale and moved on to the subject of fighting trolls. Erik was reciting half-verses of love poetry to Inga and Asa.

Like flower petals full
Lips bloom out from your face
In your eyes, like lake blue skies,
I linger in the reflection

Inga tilted her head and frowned. "Did you compose that verse, Erik?"

Erik smiled and smoothed his yellow hair. "Yes, I did, just this morning actually."

Asa nodded. "We could tell." Erik's face fell as the two sisters walked past him on the trail.

At last they approached the foot of Frostridge Falls. Surging water tumbled down from off the top of the sheer cliff and crashed into a deep pool far below. Swirls of steam rose up out of the pool and off the column of falling water, foam-white and misty.

The roar of the falls was deafening and Torin could hear little more than his own thoughts. Even fifty paces back from the water's edge, he was buffeted by an unnaturally warm breeze. Drops of temperate vapor coated his face and cloak. All kinds of moss and algae, green, brown, red, orange, and yellow, made the rocks so slick that he could barely keep his balance.

Grimsa slipped over onto his back and cursed loudly. Everyone laughed and soon he too began to chuckle as he attempted to stand, his hand slipping on a boulder or his foot sliding off a wet rock. He collapsed again, laughing so hard his belly shook. "It is no use. Leave me here as troll bait!"

"I don't think even a troll would have much of an appetite for you in this state, sweaty and covered in slime," said Torin, "I think you are more likely to attract frogs and slugs."

"Well then, by the gods, leave me here to the toads or come help me up!"

Wyla and Torin each grabbed one of his arms and heaved Grimsa to his feet. He wheezed and steadied himself. "That is the problem with being top-heavy. Balancing comes with great difficulty."

Bryn, who was now closest to the foot of the raging falls, turned back toward the company. "You are not top heavy, Grimsa."

Grimsa's eyes shot wide open and his nostrils flared. "Not top-heavy? You are one to speak, you spindly twat!"

"No, my friend, you are heavy all over!"

At this Grimsa laughed and slapped him on the back, then the two of them followed the rest of the company up the loose pebbled path to the foot of the falls. Warm mist soaked them from the pointed hoods of their cloaks to the worn toes of their leather boots.

Torin dropped his bag and shook out his shoulders. "Will any-one else join me for a swim?"

"Not here," said Wyla. She had to shout over the noise of the falls. "The water is tepid. It is much hotter at the top." She squint-ed as drops of warm water off the falls splashed her face. "And the view is much more impressive."

Asa's eyes opened wide. "The top? You mean up there?" She pointed to the frothing mouth of the falls high over their heads. Wyla nodded and grinned.

Grimsa scratched his head. "Do you mean to climb this? I can barely stand on these moss-ridden stones. I have no mind to scale a wall covered in slime."

Bryn flapped his arms. "Perhaps we are to grow wings like a bird and fly?"

Wyla ignored him. She had a confident smirk on her face. With both hands she pulled up great tangles of soggy brush from the base of the cliff, roots and all, and tossed them down the slope. After she had cleared a certain section, she ran her hands along the slick cliff face at about knee height. Her fingers found the groove she was searching for and she gripped it. Braced against the slippery stones, she pressed her shoulder against the rock face.

She yanked hard and a piece of the cliff swung out toward the company. It was not a rough chunk of stone but a neat arch, tapered near the top, that hinged in place somehow like a door. Though the outside was rough and covered in moss, the inside of the door was flat and etched with strange inscriptions. Beyond the archway an unlit tunnel ran straight into the mountain.

"By the gods," said Bryn, "that must be the work of the *nidavel*!"

Wyla wheezed and wiped the mist off her face. "Yes, long abandoned, I think, but finely made."

Torin picked up his bag and ran up to the archway. He peered inside. "Are there many of these secret tunnels in the valley?"

"This is the only one I know of. I found the door handle accidentally while trying to climb the wall in winter. I could not open it wide enough to get inside because of the ice, so I came back in the spring. There is a staircase inside that leads straight to the top of Frostridge Falls." For the first time, Wyla smiled without sneering. The others all crowded around the secret passage to get a better look.

Wyla ducked down and crawled into the tunnel. "Follow me, first straight, then up and to the left." Torin followed, Inga and Asa after him. Grimsa needed an extra push from Bryn to squeeze his way in through the small entrance but, once inside, had just enough room to move. Then Bryn crouched into the dark tunnel, leaving only Erik outside in the mist.

Erik stood at the gaping entrance and peered into the dark after the rest of the company had disappeared inside. He shouted into the tunnel over the roar of the falls. "I don't like tunnels. Cramped spaces make me dizzy. And I hate the dark." No response came from inside the mountain. Erik cursed, then sucked in a lungful of air, closed his eyes, and clambered after the others.

Inside the tunnel, the air was dank and the darkness was thick. Torin felt the walls with his fingers to find they were cold, smooth, and dry. The passage was wide enough, but the ceiling hung so low that he had to squat down in order to shuffle ahead. This must be the work of the *nidavel*, Torin thought. Then he remembered his encounter with Drombir and the stories Gavring had told them in Fjellhall. A quiver rattled his hunched spine.

Wyla led the way. The noise of her scuffling knees on the floor and the sound of her cloak brushing against the wall echoed in the small stone hallway. In fact, every word, whisper, and breath seemed to echo down the tunnel half a dozen times or more. Grimsa's grunting echoed loudest through the cramped tunnel in low, rumbling tones.

Grimsa knocked his head against the ceiling again. "By the gods, how much farther?"

Wyla kept moving forward. "There is a staircase to the left. Not far."

Bryn was in no hurry to leave the *nidavellish* passage. "What craftsmanship! I had heard of the tunnel-making technique used by the *nidavel*. *Adretta* they call it, 'to make a straight way', but I never dreamed I would see it for myself."

"Stop drooling over this musty rat-hole," Grimsa said, "there's plenty enough slime outside."

"Rat hole? This is a wonder! How do they make the tunnels so straight? How do they know where to go?"

Inga laughed. "You two argue more than our mother and father."

"This way," said Wyla. Torin followed her through an opening to the left and then climbed up a spiral set of stone steps.

Up they climbed for what seemed to be a very long time. The stairway was narrower than the main passage and it curved around in a tight angle. In the opaque darkness Torin could not even see his own hand when he waved it right in front of his eyes. Because of this, he became more acutely aware of his other senses as his fingers brushed the smooth, cool stone to feel the way forward.

His nose drew in musty draughts of damp air and his ears caught every thump, grunt, and echo in the stairwell.

Torin bumped straight into Wyla. Apparently, she had stopped. Asa and Inga also stumbled into them before Wyla shouted back at them. "Stop! We've reached the top. Step back and give me some room."

In a moment, everyone managed to shuffle back a few steps. Wyla groaned as she strained at something and Torin heard a grinding noise. A piercing ray of light then sliced into the darkness. Fresh air, moist and warm, rushed through the tunnel, down the stairs, past the company, and deep into the mountain. Wyla hoisted a stone slab up and out of the way, as if it were the lid of a hatch, then pulled herself out the tunnel.

Torin followed her through the opening, his eyes blinded by the daylight. His fingers felt damp stone and he heard the gurgle of water nearby with the rumble of roaring falls farther off. Then the world came into view and he saw where he was sitting: a wide ledge overlooking the whole valley at the very top of Frostridge Falls.

Gatewatch lay far to the west, a cluster of miniature houses with little columns of white smoke rising from their stone chimneys. Stonering Keep was a perfect circle of crumbled stone, and the timbers of Fjellhall rose up higher than the rest. Beyond that, Torin could see the wilds, craggy old forests and sapphire blue lakes, which stretched on to the end of the horizon.

The fields below him were green and lush. Patches of wildflowers coloured the valley like strokes from a giant's brush, purples and blues in one place, reds and yellows in another. He saw the creeks and streams they had crossed earlier as a complete tapestry; each thread was knit together from further up the valley or woven in from one of the waterfalls along the valley. Gusts of wind sent ripples through the grass and made the water sparkle in the afternoon sun.

Then he looked eastward, to where they had come from three days ago. He saw the forest with the icy creek which had led them back to the road. The scree slope they had tumbled down shot straight up to a narrow clearing between two jagged peaks which were grey, but in so light a tone that they were nearly white against the pale blue sky. Black rubble, the rocks of Shadowstone Pass, marked the field of grim statues and shattered bones. Torin's heart thumped against his ribcage when he recalled the legion of smoldering ember eyes, the Watchers, each embedded in a wispy form that had hovered over the rubble and the bones.

A gruff voice shook the image from his head. "By the gods, can I get a hand or two to help me up?"

Torin turned and saw Grimsa's hands sticking up out of the tunnel hole. Torin and Asa grabbed one hand while Wyla and Inga grabbed the other to haul the huge man up. Bryn hopped up onto the ledge with an easy jump. Erik was helped up last and then the whole company stood together on the ledge and took in the view.

Bryn shook his head. "This must be what it is like to be an eagle soaring over the world."

"It is beautiful," said Grimsa, "but I must admit that the sight of Fjellhall makes my stomach rumble."

Wyla scoffed. "You and your damned stomach."

"Do you think we will make it back for the evening meal?"

Torin laughed. "Not likely my friend, but here seems as good a place as any to eat. Unless, of course, Wyla has any other hidden passages to show us."

Wyla smirked and threw down her pack. "This is the best kept secret in all the valley. I don't think I can top this one."

They dropped their packs well away from the precipitous ledge and let the warm mist blow past their faces. The company's spirits were as high as the outcrop they stood on and everyone, even Erik, had a smile on their face. But now, with the weight of the packs off their shoulders, stomachs began to rumble.

All together they managed a fair meal, at least as far as trail fare is concerned. They sat in a circle and each of them placed their contribution on a cloak in the center. Torin unpacked two heavy honey loaves, Bryn a leather pouch of wild nuts and dried fruit that he had bought from the market, and Grimsa a small cask of ale. Asa and Inga brought out strips of cured meat and salted fish. Erik produced a small bottle of fruit wine from the folds of his cloak which, Bryn pointed out, was already half empty. Last of all, Wyla took out a small bottle made of delicate crystal filled with a dark red liquid which glowed in the afternoon sun.

Inga leaned forward and peered into the clear crystal glass. "By the gods, what is that?"

Wyla grinned, her eyes drawn narrow. "This is a rare liqueur."

Bryn also leaned in closer. "Did Brewmaster Signy make it?"

"No, this was made by far craftier hands."

Bryn scratched his head. "The *nidavel*?"

"No, the fingers that worked this liquid to perfection are far more skilled than that."

Torin wondered what she could mean. He tilted his head and narrowed his gaze. "Witches?"

Wyla laughed. "No, I would not deal with witches, much less drink any of their foul concoctions." She held up the crystal bottle to the sunlight. "I purchased this at no small cost from a travelling merchant. He had come from the wild lands beyond Gatewatch." Every eye widened and each one leaned in closer.

"This wandering merchant was visiting the lands far north and to the west where the rushing river Noros is born, where snow and wind is made, and where giants, the ancient *jotur*, dwell. He learned many secrets and heard many tales in the great halls of the giant lords. In fact, he shared some of them late at night beside the hearth in Fjellhall to those who dared to listen. He was delivering a message to one of these giant lords from King Araldof Greyraven himself."

Torin had heard tales of the *jotur* in his father's hall, ancient giants who were said to live on the frozen glacial plains far north in magnificent castles made of ice and stone. All these tales agreed on three things: the *jotur* were very old, very wise, and very dangerous.

"What did they look like?" said Asa. Her voice was almost a whisper.

Wyla grabbed a strip of cured meat and leaned back with her legs crossed, and her gaze set far off down the valley. As she tore a bite off the tough strip, the others remained silent. "They are like us, at least in appearance, but much taller. The wanderer said he saw giants three times the height of the tallest man to be found in Gatewatch." Torin thought of Gavring and shuddered. "He also said their skin, pale as ivory, had a tinge of silver to it. Their hair, worn long and in braids, was red like tongues of fire or white like the clouds. Every one of them was greatly skilled in song and verse, in craft and magic, and most of all, in battle. It is even said that they might, at times, contend with the gods themselves."

For some time, they all sat in silence satisfying their hunger and relishing Wyla's description. Everyone took a hearty chunk of the sweet, honeyed bread. The cured meat that Asa and Inga brought had been made by their father and was richly flavoured with smoked cedar, almost as rich and sweet as the strips of dried fruit. Grimsa's cask of ale was passed around, a crisp golden liquid with sharp flavours and a bitter aftertaste. It went well with the salted fish and wild nuts. Besides Erik's fruit wine, which Torin suspected had been watered down, the meal was nearly as rich as those they had enjoyed in Fjellhall.

After everyone had eaten their fill, Torin leaned forward and inspected the crystal glass. "So, what about this liqueur makes it so special?"

"That was brewed from the juice of tart wildberries found only on the northern icefields mixed with water from the Everspring where the Noros River is born," said Wyla. She paused for a moment before she added another detail. "And one more thing: trolls' blood."

Grimsa nearly spat out the mouthful of ale he had just taken. "Trolls' blood!"

"Trolls' blood is like venom," Bryn said, "Do you mean to poison us all?"

Wyla chuckled. "The wanderer said that this draught is poisonous only to the coward. All others need not fear. So I am prepared to take the blood-oath with anyone here brave enough to share this drink with me." She grabbed the crystal glass, unscrewed the top, and took a swig. After a moment she shook her head and coughed.

The sun had started its slow descent toward the horizon, the sky already dusky orange. Wyla held up the open bottle, offering it to whomever would take a sip. The ruby liquid glowed and glimmered like a flame in the falling light. Torin narrowed his gaze, reached forward, and took the crystal glass.

"Long live the Greyraven," he said. The crystal glass was smooth against his lips and the red liquid dripped from the vessel onto his tongue. It burned in his throat like fire and filled his head with a throbbing ache for a brief moment. Then the burning and the throbbing melted away and he felt a warm sensation, like the heated stones of a homely hearth, deep in the center of his chest.

Wyla looked at him, he thought, for the first time without malice or spite. "Torin Ten-Trees, I swear the blood-oath to you. May we be as kin, blood for blood." She spit in her palm and extended it to Torin. He did the same and grasped her hand firmly.

"Blood for blood."

Each in turn, Bryn then Grimsa, Asa and Inga, and finally even Erik took the draught and joined in the ritual. As the sun continued its descent, a blaze of fiery orange and red which lit the sky. Now they were bound together in kinship to protect each other against the trolls or any other danger and to avenge any death with steel and fury. Then they sat silent as their stomachs settled and they took in the view of the setting sun.

After a while Torin stood and stretched, first up then side to side. "Who will join me for a swim?"

"Aye," Grimsa said, "a boil in a hot bath seems just the thing. My joints are stiff from the hike and my back is sore from crouching over in that damn tunnel."

There was a shallow pool, swirling with bubbles and steam, beside the mouth of the falls. At its edge, the water dropped straight off the cliff. It was waist-deep with plenty of room for the seven companions. Each one threw off a mist-soaked tunic and waded into the natural hot-spring. Torin drew the mineral-soaked vapour into his lungs and sat back against a warm smooth rock.

The horizon now blazed with colours; red and orange and purple streaks filled the wide canvas of the sky. Then the light faded. Far down the valley, past Gatewatch and the wilds beyond, the sun set the peaks of one hundred distant mountains on fire as the dying light flickered against the ice and snow. The wind shifted. Now a draft came up the valley, rich with the scent of evergreens, softer and cooler than the midday breeze. Above them the half-moon shone clear and the stars speckled the sky in the wake of the vanishing light.

A loud slam, stone against stone, shook Torin to his senses. He leapt up, along with the rest of the company, splashing water in every direction. Erik shrieked and his cry echoed out across the valley.

"What was that?" said Bryn.

Wyla's expression darkened in the dim moonlight. "Nothing good."

Torin pulled his tunic on over his shoulders and crept along the ridge toward the place where he had heard the sound. The rest of the company followed close behind.

The sound came from where their provisions had been laid. Torin inspected these and found that none had been disturbed. Besides the company and their belongings, Frostridge was empty and silent.

Bryn rushed past Torin and kneeled on the ground. "Wait! What about the entrance?"

"The entrance?"

"To the tunnel!"

Torin's heart dropped in his chest with a violent thud and his eyes widened. He looked to the place where he first gazed out at the valley then retraced his path to where the entrance was, or where it should have been.

Torin looked at Wyla and saw her face was pale. Grimsa's mouth gaped, his jaw hung loose. Bryn frantically felt the ground in the silver moonlight as he tried to find grooves in the stone or a handle to pull the hatch up again. It was no use. Even when everyone backed away to let in the light of the moon and the stars, there was no trace of an opening or a door.

Wyla pulled at her hair as she crouched down beside the hidden entrance. "The hatch was laid wide open. How could it have closed?"

Grimsa growled and tugged on his beard. "I know exactly who closed it. It must have been the same ones who made it: the *nidavel*."

Torin thought of Drombir once again and shivered. If it was the *nidavel*, this was far more foul work than swindling them out of their horses. He peered over the precipitous ledge then took a quick step back. There would be no climbing down the wall from such a height.

Erik paced back and forth. "What will we do now? Are we stuck up here until we starve? Will they come looking for us or just assume we are dead?"

Asa gritted her teeth and stomped her foot. "If we do not make it back to Gatewatch by sunrise, Almveig will have us thrown out of the company. We will be sweeping kitchens for the next two years!" Inga nodded and Bryn shook his head.

Wyla did not turn back toward the company but rocked on her heels and pulled on her long, beaded braids. Grimsa looked more miserable than usual and Bryn was thinking with his arms folded over his chest and his neck bent down toward the ground. Asa and Inga crouched down, faces darkened, brooding over the situation while Erik continued to pace and to breathe heavily.

Torin grabbed Erik by the shoulders and shoved him down. "By the gods, sit down." Everyone but Wyla looked up at Torin. "We have to get down from Frostridge tonight to meet the others at Stonering. I do not plan on wiping tables for the next two years and I reckon neither do any of you. Besides, my guess is that we will find ourselves in situations worse than this once we cross over into the wilds. Do not despair. Think! We all took the oath of kinship, now let us prove our worth to each other and to the Gatewatch. We have until sunrise."

Everyone nodded, but their faces stayed glum. The chill of night was in the breeze and so each one pulled their cloak over their head. Torin kept his expression calm, just as his father had taught him, but his heart raced and beads of sweat formed on his brow and down his back. He took one more look over the edge of the cliff and cursed. For a moment he thought of diving into the pool at the base of the falls, but then shuddered at the thought of his broken corpse strewn across the rocks if the water proved too shallow. The lip of the ridge receded back into the steep mountain face on either side of the falls so there was no going up or down the valley. At last he turned to the rock face behind them and craned his neck up toward the top of the ridge, a jagged spine that rose up about five times his own height.

Bryn walked over to Torin and leaned close. "I hope you are not thinking what I suspect you are."

Torin grinned and tucked in his cloak. "Sorry to disappoint you." He gripped a crack in the rock face in front of him and scanned the ridge wall. He pressed his body close to the cold stone and found a foothold. With a grunt he managed to push himself up to the next crease in the rock and hooked the exposed edge with the tip of his fingers. Little by little he made his way up the wall until he reached the very top of the ridge.

Grimsa laughed as Torin swung his leg over the top of the ridge. "How is the view from up there Torin?"

He looked out over the dark valley toward Gatewatch, his companions far below him. "Incredible," he said, "If I was a bit higher, I might be able to see all the way to Ten-Tree Hall." Grimsa's laughter was swept away by a rush of wind. Wyla and Bryn were already halfway up the wall.

The low places were filled with shadows and the peaks of the ridges and mountains glowed in the moonlight. In some places, clouds filled distant valleys, in others, they hovered above sharp peaks like halos. His eyes traced the jagged spine of Frostridge down toward Gatewatch. The path did not look promising.

Wyla reached the top first and Bryn, right behind her, breathed heavily. "Not everything is a race."

Wyla laughed. "Maybe not for you."

Torin pointed to a dip in the ridge. "What do you think about that?"

Wyla nodded. "It looks passable. If we shuffled along the ridge, we could make it down that way."

Bryn leaned over to see past Torin. "That would take us down the other side of Frostridge. We would have to work our way through the wilds back to the West Gate."

"Well," Torin said, "Almveig failed to specify which side of the West Gate we have to meet her on."

A wide grin broke over Wyla's face. "Imagine the look on her face when we show up at sunrise outside of Stonering Keep!"

Bryn shook his head. "By the gods, I think that troll blood has gone to your heads."

They called back down to the others and, one by one, each made their way up to the top of the ridge. Everyone cheered whenever another member completed the perilous climb, especially when Grimsa, who fell from halfway up on his first attempt, swung his leg over the top of the ridge. After some persuasion, even Erik agreed to try and scale the wall, his options limited severely by the precipitous drop off the top of Frostridge Falls. Asa and Inga hauled him up the last few feet and he clung to the ridge as closely as he could.

A whistling wind rushed over the ridge as they shuffled down the gradual slope. Soon they reached the lower section that rolled gently down into the wilds. As long as they kept Frostridge on their right, Torin thought, they should be able to work their way around the end of the mountain to the West Gate. At last they slid off the jagged spine onto the other side of the slope. One by one they descended into the darkness of the wild valley below.

7

◇ TROLLS ◇

ALONG THE TOWERING SPINE OF FROSTRIDGE, the light of the moon and the stars had been enough. However, as the company delved further into the dim tangled woods, the darkness became thick as stew. To make matters worse, a chill fog was setting in low to the ground so that it was impossible to see where they were stepping.

Bryn swatted another branch away from his face. "By the gods, I think there may have been more light in that *nidavellish* tunnel."

Grimsa stubbed his toe on a large tree root and cursed. "First, I am dragged over slimy rocks, then I am shoved into a *nidavel* hole, then I am forced to scale a sheer rock face, and now this! Whose harebrained idea was this anyway? I could be sleeping soundly with a belly full of mead in Fjellhall right now."

Asa cried out as she tumbled into a thorny thicket. Inga tried to catch her but tripped and fell into the bush along with her sister. "Damn these woods!"

"We all know exactly whose idea this was," Erik said.

Torin could barely make out Wyla's shadowy figure as she forged ahead through the forest. She did not slow or respond but kept stomping and snapping branches as she went. He sighed.

"Keep complaining," said Torin, "That way we can all stay together. If the moaning starts to sound too distant then we will know we have almost lost you. Besides, we all agreed to come along of our own free will. Now our fates are bound."

After this no one spoke for some time. Behind Wyla each one followed the sound of snapping branches, rustling brush, and cursing ahead of them. The fog thickened, not white but a sickly grey in the shadows. The forest air smelled of damp moss, sweet cedar, and rotting wood.

They marched through the dark woods for what seemed like a very long time. Torin watched his breath rise in front of his face in faint swirls as the air became more frigid. His legs ached and his feet were bruised from all the roots and stones he had tripped on.

Hunger set in like a wild cat prowling and pacing back and forth inside his ribcage. He thought then of Ten-Tree Hall with its wide rafters roaring hearth, of his father, and of steaming loaves of harvest bread. He had been so eager to leave and now would give almost anything to have a raven or an eagle whisk him back. A sharp breeze through the trees made him shiver and his stomach growled again. All he could do was keep placing one foot ahead of the other.

Torin bumped into something in front of him, not a rock or a tree, but something softer. Then a sharp elbow jabbed his ribs and he knew who it was.

Wyla spoke in harsh, hushed syllables. "Watch your step Ten-Trees."

"Why did you stop?"

"Are you blind? There is a light up ahead. Look."

Torin squinted in the dark. Far ahead, against the mountain, there was a dim orange glow. It flickered.

"Looks like a fire. Do you think it could be a Greycloak patrol from Gatewatch?"

Wyla scratched her head. "Perhaps."

The others soon caught up and all agreed to investigate the light. Each one could hardly repress the fantasy of warming up beside a roaring fire. Perhaps the makers of the fire, if they were friendly, would have food and ale as well. Torin's mind rushed to all sorts of comforting possibilities.

The place where they stopped was a little clearing that let a bit of the moonlight through. Every face was muddied and battered, everyone's hair knotted with branches and leaves.

"What if it is not a patrol?" said Asa.

Erik threw up his hands. "Who else do you think makes fire in these woods? The ravens? The wolves?"

Bryn nodded. "I agree with Asa. Perhaps one or two of us should go scout ahead."

Wyla frowned. "How will the scouts find their way back to our party?"

"Maybe we can signal with bird calls."

Inga laughed. "How many birds have you heard in the forest tonight? It is as silent as a graveyard."

Asa nodded. "If we are going to make a racket we might as well just call out."

"Let's get closer," said Torin, "then we can decide what to do." Everyone agreed to this and so they crept ahead, as quietly as they could, stifling curses as they tripped on roots and stubbed their feet on stones.

The glow of orange firelight came from the mouth of a cave, though from the edge of the forest they saw only shadows that danced with the flicker of the flames. A breeze picked up and carried with it a scent, sweet and savoury, of wild game being roasted over the hearth.

Torin's stomach seized up and his mouth watered. It had been a long time since they had eaten and in that time he had scaled a mountain and walked countless hours through a dark wretched wood. Now that he had stopped moving, the dampness of the night air chilled his bones and he longed to warm himself by the fire.

Grimsa licked his lips and peered out from behind a large stump. "Surely this must be a Gatewatch patrol. Would a troll cave not reek horribly? And would we not hear stomping and munching and crunching?"

Bryn stretched his neck out into the clearing. "I am with Grimsa on this. Besides, even if it were a troll lair, at this point I would gladly wrestle a troll for a warm place to sit and a bite to eat."

Asa pulled him back into the woods. "Don't poke your head out so far!"

Wyla crept out of the brush and into the clearing. "I will go scout out the cave. You are all in this miserable position because of me anyways. If I do not return, then do not come after me."

The others watched her move silently toward the mouth of the cave. She crouched down low and crawled up to the edge of the radiant entrance. Then she slipped inside, out of sight.

They waited there at the edge of the wood for what seemed like hours. Torin watched the moon float across the sea of stars. He imagined the silver crescent was the sail of a great ship that might swoop down and take him back home. Ten-Tree Hall, which a few short weeks ago seemed like a prison, now glowed in his memory with warmth and welcome. He looked at his company, each ragged and weary, and imagined what reception they would have if his father's great hall lay over the next hill. The ten great oaks, the feasts and the banners, the ale and the dancing, the riddles and the wrestling, all of it seemed as distant as another land across the sea.

Snoring sounds started from behind the tree where Erik and Grimsa were hiding. Torin went to wake them but Asa protested. "Why not let them sleep? We have been up all night and we hardly need twelve pairs of eyes on watch."

Inga agreed. "We may need our strength again soon. Perhaps it would be wise to rest now."

Torin's stomach twisted into knots as he thought of all the evil that might have come upon Wyla in that cave. "I cannot sleep. Wyla has taken far too long. I am going after her."

"I am with you," Bryn said, "I have been thinking too much of the Watchers and their smoldering ember eyes. We may be far from Shadowstone Pass but I won't risk sleeping outside in this foul place."

Asa sighed. "I could sleep a whole day and night straight through, but you are right. We should go after Wyla."

"Then let's go together," said Inga. She roused Grimsa and Erik and then the whole company fastened their cloaks, tightened their belts, and gripped their axes as they crept toward the cave.

Torin expected to see a tunnel but instead discovered a high-roofed cavern. A roaring fire blazed at its center, fueled by tree sized logs. The fire itself was much taller than Torin and the heat that radiated from its embers warmed the entire room. The walls were rugged stone, empty and bare, but around the edges of the room lay all sorts of wares. Three or four dozen unopened barrels were stacked against the wall, giant sacks tied with rope were piled up in several places, and three great chests with crude iron locks sat at the back end of the hall. There was also a wide table, its frame of rough-hewn wood, which was set for a feast. Enormous chunks of salted meat, of various types, had been set on silver platters which glimmered in the firelight. Instead of bowls of fruit there were large pots with fruit trees planted in them. Some had berries that were small and bright red, others had purple fruit the size of a closed fist. The rest of the hall was empty. Nothing stirred but the flames.

Grimsa stepped into the cavern toward the welcoming fire and breathed deep. "By the gods, what luck—nobody home! I don't suppose whoever lives here will mind if we sit down to that wonderful feast."

"I think not," said Erik, "Perhaps it was prepared for guests? Who could eat such massive portions?"

Bryn edged further into the room with careful steps. "Listen to yourselves! 'Who could eat such massive portions?' Trolls, of course."

A shudder rattled Torin's spine. "I agree with Bryn."

Inga crept closer to the finely laid table. "All the more reason to help ourselves."

Grimsa nodded and followed her to the table. "And once we've had our fill, we will set a trap and kill the troll. Certainly, we don't have the strength to slay trolls on an empty stomach."

Grimsa and Inga were already at the table and Erik was chewing on a piece of salted venison. Bryn, eyes wide and hands extended, drew closer to the table. "Yes, perhaps just a few bites then we will set a trap."

Torin's stomach groaned but he swore to himself that he would not eat until he found Wyla. While the others tore strips of spiced meat from the slabs on silver platters, bit into the rich red fruit, and guzzled giant goblets of heady wine, he searched the cavern. Spider webs hung thick between the stacks of barrels which smelled of rotten apples or were sticky with spilled beer. Some had collected a thick layer of dust as they waited to be opened. There were many large canvas bags, roughly but tightly stitched together. They were stacked in great heaps around the edge of the hall. From what he could feel, they seemed to be full of wares, hard like wood or metal.

From behind one of the great wooden chests he saw a hand protruding. He ran over to the chest and behind it found Wyla sprawled out of the ground. At first his heart dropped in his chest for there was a red liquid around her face and on her neck that he thought was blood. However, he then saw a fruit in her outstretched hand dripping with red juice and heard a soft snore from her nectar-stained mouth.

"You imp," said Torin, "Eating your fill and falling asleep while the rest of us freeze out there in the forest." He nudged her ribs with his foot. "Come on now, join the rest of us and explain why you didn't come get us hours ago."

She did not stir but continued to snore. Though Torin was quite relieved to have found her in one piece, he still felt a surge of anger tighten his chest. Besides, he was tired, hungry, and sore himself, so his temper was strained. Torin crouched down with his hands cupped to his mouth and began to shout. "Wake up, Wyla."

His words echoed in the cavern, which he then realized had become very, very quiet. The table, freshly disturbed by the rest of the company, was a mess of meat and fruit and wine. All around its edge his companions lay sleeping, Grimsa's loud snoring audible from beneath the table. Each one lay as still as a stone, lost to dreams.

Torin's stomach groaned again and he felt sick. He looked at the fruit in Wyla's hand and the juice on her face and suddenly understood. He cursed. Before he had time to think of what to do, he heard rumbling steps outside the cavern entrance. He leapt into the mess of dust and webs behind a stack of unopened barrels.

"Told you. More in the bush."

"Tricky devils aren't they, Cragh?"

"Yes, Bhog, tricky but tasty."

"Look. So many."

"Never caught this many all at once."

The voices of the two creatures were like shifting gravel or scraping stone. The deep resonance of their grinding syllables was interrupted by creaks and squeaks like a rusted hinge being forced to turn.

Torin's heart thrashed inside his chest like a trout out of water and he had to wrestle his lungs to keep his breathing quiet. He drew in a few steady breaths with his eyes closed then forced his shoulders down from his ears. With great caution he twisted his body around so that he could peer through the crack between two barrels.

What he saw were two enormous figures, at least twice his height. Had he been walking through the forest, he surely would have mistaken them for boulders covered in moss and mud and twigs. Ratty knots of brown hair strewn with leaves and bark hung down from their swollen heads and tumbled in every direction over their shoulders. As for their faces, their noses and eyes looked bulbous and rotten, the tone of their skin a sickly stone-grey colour. Each had broad slumping shoulders, a large round belly, stubby knees, and feet that looked like gnarled tree roots.

The shorter one slapped its stomach with a clawed fist. "Our bellies will be full tonight."

"No, Bhog, not tonight."

This creature, Bhog, frowned and wrinkled up its sagging nose. "Why not, Cragh?"

"We'll take these to the *Trollting*."

"Tomorrow night?"

"Yes."

"Why not eat them now? They all look so juicy and I'm hungry."

"Because," Cragh said, "if we bring them to the *Trollting* tomorrow, all the other trolls will see."

Bhog's awful yellowed eyes lit up and he nodded. "Ah, and they'll be jealous."

"Jealous of crafty Cragh and beastly Bhog."

They made a noise which Torin reckoned was laughter but sounded more like gargled water or choking. Their gaping jaws were hinged open and, though not in any way that resembled a smile, each had its lips pulled back to reveal two rows of jagged yellow teeth, a slimy green tongue, and a dark cavernous throat. Rolls of leathery grey skin jiggled over their bellies, and their flabby jowls shook. Shortly they stopped and stared at the sleeping bodies around the table.

The one called Cragh lifted its arm and pointed. "You put them in the sacks. I'll make up the table."

As Bhog stomped toward the pile of barrels, Torin's heart raced. The creature stopped and stared toward him with bulbous yellow eyes. It tilted its head and scratched its chin with clawed fingers. Torin could hear the scraping, like stone on stone, with every stroke.

"Wait."

Cragh grunted. "What?"

"I see another one."

Bhog took a few more steps toward Torin. He held his breath. Then it turned toward the old rusted chest. It reached forward, its moss-covered limb just a few feet from Torin's face, and grabbed Wyla by the waist. Torin was so close he could smell the troll, an aromatic mixture of rotting wood and brackish algae. Bhog carried her back to where the others lay and tossed her sleeping form, which landed with a thud, on top of Asa and Inga.

"That makes three."

"No," said Cragh, "That makes six."

Bhog shook his head. "Three for you and three for me."

Again, there was the gurgling, choking noise. Bhog trudged over to the other side of the room where the sacks were, picked up an empty one, and stomped back toward the table.

As Bhog tossed each snoring member of Torin's company into the empty sack, Cragh began to chant. It groaned with a noise like swirling gravel and made clicking sounds with its tongue like rocks banging together. Slowly the dishes on the table rearranged themselves and those on the floor floated back up into place. The cured meat swelled and grew until each had reached its original form. A gurgling noise came from the wine bottles which filled up to their brim and the potted trees quickly grew their fruit which squeaked as fresh juice filled the fruit skins. Last of all, the chairs shuffled across the floor back to the places they had been. The feast was set again; it was a devilish trap.

After this, the trolls began to stack stones in front of the entrance. Each grunted as it piled up the massive boulders. The dim signs of dawn outside were snuffed out as the last rock was put into place. Now the massive fire had died down and only its embers lit the cave.

Bhog looked again at the sack which held Torin's companions and licked its lips, a green residue left where the slug-like appendage had trailed. "I'm hungry."

"Not until the *Trollting*, Bhog," said Cragh, "Go look through the barrels."

Bhog trudged toward Torin once again. While the trolls had been stacking stones, Torin had secured a better hiding spot behind some of the canvas sacks. Though it was still dangerously close to the stack of barrels, Bhog was in no mood for close inspection. It ripped the lids off the barrels with its clawed fingers and tossed them over its shoulder.

After opening the third one Bhog sighed. "Apples. Nothing but apples." It emptied the entire contents of one of the open barrels into its mouth. Then it peeled off the iron strips holding the barrel together and chewed on the thin wooden planks. Torin thought its shoulders were more steeply slumped and its face more wretched and twisted than it had been before.

Cragh laid down on the other side of the hall. "Don't chew the wood, Bhog. Remember what happened last time?"

Bhog dropped the barrel and spat out the plank. "I hate apples."

It then trudged back over to the fire and fell over onto its side. Soon both Cragh and Bhog were snoring, great grinding snores that seemed to shake the floor. After they had slept a few moments, Torin dared to sneak out from under the canvas sacks to look around.

Each troll looked like a small boulder covered in moss and, if Torin had been in the woods, that is exactly what he would have mistaken them for. But here on the stone floor he could see their twisted root feet, their knobby knees, and their bloated rat-nest heads. The embers of the fire still glowed enough to light the room and the canvas bag that held his companions lay near the three chests.

Torin drew out his axe and chopped at the knotted cord that sealed the mouth of the sack. The sound of his companion's snores was just audible through the thick canvas. Soon he realized that this was no use as his axe was becoming dull and he had not even scratched the rope. Perhaps it was another enchantment, he thought. He tried his hand at untying the massive knot, twice the size of his head, but it would not budge in the slightest. Not even the canvas itself showed as much as a scratch despite his desperate strokes. After close to an hour of muted grunts and groans, he fell back panting.

He looked again to the trolls and cursed. If he could not free his companions, he would have to slay these two creatures himself. His axe, now a bit dull but still finely made, might prove heavy enough to bludgeon them. Torin reasoned that Cragh was the leader, also larger and smarter, and so that was who he planned to kill first.

Torin crept over to where the massive troll slept. The same smell of dank rot filled his nostrils as he planted his feet on either side of the troll's bloated head. With both hands he gripped the handle of his axe and, as if to split a large piece of wood, he brought the axe-head down with all the force he could muster. It struck the creature right in the middle of the forehead.

Torin had hoped that he would feel the blade sink deep into the troll's skull, much like Captain Calder had sunk his axe into the wild bear the day before. However, it did not stick. In fact, it bounced off without so much as a mark. Worse, the troll stirred. Torin dove behind a sack of canvas bags just before it opened its eyes.

"Bhog?" said Cragh, "Bhog, wake up."

Bhog sat up and scratched its head. "What is it?"

Cragh felt its forehead and frowned. "I think we may have a leak. I thought I felt a drop of water fall on my head while I slept."

"Strange," Bhog said, "Better move somewhere else."

So Cragh shuffled around the fire to another place on the flat stone floor and lay down. Soon both trolls fell asleep again, their grinding snores filling the cave with a terrible racket.

When Torin finally worked up the courage to peer out from under the pile of sacks he looked out, wide-eyed, at Cragh. A blow like that would have shattered the skull of any creature he had ever seen before. Yet there it lay, arms sprawled out on the floor, asleep as soundly as ever.

Torin's head felt like a bowl full of muddy water; his thoughts emerged and then disappeared in the muck. He had not slept since the day before and the last time he ate was at Frostridge. All that had happened with the trolls seemed so absurd that he wondered if it was a dream. But it was not. A few firm pinches on his arm assured him that this dreadful situation was really happening, and he doubted then if he would ever be able to save Bryn and Grimsa and the rest of the company.

He looked across the cave to the barrels of apples that Bhog had opened. A growl came from his stomach that was so loud he thought it might wake the trolls, but it did not. He stared again at the enchanted feast, the meats and fruits, and licked his lips. Then he shook his head and crept over to the apple barrels.

The apples were mostly rotten. After digging through the sweet, sticky mush, Torin found one that did not look entirely decayed. He tucked himself in behind the stack of canvas sacks and ate the apple, the flavour slightly off but the juice sweet and the flesh filling. For a moment he worried that it might be enchanted because a haze of sleepiness came over him. However, he did not fall asleep but lay there for some time and imagined what awful things might happen to the rest of his company if he could not free them. As he tried to devise another plan to slay the trolls, he slipped off into a shallow, restless sleep.

Torin woke to the sound of grinding rocks. As he peered out from underneath the dusty, web-covered pile of canvas sacks he saw Cragh and Bhog removing the pile of stones from the entrance. It was night again. The air inside the cave had become insufferably damp and smelled of mold, so the fresh breeze that wafted in through the entrance was a relief. He had not slept well or long, and the taste of the bad apple lingered in his mouth.

"Quickly now Bhog, quickly! The *Trollting* will be starting soon! We can't be late."

Bhog panted like a dog, mouth wide open and tongue extended out. "I'm going! At least I'm going as fast as I can on an empty stomach. If I could just munch one of those tasty *madur*, just one of the small ones."

Cragh cut him off. "No, we are saving those for the *Trollting*. Stick to the plan."

Bhog shook in a manner Torin thought might be whimpering. "Just one nibble, a crunchy foot or a juicy head." It trudged toward the canvas sack full of Torin's companions and extended its clawed hands.

"No, no, no," said Cragh. It shoved its companion and Bhog fell over with a great thud. "I'll get a stick while you grab the treasure. Hurry up, we can't be late."

Bhog moaned and stood up slowly. Cragh stepped outside and pushed a tree over. After ripping the tree from the ground, it dragged it back to the cave entrance. Like a farmer plucking the feathers from a bird, it removed each branch with a quick flick of the wrist and soon had a long smooth pole. Bhog dragged over three other canvas sacks from the back of the cave. One by one they strung each bag onto the pole by the cords that tied it shut. Torin thought he saw the sack full of his companions stir. His stomach retched. After the three sacks were all strung, they picked the pole up by both ends, Cragh in the front and Bhog at the back, and walked out into the shadowy forest.

Torin scrambled after them, careful to mind his distance but hard pressed to keep up with the grisly pair. As with the night before, it was nearly impossible to see the forest floor. Despite this he managed to keep up, a steady rhythm of short sprints and silent stops, as he chased the trolls deep into the dark forest.

◇

◇ THE TROLLTING ◇

Through the dark forest, Torin followed the trolls. As the ground pitched downwards and descended into the wild valley, he worried he might slip or tumble all the way to the bottom. The twisted tree roots and ragged bushes on the slope barely gave him enough to hold on to as he pursued the beastly creatures. Still, Torin watched the canvas sacks sway back and forth on the log pole with a nauseating rhythm. The kin-oath he had taken on the ledge of Frostridge Falls rang in his ears and pushed him onward through the forest.

After some time, the ground leveled and the trees thinned out. Under the silver moon the trolls stopped at a shallow creek which was knee deep and about twenty paces across. Each of them guzzled great mouthfuls of water before swallowing it all in a single gulp. Bhog choked on a fish it had swallowed by accident and spat it back up with a belch.

"Remember," said Cragh, "stay quiet and let me talk."

Bhog nodded but then frowned. "What am I supposed to do then?"

"Guard the treasure sacks."

Bhog pulled back its grey lips then licked them with its pointed green tongue. In the dim light Torin could just make out their bulky forms, shadowy grey figures, but what stood out most was the sickly yellow glow of their eyes. Their eyes were like giant torchbugs, or little anemic moons, full in shape yet pallid in colour. It reminded him of the fearsome ember eyes of the Watchers, their smoking, smoldering stare which still haunted him. Torin shook the thought from his mind.

Cragh bent down and took one more mouthful of water. "Almost there."

Bhog hoisted its end of the pole up over its shoulder. "Won't be long now."

With that the trolls turned straight up the creek, sloshing and splashing as they went. Torin raced down to the edge of the water further downstream and drank his fill. Through the whole ordeal, he had forgotten his own thirst. After he had slaked it, he ran, refreshed, alongside the creek, in pursuit of the trolls under the star speckled canvas of the night sky.

The path up the creek took them to the base of another mountain across the valley. Cragh and Bhog grunted and snorted as they stepped up the trickling waterfalls and swirling pools. The log pole they carried creaked with every bouncing step. Torin worried he might fall behind when the path beside the river reached its steepest point, but the trolls stopped there.

The two creatures were staring up at the mouth of a wide cave in the mountain side. Out of its center flowed the creek they had been following, like a long serpentine tongue out of a gaping throat. Stalactites on the cave roof and stalagmites on the cave floor near the entrance gave the impression of a set of vicious teeth, thin and sharp. During the day, Torin thought, the light might reach far down into the cave, but in the dim starlight it seemed like a void of utter darkness.

"The Teeth of Fanghall," Cragh said.

Bhog nodded. "Long time since we were here. Do you think it is true?"

"We'll soon find out."

Cragh and Bhog trudged on into the mouth of the cave. The disturbance sent a flurry of small winged creatures out into the forest, little zipping shadows. Torin cursed his luck, tightened his cloak and then hurried in after them.

It was easy enough for Torin to find his way through the cave. He followed the sound of splashing ahead of him and did not let it get too close. He tried, as best he could, not to splash too much himself. Near the edge of the underground creek he groped stalagmites along the edge of the water, ready to dash among them if the trolls turned back toward him. The cold water of the underground creek soaked through his boots and his feet went numb. All the better, he thought, because they were so sore by then that he did not want to feel them anyways.

A dim light at the end of the tunnel appeared and then grew with every step forward. It was a soft, flickering light, like that of the fire in Cragh and Bhog's cave the night before. There were also noises: a raucous, rumbling sort of commotion. The closer he came to the light the more the noises grew and the better Torin could see Cragh and Bhog ahead.

The two creatures said something to each other as they came around the last corner into the place where the fire was, but Torin could not hear it because of the noise. When he snuck around the corner, careful to stay low and out of sight, he saw a most terrible and festive sight.

The large domed cavern was filled with trolls, dozens of them. They were all gathered around a monstrous fire at the center of the room, its embers crackling in a roaring rhythm. Some trolls danced, if it could be called that, around the flame. Their flailing bodies sent wicked shadows sprawling across the cavern floor and up onto the walls. The others cheered with deep, gravelly grunts. One that pranced around the fire was just a little taller than Torin himself. Another who was feeding the fire with splintered tree trunks was taller than either Cragh or Bhog and looked far fiercer. Thin trolls, wide trolls, old and young trolls, Torin saw them all. Some looked like standing stones, others like rugged trees, and still others like something dredged out of a slimy bog.

The sight might have overwhelmed him if he had not heard footsteps from the tunnel behind, sloppy splashes through the underground creek. He dove into the stalagmites as if they were bushes and crawled back between the jagged deposits until he was sure he could not be seen. He watched a gangly-armed troll pass by and join the crowd around the fire, then a short, stocky one, then another and another.

Time passed and more trolls gathered. Torin groaned and knocked his head against the stalagmite he was leaning on. How could he save his company with the horde of trolls gathered around them? Hope drained from him like fresh ink in the rain as he imagined all the awful ends his friends could meet at the hands of such beastly creatures.

The noise and the commotion around the fire stopped. Torin peered out to see what was happening. All the trolls faced toward the back end of the cavern. He thought he heard a horn, but then doubted himself and thought that it must simply be the wind blowing through the tunnel. Then he heard it again. That must be a horn, he thought. All the creatures around the fire gasped and looked at each other wide-eyed. He could not see over the crowd to what had drawn their attention.

Behind the fire there was a large flat stone into which a set of rough steps had been carved. Through the crowd Torin could see that some enormous figure was walking up to the top with slow, confident steps. The cavern buzzed with excited murmurs and all eyes were fixed on the stone platform.

As the figure rose above the crowd, Torin could see that he had the shape of a man but was more than twice the size. His cloud-white hair gleamed like ocean pearls and his skin was translucently pale with freckles of azurite blue. Sharp cheekbones and a broad chin framed the grim and noble expression on his face. His eyes were the green white of sea ice. Torin marveled at his long hair and beard, which were both finely braided, interwoven with gold beads inlaid with precious stones. Over his broad shoulders hung a cloak of bear pelts, but instead of black or brown, the fur was white. It was fastened at the neck with a gold clasp which matched his many gleaming arm-rings. A silver coat of mail hung down to his knees and shimmered in the firelight with every step. At his waist hung a mighty sword sheathed in a scabbard so richly adorned that it looked like it was made entirely of glittering gemstones.

From the top of the stone platform he turned toward the crowd of trolls and faced them in silence. Hardly moving, hardly breathing, the grisly creatures waited. The narrow sea-ice eyes of the giant figure inspected each troll with stern judgement. The fire flickered as it died down to glowing embers. Not a word was spoken.

Torin thought back to Wyla's description of the troll-blood wine, to the wandering traveller and the description of those that he had visited. Tall and pale skinned with white or red hair, the shape of men but taller and far stronger, noble and wise, skilled in craft—this was certainly a *jotur* from the far north. He was both puzzled and stunned at the sight of an ancient giant standing before a horde of trolls.

At last the *jotur* threw off his white bear-skin cloak and addressed the crowd in a deep, rumbling voice. "I am Ur-Gezbrukter, son of Gezbrukter who was once king over these mountains. I am here to claim my father's throne and win back his domain." The gestures of the trolls reminded Torin of the dogs that would salivate at his father's table. The giant's face soured, and he spat. "You are all cowards. When my father gathered forces to defeat the insolent *madur* you did not join him. At the great battle of

Gatewatch your kinfolk suffered the sun-death and my father was slain. Now I am giving you a chance to redeem yourselves."

One of the largest trolls, the one who had been stoking the fire, stood up and roared. "Coward? I'll squeeze the marrow from the bones of any who dare call me a coward!"

This troll rushed at the *jotur* in a black fury. As it fell upon Ur-Gezbrukter, Torin saw the flash of a glittering blade then heard a mighty crash. The whole cavern seemed to shake for a moment. Then the *jotur* emerged again from behind the stone platform dragging the troll's severed head up the steps behind him. The glittering hilt of his blade sparkled as he tossed the head across the cavern and into the fire. It landed in the heart of the embers which crackled and hissed. All the other trolls stared wide-eyed at the gory blaze for a moment. Then a cheer came up from one of the smaller trolls and soon all were chanting and whooping like lunatics.

"Long live, Ur-Gezbrukter!"

"Death to the *madur*!"

"Glory to trolldom!"

As the trolls cheered Torin looked over at the pile of canvas sacks that Bhog had left near the door. One of them started to wriggle and Torin knew then that his companions were awake. He felt his stomach turn and he thought he might vomit. He had to do something soon or else all hope for his friends would be lost.

As the whooping settled down, a stout troll with long, mossy hair stepped toward the stone pedestal and hailed the self-proclaimed Troll King.

"Hail Ur-Gezbrukter, son of Gezbrukter. We have long been waiting for you. My name is Rhott. As a token of my loyalty I present a gift to you, a prisoner." The troll waddled over to the pile of canvas sacks and untied the knot. It shook the bag roughly and out tumbled a *nidavel*. He did not look young, nor did he look well kept. His hair was wild, his clothes tattered and soiled.

Ur-Gezbrukter relaxed his shoulders and nodded. "This is a good gift, Rhott. I accept it." The old *nidavel* stood there frozen. His knees shook and his arms quivered. The Troll King smiled. "For your initiative and your loyalty, I will reward you with a place on my council."

Another troll jumped up and pushed Rhott aside. "Troll King, wait! I also have a gift for you." This troll was taller and much more gangly. Torin did not know the age of the trolls or even how to determine it, but he thought this one looked younger than the rest. It stretched a thin arm out to the piles of sacks and untied it at the top in quick, jerky motions. When it shook the bag, another small figure rolled out and onto the ground beside the old *nidavel*.

"I am Pitt and I swear my loyalty to you! This prisoner is my gift."

Torin strained his neck to see the next figure. From the bristling beard he knew it was another *nidavel*, though much younger than the first. The captive looked around with wide eyes, then cursed and crouched down like cornered rat.

"Well done, Pitt," the Troll King said. "You will have a place at my side in battle."

The other trolls were nearly tripping over each other trying to get to the canvas sacks so they could present their tokens of allegiance. Two trolls, Cragh and Bhog, pushed the others out of the way and addressed the Troll King.

Once they cleared a space in front of the stone pedestal Cragh spoke. "Mighty Ur-Gezbrukter, your father was wise and cunning. I, Cragh, once gave him council. I offer my service again." It bent over in what appeared to be a gesture of servitude or worship. "My brother Bhog and I have a gift for you as well."

Bhog looked over at Cragh and frowned. "We do?"

"Yes, a gift much more generous than both Rhott and Pitt."

Bhog whispered, far too loudly, in Cragh's ear. "We did not bring anything."

Cragh pushed Bhog aside and picked up the sack with Torin's companions in it. It untied the bag and shook it vigourously. Out tumbled Asa and Inga and Erik. Grimsa landed next with a thud on the stone floor, with Bryn and Wyla coming down right on top of him.

All the trolls gathered there gasped at the sight—six young *madur*, none of them dead or crumpled, all pink and delicious. On every side, the creatures salivated and licked their crooked lips. Ur-Gezbrukter leaned in toward the pile with a wide-eyed stare. Torin saw his company stumble to their feet, each stiff and groggy. As their eyes adjusted to the firelight, each jaw dropped and every face went pale. None of them made a sound.

Torin clenched his teeth and gripped the stalagmite in front of him until it hurt his fingers. Inside his chest his heart throbbed, and his breath became short and forceful. If he did not act soon his friends would surely perish by the claws and teeth of those awful creatures.

The *jotur* leaned back on his stone seat and clapped his hands. "This is a fine gift, and I suspect there is some tale of trickery involved in their finding. I give you the name: Cragh the Cunning."

At that moment, Torin shouted. He later wondered if he had shouted of his own will or if his lungs had simply burst open in desperation. "I also give you names: Cragh the Stone-Brain, Cragh the Swamp-Reeker, and Cragh the Fat-Nose."

Every troll in that cavernous hall turned toward the dark tunnel through which the creek ran. Cragh's eyes were ablaze with fury and its nose flared wide. It took a step closer to the mouth of the tunnel, its feet splashing as it plunged into the creek. "Who dares to insult me from the dark?"

"One that is much more cunning than you, Cragh the Cave-Rotter."

Some of the trolls chuckled and a grin stretched out over the *jotur's* face. Cragh's voice grew higher in pitch and it waved its fists. "That is no name! Who is this who would challenge my cunning?"

Torin saw at last how he might save his companions. He took a deep breath in and shouted with all his might. "I am called Gatar the Clever. You, Mud-Gurgler, are as clever as a mushroom on a rotting stump."

"You have not proved your cleverness to me, Gatar Shadow-Hider."

"Then I challenge you, Dung-Hoarder, to a wager of wits."

Now the trolls roared and whooped with laughter. Cragh's face flushed full of blood, giving it a greenish hue. "What sort of wager?"

"*Bardagi*, a duel of riddles. If I can outwit you, then I will have those prisoners for myself."

"And if I outwit you instead?"

"Then you can have my head, Mold-Muncher."

From his stone-pile seat, Ur-Gezbrukter laughed. It was a deep and evil noise, so chilling that even the chuckling trolls froze in place. The whole cavern resonated with the vibrations and the sound lingered in fading echoes a while after the *jotur* had ceased. He stood up and crossed his great arms over his chest.

"The prisoners were given to me and so they are mine to wager," Ur-Gezbrukter said. The *jotur* scratched at his finely braided beard and grinned. "I have already claimed one head and would not protest another. I accept your challenge."

Cragh's ears drooped and his shoulders sunk. With a vile, twisted look on its face, it grabbed Bhog and they stomped back into the crowd of trolls. The rest of the hoary company murmured among themselves.

"Show yourself, Gatar, then I will see how clever you are."

Torin's heart had not stopped pounding and it did not stop then. Beat by beat it slammed against his ribs with such force he thought it might break them. His feet told him to run, to flee the cave and sprint all the way back to Gatewatch. However, the sight of his companions, dishevelled and huddled together in front of the troll fire, stoked his courage. He thought of his father, of his friends, and of the green fields around Ten-Tree Hall that he might never see again. Then Torin sucked in a breath, threw out his chest, and leapt out from behind the stalagmite into the fire-lit cavern.

The trolls near Torin gasped and stepped back just like a group of kitchen-hands who had spotted a mouse on the table. Then each one pushed and shoved to get a closer view of the *madur* who had challenged the Troll King. Torin was deep in a forest of trolls, their legs and arms like the trunks and branches of one hundred moving trees. They closed in around him so tightly that he thought they might accidentally step on him or tumble over and crush him.

Ur-Gezbrukter growled and stomped loudly. "Move back." The trolls parted just enough for Torin to make his way up to the base of the raised stone pedestal.

There were his companions, wide-eyed and loose-jawed. They were all bruised and battered from being slung around in a sack. Their hair was dishevelled, and they did not smell particularly pleasant. Bryn spoke in a hoarse voice. "By thunderous Orr and all the gods, when we found out you weren't thrown in that awful sack with us, we figured you must be dead!"

Torin could not help but smile at the sight of his friends. "Well, I may be soon."

"You and your damn riddles," said Grimsa. "I never thought I would be staking my life on them, but thank the gods you are still alive."

The *jotur* picked up a rock and slammed it down on the stone pedestal several times to silence the crowd. Then he addressed Torin directly in a booming voice that seemed to shake the stones. "Introduce yourself, stranger."

If Torin knew anything, it was the manner in which to introduce himself and make an impression. He shook out his shoulders and threw back his head. "I am Gatar the Clever. They call me Riddle-Knower, Answer-Seeker, Truth-Keeper, and Wit-Weaver. I have travelled far and learned much."

"Gatar Wit-Weaver, you have arrived at the hall of Ur-Gezbrukter, son of Gezbrukter, ancient heir to these lands. I think you have not travelled as far or learned as much as I have, but we will see to that soon enough. These are the terms of our *bardagi*. I shall present a riddle and you shall answer. Then you will question me with a riddle, and I shall answer in turn. The first that fails to produce either a riddle or an answer in three attempts loses. If I lose, I grant you these prisoners, the six *madur* I acquired. If you fail, then I will have your severed head as an ornament for my standard of war. Do you accept?"

Torin did not trust the word of the Troll-King any more than he would trust the word of a troll, but he saw no other way to free his companions. He felt like a mouse being batted about by a wolf for sport. He looked again at his ragged friends. A chance was, he thought, still a chance.

"I accept."

And so, the duel of riddles began.

9

◇ A GAME OF RIDDLES ◇

UR-GEZBRUKTER SAT BACK on his rough chair of piled stones and stroked his beard. Torin kept his gaze firmly locked on the ancient *jotur* and pushed the thought of being devoured by the swarm of trolls from his mind. He thought of Ten-Tree Hall, of its smooth-worn wooden benches where he had listened to so many riddles, of its hearth fire and the sound of his father's voice telling stories through the dark winter nights. His breath became less hurried, his heartbeat slowed, and his shoulders relaxed. Still, the smile on the Troll-King's face put him ill at ease.

"My first riddle is an old one," said the *jotur*, "listen carefully."

> *Six legs, one tail, and four keen eyes*
> *Swifter than the raven flies*
> *O'er valley, hill, and flowering field*
> *To none but rushing water yields*

"Answer, listener, if you can."

Torin nodded but did not answer immediately. He knew to let the others ponder the riddle first, to let them wrestle with it in their minds, so that when he answered he would win their admiration. This one he had heard once, long ago, from a travelling merchant.

He paced back and forth in front of the fire for a time then turned toward Ur-Gezbrukter.

"Your riddle is a good one, Troll-King, but I can answer it. Between a horse and its rider there are six legs, one tail, and four eyes. They may travel faster than even the raven but must yield to rushing rivers."

The Troll-King laughed and clapped his hands. The trolls, though for the most part dim-witted creatures, yipped and hollered with frenzied excitement. Torin's friends let up a cheer. Then every eye turned to Torin and all was silent except the crackle of the fire and the trickle of the creek.

"Here is a riddle I heard once," said Torin. "See if you can find its meaning."

> *Ferocious fiend, grim appetite*
> *A taste for all within its sight*
> *One thousand tongues but not one tooth*
> *Held captive under every roof*

"Answer, listener, if you can."

The ancient *jotur* furrowed his white-wisp brow and tugged at his beard. Every set of eyes flickered between the giant high up on the stones and Torin, the tiny *madur*, at the base of the fire. All at once, Ur-Gezbrukter raised his brows and smiled wickedly.

"An answer I have for you. What could be ferocious with many tongues but not have teeth? What is held captive in every hall though it threatens to destroy it? Flames of fire, *logi*, burning in the hearth."

A cheer went up from the trolls and some of the creatures around Torin's company began to poke them and lick their lips. Erik, especially, looked very pale.

Torin kept his voice calm. "That is correct. What is your next riddle?"

Ur-Gezbrukter leaned forward in his seat and narrowed his eyes.

> *In its jaws a finger gnaws*
> *Binding two by ancient laws*
> *Crowned with glorious glittering gem*
> *Beginning when it meets its end*

"Answer, listener, if you can."

Torin had not heard this riddle before but by luck caught its meaning in this first hearing. "This I think I can answer. What gnaws fingers and never meets its end? A ring. And what ring binds oaths between two people and is crowned with a gem? A wedding ring."

"Well-spoken, Gatar Wit-Weaver," Ur-Gezbrukter said. All around them, trolls stomped and clapped while Torin's company chanted. The *jotur* waited for the din to quiet then cleared his throat and opened his arms wide. "Where I was born, drink must be given after three riddles. Fetch *Glediketil*, my cauldron."

From behind the stone throne two trolls lifted a cauldron so large that Torin thought both of them could hide inside it. With awkward shuffling steps they moved over to the creek, then tilted the giant pot on its side to fill it with water. Once it had filled a ways, they set it upright on the smooth river stones. Ur-Gezbrukter, unhurried, walked down the stone steps and murmured something indecipherable. When he reached *Glediketil*, he untied a long, spiralled horn from the belt of his tunic, a drinking vessel inlaid with silver and precious stones, and dipped it into the cauldron. First there was a hissing noise, then from the giant pot came sparks of light in every color and swirls of steamy vapor. The trolls shrieked and cheered all at once, as some leaned in toward the spectacle and others cowered in fright. The Troll-King lifted the vessel to his lips then emptied it all in one draught.

"*Glediketil* is the finest of cauldrons," he said. He wiped his lips and filled it again. "The mead-vat is full, so let us drink!"

Every troll then scrambled to find its drinking vessel. Some pulled out stone cups or wooden bowls, others had skulls of various shapes that had been fashioned into goblets. The drummer troll beat its drum again in a frantic, festive rhythm. One by one each troll danced past *Glediketil* and filled its vessel, some returning to the line twice or even three times. Those that did not have a vessel dunked their heads in for a mouthful. One fell in headlong and had to be dragged out before it drowned.

To Torin the sight was both terrific and terrible all at once. He had nearly been trampled when the trolls first rushed over to *Glediketil* and now he was at the center of a ring of dancing, drinking trolls. Torin thought that the rumble of their heavy feet on the floor might cause the cavern to come crashing down on their heads, but it did not. Through the festive frenzy, he heard a voice call out.

"Torin! The cup! Get us a drink! We are nearly dead from thirst!"

He turned toward his company and saw it was Grimsa shouting above the din. With hands and feet bound, the huge man motioned with his head toward Drombir's cup which still hung from his belt. Torin ran over to fetch it. Just as he loosed the knot, he heard the voice of the Troll-King.

"Where is Gatar Wit-Weaver? Will he not drink?"

Torin turned toward the stone pedestal and raised Drombir's cup in salute. "I will Troll-King. But what of these prisoners? Surely a good host would fill their cups with drink as well."

The *jotur* grunted and sneered. "They are prisoners. Besides, I have no vessels for them."

"What if I gave each a drink out of my own cup?"

The giant laughed at this and the trolls, now giddy with mead, joined in. "From your own cup? Will you water them like cattle, running back and forth from the trough?"

"No, I need but one cupful to fill this whole company."

At this Ur-Gezbrukter roared and slapped his knee. "The whole company? Out of that thimble-head? It is already small, well apportioned for a tiny *madur* like yourself. But for sport I would gladly see you try."

Torin walked over to *Glediketil* and tied Drombir's cup to his belt. He jumped up as high as he could, caught the rim, and pulled himself up. As he straddled the edge of the vat, he reached down with Drombir's cup and filled it with the golden, sparkling mead.

"Don't fall in," said one of the trolls.

"I hope he does," said another.

Torin slid down the outside of the giant's cauldron. Some mead sloshed over the edge of the cup and onto his cloak which sparked another round of chuckles and jeers from the trolls. Then, one by one, he took the cup to each one in his company and quenched their thirst.

"By the gods," said Bryn, "I am so thirsty I can barely speak." The rasp of his voice was terrible, but when he had his fill his eyes brightened and he smiled. "That is the best mead I have ever tasted!"

One by one each of Torin's company drank, Grimsa more than the others, and soon all were in better spirits. Everyone, that is, except for Erik, who whimpered quietly to himself. After Torin had finished with his company he also offered mead to the two *nidavel* prisoners who were glad of it and soon had their fill as well.

Then Torin turned to the Troll-King and the host of trolls and drank down the last of the mead in generous gulps. The trolls watched with wide eyes and slack jaws. When he had finished, he wiped his lips on his sleeve. "This is indeed fine mead!"

Ur-Gezbrukter clapped slowly and grinned at Torin with narrow eyes. "It seems I have underestimated you, Gatar Wit-Weaver. You are proving to be even more entertaining than I expected. Present your next riddle."

Torin paced back and forth in front of the fire several times, then turned toward the Troll-King. "My next riddle will not be so easy."

> *Warriors with helms of white*
> *Charge ahead both day and night*
> *Each falls in turn with crashing blow*
> *Yet none can slay their ancient foe*

"Answer, listener, if you can."

The *jotur* nodded, sat back in his seat, and mumbled to himself. "Helms of white, crashing blow, ancient foe." His eyebrows lifted for a moment and his mouth opened as if to speak, but then he furled his brow and pursed his lips. The cavern was silent, every set of eyes, troll and prisoner alike, fixed on the *jotur*.

Torin looked at his friends, a miserable bunch, tied together with ropes. One of the smaller trolls kept trying to lick them with its slimy, green tongue. It gnashed its teeth when one of the larger trolls shoved it away. Asa and Inga comforted each other and Bryn and Grimsa sat together back to back. Wyla looked wracked with guilt and Erik lay on his side, curled up and whimpering.

Ur-Gezbrukter broke the silence. "Aha! I think I have unlocked the meaning. What constantly charges ahead, ends in a mighty crash, and is capped with white? The waves of the sea. The seafoam is the helm of white, their foe is the shore on which they break, and they march ahead in rows like warriors to battle."

Torin nodded and the trolls burst out into riotous cheers. A sick feeling swirled around in his stomach as he thought of his friends being eaten by trolls, one by one. He shook out his shoulders. The Troll-King seemed very pleased at his success so far and might soon let down his guard, or so Torin hoped. The giant motioned for silence and all went quiet.

"Now I have another riddle for you, Gatar the Wise, though I must say no *madur* has ever come this far in a duel of riddles with me. Perhaps I shall preserve your severed head after I have carried it into battle so we can continue this game of riddles."

"You have not defeated me yet, Troll-King. My head is still my own."

"True. Now ponder this."

> *Inspires speech yet stops the tongue*
> *Dear to both the old and young*
> *Listens long to mournful weeping*
> *And to laughter fast increasing*

"Answer, listener, if you can."

Torin nodded and crossed his arms. Trolls jeered and his company cheered as he paced back and forth in front of the fire. The drink had been sweet and strong and now his head swirled just enough to ease his nerves and loosen his mind. Drombir's cup bounced against his leg as he walked and, when he looked down at it, Torin saw the meaning of the riddle.

"What makes men and women want to speak, yet ties their tongue? Where do both the old and young seek comfort in mourning and pleasure with friends? The answer is clear—good ale, mead, wine, or any sturdy drink."

The Troll-King clapped and nodded. "You have answered correctly, Gatar Wit-Weaver. Give me another."

Torin stumbled up to the stone pedestal and steadied himself on its base. "This is a riddle I once wrote. See if you can solve it."

Catching what cannot be seen
Most have two but none have three
Ever filling, never filled
Empty when all else is still

"Answer, listener, if you can."

The Troll-King closed his eyes. He mumbled and groaned in a laboured sort of way as he thought. Then he rubbed his temples and tapped his foot against the floor of his stone pedestal. All at once the *jotur* jumped up, startling those trolls seated around him, and shouted his reply.

"Aha! I think I have deciphered the meaning. What can be filled endlessly without ever being full, yet also becomes empty when everything else is still? The ears." He tugged at his own ears and laughed. "And all creatures have but two."

"That is correct," Torin said. He forced a smile but felt hollow in his stomach. He was running out of riddles.

The giant clapped his hands and laughed. "In the land of my people, far to the North near the gaping Everspring from which all rivers flow, it is the custom for the host to serve sweet bread, spiced meats, and strong cheese after six riddles."

Ur-Gezbrukter whistled a haunting melody. Soon the sound of hooves splashing in water came from deep within the cave. From the dark tunnel came two horses, each larger than any horse Torin had ever seen, well-groomed and finely decorated with braided manes, red ribbons, and woven blankets. One was pure black, so dark it looked like a shadow walking. The other had a coat of light-brown hair which glowed like gleaming gold in the flickering firelight.

"I see you admire my horses, Gatar Wit-Weaver," the Troll-King said. "These are *Trur* and *Sterkur*, bred and raised by my grandfather. No finer horses are to be found in these mountains."

Trur and *Sterkur* both drew an enormous cart loaded with all manner of breads, piles of cured meats, and stacks of wheeled cheese. The trolls swarmed the cart and filled their mouths with as much food as they could. Each one pushed and shoved the others away from it only to be thrown back or muscled out by another troll. Then the Troll-King roared, and all the trolls scattered.

"Have your fill, Gatar Wit-Weaver, if you can reach."

At this the trolls laughed in an awful squawking manner, pointing and cackling like a flock of horrid birds. Torin's face flushed red. His stomach growled and ached so badly he thought it might leap right out of his body. The base of the cart was well over his head and the stone wheels offered little in the way of grip holds. He leapt up and caught the top edge with his fingers, but just as he did, both *Trur* and *Sterkur* lurched forward. He tumbled back down to the ground and the trolls mocked him with sneers and howling laughter.

Torin dusted off his cloak and drew out his axe. He jumped up again and this time swung his axe high overhead so that it lodged into the wooden cart. Again the horses lurched, but this time he held onto the axe shaft. With a heave he pulled himself up onto the cart and dislodged his weapon. Then, with eager blows, he hacked off pieces of cheese, meat, and bread with his axe blade until he could carry no more.

The Troll-King clapped. "Well done, Gatar Wit-Weaver. It seems you are also an acrobat and a butcher. Now your greatest feat will be to finish all that food in your cloak."

Torin jumped off the edge of cart, his cloak wrapped up full of food. With a chunk of cheese in his mouth he walked back to his place in front of the fire. As he approached the stone pedestal he tripped, or at least pretended to trip, and threw all the food bundled up in his cloak high up into the air. Most of it landed right on top of the prisoners and before a word could be said about it, they gobbled it up.

"What misfortune," said Torin, "Here I thought I'd have a feast and now I've spoiled it." His companions and the other prisoners cheered as he stood up and dusted off his cloak.

The trolls still laughed stupidly, but the Troll-King's face darkened. "I begin to suspect that you are not who you say you are. But we shall see that soon enough. No more easy riddles. Brace yourself, Gatar Wit-Weaver."

> *Skin without the bones and flesh*
> *Moves about yet draws no breath*
> *Flees the lovely summer flowers*
> *Then, in winter, men devours*

"Answer, listener, if you can."

Torin picked up a piece of cured meat that had fallen nearby and chewed it as he thought about the riddle. Though he was still hungry, the thought of his friends being eaten by trolls made him so sick he could hardly swallow a bite. The gristle of the meat inspired in him the thought of their bones being chewed and he almost vomited. He tossed the morsel away. With eyes closed he furrowed his brow and drew in slow, deep breaths.

"Skin without the bones and flesh? That seems to me to be the hide of some animal. Yet how would it move with no breath?"

He opened his eyes and stared at Ur-Gezbrukter. The *jotur* did not look pleased and Torin took this to be a good sign. He continued to think as he felt beads of sweat trickle down his back. His heart was pounding so loudly he could hear it in his ears and the silence of the captivated crowd was absolute. Then, all at once, he saw the answer in his mind.

"What is hidden in summer then emerges in winter? What devours men, yet shies away from flowers? It can be nothing other than a fur cloak which is made from all but the bones and the flesh of a beast. It moves because it is draped over a living person."

The *jotur* nodded and Torin's company cheered once again. He forced a smile and swallowed hard.

"This is a riddle of my own making. I presented it at Fjellhall, the great feasting hall at Gatewatch. None there could answer it. Surely you, mighty Troll-King, can find an answer."

> *Stags and rabbits both it catches*
> *Chews on roots from garden patches*
> *Every night it has its fill*
> *Yet in its place stands ever still*

"Answer, listener, if you can."

Ur-Gezbrukter frowned and sank back into his stone seat. The *jotur* grumbled and groaned as he rubbed his forehead and wrestled the riddle in his mind. After a while the trolls began to fidget and whisper among themselves but were silenced when the Troll-King stomped his foot.

"How can something catch the swiftest beast without moving? And what chews both flesh and roots? This riddle is most vexing."

Ur-Gezbrukter stood up then paced back and forth across his stone pedestal. Torin's company looked hopeful, but he kept his expression long and grim. It was too soon, he thought, to know if he had stumped the old giant. Even if he had, he could not be sure that the Troll-King would keep his word.

"How can something have its fill every night if it does not stalk or hunt?" said Ur-Gezbrukter. "There is only one way—if someone else brings it food. Does it lay a trap? No, there is no need to trap roots. What would be brought meat and roots of vegetables every day?" He stopped his pacing and looked up; a cruel grin spread across his face. "I think I have solved it. What catches the meat of both stags and rabbits, as well as the roots of vegetables out of the garden? What is filled every night though it stands in the same place? It can be none other than the stew pot."

Torin nodded and forced a smile though he thought he might faint. He had spent all his most difficult riddles.

"Aha, so I have surpassed the minds of Gatewatch. Though I hear there are fewer men of wisdom there and more that are but brutes and criminals. While I enjoy this sport, and indeed indulge it perhaps too richly, I have business to attend to in my newly formed court. So, Gatar Wit-Weaver, present your best riddle as I will present mine. If no winner is found between us, then I shall declare a draw. Half your company will go free and I will take only the top half of your head."

At this the trolls laughed and cheered. They continued to take food off the cart pulled by *Trur* and *Sterkur*, and the *jotur's* enchanted vat of mead was still full though the trolls tried their best to drain it. The Troll-King sat back on his pile of stones. Torin gritted his teeth but said nothing, as he could think of no other way to save his friends.

"This is my final riddle. There are those in the courts of *jotur* in my father's time who could not answer this question. Ponder it carefully."

> *Stalking man and beast by day*
> *Every night it hides away*
> *Fast as quickest creature found*
> *Has no eyes and makes no sound*

"Answer, listener, if you can."

Torin walked back and forth in front of the fire which, by this time, had burned down to embers. His company and the two *nidavel* prisoners cheered him on. The trolls made horrid faces at him or whooped and beat their chests. With his arms folded over his chest he closed his eyes and tried to shut out the noise.

"What sort of predator would stalk man by day and then hide away at night? And how, with no eyes, could it stalk a man at all?"

As he was speaking, the answer emerged like a horse and rider out of the fog. "Aha! It can be only one thing—a shadow. Shadows stalk every living being by day and then disappear at night. They have no eyes, they make no sound, and they are as quick as whatever they follow."

The Troll King's shoulders dropped, and his mouth twisted into a foul grimace. Victory had eluded him. Either Torin would now stump the *jotur* or the *bardagi* would meet its gruesome end.

Torin cleared his throat and waited for everyone present to be quiet. He reassured himself that there was a chance at least half his company would be freed if the Troll-King kept his word. However, that thought gave him little hope because of the matter of losing half his head. He knew had but one chance, this last riddle, to win the *bardagi* or die.

His mind raced back to home, to far-off comforts and familiar faces. Torin wrestled it back to the present and focused every ounce of energy left within him to forge a final riddle. When he tried to recall all that had happened over the past two days, an idea sprang up in his mind. He took a few deep breaths, then stepped forward.

"This riddle will decide this *bardagi*, Troll-King. Let us review the terms before I present my final riddle."

Ur-Gezbrukter, deflated, nodded. "Yes, of course. If you win, all the prisoners here will be in your possession. If we draw, then I will release half the prisoners and take only half of your head." His lips peeled into a grin.

"So all here have heard the terms," Torin said. He looked at the crowd of trolls before him, evil, snarling creatures. Their tolerance for treachery, or perhaps their delight in it, was grossly apparent. Then he saw his companions, wide-eyed and desperate. This was his only chance.

"This riddle is inspired by another that I heard some time ago. I have altered it to my purpose."

> *A golden chest so small and fair*
> *The key, a tooth, to lay wide bare*
> *The treasure hid, the tiny stones*
> *Each worth one hundred chests alone*

"Answer, listener, if you can."

The wicked smile drawn across the *jotur's* face quickly warped into a contorted mess, brow furled and lips curled. Ur-Gezbrukter gripped his head and leaned forward, breathing heavily as he pondered Torin's riddle. Neither the trolls nor the prisoners dared to make a sound. Then, Ur-Gezbrukter began to groan like a man struck with a toothache.

"How can just one stone be worth one hundred? This repulses the mind. I suspect treachery from you, Gatar Wit-Weaver. It is an unsolvable riddle."

Torin steadied his gaze and crossed his arms. "If you ask me, I will tell you the answer, Troll-King, but then you will have forfeited most dishonorably."

Ur-Gezbrukter spat onto the ground and settled himself on the pile of stones. He rubbed his head, then banged it with his fists. His groans turned to roars. At last the giant jumped up and hurled a stone toward the fire. The rock barely missed Torin as it flew over his head and struck a troll dead.

"To kill me would also be cowardly," Torin said. "And what's worse, you would never know the answer."

The Troll-King's eyes burned with fire and his hand went to the hilt of the mighty blade strapped to his leg. Before he drew it, he paused, thought better of disgracing himself, and fell back into his stone seat.

"Damn your confounded riddle."

"Do you admit defeat, Troll-King?"

Ur-Gezbrukter narrowed his eyes and pulled his lips tight across his face in a sneer. "No. According to the old laws I have until sundown tomorrow to give my answer. Until then, I name you Gatar Mind-Thorn, intruder and nuisance-maker in Fanghall, seat of Ur-Gezbrukter son of Gezbrukter, King of Trolls." The *jotur* motioned to Rhott and Pitt, the two trolls who had gifted him with the *nidavel*. "You two, house the prisoners in a cavern cell deep below. Tomorrow I will have my answer and then we shall sip their blood and chew their bones." At this the crowd of trolls cheered and chanted the Troll King's name.

Torin's heart fell in his chest. He had bought his companions, and himself, more time, but he feared great treachery was in store. Rhott and Pitt rounded up the prisoners by prodding them to their feet and forcing them into line. Then Pitt grabbed Torin by his cloak and shoved him into line behind his companions. From the crowd of trolls, hundreds of glowing eyes, sickly yellow and luminescent, watched the prisoners march away, deep down to the depths of Fanghall, the dungeon beneath the mountain.

10

◇ TO MYRKHEIM ◇

THE FURTHER DOWN THEY MARCHED, the darker, damper, and colder it became. Rhott held a flaming torch which sizzled and flickered every time a drop of water fell onto it from the stalactites above. A few drops splashed right onto Torin's head and soaked his tunic all the way down his back. When they finally arrived at the dungeon, every member of the party was nearly soaked.

At the far end of the chamber, they came to a gap in the wall which appeared to be their cell. Inside, the dewy floor was littered with ancient bones and the air smelled of must.

"All right, you maggoty *madur*," said Rhott, "Get in. All of you. Any who try to escape will be squished into jelly."

Pitt sneered with a smile and rubbed its leathery hands together. "And any that don't escape will be eaten tomorrow!" Both Rhott and Pitt laughed horribly and Torin thought the sound more awful than he imagined the cackling of witches to be.

"Now," Rhott said, "Pitt is going to guard you very carefully."

Pitt frowned and wrinkled its knobby nose. "Why me?"

"Because," Rhott said, "your eyes are so keen. I am old and my eyesight is poor."

Pitt snorted. "Damn your eyes. My nose is stuffed up and I can't smell a thing. It would be much better to sniff out these creatures in the dark. You should watch the prisoners."

"Damn your nose! You will guard the prisoners and that is that. I am going back to the *Trollting*."

The old troll turned to leave, but before it could stomp away Pitt shoved it into the wall. Rhott returned the favour. Then the torch that Rhott had been holding fell to the ground and erupted in sparks and smoke. The prisoners shuffled back as the two trolls grappled in the dark dungeon.

Torin looked up at the stalactites above his head and worried that the trolls might knock one loose with their wrestling. Snorts, grunts, and curses echoed in the dungeon as their enormous shadows flickered high up against the rock wall.

Just then Torin felt a frantic tug at his cloak. "Gatar Wit-Weaver, come with us!"

Torin looked down and saw the face one of the *nidavel* prisoners. The other *nidavel* had used a small knife to cut the bonds off the others with hasty slashes.

Torin did not hesitate for a moment. He and the rest of his company hurried after the *nidavel* into a dark corner at the back of the dungeon. The trolls were still engaged in their dispute and did not notice them move to the back of the cell.

"Shouldn't we be running out of the dungeon and not into it?" Grimsa said.

"No time for thinking," Bryn said.

Torin shoved Grimsa forward. "Just follow the *nidavel*!"

Both *nidavel* ran their hands along the back of the dungeon wall. They bent low and stretched high as they searched the rough rock face. Torin could see nothing in the dim light but an impenetrable wall of grey granite.

"I found it," the smaller *nidavel* said, "Help me get it open!"

The second *nidavel* placed his knife blade where the first had pointed and wedged it in. With a heave, a slight crack in the rock appeared, well rounded, the size and shape of a small door. Torin thought again of the door that Wyla had found at Frostridge Falls, how it had appeared out of the rock face from nowhere and then disappeared when it closed.

The older *nidavel* wheezed and gasped. "One more time, Bari!"

They heaved on the knife grip and the door swung open. The two *nidavel* shoved the others through the door, first Erik, then Asa and Inga, then Bryn and Wyla and Torin. Grimsa was the last to squeeze through the narrow passage and managed it only with many huffs and grunts. The older *nidavel* shuffled in after the others and the younger one hurried through last. With a groan they managed to pull the door shut behind them. The roars and grunts of the wrestling trolls now sounded muted and distant.

Every member of the company, *nidavel* and *madur*, dropped down against the stone walls of the lightless tunnel. In the dark, he heard the pulse of his own heartbeat against his eardrums and the exhausted gasps of the others. For a few moments, they lay still without saying a word. Then Torin heard someone stand up and rummage around in a bag. It was one of the *nidavel* back near the tunnel entrance.

"*Skina*," the older *nidavel* said. Down the tunnel Torin saw a burst of green light. In his hand the older *nidavel* held a fist-sized stone which glowed brightly. He shuffled past the others and approached Torin.

"Gatar Wit-Weaver," the *nidavel* said, "I am Brok, servant of Mastersmith Ognir. My nephew Bari and I owe you two favours. First, you saved our lives. If you had not wagered us in your *bard-agi* with the dreaded Troll-King, they surely would have made us prized delicacies at their horrid feast. Second, through wit and cunning you gave us food and drink which we have not had in many days. We have repaid the first debt now that you are safe from the trolls. Next we will repay the second. Will you come with us to Myrkheim?"

Torin's eyes had not yet adjusted to the strange light and he was still dizzy. He shook his head then nodded. "Myrkheim? How far is it?"

"Yes, Myrkheim, the city of the Mastersmith," said Bari, "It's not far. Maybe half a day's journey."

"I will only come if the rest of my company can join us."

"Certainly," Bari said, "Mastersmith Ognir's table is never short of food or drink."

Brok frowned. "Do not be too hasty to extend invitations to strangers Bari. We have no debt to the others."

"But the Mastersmith will want to meet them, won't he? Anyone who defeats a *jotur* in a *bardagi* must surely be worthy of an audience with the Mastersmith. And his companions no less!"

Brok sighed and tugged at his beard. "Well, I suppose. But I warn you, the Mastersmith is not overly fond of visitors."

Torin stood up, though not all the way as he had to crouch under the low ceiling. "I am sure we will be more welcome in his hall than in the hall of that fiendish Troll-King."

In time the others each caught their breath and stood up. Though everyone looked ragged and smelled worse, all smiled. In the light of Brok's stone, their white teeth glowed green. Torin thanked the gods that for the first time in two days they were free of their bonds and did not have to worry about being eaten, or at least not by trolls.

Bryn stretched out his arms and groaned. "I will go anywhere as long as it is not back to that horrid troll-ridden cave."

Grimsa spat on the ground and shuddered. "Aye, that is the foulest place I have ever been."

Brok nodded and motioned with his hand. "I've been to many foul places and even I must admit that I agree. So let's be off. Food and drink await us in Myrkheim!"

And so, they all trekked deeper down into the mountain. The steepness of the descent surprised Torin. He reckoned they had already gone quite far underground in the troll dungeon and now it seemed that they were bound for some place much deeper. After a short while, the small tunnel intersected a larger one which was so spacious that even Grimsa could stand straight up.

Brok placed the green glow-stone back in his pocket. "*Skina!*" At this, whole length of the larger tunnel lit up, this time a luminescent blue. Hundreds of glowing stones were embedded into the tunnel walls and ceiling in a geometric pattern. In the eerie light, Torin could see as far as his vision could stretch in either direction down the arrow-straight tunnel.

"By the gods," Bryn said, "what a wonder."

Brok laughed. "Ha! You have seen nothing yet. Myrkheim, the dwelling place of Mastersmith Ognir, is truly something to wonder at."

Torin scratched his head and looked again in both directions. "How do you know which way to go?"

Bari pointed at the wall and then ran his finger through a thin groove about a thumb-width deep. "This is called a guide notch. Keep it on your right and you will end up in Myrkheim. Keep it on your left and you will end up above ground."

"Isn't that where we want to go?" said Erik. "Why are we going deeper into these horrid tunnels rather than out?"

Brok marched up to Erik and eyed him hard. "Above ground? Back in the wilds? A great bit of mischief you found last time you wandered around in the woods."

Wyla shook her head. "For once I have to agree with Erik. We need to go back to Gatewatch and warn the others about the Troll-King."

Bari crossed his arms and frowned. "It's a two-day journey from here to the surface. You'll find no comfort or company along the way, just tunnel rats and cave snakes and roving bands of goblins, *skrimsli* as we call them. But Myrkheim isn't far. Much better to meet the Mastersmith and feast at his table there, I think. Then you can leave refreshed and properly outfitted for the journey."

The others agreed and so the company followed Brok, who proceeded down the path with a brisk step, the guide notch on his right. The old *nidavel* hummed a tune unfamiliar to Torin's ear. Bari joined in, sometimes with an echo of the refrain, other times with harmony. It had a merry ring to it and the rhythm fell in time with their steps. Soon the rest caught on and so they carried on together humming the *nidavellish* melody. Bryn, Asa, and Inga began to dance in a circle. As they twirled, they caught Bari and spun him around. The young *nidavel* got dizzy and toppled over. Everyone laughed, Bari more than any other. Then they all clapped as they went along and, for the first time in many days, spirits were high.

Torin found Wyla at the tail end of the company. "You have been very quiet since we escaped those trolls and by the look on your face it appears that perhaps you would rather be back there?"

"This is all my fault, isn't it?" Wyla said. "If I had just stayed in Gatewatch we would all be stuffing ourselves at Fjellhall then drifting off to sleep on soft beds."

"You don't look like one who has ever been contented with soft beds."

"No."

"Well, the rest of us came to Gatewatch looking for adventure and here we are. If we ever make it back, we'll all have a few good stories to tell. For better or for worse, we've got you to thank for that."

She sighed and stood up a bit straighter. "I guess that's true. You don't think Erik plans to compose one of his awful rhymes about our adventure, do you?"

Torin chuckled and nodded. "I certainly hope we get a verse! Though I would rather hear it from Bryn. If our journey so far hasn't been worth a line or two, I don't know what is." Wyla smirked and said nothing more as they continued down the *nidavel* passage.

In a small alcove carved out of the tunnel wall, they saw a fountain. At its base there was a smooth square stone basin full of cool, clear water. At its center were smaller square basins stacked on one another so that the water that gurgled out from the top trickled over the edge of each level into the slightly larger one below it. The cascading water glimmered in the blue light of the glowstones. Along its edges Torin saw *nidavellish* inscriptions carved in long, graceful runes.

"Ah," Brok said, "Nori's Well. We are very close to Myrkheim now."

Bari stepped up to the edge and dunked his face in. He slurped great mouthfuls of water and rinsed the grime from his face. The others followed his example and soon all had quenched their thirst.

Grimsa guzzled the water up in great gulps. Asa looked at him with a frown and wrinkled up her nose. "This is a fountain Grimsa, not a slop trough."

Grimsa looked up at her with a mouthful of water. Though his cheeks bulged out and his lips were closed tight, he managed a bit of a smile. Then, all at once, he sprayed the mouthful out over Asa, as well as Erik and Bryn beside her. He laughed a deep belly laugh and nearly fell over with glee. All three groaned and stepped back from the fountain.

"You really are a pig," said Asa.

Just as Asa spoke, an arrow whizzed out of the dark ahead of them and sunk into Brok's thigh. He roared with pain and stumbled back against the fountain. Torin saw a gush of hot red blood soak through Brok's pant leg as Bari rushed to catch the old *nidavel* before he fell over. The arrow that stuck straight out of his leg was greasy black and had a crooked shaft.

Bari's face went pale and his eyes shot wide open. "*Skrimsli*!"

The whole company pressed themselves back into the alcove of Nori's Well to stay out of range. Three more crooked arrows flew by and bounced off the walls. The trolls had taken every weapon except for Torin's axe though a few of the companions had short daggers hidden away beneath their tunics or tucked into their boots. For a moment it was very quiet, then Torin heard feet shuffle toward them down the hall.

A hoarse voice called out from blue-lit tunnelway, squeaky and high pitched. "Surrender, *nidavel*, and we'll ransom you for gold. Resist and we will slit your hairy throats!"

Brok groaned, straightened himself, and shouted back. "Surely one old *nidavel* isn't worth your energy to ransom or to harry."

"Lies! There are at least two of you. We saw your shadows and heard voices."

Grimsa picked up one of the arrows that had fallen to the ground. He snapped it in half to make a small shiv. "I'd sooner meet my ancestors than become yet another creature's prisoner."

The others nodded and Torin felt his heart beat hard in his chest like a war drum. Shoulders swelled, eyes narrowed, and jaws clenched as they all prepared to launch the attack.

Again the shrill voice called out. "This is your last chance *nidavel*! Surrender or we'll stick you with our knives!"

Torin counted down silently with a wave of his hand, then Bryn tossed his empty cloak out into the tunnelway. Three arrows struck the cloak and it fell to the floor. The next instant, before the *skrimsli* archers had time to draw another arrow, the whole company charged out with loud war cries, weapons drawn. Within the confines of the tunnel, the roar seemed to shake the stone.

The *skrimsli*, who thought their prey injured and far fewer in number, had crept too close to Nori's Well. When the company of *madur* sprang out they nearly landed on top of the band of *skrimsli* stalkers. Moreover, they had expected *nidavel*, not *madur*.

The sight of Grimsa, who towered high over their heads, and the sound of the company's mighty roar struck them with panic. They shrieked and squealed, just like pigs Torin thought, and those that didn't drop their weapons could barely handle them.

Wyla managed to steal a long dagger off the belt of the creature she grappled with, one of the larger ones, and stuck it deep between its ribs. When another jumped on her back to strangle her, she flipped backwards, just as she had done to Torin in Fjell-hall, and it fell to the ground with a slit throat.

Grimsa had tossed away the tiny shiv and instead had two *skrimsli* by the ankle, one in each hand, which he smashed against the wall. He continued to smash other *skrimsli*, using the two in his hand like clubs, or stomped them with his massive feet.

Bryn danced around the chaotic squabble. He dipped in and out with the dagger he had kept hidden in his boot. Two *skrimsli* came at him together, so he ducked and rolled right between them such that they collided, and their blows fell upon each other.

Torin had his axe in hand and cut down another *skrimsli* with every stroke. He felt the fire frenzy of battle in his chest and his eyes were wide and wild. He smashed the creatures' weapons, cracked their skulls, and felt the splatter of *skrimsli* blood burn like itchweed on his arms.

Asa and Inga fought back-to-back with daggers. The long, thin blades flashed with glints of blue from the glowing lights. Three *skrimsli*, then four, fell at their feet. Down the tunnel Torin saw one of the largest of the creatures barrel toward the twins with a tree-root club. Before they had time to maneuver, it swung its club at Inga. She covered her head with her arms and ducked, but the blow still sent her sprawling. As she tumbled over, Inga cried out. Asa, quick as a rabbit, dashed around the burly *skrimsli* and jumped up on its back. Before it had time to lift its club or reach around to grab her, she had yanked its head back and slit its throat.

In the end, nearly every *skrimsli* was dead. Even Erik had managed to kill the *skrimsli* that had jumped on him. However, two *skrimsli* fled the fight and tried to escape down the tunnel. As Wyla raced after them, Torin called out to Bryn. "Take this! Go with Wyla!" Bryn caught Torin's axe by the shaft as it was tossed to him, then sped after the two deserters.

All the others breathed heavily, leaned back on their heels, and wiped the gory ooze of black *skrimsli* blood off their hands, arms, and faces. Inga's face was contorted and flushed as she clutched her arm, but she did not groan or cry. From among the dead *skrimsli* they scavenged a bow, an odd assortment of trinkets and coins, and a variety of knives, daggers, and short swords. Asa took the bow while the rest helped themselves to whatever they thought might be useful.

Bari and Brok emerged from the alcove. The old *nidavel's* wound was still bleeding, but Bari had managed to bandage it. He limped along with the help of his nephew and beamed at the sight of the dead *skrimsli*.

"A whole *skrimsli* troop!" said Brok, "Thank the Mastersmith you all were here. Being captives for ransom of a gaggle of *skrimsli* might have been a worse fate than being a prisoner of trolls. Once again, my nephew and I are in your debt."

Inga looked at Brok and shook her head. "Your leg looks bad."

Brok chuckled and raised his eyebrows. "So does your arm. We should get moving."

Torin stood up. "What should we do with the dead *skrimsli*?"

Bari was still pale. He stammered for a moment, then wiped the sweat from his forehead and nodded. "Those foul creatures? No need to worry about them. The tunnel rats will nibble their corpses soon enough. Let's be off! Myrkheim isn't far."

The company lost no time. Those with weapons kept them in hand. After a short while they met with Wyla and Bryn who had gone ahead to finish off the deserters.

Torin called out when he saw them down the tunnel. "Did you catch the two that fled?"

"I caught one," Wyla said, "but the other one slipped through that crack in the wall."

Bryn handed the axe back to Torin then turned to Brok. "Are *skrimsli* vengeful creatures or are they cowards?"

Brok frowned. "In truth they are cowards, but in great enough numbers they might be bold enough to retaliate. We should move quickly."

Bryn offered his shoulder to Brok so that both he and Bari could help the old *nidavel* along. The others constantly glanced up and down the glowing tunnel for any sign of *skrimsli*. At times they thought they saw shapes in the shadows or heard the scurry of clawed feet, but nothing ever emerged from the dark.

The farther down they trekked, the hotter it became. Up near the troll dungeons, the air had been damp and clammy, but now a warm breeze blew through the tunnel. The air still had a dank mustiness to it, but Torin thought either it was better than before or that he had become used to it. As for the company, each one battered from their encounter with the trolls and bloodied from the skirmish with the *skrimsli*, Mrykheim could not appear soon enough. Stomachs gurgled and grumbled at the thought of a feast in the Mastersmith's hall and every throat ached for ale or mead. Bari's elaborate descriptions of such things only stoked their hunger and their thirst. Though their feet were blistered and sore from walking the stone road, that hope kept them going.

At last the path levelled out and the road curved to the right. For the first time since they had joined the main tunnelway, the passage grew higher. It continued to curve and widen until they came upon a vast underground cavern. Ahead of them a wide stone bridge spanned a dark abyss so deep that the bottom could not be seen. All the way down, the face of the precipitous drop glittered and glowed with precious stones and luminescent minerals. Across this bridge, on the other side of the gap, Torin saw the radiant glow of a walled city.

Brok sighed with relief. Torin saw in the old *nidavel's* eyes the same look he might have if he were to come upon Ten-Tree Hall after such trials. As his nephew helped him stand straighter, Brok winced. "By the Mastersmith, as I sat in the stench of that troll den, I thought I would never see this city again. Ahead! Across the bridge is where rich food, sparkling drink, sweet music, and warm beds wait for us!"

Across the stone bridge they went, their feet light and their spirits lighter. On either side of the bridge there were magnificent stone statues of mighty *nidavel* warriors, each one positioned across from another statue of a terrible monster. Everyone in the company, especially Bryn, marvelled at these, both because of the splendid look of the warriors and the awful aspect of each creature.

"There is a great tale to every statue," Bari said. "Perhaps when we have had our fill, I will sing you the lay of Eikinskjaldi the Bold, or Fraegr the Fearless, or Bumbur the Fat."

"So you are a singer, Bari?"

Bari beamed. "One of the best under the mountain."

It took them some time to cross the bridge, but at last they came to the other side. An iron gate blocked their way into Myrkheim. It was made of twisted metal tied in knots and crisscrossed as if it had been knitted together. The walls around the city were high and smooth so that an outsider could do nothing but wonder what lay on the other side.

Brok cleared his throat and stood up as straight as he could. "*Opna!*"

Over the top of the gate, high up on the stone wall, a small *nidavellish* face emerged and peered down at them. It frowned and scratched its head then replied. "Who is it that wishes to enter Myrkheim, city of the Mastersmith Ognir?"

Brok's face burst into a crimson red and his expression soured. "Lofi, you oaf! It's me, Brok the Silversmith, cousin to Ognir, and uncle to Bari the Bard, who is also with me. We've been bundled and bruised by trolls, starved, parched for water, and harried by *skrimsli*. I have neither time nor patience to deal with any more of your miserable questions so, by the Mastersmith, let us in!"

The *nidavel* atop the gate, Lofi, as Brok had called him, scuttled away from the edge and cranked the gate winch as fast as he could. As the iron bars rose, Torin remembered Gavring and his first view of Gatewatch. Though he had spent only a short time there, he felt the pain in his chest that one feels when they are reminded of home. He thought of Gavring's stories about the *nidavel* swindlers, about the food and the song in Fjellhall, and about the lush fields of green grass and alpine flowers outside of Gatewatch.

Myrkheim was a different sight to behold. Though there was no sunlight, the whole city glowed with a luminescent blue. It was difficult to tell where the glow came from, either from the rigid, flat-faced structures of stone or some other mysterious source. As they stepped through the gate of the city each gazed at the columnar buildings that rose up high up over their heads.

Lofi, the guardsman who had opened the gate, waddled over to their company and gave a quick bow. Even for a *nidavel* he was short. He wielded a spear and wore an oversized helmet which fell down a bit too far over his eyes. "Welcome home, Silversmith Brok, cousin of Mastersmith Ognir! The city gates open wide for you, forger of the seven shining rings. The streets welcome the weight of your step, crafter of the great ale drum, *Hatidlegr*. Long may your beard grow, welder of the whirling wheels."

Brok frowned and sighed. "Enough, enough! We need food, drink, and rest. Send ahead to my good cousin that we are coming to hail him." Lofi stood silent and dumb for a moment. Brok's face boiled again. "Go! Use those stubby little legs of yours before

I break them off!" Lofi jumped with a start and sprinted away as fast as his legs would take him.

11

◇ SECRETS AT SUPPER ◇

Bari led them deep into the city, a stone labyrinth of strange flat-faced structures. Myrkheim itself was made up of enormous interlocking six-sided columns, all of which were exactly the same size. The lowest of these columns served as streets, the shorter ones as small shops or homely halls, and the tallest as barracks or watch towers. In addition to the bizarre arrangement of six-sided buildings within it, the whole city also seemed to rise to a peak at its center; like a mountain within a mountain.

Torin saw now that the blue light that emanated from the city came from tiny blue glow-stones naturally embedded in the rock. These deposits swirled up the sides of buildings and spread over streets like strokes of a painter's brush. Set as they were against the dark grey stone canvas of the city streets, they reminded Torin of the glimmer of stars across the night sky.

Bryn pulled at his hair and shook his head. "How did you do it? Each of these pillars is the size of a house, yet they all are smooth-faced and perfectly matched with the rest so that they fit together. The tunnels were impressive, but this is unfathomable!"

Brok chuckled, then readjusted his grip on Bryn's shoulder. "The craft of the *nidavel* is surpassed by that of only one other, and that is nature herself. These basalt columns are natural wonders.

When the deep belly of the earth grumbles so that her founda-
tions crack, she bleeds a great storm of molten rock. If the condi-
tions are right the rock may cool in such remarkable formations."

"The poets say it best," Bari said, "*In nature perfection, all craft
mere reflection.*"

Grimsa, a few paces behind the others, leaned over to Torin.
"Sounds like some *nidavellish* non-sense to me. This place reeks
of magic."

Wyla pulled Grimsa and Torin in close. "I agree. We must
keep up our guard. It is never wise to trust a *nidavel.*" She turned
to Torin. "This was a bad idea, coming here. We should have
gone straight back to Gatewatch." Torin shook his head and kept
walking.

Through the winding street, past markets and lively street-side
vendors, they continued up the city's slope. Wherever they walked,
the crowds fell silent. Young *nidavel* watched the strange company
of *madur* with wide-eyed wonder while the older ones regarded
them with suspicion through squinting stares. A few of the children waved and giggled as they hid behind the cloaks of their
mothers. When others threw small rocks or bits of scrap at them,
Bari waved them off.

"Very few *madur* ever travel to Myrkheim," said Bari, "In fact,
I reckon most of the *nidavel* here have never even seen a *madur*
before."

Torin chuckled and nodded. "They certainly do not seem keen
on strangers."

Brok snorted. "Never mind them, they are ignorant fools. Most
here have their heads stuffed so far down their coin purse they can
hardly tell up from down. They care little who or what you are as
long as you have gold or silver."

They stopped in front of an arched doorway carved into the
basalt face of a particularly tall pillar. The double doors swung
open at their approach. From the gaping mouth of the curved
door frame two *nidavel* robed in red shuffled toward the company.

The first carried a silver pitcher in the shape of a swirling shell that was so large she had to carry it with both hands. The second followed behind the first with a silver platter etched with knotted vines upon which was stacked a dozen small drinking vessels. The cups were also of silver and had the same swirling shell design as the pitcher.

"Welcome home, Master Brok and Master Bari," the first *nidavel* said, "We have been sick with worry since your disappearance." She had strands of white in her coal-black hair which was tied up neatly in a twisted bun. Wrinkles creased around her smiling eyes, yet her face still held a youthful beauty. When she saw the bloody tourniquet around Brok's leg, her face fell, and she knelt to inspect it. "By the Mastersmith, I knew something serious must have kept you away so long. I worried you might never return!"

"Dani, keeper of my hall, do not worry about me. You have kept everything in order. In fact, I am quite sure you ran my estate with more diligence and keen judgement than I myself could muster. And as for this wound, stories shall be told! But first, a drink for my honoured guests."

Bari laughed and helped the other servant hand out the drinking vessels. "It is said of the *nidavel* that you are not truly welcome unless the taste of ale or spirits is on your lips as you pass over the threshold." Grimsa's eyes lit up and as the golden liquid was poured into his cup, a wide, stupid smile spread across his face. Despite his protests a few moments before, he guzzled the golden liquid down with glee. Wyla was more cautious than the rest. She waited until Bari and Brok had taken a draught before she drank her cup dry.

Brok was still in great pain but insisted on standing as he gave the toast. "Here is to friends made under strange circumstances, to dodging death, and to a quick recovery. Long live the Mastersmith!" The others hailed him then drank a second round together.

Brok led them into the hall, helped by Bari and Bryn. A smooth floor of swirling white marble welcomed their weary feet. The dark basalt walls that rose up around them had been polished so vigourously that Torin could see his own reflection. Up over their heads, spiral columns carved into those same walls arched inwards and met high above the center of the six-sided room.

The old *nidavel* sighed and smiled. "Now, let's have a bath prepared. Then we will feast!"

Dani slipped under Brok's arm and helped him forward. "I've already sent two servants to prepare the bath, and the cook should be back from the market any minute now. But your wound needs attention. I'll see to that while your friends go to the baths."

Brok smiled and raised his arm toward Inga. "This is Inga. She took a blow to the arm while defending me against *skrimsli* in the tunnels."

Dani's eyes grew wide. "*Skrimsli*? Are they so bold as to attack a cousin of the Mastersmith?"

Brok shook his head. "They are stupid creatures, greedy and violent. But the stories must wait. Come with us, Inga, and we'll see that your arm is tended to." Asa moved to follow her, but Inga motioned for her sister to join the others.

Bari squeezed Brok by the shoulders. "Rest well, uncle! We'll see you at dinner. Everyone else follow me to the baths!"

Bari led them through one of the interior doors and down a set of spiral steps. The *nidavellish* draught on an empty stomach made Torin's head swirl just enough to forget the blisters on his feet and the bruises on his ribs. The baths below Gatewatch came to his mind and he smirked at how desperately he felt he had needed them then. Their journey over Shadowstone Pass now seemed almost laughable compared to the past two days. He breathed deep the rich, familiar scent of the mineral baths and felt the radiant heat of the stone steps in his feet.

Bari stripped as he ran down the stairs and then jumped straight into the white shroud of steam at the bottom of the stairwell. He made a mighty splash and water sprayed in every direction. The others rushed to rid themselves of their reeking clothes and then waded in after him.

The pool was wide and chest deep for a *nidavel*, about waist-height for the company of *madur*. It was not a natural spring as had been the case in Gatewatch. A mosaic of smooth ceramic tiles covered the floor and edge of the bath, and water poured in through the wall out of a decorative spout. The water was steaming hot and smelled strongly of aromatic oils, cedar, and cinnamon.

"By the gods!" Grimsa said, "I have never been so glad of a bath!"

Bryn called back through the white cloud. "You are not as glad of the bath as we are for you taking it! You smell as foul as a troll and I can say that now that I know of it first-hand."

Grimsa sent a wave toward Bryn and it doused him completely. With wet hair hanging down over his eyes, Bryn laughed and threw himself back into the water. Then Erik splashed Asa and she shoved him over into in the bubbling pool.

While the others splashed and scrubbed away the grime, Torin found Bari near the back of the room. The young *nidavel* sat reclined on a submerged seat with his hands behind his head.

"Your uncle's hall is impressive. It is like nothing I have ever seen."

Bari chuckled and nodded. "It is one of the finest in all of Myrkheim, inherited from his grandfather who was the brother of the last Mastersmith."

"And he lives here alone? No wife or children to greet him after his long journey?"

"Now there is a tale." Bari sat up in his seat and straightened his shoulders. "You see, my Uncle Brok was young when he found love. Yet it was not in the halls of the great families nor in the goldsmith's workshop when he found it, but in the market. Worse than that, not even a commoner! A servant. Her name was Dani."

"Dani? The woman that met us?"

Bari smiled and winked. "Yes. My uncle planned to renounce his family and use what little wealth he had then to free her. He thought they might flee the city and live a life together in the deep tunnels. She would have none of it though. Instead, she counselled him to establish his own house and make her the master of his staff. That way there would be no quarrel with his family, as they would never accept her anyway, and they could live then as they pleased. With her by his side he has achieved great stature among the people of Myrkheim, even with the Mastersmith himself! Few know him well, but those that do know that the secret to all his success is the wisdom and discernment of Dani."

Torin laughed and shook his head. "That is quite the tale. Your uncle has even more luck than I thought."

Bari sighed and shook his head. "Sometimes I worry that luck is the only thing keeping him alive, but yes, you are right. Come and sit if you wish. There is another chair here under the water."

Torin then sank down to his neck and breathed deep as he lay back in the chair. "When do you think we will get an audience with the Mastersmith?"

Bari twisted his mouth and scratched his head. "I doubt my uncle will be in any condition to travel to the Mastersmith's hall tonight, but there is a good chance you may get to meet him tomorrow."

"What is he like, this Mastersmith Ognir?"

Bari pulled at his beard and frowned. "The Mastersmith? He is a cousin to my uncle Brok, and the skill of craft that runs in our family runs deepest in him. He is shrewd and short-tempered but also inquisitive and inventive. His lust for wealth has spilled down from his coffers into the rest of the city and for that most hold him in high regard. However, he also delves deeply into the magic. Too deeply some would say. Certainly, a Mastersmith must be bold in his experiments, but there are some dark areas of study which many think it unwise to explore."

"Such as?"

Bari lowered his voice and motioned to Torin to lean in. "I've heard rumors that he strives to lengthen his own life. Some say he has tampered with souls while others say that he communes with the dead." Bari shivered and shook his head. "It is unwise to be picking at the threads of life itself, treading the edge of death, if you ask me."

"Has he had any success?"

"I can't say for certain. And surely any mention of the subject will turn his mood bitter." Bari's bright eyes darted back and forth. "Probably best not to mention it to the others as that Wyla girl seems to have a bitter dislike for us *nidavel* already."

Torin nodded then leaned back in the submerged chair. He let the steamy vapour pour into his lungs and the heat of the bath soak into his sore skin. However, as his body relaxed, his mind darkened. Memories of the Watchers, those ghostly figures with burning ember eyes, again haunted his thoughts. Their grotesque forms, outlined by the chilled fog, seemed to be permanently etched in his mind.

Then the white steam around him swirled as it had that night at Shadowstone Pass and a chill ran over the hot bath. Through the steam of the bath, Torin saw two dim red embers appear. He shook his head, but the embers were still there. He drew a quick breath and nearly sucked in a lungful of water. His heart railed against his ribs like an animal clawing at a cage, but his body froze in fear and refused to move. The two embers swayed back and forth in an eerie rhythm as they moved slowly toward him through the churning clouds of white vapor.

Just when Torin thought he might call out or dash away, two forms appeared below the burning embers. At first, they were just shadows, but as the steam swirled away he saw two *nidavel* servants holding torches up high. Both stood at the edge of the pool and squinted in the steamy darkness.

"Master Bari? Are you still in the bath? Dinner is prepared and waiting. You and your friends are now welcome to join Master Brok in the dining hall."

Bari sighed and stretched out his arms. "Yes, very good! We will be up right away."

Torin exhaled and shook his head, but the image of a Watcher in the mist lingered in his mind. He was glad to jump out of the steaming bath along with the others to dry off with the towels that the servants had brought. They then passed out fine robes, the largest in Master Brok's wardrobe. Each of them found a decent fit with the unfortunate exception of Grimsa. In the end, he simply wrapped himself up in towels.

Bari led the whole company up the stairs and into the dining hall. As with all the other rooms, the hall had six sides with floors of white marble and walls of dark polished basalt. Banners of gold, red, and silver hung on the walls and a ring-shaped table ran around the room. There were no benches, but there were twelve seats of stone which had been carved to look like the petals of giant flowers. These petals formed the seat and back of the chair while a thick carved stem connected each one to the floor. At each seat a round crimson pillow made the flower's face. A tablecloth of the same hue had been spread along the curved ring table, as well as fine silver platters and goblets which were laid out before each seat.

Brok rose from his chair opposite them and opened his arms wide. He wore a fine robe of crimson with a gold chain belt. From his neck hung a silver pendant which rested on the curly hairs of his chest. In the tunnels, his appearance had been wild, but now both his hair and beard were combed, oiled, and neatly braided. Dani sat beside him arrayed in a red silken gown, long silver earrings, and a glittering headband which had been woven into her braided hair. "Come friends, soon dinner will arrive from the kitchen."

When they had taken their seats, a round door opened from the floor at the center of the ringed table. Sweet and savoury smells floated up from it as servants brought up lavish platters from the kitchen below. Each held fist-sized mushrooms stuffed with strong cheese, strange cave-dwelling fish fried in herbs and spices, and a slab of thick-rooted boiled vegetable. After the platters had been set out, the great goblets around the table were filled to the brim with amber honey mead.

"A toast," said Brok, "to all our friends and to our good fortune in the past days. Especially to Torin Ten-Trees, known now as Gatar Mind-Thorn among trolls. Now I name him Riddlesmith among the *nidavel*. To the bravery of the whole company at Nori's Well who defended me from a troupe of *skrimsli* which surely would have taken me hostage or worse. And last, to luck, which favoured us when death seemed close. Let us drink! *Skal!*"

The whole company, including the servants who themselves had also been given drink, saluted together. "*Skal!*"

Their appetites were so great that nothing more was said until each platter had been picked clean. Torin savoured the cheese-stuffed mushrooms while Grimsa gulped each one in a single bite. Bryn praised the fried fish and Wyla conceded that the mead was of good quality, though not as fine as in Fjellhall. The only one of them to shy away from his platter was Erik who said he did not have much of a taste either for mushrooms or for fish. As soon as he spoke, Grimsa reached over and devoured all of Erik's mushrooms and snatched up his fish. Erik was then left to chew on the boiled vegetable.

Brok sat back with a sigh and swirled his mead. Torin noticed wrinkles around his eyes and that his gaze was distant and troubled. His eyes caught Torin's and he leaned over. "My friend, we have something important to discuss. But first, as a good host, I must provide some entertainment."

"Look no further, Uncle." Bari, who had overheard, stood up and walked around the table. At the far end he lifted a slot out of the table and stepped into the middle of the ring.

Dani smiled wide and clapped. "We have missed your songs and your stories, Bari. This hall is empty without them."

Brok also clapped and nodded. "Servants, fill everyone's mead flask then call up the others from the kitchen so all can hear!"

So each glass was filled to the brim and the servants gathered around the outer edge of the room. Torin thought again of Ten-Tree Hall, of the long winter nights and the epic tales his father would tell. Retainers and free folk would gather around the fire with steaming cups of spiced wine, each wrapped in thick furs or soft sheepskin. Before his mind had wandered too far, a hush fell on the room as Bari began his tale.

"My *madur* friends," said Bari, "you might recall that as we walked across the bridge into Myrkheim there were many mighty statues. On one side, the heroes, on the other, the beasts. And indeed, I do believe, as a teller of tales, that a hero is nothing without a foe to fight and that each monster secretly begs the bold and the brave to meet them in battle. Moreover, I think we may be nearing a time when fiends as fierce as those in the old stories will call for the rise of a new generation of heroes. So tonight, I present to you a story of one such hero. He cannot be missed while crossing the bridge for he is the largest of the heroes there by girth, if not by deed, and perhaps most loved by the tellers of tales. It is now my great pleasure to sing for you the Lay of Bumbur the Fat, slayer of the Great Snake Vitormur." Bari hummed a note to himself then began a strangely syncopated minor melody.

> *In the reign of Lord Thrain*
> *Of the Mastersmiths sixth*

Vile Vitormur bore
Venom fangs long and dread

Measureless treasure, told
Thrain, would be given to
He who slew Vitormur
Dread snake so hated

Fierce young nidavel fell
To strong Vitormur's fangs
In vain, Thrain's vast treasure
Laid untouched in its vault

So sat Bumbur the Fat
City gate long guarding
Heavy did his eyelids
Fall that fateful hour

Ringing bells broke sleep's spell
Eyes wide, he saw dread come
Vile Vitormur bore down,
Wide open gate in view

"Drop the gate! Drop the gate!"
Bumbur heard the guards cry
'Neath the gate, loosed too late,
Slipped Vitormur's long fangs

Yet scaled neck got not through
Caught 'neath gate iron-wrought
Still, for fear, none drew near,
Those fangs venom spewing

But Bumbur, clumsy glut,
By chance off the wall fell
Down on that dreadful head
Vitormur, vanquished, died

With words profane Lord Thrain
Cursed the clumsy watchman,
But stayed true to his oath
So Bumbur treasure won

And so, though bold or brave
Oft deal the final blows,
Great luck and fate may make
Mere fools into heroes

Bari bowed as he sang the last line and the room erupted in cheers. Servants clapped with vigour and Torin's company cheered. Brok and Dani held hands and smiled at each other. Once the applause died down, Brok stood up and addressed the company.

"My dear nephew, your skill at the word-forge never ceases to delight us. I thank you for your tale. And though I would gladly listen to your songs and stories through the night I now must speak of heavier matters."

Silence took the room and all eyes fell on the old *nidavel*. Though it clearly pained him, he stood and used the table as a support. Slowly he worked his way around the table and entered the center of the ring by the same opening Bari had used.

"Some here might think it strange that two *nidavel* would end up in the clutches of the trolls, those most despicable creatures, particularly two *nidavel* of renown such as Bari and myself. Indeed, it is strange, for we have many tunnels and are not prone to being captured within our realm of stone. But it was at the Mastersmith's bidding that Bari and I journeyed far from here in secret. We were sent above to the sun-realm with a special purpose which I now regret that I must reveal."

The old *nidavel's* eyes were soft and his brow drawn tight together in a frown. Torin wondered if it was his injured leg that made him look so miserable or if it was the pain of revealing whatever this secret was before friends.

"As most of you know, our beloved Mastersmith has an obsession of late with the extension of his mortal life: with attaining immortality. Though many ponder this in old age, he has taken his research to extremes. This has drawn much criticism from many in Myrkheim, including me."

Torin glanced at Bari who had moved off to the side of the room. Bari's arms were crossed tight and his face was dark.

"I think that perhaps he is becoming desperate as he feels the strain of age upon his bones, for when he heard of the arrival of an heir to the troll-throne he asked his closest advisers and kin to send a secret delegation."

At this the room went deadly quiet. Torin felt a surge of blood rush to his face and his chest tightened. With slow breaths he pushed down the anger that threatened to boil over within his chest. He kept his face still as memories of Ur-Gezbrukter, laughing above the throng of trolls, flashed behind his eyes.

Brok's eyes widened as he saw the faces around the room. A drip of sweat ran off his forehead and down his nose. "I must beg your forgiveness for not revealing this sooner. But I hope to convince you that I took the assignment with good reason."

Wyla stood up and slammed her goblet on the table. Her nostrils flared and her eyes were wild with fire. "What good reason could you have for conspiring with the Troll-King against us and our ancestors who bled to keep Gatewatch free of those horrid creatures? Does your Mastersmith plan to restore Ur-Gezbrukter to his throne so that trolls can terrorize the land once again? What of our alliance? What of the gold and silver he has grown rich on from trade with King Araldof Greyraven? Does one hundred years of friendship mean nothing to you *nidavel*? Traitors! Fiends!"

By the time she had finished everyone in the room was on their feet. Wyla leapt over the table and grabbed the old *nidavel* by his beard. Bari shouted and Dani screamed. Asa and Inga each grabbed a wriggling servant before they could scuttle off while Grimsa blocked the door.

"Please, please," Brok said, "give me a chance to explain myself!"

Wyla drew out the long cruel dagger she had taken from the *skrimsli*. "I have no mind to listen to a liar and a traitor." She pointed the curved blade at Brok's heaving chest.

Torin leapt over the table into the center of the room where Wyla and Brok stood. "Stop!" His shout came with such force and volume that he even surprised himself. The servants quit squirming and Wyla turned her wild gaze toward Torin as the dagger trembled in her hand.

"What would we gain by harming him?"

Wyla spat and bared her teeth. "Is there nothing to gain in justice?"

Torin nodded and shrugged. "Perhaps, but there is much more to be lost with a rash decision."

At this, Wyla whirled around with lightning quick speed and aimed the dagger at Torin's throat. "I am sick of hearing you talk. I told you not to trust the *nidavel*. Are you a traitor too?"

"I'm no traitor," said Torin, "and you know that."

Wyla frowned. "Do I? What I know is that I was right and you were wrong. But everyone listened to you and went along with these back-stabbing *nidavel*." Her eyes smoldered with some mix of jealousy and hatred which made Torin's heart shudder. "Now they have us trapped in their miserable city of stone! We should be trekking back to Gatewatch right now to warn the others. They have no idea what is coming. Instead we are drinking and singing and feasting with a lot of traitorous *nidavel*."

Torin took a deep breath and forced his shoulders down. "You are right. We need to warn the others. But might the Mastersmith offer aid now that he knows the true nature of this Troll-King,

Ur-Gezbrukter? I would hear Brok speak." The others in the company nodded silently.

Brok limped toward Wyla and Torin. "I, more than anyone on the council, disagreed with the Mastersmith's plan. That is why I took the assignment. I meant to sabotage any possible allegiance between this rumoured Troll King and our beloved Mastersmith. It turned out that my suspicions were well founded, for when we made contact with the trolls, they took us captive and treated us worse than prisoners. When we were presented to Ur-Gezbrukter, it was clear that he regarded us as less than maggots. Now I am bent on destroying that horde of evil trolls and their wicked king. The Mastersmith must be convinced to fight against this abominable threat. But to convince him, I need your help."

Wyla sneered. "You need our help, but do we need yours?"

Brok's beard bristled and his eyebrows shot up. "Gatewatch may have strength of arms, but you'll need far more than that to defeat the son of Gezbrukter. You saw him work spells upon his cauldron, didn't you? That *jotur* has knowledge of ancient magic and for that Gatewatch is wholly unprepared. I admit that even I have my doubts that our Mastersmith could match him but still there is a chance. So yes, you do need us."

For a moment the room stayed quiet save for the sound of Wyla's slow shaky breaths. Then her eyes began to fill with hot angry tears, and she let out a wretched scream. The dagger trembled in her grip and she threw it on the floor with a ringing clang.

Brok collapsed onto the floor as Dani and Bari rushed to help him. Wyla stormed toward the door and pushed past Grimsa. The others breathed easier and sat back in their chairs. Torin leaned back against the table and rubbed his throbbing head.

The old *nidavel* groaned as he stood again with Dani and Bari's help. "So, does this mean you will help us?"

Torin narrowed his eyes and nodded. "We have a common en-emy and I would like to see you as a friend. However, if you betray our trust again, we will not hesitate to see justice done."

Brok nodded and pursed his lips. "Very well. For your sake, Torin Riddlesmith, I will forgive Wyla's threats. Now take some rest, for tomorrow we go straight to the Mastersmith."

12

◇ THE MASTERSMITH ◇

TORIN WOKE UP AFTER AN UNEASY SLEEP. Many scenes of terror had flashed through his mind that night, but the worst of all had been a vision of Ten-Tree Hall burning. In that dream, trolls danced around the hungry flames, while Ur-Gezbrukter gloated in the light of the fire. However, it was not the fire or the Troll-King that disturbed him most but what lurked in the shadows around the fire—the Watchers. Those silent swaying forms looked upon the destruction with quiet approval in their unblinking ember eyes. From within the flames Torin could hear his father cry for help, yet he was too terrified to move, frozen by fear of those ghostly apparitions.

Now, the strange shape of the room and the firm feel of the stone bed brought him back to where he was, safe in the center of Myrkheim. His head throbbed as he recalled the uproar Wyla had caused the previous night. Afterward, she had shut herself away in one of the rooms and refused to speak to anyone. He wondered whether a good night's rest had doused her temper. He doubted it.

A light knock came at his door and a small figure stepped into the door frame, a *nidavellish* servant. "Greetings, Master Torin Riddlesmith, crafter of fine riddles, frustrater of Ur-Gezbrukter, and slayer of many *skrimsli*. May one thousand golden rings fall softly into your lap."

Torin sighed in the darkness. "Just Torin will do."

"Certainly, Master Torin. Yet it is the custom of the *nidavel* to address a superior by recalling their greatest achievements. You are young and already have accomplished so much."

"I don't feel like I've accomplished much more than getting lost in the wilds, becoming a prisoner of trolls, and being surprised by a rogue band of *skrimsli*."

"Few would call surviving all that a small feat. Yet I think more here in Myrkheim will know the name Torin Riddlesmith before this day is over than those who don't."

Torin scratched his head at this and watched the servant use a small device to light an oil lamp in the corner of the room. Then he brought Torin's clothes, washed and folded, and laid them on the edge of the bed. With a wheeze of exertion, the servant twisted a ring on a pipe that protruded from the wall and, to Torin's surprise, steaming water leaked out. Right underneath the gurgling stream of water was a copper bowl set into a wooden table. When the bowl was nearly full, the servant again twisted the ring and the flow of water stopped. From a drawer beneath the table he took a long, thin blade, wrapped it in cloth, and laid it beside the bowl.

As he stood in the doorway, the servant smiled and bowed. "The others are just waking up now, but soon breakfast will be ready. Make sure to wash your face and shave because you and your company have been given an audience with the Mastersmith. It is the greatest honour anyone in Myrkheim can be granted."

"Today? Already?"

The servant nodded and clapped his hands, a grin spread wide across his face. "Yes, this morning in fact. Master Brok is highly respected and news of a company of *madur* in the city caught the Mastersmith's attention right away. Though his injuries will keep Master Brok home, Master Bari will accompany you. You are lucky, as most *nidavel* must wait months before being granted an audience. I'll leave you to clean up now. Breakfast is in the dining hall. Don't be too long!"

The servant scurried away as fast as he had come and Torin was left alone. His head still ached, and his legs were so sore he could barely stand. However, he managed to stumble over to the washing bowl and rinse his face. The hot water was a balm to his skin and the steam filled up his lungs with warm, moist air.

Torin picked up the long, thin razor blade that the servant had left. The itch on his neck from the stubble had grown worse over the last few days. He soaked his neck with hot water then pulled the thin blade back over the stubble, careful to shave close so that his skin was smooth.

On the table beside the washing bowl there lay a polished silver dish. He picked it up and looked at his neck in the reflection. He had missed a small patch, so he soaked it again and cleaned it up with the razor. Satisfied, he drew the mirror farther away to look at himself.

Torin saw something then that he had never seen before. When he caught a glance of his whole face there appeared to be a flash of his father. Never before had Torin seen it, but now a slight gauntness of the cheeks, a strain across the brow, and a tiredness around the eyes drew his features closer to those of his father. His heart dropped in his chest as he felt the great distance between himself and the place he had been raised. He wondered what his father might do in his position, what advice or guidance he might offer a young man who found himself strung between a looming troll war and an eroding company in a strange city.

The servant called again from the hallway. "Master Torin, breakfast is waiting!"

Torin shook his head and wiped his face. With slow, sore movements, he tightened his belt and pulled his tunic over his head. Then he bent down with a groan, tied up his boots, and descended the spiral steps.

Most of the others were at the circular table when Torin stepped into the dining hall. Bryn sat at one of the stone seats next to Bari. Asa slurped a bowl of thick, steaming mushroom soup, while Inga, with her free arm, chewed a strip of dried meat. Grimsa and Erik still had not come down from their rooms and no one had spoken to or heard from Wyla since the night before.

"Torin," said Bryn, "good news! The Mastersmith has given us an audience right away."

"That is good news."

Bari motioned to Torin to come sit with them. "Yes, but we must leave soon. Come and eat some soup, then we'll be off."

Torin sat down beside his old friend and the young *nidavel*. Servants from the kitchen placed a steaming bowl of mushroom soup in front of him and laid a strip of spiced meat, dried and cured, beside the bowl. The soup was dark grey and slimy, but the flavour was good and it filled his grumbling stomach.

Bari shifted in his seat and wiggled his arms. "Keep in mind that the Mastersmith is no fool and will cross-examine us carefully. This is what we agreed on last night. After Brok and I were captured by the trolls, we were taken as prisoners to the *Trollting* at Fanghall. Then your company, a regular patrol from Gatewatch, tracked troll prints to the cave. Hiding in the shadows, you heard the Troll-King announce his hatred for the *nidavel*, especially the Mastersmith. Then the Troll-King picked me and Brok up, one in each hand, ready to eat us. Your company jumped out of the shadows and startled the trolls. In his confusion, the Troll-King dropped us and we escaped. When all had settled, you were taken prisoner and thrown into a dungeon cell. Brok and I snuck down and helped your company escape through the tunnels where we were attacked by *skrimsli*. We barely made it back alive."

Bryn smirked as he nodded. "There is enough truth in that story to make me believe it, and I was there."

Just then, Grimsa and Erik stumbled into the hall, shoulders slouched and eyes baggy. The servants pulled them over to the table and gave them each a bowl of soup.

"Stone beds," Grimsa said, "Whose idea was it to make a bed of stone? How does anyone sleep on such a thing?"

"If not the stone beds, I did appreciate the stone walls," said Bryn, "it was the first time your snoring didn't wake me up at night. I'd gladly sleep on a stone bed every night if it meant I didn't have to listen to you snore." Grimsa growled and slurped his soup.

Torin finished the last of his soup and picked up the cured meat. "Has anyone seen Wyla this morning?"

Bari shook his head. "No. She shut herself away in her room last night. As far as I know she refuses to open the door or speak with anyone."

Torin sighed. "Alright then, I will see if I can convince her to come down."

Out of the dining hall and up through the staircase that led to the guestrooms, Torin found the door to Wyla's room. He knocked, but there was no reply.

"Wyla, we have an audience with the Mastersmith right away. Are you ready to leave?"

Torin pressed his ear against the door and listened for any sign of movement. There was none. He knocked again but the room behind the door was silent. He frowned and gripped the doorknob. When he turned the filigreed copper handle, the latch popped and the door fell open just a crack.

"Wyla? Are you there?"

He waited another moment before opening the door and stepping into the unlit room. It was empty. The blankets on the stone bed were still neatly folded as Torin's had been when he first entered his own room. The pillows were not disturbed. It appeared to him that no one had been in the room at all, except for one thing: an open window. He peered out saw the roof of the next building not too far below. Column by column, roof by roof, his eyes traced a pattern that led down to the streets of Myrkheim.

He scratched his head and turned back toward the door. He wondered what Wyla thought to do by leaving. She must be headed back to Gatewatch, he thought. But how would she know the way? Torin shuddered as he remembered the *skrimsli* troupe and Bari's tales about giant rats and worse.

When he returned to the dining hall, he called to everyone at the table. "Listen! Wyla is gone. I went to see if she was in her room, but it was empty. I think she left through the window last night."

Bryn leaned back in his chair and frowned. "Where is she now I wonder? Doesn't she want to meet the Mastersmith?"

"Apparently not," Grimsa said, "if she goes sneaking off in the middle of the night."

"Did she say anything to anyone last night after dinner?"

Everyone around the table shook their heads. Torin felt a twinge in his stomach and cursed under his breath.

"Honestly," Asa said, "since she nearly murdered our host last night, perhaps it is better that she is not with us when we meet the Mastersmith."

Torin frowned. "We all took the blood oath. We are all part of this company and so we should go after her."

Bari stood up and wiped his lips. "No time, I'm afraid. We must be off at once. The Mastersmith has many virtues, but patience is not one of them." He waved the servants over and called out in a loud voice. "Alright everyone, we must not keep the Mastersmith waiting. He has given us an audience first thing this morning. Let's get ready to go." Then all the tables were cleared, and the company was rushed down the hall and out the door.

The shops along the streets of Myrkheim started to open their iron-wrought doors and their copper window shutters. From these doors and windows, curious vendors and artisans peered out at the group of foreigners. A few of the *nidavel* children dared to wave or smile, but most kept quiet and stared at them with blank faces.

Grimsa especially looked far too wide and tall for the city. The twins, Asa and Inga, fascinated the *nidavel* with their identical features and fiery red hair. At every corner, Torin saw astonishment in the eyes of the local people and wondered what he might think of a man twice his own height approaching Ten-Tree Hall. Then he thought of Ur-Gezbrukter, the *jotur*, and his dream from the night before. A cold chill rattled his spine. He worried that if they could not convince the Mastersmith to help them defeat the Troll-King, that dream might become all too real.

Bryn walked up beside Bari. "How do you know if it is night or day? Don't the minerals in the stone glow all the time?"

"Ah, yes. Since you came in the evening last night you have yet to see what Myrkheim looks like in the glow of day. See, the Heart of the Earth is the source of all magic and it beats with a regular pulse. With every pulse a surge of magic emanates from deep below us where the heart resides. The next pulse should come at any moment and light up the streets, then that light will slowly fade until the next morning's pulse. That is how we count our days here in Myrkheim."

Bryn laughed and shook his head. "Perhaps one day I will return and live here in this strange city. Then I could travel all over Noros, travelling from great hall to great hall, telling stories of the *nidavel*."

"You could," Bari said, "but none of the sun-dwellers would believe it. More likely you'd end up locked away for having lost your mind." Torin and Grimsa laughed as Bryn's face fell.

Up the polished basalt streets they climbed, level by level, until at last they reached the door of the Mastersmith's hall. It was arched like the door at Brok's hall, but it rose up much higher and was more intricately decorated around the frame. Torin had expected a large courtyard or a bridge to separate the great hall from the rest of Myrkheim. Instead, the narrow streets wound right up to the entrance with other columnar buildings huddled right against its walls. Like everything else in the city, it felt too crowded.

Bari stepped forward and gripped one of the two iron torcs that hung from the door. With a grunt he lifted it and let it fall against the towering door. Again, he lifted the torc and dropped it. A dull metallic hum resonated through the air each time it struck. After knocking the door a third time, Bari stepped back. His face was speckled with beads of sweat and he wheezed quietly.

For a moment all was quiet, save for the last echoes of the ringing metal hum. Then, like a giant waking, the doors opened. First there was a click, the release of a latch from somewhere on the other side of the door. Then a groaning creak came as the hinges bore the shifting weight of those hulking plates of iron. When the door had opened a small way, the creaking stopped.

A *nidavel* servant scurried out through the crack in the door and bowed ceremoniously. A long red cloak hung down from his shoulders and was clasped at his throat with a golden ring. "Greetings Master Bari, singer of one thousand songs, crafter of the great Lay of Eikinskjaldi the Bold, chanter of the ancient tales, and traveller to the dreaded sun-realm above."

"Greetings. We are here to answer the summons of the Mastersmith."

The servant pursed his lips and inspected the company with wide eyes. "So, it is as he said. Very well, then follow me."

Bari disappeared into the hall and the others shuffled after him. It was a tight squeeze as the door was only opened wide enough for a *nidavel* to enter comfortably. Grimsa had to be shoved by the others to get through and that put him in a foul mood. They followed Bari and the servant through a dark empty hall and up a set of spiralled stairs. Around the corner from the last stair, they entered a room, tall and airy, through which a cool breeze blew. With a wave of his hand, Bari motioned for the company to stop then pointed. There at the far end of the room, with his back toward them, stood the Mastersmith.

Torin had expected a wizened old *nidavel* robed in finery and decked with all the treasures of the deep places, rubies and emeralds and sapphires. This figure wore neither a robe nor rings of gold, just dark leather pants and simple leather boots tied up at the knee. A knot of steel grey hair was tied up at the top of his head. His bare back, thick shoulders, and muscled arms were tattooed with swirls of blue dye. Between the swirling azure knots Torin could make out runes, the ancient language of the *nidavel*, but what they said he did not know. The figure stood hunched over a bench in front of a giant furnace which glowed red hot in the dim light.

The Mastersmith raised an iron hammer in his right hand and held up a lump of glittering metal with a pair of tongs in his left. He shouted an order with a deep, rich voice that boomed through the empty hall. "Bellows! Bellows!" Torin then saw another small figure step out from the shadows and pump a giant lever. Great gusts of air were sent through the vents and the whole company felt a blast of heat as the furnace roared to life.

With mighty blows the Mastersmith began to shape the lump of metal. His shoulders swayed back and forth with every strike and his feet danced to the rhythm of the ringing hammer. Each clang had a different tone and the knot of grey hair on top of his head bobbed side to side in time. At every fourth stroke of the hammer, the bellows pumped again with a hiss and a wheeze which sent a burst of red light and a wave of sweltering heat through the hall. A trance fell over the company as they watched the hammer rise and fall, saw the sparks fly off the table, and felt the rippling heat of the furnace. Torin's body began to sway in rhythm with the ringing strikes and, as soon as he caught himself, he saw that the others had done the same.

At last the trance was broken when the Mastersmith stopped swinging his hammer. "Bring the basin! Quickly now!" Two *nidavel* clambered through one of the doors at the opposite end of the hall and brought a large cauldron, brim-full of water. Torin thought they might trip and spill the water everywhere, but they managed to drop it right at the Mastersmith's feet.

The Mastersmith dipped the tongs into the sloshing basin. Squealing swirls of steam billowed up and rose to the lofty ceiling. He knelt and whispered words in the old *nidavellish* language. As he did, both the water in the basin and the knotted azure tattoos on his arms and back glowed a luminescent blue. Neither Torin nor any of the other *madur* could understand what the words meant, but all could feel a strange hum or vibration in their chest.

Half of Torin's mind was completely enamoured in watching the craftsman work, while the other half urged him to run. However, before anyone had dared to move, the Mastersmith lifted the tongs from the basin and turned to face their company.

"Torin Ten-Trees, who is also called Riddlesmith, welcome to you and your company. And welcome to you, Bari Wordsmith, nephew to my cousin. A gift I have for each of you, a token of thanks for protecting my cousin, Brok Silversmith."

As the craftsman drew closer, Torin saw that many arm rings rattled along the length of his tongs. Each was made of three gold strands twisted together in a knot with two golden serpent heads that connected the ends into a ring. The *nidavel* slid one off the tongs and into Bryn's hands.

"By the gods, I can still feel the warmth of the forge," Bryn said, "Many thanks, Mastersmith Ognir, for this rich gift."

An arm ring he gave to Grimsa next, then Asa and Inga, and finally Erik. Each one bowed with reverent awe as they received it.

"The arm-rings are enchanted," Ognir said, "Whichever arm you wear it on will have more than its natural strength." Torin watched the others stare at the rings with wide eyes.

From his pocket the Mastersmith slipped a silver ring and placed it on Bari's finger. "This is an ancient bardic ring, *Havaerari*, which greatly increases the volume of its wearer's voice. Long has it been in the possession of great skalds here in Myrkheim. Now it is in your keeping." Bari clasped his hands together and bowed several times with haste.

Last he turned to Torin. Sweat and soot blackened the old *nidavel's* face and his large calloused hands rested firmly on his hips. Torin could smell the greasy coal grit and the strong scent of sweat. The gaze of Ognir's wild grey eyes bore into his mind like an auger. Still, Torin held his eyes level and did not look away.

After letting the silence linger, Ognir smirked and recited a riddle.

> *A golden chest so small and fair*
> *The key, a tooth, to lay wide bare*
> *The treasure hid, the tiny stones*
> *Each worth one hundred chests alone*

Torin felt the blood drain from his face as he recognized the verse. His stomach turned as he wondered how Ognir had heard of his final riddle to Ur-Gezbrukter. Before he could ask this question, the Mastersmith motioned to his servants who brought a small copper chest little larger than the size of a closed fist.

"That was a finely crafted riddle, but I have the answer."

The Mastersmith opened the chest carefully to reveal a small apple made of a silvery gold metal. The skin of the fruit was perfectly smooth, and its stem had three finely crafted leaves. Even in the dim light, it glowed like an ember.

"An apple is like a small golden chest and is opened by a tooth biting into it. Inside this chest, you find seeds, each of which will produce in turn one hundred more apples."

Torin nodded, eyes wide, and the old *nidavel* laughed. It was a deep bellow which rumbled through the open hall. Torin was not certain that it was friendly. "Then I have bested this Troll-King, Ur-Gezbrukter, arrogant fool." With that, he closed the lid on the chest and passed it to Torin.

Torin wasn't sure what the apple was for, but he thanked the Mastersmith, nonetheless. "How did you know about the riddle?"

A sudden shadow came over Ognir's face as he drew his eyebrows together in a frown. "No one keeps secrets from me, at least not under the surface of the earth." A fire like a furnace blown by bellows lit his eyes, then died down. "But let's not dwell on things past. Ask me what you have come to ask."

Torin stood silent, copper box in hand, as the others looked at him. He glanced over at Bryn, who shrugged, and at Grimsa, who puffed his cheeks out and shook his head.

When he turned back to Ognir, the *nidavel* swung his hammer up toward Torin's head just shy of his nose. Ognir levelled his gaze at Torin down the shaft. "Ask!"

Torin forced his stiff shoulders down and drew a deep breath. "How do we defeat Ur-Gezbrukter?"

"No," Ognir said, "that is your second question. Ask the first one!" He poked Torin in the ribs with his tongs and held the head of the hammer within a finger width of his nose.

Torin narrowed his eyes and gritted his teeth. "Will you betray us and all of Gatewatch to the Troll-King?"

Ognir lowered his tools and laughed again. "Yes, that is the first question." He smiled and motioned for them to follow him. "But first, let's see the morning break over my city."

The uneasy company followed him to the far side of the hall to a set of large iron doors behind the furnace. Though the bellows had not been blown for several minutes, Torin could still feel on his cheeks the heat of the hungry fire in the belly of the furnace. The Mastersmith stepped up to the doors and raised his tools above his head.

"*Opna!*"

The doors opened with a grinding creak onto a wide balcony that overlooked the terraced columns of Myrkheim. The city was still dimly lit, though many small figures could still be seen moving in the streets. Ognir walked right out to the ledge. The others followed but stayed away from the precipitous drop at the edge of the balcony.

A few quiet moments passed before it happened. Torin later wondered whether it had started in one place then spread or if the whole city had lit up all at once. It began with a soft rumbling boom like the beat of a great drum from deep below the earth. He remembered Bari's description of the Heart of the Earth. Ripples of blue light ran up each columnar building like flickering flames, then came to rest. It took a moment for his eyes to adjust but soon Torin could look again without squinting at the blue-lit buildings.

"This city," Ognir said, "stood long before your ancestor, Beoric the Bear, set foot in Gatewatch. I think it will stand long after the last *madur* bleeds on the surface above. And Myrkheim has long been wealthy, yet trade with King Greyraven has given this city wealth beyond any it had known before. That is the problem with wealth, you see. One might think himself wealthy, but if his wealth doubles he can never again be satisfied with what he had before. Indeed, my great-great grandfather, the Mastersmith Thrain, said it best."

> *If gold and silver flow like blood*
> *A kingdom surely thrives*
> *If riches wane and hunger gains*
> *The kingdom quickly dies*

"So I would not lightly cut my friendship with the Greyraven short. Yet for one thing, I would give everything, even a hand or an eye." He ground hammer shaft and the tongs together, sorrow and anger mixed in his eyes. "The key to life itself. Only the *jotur* lords harbour that secret."

Torin's heart beat faster as he recalled Ur-Gezbrukter on his stone throne, the finery of his robes and his glimmering sword. In his mind, he saw the trolls dancing around the fire in Fanghall and in that moment the memory morphed into his dream of Ten-Tree hall in flames.

"And yet," said Ognir, "you, Torin Riddlesmith, have shown me that this *jotur*, Ur-Gezbrukter, son of Gezbrukter, cannot know the secret, though he himself possesses an immortal body. For who could fail at a mortal riddle, as well crafted as it might be, when he has unlocked the mystery of mortality? No, this Troll-King cannot offer me the secret I so deeply desire. So, the answer to your first question is no, it is not in my interest to betray you at this time. The answer to your second question lies in that box."

The knot that had been tightening in Torin's stomach unravelled all at once and he nearly dropped the copper box that Ognir had given him. He unlocked the clasp with shaky fingers, opened the lid, and peered at the small silver-gold apple. The others stepped toward him to get a better view of the palm-sized prize.

"White light is the bane of trolls. Indeed, that is how Beoric won the great battle of Gatewatch. When the sunlight peeked over the mountains, the Troll-King's army turned to stone. However, the sun is not the only source of white light."

Ognir stepped up to the box and plucked one of the finely crafted leaves from the stem of the golden apple with his tongs.

"This is Sunblaze, no ordinary metal. It is as pliable as stiff leather and will melt in your hand if you hold it long enough." He held up the leaf which glimmered and began to wilt in the blue light that emanated from the city below. "So, take care not to let it get too warm."

Ognir held the leaf high over his head and made his way back into the hall toward the water basin he had used to cool the arm rings. "Herein lies its true power. Behold!"

Ognir tossed the leaf into the water basin and, with a crack like lightning, it exploded in a flash of white light. The force of the explosion caught Torin off guard and he nearly fell over when the blast of hot air hit him. Steam rose up from the basin like the smoke of a raging fire and all around the basin scorch marks scarred the floor.

When Torin's ears stopped ringing, he heard his companions curse, some crouched down and others sprawled on the floor. The Mastersmith was laughing again in a deep bass-toned timbre. Torin's hands trembled as he held the box and locked the lid closed.

Grimsa's roar rose above the rest. "By the gods, curse this foul magic!"

The Mastersmith looked over at the huge man sprawled on the floor and grinned. His white teeth glowed bright against his coal-smudged face. "That is not magic, young *madur*, simply a property of the metal. If that was but a leaf, you can imagine what that whole apple is capable of. Use it well and do not waste it."

Torin nodded. The others brushed themselves off and began to edge toward the door, each one careful to give the steaming basin wide berth.

"Are you leaving so soon?" Ognir said, "Perhaps it is for the best. Yet your companion, the fair-faced woman who left late last night, may already be dead."

"Wyla? Dead?" Torin said, "Why do you say that?"

The Mastersmith wiped his brow and stroked his long, braided beard. "She crossed the bridge alone and disappeared into the tunnels. No doubt she meant to return to Gatewatch to warn the others. I have heard no whispers of her whereabouts since."

"Mighty Mastersmith Ognir," said Bari, "which way did she go?"

Ognir frowned and lowered his voice. "Back the way you came."

Bari gulped hard and shook his head. He glanced at Torin then looked back at The Mastersmith. "If I may, I would like to accompany the *madur*. I know the tunnels well and can guide them."

"The way is full of danger, Bari Verse-Crafter."

Bari straightened his spine and puffed his chest out. "Great happenings are underway, Mastersmith Ognir. I would see them firsthand, so that I can return and record in song and verse all that happened and what part we *nidavel* had in it."

Ognir smiled. "Very well."

Though every bone in Torin's body begged him to flee the hall of the Mastersmith, he had one more question that needed an answer. "Mastersmith Ognir, I have one last question."

Ognir nodded. "Ask it and I shall answer if I can."

"My companions and I saw strange phantoms in Shadowstone Pass on the way to Gatewatch, the Watchers as they are called by some." Just uttering that name made Torin shiver. "What are they?"

Ognir smiled and nodded. "The sun-death is not the end of trolls. Their spirits linger long after their bodies turn to stone."

"The Watchers are trolls?" said Bryn.

"Troll spirits," Ognir said, "harmless as they are now. But magic could stir them from their slumber and with words of the ancient *jotur* tongue they could be reawakened from the rubble in which they lie."

Torin felt dizzy as his head spun. "Reawakened? Is that what Ur-Gezbrukter means to do?"

"That, Torin Riddlesmith, is a question that hardly needs to be answered."

13

◇ SCORCHED BEARDS ◇

THE COMPANY RETURNED TO BROK'S HALL and told of their meeting with the Mastersmith. Around the ringed table in the dining hall, each told in turn of how they had seen him smith the golden arm rings before their very eyes. Brok's own eyes widened at the sight of the enchanted arm circlets and at *Havaerari*, Bari's silver ring.

"These are rich gifts indeed," said Brok, "And what did he give you, Torin Ten-Trees? I see no golden ring on your arm."

Torin drew the copper box out of his shirt pocket. With great care he laid it on the table as the others took a step back. He opened the latch and pulled back the lid to reveal the small silver-gold apple.

"By the Mastersmith," Brok said, "Sunblaze! I have never seen so much of it in one place."

Torin smiled and closed the lid. "Mastersmith Ognir gave us a demonstration of what even a sliver of this metal can do. The key, he said, is white light. It will turn the trolls to stone just like sunlight."

Brok leaned back, his bandaged leg raised up on a stool, and tugged at his neatly braided beard. "So he really does mean to help then. This is no small advantage, yet a flash of white light will not harm the Troll-King himself. Nothing but a bold soul and sharp steel will defeat him."

Torin frowned and looked down at the floor. "Once we bring word to Gatewatch, Captain Calder will know what to do." The thought of the old grizzled man brought Wyla back to mind. "By the gods, then there is Wyla. The Mastersmith said he knew of her leaving late last night, but has not heard anything since."

The old *nidavel* grunted and shook his head. "She is a fool for running off alone, and more besides. This Captain Calder you speak of needs to know that Ur-Gezbrukter has returned to take up his father's throne. There is no time to search for her now. Gatewatch will stand little chance if they are attacked without warning. She made her choice. Now you must make yours."

The others had fallen silent while Brok and Torin were speaking and now the room was quiet. Torin felt the pressure of many eyes laid on him from all around the room. He crossed his arms and shrugged. Bryn frowned and Grimsa shook his head.

Bari stood up and cleared his throat. "I am going with them, uncle. I have the Mastersmith's blessing."

Brok's face darkened and he nodded. "Great things are underway, Bari. I only wish I could accompany you. However, I will outfit you and the rest of the company as best I can."

The whole company cheered for Brok and slammed the table with their fists. Then, one by one, each came over to the old *nidavel* and embraced him before gathering their belongings. At last everyone was in the entranceway ready to bid the old *nidavel* farewell.

Though Brok used a crutch, Dani still had to support his other arm to keep him upright. "I am not as young as I used to be and seeing the rest of you leave without me brings great pain to my heart. However, I must play my part in all of this, even if it is not the one I would have preferred." He motioned to his servants in the next room who brought bundles for the company. "Dani bought the biggest cloaks she could find down in the market. They are also waxed so you can stay dry once you are up above ground." Brok pointed his bony finger toward Torin's copper box. "And don't you dare let even a single drop of water into that box."

The cloaks reminded Torin of the ones he had seen on Drombir's company. There was a layer of soft grey fur sewed to the inside of the waxed fabric and copper clasps ran down the front. Though they were a bit short for most of the company, and very short for Grimsa, each was glad to have one.

"Provisions are in these satchels. Each one has two days' worth of dried fish and hard cheese, not much in the way of flavour, but hardy and light. Here is a small cask of some of my best ale. That should be enough to get you back to Gatewatch."

Brok's servants distributed thin-headed axes with long handles, each of which had a braided leather grip and a sharp pick opposite the blade. Torin tested the axe in his hand and found it to be light and well balanced. Brok grinned as he watched them admire the weapons. "*Nidavel* swords would seem like knives to you and I have heard that troll-hunters prefer long axes over blades."

Brok patted Bari's shoulders and gave a stern nod. Torin saw lines of sadness tug at the edges of the old *nidavel's* eyes. "I will expect a full rendition of your adventure, in song of course."

Bari embraced his uncle and sighed. "It will be a terrific tale; I am sure of it. Goodbye Dani. Goodbye, Uncle Brok." The couple then stood in the doorway of the hall and waved to the company as they made their way down the street and out of Myrkheim.

The blue light of the morning glow filled the vast cavern in which the city lay. It lit the precipitous fall outside the city gate so far down that, from the edge of the bridge, Torin thought he could see a dark river below. Again they passed the grim statues of warriors and monsters paired together along the length of the bridge. The whole company recognized Bumbur the Fat and the great snake Vitormur from the night before. Bari pointed out many other heroes and described the danger that each encountered during their quest against the monster opposite them. Torin wondered what a statue of Ur-Gezbrukter might look like and if they might ever carve a statue of Bari on the bridge.

The quickest way back to Gatewatch was a two-day trek back the way they came, and by lunchtime they had already reached Nori's Well. The company stopped to relieve their dry throats. While some chewed on the dried fish and hard white cheese, everyone thought it best to save the ale for the evening meal. As Torin listened to the water that gurgled up from the well and enjoyed the peaceful quiet, he marvelled that just the day before they had been attacked by *skrimsli* in that very spot. Nothing but a few scraps of cloth were left where the skirmish had taken place.

"There is no trace of the *skrimsli*," Grimsa said, "even the stones have been licked clean."

Bari chuckled. "The rats are greedy and jump at any chance of a meal. If they are not quick enough, they themselves may become a morsel for a much fouler creature. The scent of blood, *skrimsli*, *nidavel*, or *madur*, attracts the worst luck."

Bryn had been unusually quiet since they left. He peered down the tunnel ahead of them and then turned to Bari. "Wyla must have come this way."

Torin felt his face heat up with red blood. "By the gods, enough about Wyla. She thinks she can take care of herself so just let her."

Bryn turned back to Torin and frowned. "You and I both took an oath of kinship with her, Torin."

Torin felt a pulse of blood shoot up from his chest into his head and his ears burned red hot. "Did we not also swear to keep the pass clear of trolls?"

"A hard thing," said Bari, "whenever one takes two oaths, they are eventually bound to conflict."

Bryn tossed away a fishbone and took a bite of cheese. "All I am saying is that it is our duty to help her if she is in danger."

Torin stepped back and threw up his hands. "Is she in danger? It is hard to know when she runs off without a word to anyone." Torin's words came out as a shout, so he lowered his voice. "All we know is that she crossed the bridge last night. My guess is that she is halfway to Gatewatch by now."

Bryn leaned back and levelled his gaze at Torin. "She could also be a captive of a *skrimsli* band. Or worse."

Torin gave a bitter chuckle and shook his head. "And how would we know? What direction should we look? Should we call out her name as we walk along? She obviously did not want us with her, or she might have told one of us that she was going to leave."

Grimsa stepped between Torin and Bryn and straightened his belt. "I am sure Wyla is fine. If she can match Bryn in a race, knock Torin flat on his back, and almost keep pace with me in a drinking contest, she will manage. In fact, she will probably be waiting with a cask of ale when we get back to Fjellhall." Neither Bryn nor Torin looked back up at each other and they said no more. The company packed up their bags and continued to climb up through the blue-lit tunnels. Torin marched ahead with Bari near the front of the group while Grimsa and Bryn followed in the rear.

All they had seen of the tunnels before were straight sections of uniform width. Now that he had slept and eaten, Torin felt incremental changes, small pivots in direction which he had not noticed before. The paths were not merely tunnels either. They intersected caverns along the way, great empty chambers full of slimy mushrooms and orange lichens and hard-shelled insects that jittered in and out of cracks in the rock. The company passed two more fresh-water fountains and an underground brook which trickled along the side of the path for some time. Of course, there were all the smaller tunnels that led away from the main tunnel and Bari pointed out the one they had come from when they escaped Fanghall. No one spoke much, until at last they came to a flat open space within one of the larger caverns.

"I think if I take another step, my feet will fall off," said Erik.

Bryn narrowed his eyes and shoved Erik aside as he walked by. "If you complained just a little bit more, would your mouth fall off?"

Bari peered ahead, then looked behind some of the stones just off the trail. "Well, I suppose we will need to rest somewhere. We won't be walking to Gatewatch all in one day. I reckon this is a good place to set up camp. Besides, we don't want to get boxed in where the tunnel narrows."

The company set down their packs and stretched their sore backs. Torin had a blister on his right heel which had started to bleed through his boot. His knees were stiff from walking on the hard stone, and the waxed collar of the *nidavellish* cloak chafed at his neck. It seemed the others had fared no better. Bari and Bryn both sat and rubbed their feet, while Grimsa stretched out his shoulders from side to side. Asa adjusted the sling that held Inga's arm, then they took turns bandaging each other's feet with scraps of cloth from their old cloaks. Erik lay sprawled out on the cavern floor, occasionally moaning or whimpering about his feet.

"Let's make this good ale from Master Brok last a little longer," Grimsa said, "Drombir's cup will turn the trickle of our little cask into a river!"

Everyone agreed and soon each had a healthy dose of the golden liquid to wash down the dry fish and strong cheese. Then, one by one, they all lay back and stared up at the dark ceiling of the cavern. Only Bari sat up, for he had taken the first watch.

"If only I had been allowed to run away that day in Stonering Keep," Erik said, "I would be warm and dry in the kitchens of Fjellhall. But Wyla grabbed me by the collar and forced me to stay, just like she dragged us all up to Frostridge. Now look where we are. How miserable. I hope she falls into a pit or gets eaten by *skrimsli*. By the gods, I never want to see her again."

From where he lay Torin heard a shuffle and then a piercing yelp. When he sat up, he saw Bryn on top of Erik's chest with a grip on the collar of his cloak.

"Take it back, you squeaking rat. You took a kin-oath with her."

"Get off me!"

"Take it back!"

Bryn gripped Erik's cloak harder and pounded his fists into Erik's chest, lifting the scrawny figure with every blow. Erik squawked like a bird and tried, without success, to roll out from under Bryn. Torin leapt up and grabbed Bryn from behind. With a heave he pulled him away, though Bryn still kicked and thrashed like a wild horse. With a quick twist of his torso, Bryn tore himself free of Torin's grip and rolled a few feet away.

Torin breathed heavy, his eyes wide. "Bryn, what are you doing?"

"What am I doing?" Bryn said, "What are we doing? Can everyone else stand to hear this whining sop speak about Wyla like that? Am I the only oath-keeper here?"

Grimsa growled low and stood up with heavy steps. "I agree with Bryn. An oath is an oath."

His two old friends looked at him with hard eyes. Torin glanced again at the rest of the company who sat dazed and wide eyed, except for Erik who still wheezed as he caught his breath.

Bari stood up and waved his hands. "More division would not benefit this company. There is greater good in not delaying our arrival at Gatewatch than in seeking one lone renegade."

"There we must disagree, Master Bari," Grimsa said, "We *madur* believe that to honor an oath is the highest good, not to break it when it suits us. We came to Gatewatch to do deeds deserving of verse and song. What song will be sung of us if we abandon our kin-oath now?"

Bari opened his mouth to reply, then closed it with a huff. "Very well, you granite-headed oaf, trot off into the dark of the tunnels in search of your lost companion then."

Grimsa stomped his foot and picked up his cloak and axe. "I will."

"So will I," said Bryn, "Who is coming with us?"

"Not me. I'm staying right here," said Bari. He sat down and pulled out a pipe which he fumbled with for a moment before lighting it.

Erik wheezed and rolled onto his back. "So am I."

Asa scratched her head. "It doesn't sound very wise to go marching off into the tunnels. Besides, Erik is right. Following Wyla is what got us into this mess. I think it's better to stay."

Inga looked at her sister then down at her arm and sighed. "I would be of little use in this condition to fight *skrimsli* or whatever else you might find in the tunnel."

In the eerie silence of the cavern, Torin could hear blood pound against his ear drums. He sighed and rubbed his temples. "This is not a good idea."

Grimsa grinned and shrugged. "Has that ever stopped us before?"

Torin threw his cloak over his shoulder, stuffed his food satchel under his arm, and snatched up his axe. From the corner of his vision he saw Bari shake his head and Erik turn over to sleep, but he ignored them both. Without another word, he trudged off into the darkness with Bryn and Grimsa and left the others there at the camp.

Once his temper had cooled, Torin was surprised to find how diverse the climate of the tunnels could be when they got closer, or so he supposed, to the surface. Some sections were so humid and damp that drips of water fell from the ceiling like drops of rain while others were as warm and as dry as his father's hall. The longer he walked the more he noticed the sounds of that deep road. Rats scampered away at their approach, the trickle of underground creeks cascaded down the passage, and occasionally rocks shifted and groaned far below them. However, the scent was the same wherever they went: a musty odour like damp rags, which grew stronger or weaker in different parts of tunnel.

All at once, a rumbling boom came from somewhere deep below, which sent ripples of bright light through the glowing minerals above their heads. The intensity of the ripples seemed to turn the dim blue light white for a moment before they died down and the light, much stronger than before, regained its bluish hue.

"Another day begins," Grimsa said, "if you can really call this miserable glow 'daylight'."

Bryn shook his head and cursed. "Still no sign of her."

Torin gave the wall a half-hearted kick and threw up his hands. "We don't even know if she went this way."

As soon as Torin finished speaking, they heard a cry from down the tunnel ahead of them. The drowsiness that had softened their steps vanished and each companion stood stone still, ears and eyes wide open to the silence that followed. Then the cry rang again through the air from far down the tunnel.

Torin leaned in toward Bryn and Grimsa and drew out his axe. "Quickly!"

They instinctively stayed close to the wall, though it was little use, as one could see far down the well-lit tunnel in either direction. They heard the cry again three times, each time louder and shriller than before. The last time it came from behind them.

"Back there," Torin said, "we must have passed it. Yes, through that hole off the main tunnel." Bryn stepped back and peeked through the opening. His nimble frame disappeared into the darkness.

"Damn these small places," Grimsa said, "I am ill shaped for this adventure."

"Quick," said Torin, "I'll push you if you need it."

With a few grunts and many curses, they managed to get through the small entrance of the side tunnel. Soon after, it opened. They caught up to Bryn, who had stopped outside of a ring of orange light that flickered, then died out.

"Firelight," Bryn said, "something ahead."

Another shrill cry came from just around the corner. A deep grunting voice spoke afterwards but Torin could not quite make out what it said. Gusts of warm air blew by, so Torin thought there must be a large fire.

"It doesn't sound like Wyla," said Bryn, "perhaps we should turn back."

Torin narrowed his eyes. "Let's be sure."

He led the way as they crept down the tunnel, which now widened greatly. The heat of the fire and the echo of the shrieks grew more intense the farther they inched along. When Torin got to the corner, he gestured for the others to stop. He slowly leaned his head out from the tunnel and peered around the corner.

What he saw was not a fire, but rather a stream of red-hot molten rock. It sputtered and spewed sparks as it oozed through the cavern from end to end. The cavern seemed large and empty, but Torin could hear the shuffle of feet and a soft whimper in the shadows beside the molten river.

A deep croaking voice called out. "Who is next?"

Another voice squealed with excitement. "The one with the fat belly!"

Torin's eyes had still not adjusted to the light and, though he squinted, he could not make out any of the shadowy forms that scuttled about the cave down below. Bryn and Grimsa also leaned over to see what little they could.

Suddenly a great burst of flame came from the molten river. A large stick, it seemed, had been shoved into the lava flow and now blazed with orange light. In the flame's glow, Torin saw the face of a massive *skrimsli* which was twice as wide as it was tall. It had an awful crooked grin on its face and warty green skin like a toad. As it pulled the burning stick from the river, it laughed in short, stilted grunts.

The blaze of the torch illuminated a small part of the room and in it they saw dozens of *skimsli*, perhaps as many as one hundred. The torch bearer slowly moved through the crowd, which quivered with excitement. Then the light fell on a natural obelisk at the center of the cavern to which six small figures were tied. Shreds of cloth bound their hands and feet, and a rusted chain wrapped around the stone pillar kept them in place. One of the prisoners moaned with his head down, chin near his chest, while the others shrieked and wiggled.

Grimsa leaned over to Torin and whispered. "The prisoners, they are *nidavel*!"

Bryn squinted in the dark and then stifled a gasp. "Not just any *nidavel*. That is Drombir's company!"

Torin looked closer. He recognized the face of the oldest figure, Drombir, the *nidavel* who had swindled them out of their horses on the way to Gatewatch. "By the gods, it is them."

The *skrimsli* with the torch grabbed the beard of one of the prisoners and yanked on it. Then it held the flame right below his chin and singed off tufts of his beard. The prisoner shrieked and yelped and coughed and sputtered. Then the *skrimsli* held up the tufts of curly hair to the crowd of horrid creatures who croaked and cheered. The *nidavel's* face was covered in ash and the wispy remnants of his beard, odd strands here and there, smoked like snuffed out candle wicks.

"Now," said the torch bearer, "tell us the truth."

Drombir, who was next in line to lose his beard, called out in a high-pitched voice. "We told you! There was only one. It was a female. We can show you where she is, if you let us go!"

"The Great Lord told us there were seven, not one. Where are the other *madur*?"

"There were not seven, only one female travelling alone back to Gatewatch. By my beard, I swear it!"

"Is the Great Lord a liar? No. You are the liar." Again, that deep croaking chuckle came from the leader and it turned back toward the stream of molten lava to reignite the torch.

The light had died down again, so it was hard to see, but Torin fumbled in his cloak to find the little box that Mastersmith Ognir had given him. He unlatched the hinge and squinted at the golden apple in the dim light. With great care he plucked a leaf from the stem at the top, careful to keep a fold of cloth between his fingers and the metal, then latched the box closed again."

"What are you going to do?" Bryn asked.

"A diversion," Torin said, "hopefully enough to free those prisoners."

"Free them?" said Grimsa, "First they swindled us, and now they agree to betray Wyla. Let them rot."

Torin shook his head. "Drombir is our best chance at finding Wyla. We need to get him out. Once I set this Sunblaze off, Grimsa should attack the *skrimsli*, roaring and making as much noise as possible to scare them off. Then Bryn and I can cut the prisoners loose."

All three of them drew their axes and hurried forward toward the crowd of *skimsli* as quietly as they could. For the most part they stuck to the shadows, but twice they had to hurry across a patch of dim light. Another flare of orange went up as the torch was lit by the molten river. Cheers rose up from the *skrimsli* and the noise allowed the companions to sneak up behind the crowd, the closest just a few feet away.

Torin now realized the fault in his plan. He needed water to ignite the Sunblaze. With frantic, jerky motions, he looked around where they were hiding and then near the back of the crowd, but there was no water to be seen.

Torin leaned toward Bryn and Grimsa and whispered. "Water! I need water to ignite the Sunblaze."

Grimsa scratched his beard, then pulled out the small cask of ale. "There is only a bit left, but perhaps it would be enough?"

The seal at the top of the miniature cask had been broken and was stopped up with a bit of cloth. Grimsa pulled the cloth out and handed the ale cask to Torin.

Bryn leaned back from the cask. "Wedge the Sunblaze leaf into the opening, but don't drop it in."

The metal was as pliable as leather, as Ognir had said, so Torin bent it and placed it in the hole. Though he worried the top of the cask might be wet, the Sunblaze did not ignite. He could feel the last of the ale slosh around in the bottom of the container. He had only one chance.

With his free hand, Torin counted down from three, then stood up and hurled the cask high into the air. The barrel spewed a stream of foamy ale as it spun over the crowd. Just as it began to fall back down toward the monstrous crowd of spectators, it exploded with a booming crack like thunder.

A flash of pure white light blinded every creature who had stared up at the twirling object that had been lobbed above them. When they heard the deafening noise, Torin and Bryn rushed out to rescue the *nidavel* prisoners, shoving *skrimsli* aside as they ran. Grimsa leapt up onto the rock with his axe held high over his head and roared.

Such a scene of panic and chaos the *skrimsli* had never witnessed. The creatures trampled each other without a second thought as they scampered away. Their screeches echoed off the hard cavern walls which made it seem as if there were a thousand *skrimsli* in retreat rather than the hundred or so that had been gathered there.

Grimsa's new axe, sharp as a knife-blade, came down on the *skrimsli* with the torch and cleaved it right in half. Torin heard the crunchy squelch of the blow. The torch fell with the creature and the whole cavern went dark. He and Bryn felt their way around the stone pillar and began to cut the cloth bonds of the prisoners.

Torin shouted above the din as he cut away the first set of bonds. "Drombir, is that you?"

"Bless the Mastersmith! You arrived just in time," the *nidavel* said, "Me? No. Drombir is to my right."

"Help us cut the others free."

"Who are you?"

"No time to explain now. Quick, cut the bonds!"

They went to work and soon the others were cut loose. It took some effort to wriggle out from under the rusted chain but once free, in the dark, they linked arms and started to stumble toward the tunnel from which the three companions had entered.

Meanwhile, Grimsa hacked and slashed a swath clear through the middle of the crowd. Disoriented by the explosion and blind in the dark, some of the creatures ran straight into the molten river. Perhaps because of the slick of grease on their rodent-hide clothes or the natural oil of their skin, each unfortunate creature that touched the lava stream erupted in flames. With a hiss, these gory flares illuminated Grimsa, his blood splattered grin, and his great gleaming axe.

Grimsa roared again and laughed from his belly. "Gods keep the Mastersmith! His trinkets work wonders." He raised his axe and the arm-ring around his forearm glowed in the firelight. "Now hear me, Beard-Burners, the wrath of the Mastersmith is at hand!" He charged ahead and cut another swath through the crowd.

By then, enough of the *skrimsli* smoldered in the burning river to keep the cavern lit. The cavern reeked worse than a dung heap set afire, and Torin's stomach retched because of it. A few of the *nidavel* gagged as they shuffled away from the chaos. Bryn had just about reached the exit when he looked back.

"Torin," Bryn said, "look!"

Torin turned to see Grimsa charge after the mass of panicked *skrimsli*. "Grimsa, let's go!" But the axe did not slow and Grimsa did not turn around.

Torin hopped over the pile of dead *skimsli*. Then he nearly slipped when he stepped in a puddle of vomit left by one of the *nidavel*. He groaned at the scent of the burning creatures, but plugged his nose and raced toward his frenzied friend.

"Grimsa, we must leave!"

"Leave me be, Torin! I have never been so happy as I am now!"

Torin tackled Grimsa from behind and they toppled over onto the slick floor. "Grimsa! Now!"

The fire of madness flickered in Grimsa's eyes and then cooled. "Alright, let's go."

The two companions, feet soaked in *skrimsli* blood, which itched like ivy, and cloaks wet with whatever had been on the floor, raced out of the cavern after Bryn and Drombir's company.

14

◇ A NARROW DOOR ◇

THE RAGGED COMPANY tumbled out into the main tunnelway. The two *nidavel* with singed beards moaned and rolled around on the stone floor with their hands on their faces. Grimsa, slick with *skrimsli* blood, slipped right through the hole that he had struggled to squeeze through before. Torin followed him through the cramped entrance and out into the blue glow of the tunnels.

Drombir gasped for breath as he sat up. Just as he opened his mouth to speak, he caught sight of Grimsa and recognized the huge man. Without a word, he hopped to his feet and dashed down the tunnel. The others followed his lead and took off, some up the tunnel and some down.

"Quick!" Torin said, "After Drombir!"

Bryn was up before either Torin or Grimsa could make it to their feet, so he chased after Drombir. "Master Drombir, stop, you must help us find Wyla!" Torin and Grimsa stumbled after them, their boots slippery with blood and vomit.

But the old *nidavel* did not slow down. He scurried as fast as his legs would carry him to a small crack in the wall through which he meant to escape. Just as he turned his shoulders to slip through the crevice, Bryn caught him by the shoulder. The two tumbled onto the ground and rolled over each other a few times before coming to a stop. Drombir, exhausted, relented.

"Alright, young *madur*, alright. I'll help you. Just get off me."

Torin and Grimsa caught up with the two figures sprawled out on the floor then leaned over to catch their breath. Grimsa's chest heaved up and down with each raspy breath. "I always knew he could not be trusted, no more in that mountain pass than now."

From where he lay on the floor, Drombir chuckled and wiped a bit of blood off his cheek. "I rather hoped to never meet you again, bear cub. How strange that you three should be my rescuers and now, it seems, my new captors."

"You said you knew how to find Wyla," Torin said, "Help us do that and we will leave you alone."

Bryn got up onto one knee and leaned down toward the *nidavel*. He took out his axe and fingered its sharp edge. "And *Isnif*, the knife traded for my horse, didn't work. The blade melted as soon as I dripped blood on it." He pointed the axe at Drombir. "Unless you plan on returning my horse, I believe you owe me another blade."

Drombir looked wide-eyed at the axe-blade that hovered in front of his nose and nodded with a gulp. Then Grimsa laughed and patted the goblet that hung from his belt. "The cup, however, is absolutely magnificent. It has got us into and out of trouble several times already."

Drombir's face darkened and he scowled. With stiff, jerky movements the old *nidavel* stood then brushed off his tunic. "Well, then let's get going. The *skrimsli's* fear will soon turn to anger, especially since you slew one of their most dreaded leaders. Though if you had come a little earlier, she would not have burned the beards off two of my company."

"She?"

"Yes, she. Her brood is one of the largest and cruelest in this region of the tunnels. They are, or were, infamous for burning the beards off *nidavel* then either killing them outright or leaving them to live their lives looking like scar-faced babies."

A nasal whoop came from behind them. In the distance Torin saw a small *skrimsli* jump and point in their direction. From far off, the shuffle of feet and the clang of arms began.

"No time to lose!" Drombir turned to run away and the companions were quick to follow him.

Down the tunnel they raced as fast as they could. Whether Torin's thighs burned from exhaustion or because of the *skrimsli* blood that had soaked through his pant legs, he could not tell. However, he did know that he could not keep up the pace for much longer and that Grimsa's legs would likely give out before his.

Drombir wheezed and coughed. "Here, here. Stop."

Bryn looked back down the tunnel where the sound of *skrimsli* grew louder with every moment that passed. "Why have we stopped? There is nothing here."

Drombir said nothing but took a small knife and began to feel the wall with his bare hand.

Torin rolled his eyes. "Another door?"

Grimsa shook his head and his eyes bulged. "You *nidavel* and your damn tunnels! It's a wonder that this entire mountain doesn't fall down on our heads with all the little wormholes you've wheedled into it."

Bryn pointed at the group of *skrimsli* that was charging down the hall toward them. "Faster!"

Drombir's finger found the spot. He placed the blade on the hairline crack and tapped the butt of the knife with his fist. A narrow door opened up, well-wrought in the shape of a graceful arch like all the others he had seen. Drombir disappeared through the opening. Grimsa stepped forward to follow him but got stuck, his shoulder caught on the top of the archway.

Bryn and Torin both shoved Grimsa as hard as they could but he still did not fit through. He wriggled and twisted but before he could get his shoulder under the arch the *skrimsli* were less than twenty paces away. Torin stepped back and drew out his axe. "Keep pushing him through!"

Torin roared as he charged forward with his axe raised high. He saw fear light the faces of the first half dozen *skrimsli* that ran toward him. When he brought the axe down, three *skrimsli* crumpled under his blade. Then he kept himself grounded, both feet planted in a wide stance, and refused to give way. He shifted his feet back and forth as he dodged blows and dealt death with both sides of his weapon, the long thin axe blade and the sharp pick. Then he pushed the enemy back with the blunt end of the axe shaft and slashed again. Soon he found his rhythm as he stepped back to draw them in and then surged ahead to cut them down. In the corner of his vision, another axe appeared beside him. It was Bryn who had stepped up by his side and now also hacked away at the horde.

Torin stepped back and spit out a bit of blood. "Did Grimsa make it through?"

Bryn knocked a *skrimsli* over the head then fell back in line with Torin. "Not yet, the door is too narrow."

Torin looked behind him and saw Grimsa's feet flail, torso wedged into the small entrance. Grimsa's muffled voice came from the door. "By the gods, let me at them! Damn these accursed doors!"

A sting, like the burn of red-hot metal, touched Torin's right side. A jagged spear head had cut through his cloak and glanced his ribs. Torin cursed as he glanced down at the wound. As he stepped back, Bryn hacked the spear-wielding *skrimsli* at the neck and it dropped the spear on the stone floor with a clang.

Torin bellowed and turned again to face the horde. The burning pain drove him to fury like he had never felt before. No longer did he draw the enemy back; now he stomped forward without fear. With every swing his axe felled two or three *skrimsli* until, at last, the dozen or so that remained turned and fled.

In that moment, Torin felt dizzy. He touched the place where the spear had slit his shirt and found it was wet and stained with dark red blood. The tunnel started to wobble and he felt unsteady, but Bryn caught him before he fell. Grimsa had finally removed himself from the tunnel and rushed over to help ease Torin down to the stone floor.

Drombir poked his head out from the narrow door and looked at Torin with wide eyes. "The *skrimsli* defeated? You killed them all? I was certain that horde would be the end of all of us."

"Master Drombir," Bryn said, "our companion is cut, badly."

For a moment Torin thought Drombir might just run away and leave them to bleed in the tunnels but, instead, he heard the *nidavel's* footsteps grow louder. Then, from where he lay on the floor, he saw Drombir's bearded face peer down on his wound and grimace. For a moment, Drombir stroked his beard and shook his head. "Alright. Follow me. I know another passage further down with a bit more headspace."

Grimsa offered to carry Torin, but he declined and walked instead. He draped one arm around Bryn's shoulder to steady himself and the used other to put pressure on the wound. Though it was not too long a distance to where Drombir turned off from the main-tunnel way, Torin would have collapsed if it had been any further. They followed a smaller passage for a while and the air became warm and damp. At last they reached a wooden door. At the center was a round iron ring which hung from a hinge.

Drombir grasped the iron ring and knocked six times. Then, after a moment, he leaned into the doorframe and whispered. "*Vinir.*"

The lock that held the wooden door rattled and creaked in the narrow passage. Then the door swung wide open and a dishevelled *nidavel*, one of Drombir's company, met them.

"Thank the Mastersmith," the *nidavel* said, "We thought that great horde might have caught up with you."

"They did," said Drombir, "but these young bear cubs from Gatewatch saw to it that I was not skewered to death by the knives and spears of those cursed *skirmsli*. The others?"

"All here."

"Well then, luck has turned its face toward us today." Drombir motioned to the companions as he stepped over the threshold. "Come, friends. There is food and drink and a warm fire here in our hideout. But first we will take care of that wound so that the unpleasant business of closing it will be over."

Once everyone was inside, they cleared a table. Torin peeled off his shirt and sat down on the rough wooden planks. Drombir rinsed his hands in a basin then found an iron rod and placed the tip in the heart of the fire. Another one of the *nidavellish* company came around with small cups of a harsh spirit which reminded Torin of a nasty batch of *skog* they had sampled on their journey to Gatewatch. It was so bitter that it made his spine rattle when he swallowed it. The *nidavel* offered him a second cup and Torin took it. Then he laid down on the cool wood planks of the table and gripped the edge. Bryn held down his shoulders and Grimsa kept a firm grip on each of his legs. Last, he bit down on the wooden shaft of his axe and closed his eyes.

Drombir pulled the red-hot iron rod from the fire. "This will only take a second." Torin felt the heat of the iron close to his skin right before a burst of white-hot pain exploded in the side of his chest like a blast of Sunblaze. The sizzling sound of burning flesh was drowned out by his muffled cry but the smell flooded the room in an instant. Though he fought the urge to flail, his body re-fused to obey and thrashed like a snared animal. He felt Bryn's full weight hold his shoulders down and Grimsa's heavy hands kept his legs pinned to the table. Two of the other *nidavel* grabbed his arms before he knocked anything over. However, by then the deed was already done and, after that minute of madness, Torin lay still.

Bryn and Grimsa sat down on the miniature benches around the table and Drombir took another cup full of the foul spirit. After taking a sip, he shook his head and cleared his throat.

"I must indulge in a moment of honesty if only because you have saved my life twice today. The newly crowned Troll-King, Ur-Gezbrukter, has put a price on your heads, and every villain and monster in the tunnels below is searching for you.

Bryn raised his eyebrows. "What price?"

"Your weight in gold."

Torin sat up with a groan and then turned toward Drombir. "So that is why you promised to show the *skrimsli* how to find Wyla, because they wanted her ransom?"

"As opposed to having my beard scorched off, yes. Of course, I wouldn't mind having your weight in gold bouncing around in one of my chests either. However, our last encounter with the *skrimsli* has persuaded me that a future with Ur-Gezbrukter as king would be quite unprofitable, at least for us."

"By that you mean there would not be a steady stream of Gate-watch recruits to swindle?" said Bryn.

Drombir sighed and rolled his eyes. "While I may not always see eye to eye with you *madur*, I would rather have dealings with you than those stupid, stinking *skrimsli*." He raised his finger and wagged it back and forth. "And before you get your nose out of joint, you should know that the *skrimsli* ambush we fell into was meant for your company. If they had captured you instead, we both know how that would have ended."

Torin shook his head and chuckled. "How noble you are, Master Drombir."

"Besides," said the *nidavel*, "if it wasn't for us, your companion would have run straight into that ambush. At the very least you should be thanking us for rescuing her!"

Bryn leapt to his feet. "You actually know where Wyla is?"

"Of course. Didn't I say I knew where to find her?"

"I thought you were bluffing. Where is she?"

Drombir blushed and he pointed to a door across the room. "She is," he said, "asleep, in that back room."

Bryn and Grimsa dashed over to the door that Drombir had pointed at and threw it open. Torin hobbled after them. As soon as they entered the room, they heard a frantic knock that came from a tall wardrobe shut up with a lock.

"By the gods," Grimsa said, "Locked up? Wyla, are you in there?"

There was a muffled shout from inside the old wardrobe though they could not make out the words. Grimsa took his axe and, with a single swing, shattered the lock that held the door closed. Wyla stumbled out from the stuffy closet and fell onto the floor.

Before any of them could speak, Wyla jumped up and dashed out of the smaller room into the main hall. Torin heard a squeal followed by a clatter of pots and pans and chairs crashing to the floor. When they returned, they saw Wyla had pinned Drombir to the floor and had started to strangle him.

"You moldy mushroom-munching maggot," she said, "how dare you lock me up!"

Drombir gasped for air and wriggled like a fish. "Look! I rescued your friends and brought them here."

"You rescued us?" said Torin, "That is not quite how I remember it."

Grimsa and Bryn each grabbed one of Wyla's arms and pulled her off Drombir. For another few seconds she kicked her legs, then went limp from exhaustion. Drombir gasped for air on the floor.

With heavy breaths, Wyla calmed herself and stood up. Grimsa grinned like a fool and lifted her off her feet with a bear-like hug.

"Grimsa, I can't breathe!"

The huge man let go and she stumbled back into Bryn who caught her before she tumbled over. "Thank the gods you are still in one piece. We thought you might have been captured by *skrimsli* or worse."

Wyla laughed as she pushed Bryn away and steadied herself on one of the chairs. She looked over at Torin and her eyes softened. "Torin, you're hurt."

Though he had been furious about her abrupt departure, Torin now could not hold back a grin. "Just a scratch."

The rest of Drombir's company had fled in terror at the sight of Wyla's rage. Now Drombir himself tried to crawl away before they noticed, but Torin saw him and grabbed his axe. "Master Drombir, I think you had better stay." The *nidavel* cursed under his breath and shook his head, then pulled out a long, slender pipe and lit it there where he sat on the floor.

Wyla stretched out her shoulders and pulled her hair out of her face. Bryn offered her some of the bitter *nidavel* brew and she took the bottle. After a swig, she sighed and let her shoulders down.

Grimsa sat down on one of the tables which gave a concerning creak under his weight. "Well, it's a good thing we caught up to you. Most of the others thought you would already be dead!"

Wyla glared at Drombir and stomped her foot. "I was fine until these idiots locked me in the wardrobe."

Torin sat down against the table, careful not to touch the seared skin under his left arm. Because of the wound, he tried not to laugh but a chuckle slipped out anyways. "The wardrobe? How did they manage get you in there in the first place?"

Wyla's ears went red and she narrowed her eyes. "I met them in the tunnelway. They said they could take me to Gatewatch. I was tired and hungry so, like a fool, I trusted these *nidavel* to show me the way. We came here where they had prepared a feast which they said could not wait. So, I ate with them. They told me about Ur-Gezbrukter, the gold-price they had put on our heads, and the *skrimsli* bands that were roaming the caverns. Then, just as the meal was finished, one of them burst into the room and started screaming that the *skrimsli* were about to attack. Drombir said he would pay off the *skrimsli* captain with a bribe if I would hide in the backroom."

Wyla shot a foul look at Drombir who pretended not to see it. "I was not in fighting shape by that point as I hadn't slept, really, since that awful night in the troll cave. So, I agreed to hide and, when the door was shut, he locked it!"

Torin, Bryn, and Grimsa burst into laughter and wheezed at the thought of Wyla locked up in the wardrobe with a pile of *nidavellish* night robes. As she recounted the tale, Wyla looked determined to stay angry but, as she heard her own words, a grin broke on her face. "Don't laugh," she said, "how would you like to be locked up in a wardrobe full of stinking *nidavel* rags?"

Wyla took another draught of the spirits and continued. "Well, it gets worse. As soon as I heard the click of the lock, I knew I had been tricked. Then this stone-brained moron had the nerve to propose marriage to me. *Marry me*, he said, *or I will sell you to the skrimsli for gold.*" She picked up one of the small cups on the table and hurled it at Drombir. It flew right over his head and smashed into pieces against the stone hearth behind him

Bryn stifled a giggle at the thought. "You? A *nidavel's* bride?"

"So I gave him my mind on the matter, and he stomped out of the room. That is the last I heard until you showed up. I thought they were torturing some poor creature out here when I heard all the noise."

Torin looked down at the burnt flesh on his side and winced. Then he looked up at Drombir. "So," Torin said, "you didn't run into the *skrimsli* ambush by accident. You met with them to collect Wyla's ransom. Then, when the *skrimsli* decided they would rather torture you than pay for her whereabouts, we found you in the cave."

Drombir began to crawl backwards. He dropped his pipe and smoky ashes spilled out on the floor. He would have stood up, but he shook so violently he could not. Grimsa growled low and stood over the old *nidavel* who cowered on the floor. "You, Master Drombir, had better take us to Gatewatch right away."

Drombir nodded eagerly. "Yes, of course, certainly."

Then they heard the sound of footsteps. Everyone froze. It seemed they came from outside the locked wooden door. Torin was certain he heard the sound grow louder.

"Drombir, is that your company?"

The *nidavel* shook his head and replied in a coarse whisper. "No, my company uses the smaller secret entrances."

"*Skrimsli*," said Bryn. Each of them grabbed their weapons, axes for the three companions and, for Wyla, the long, jagged dagger she had acquired at Nori's Well. As quietly as they could, they moved to either side of the door to ambush the intruders. Grimsa gripped the collar of Drombir's shirt and dragged him along to make sure he did not slip away.

As they stood in silence, backs pressed against the wall, they heard the locked door handle turn slightly. There were whispers from the other side of the door and then, again, the shuffle of feet. Next Torin heard a metallic grind as the lock joints squeaked and creaked.

Drombir pulled away from Grimsa but he could not get loose. "You boulder-brained bear, can't you hear they are trying to pick the lock? We must escape while we have a chance!"

But it was too late. The lock clicked open with a low-ringing hum and the door, as its hinges creaked, slowly fell open. A breeze from the tunnel, dryer and cooler than the humid air in the room, blew in past their feet. Bryn raised his axe to strike the first *skrims-li* through the door.

A figure dashed in through the doorway and Bryn, who had been poised to strike, stopped mid-way through his swing and lost his balance. Torin stepped forward to strike where his friend had failed but then saw the reason for Bryn's hesitation.

"Bari?"

"Torin, we thought you were dead! And Wyla, is that you?"

In through the door stumbled Asa, Inga, and Erik also. Inga embraced Wyla with her good arm and laughed.

"There were so many dead *skrimsli*," Bari said, "and from the streaks of red *madur* blood I feared the worst sort of fate had found you. Yet here you are. Thank the Mastersmith!"

Bryn scratched his beard. "How did you get here so quickly?"

"That was Inga's doing," said Asa, "We laid down at the camp for about an hour but none of us, except Erik, could sleep. We heard all sorts of strange sounds in the cavern and Inga said it would be better to die trying to find our friends than to get stabbed in our sleep."

Bari nodded. "Even when we argued, Inga insisted, despite her broken arm. We packed up camp and followed the main tunnel-way until we reached the carnage."

Erik's voice wavered as he recalled the scene. "How many *skrimsli* were there?"

Grimsa grunted. "How many? I would say well over one hundred."

Torin shook his head and chuckled. "How would you know Grimsa? Your head was stuck in a hole while Bryn and I fought them off. It was more like two or three dozen."

Grimsa's ears went red and he shrugged. "Well, it certainly sounded like well over one hundred."

Bari pointed to the seared flesh on Torin's chest. "I assume they gave you that wound?"

"Yes, and more of us may bleed by *skrimsli* blades if we don't get out of here soon."

Drombir stepped forward but fell back a little when Grimsa tugged him by the collar of his tunic. "I can show you the way to Gatewatch. I know the quickest way to get there."

Bari's eyes opened wide at the sight of another *nidavel*. "Who is this?"

"This is Master Drombir," Bryn said, "our somewhat reliable acquaintance."

Wyla frowned and sneered. "I'd say far less than reliable."

"Drombir? The famous renegade?"

As Drombir smiled at the title, his crooked yellow teeth peeked out from under his bearded lips. "Yes, I am he." He tried to bow but, as Grimsa still gripped his shirt collar, he could not quite get down all the way.

"I am Bari Wordsmith, nephew to Brok the Silversmith who is, in turn, cousin to Mastersmith Ognir himself."

Drombir stroked his beard and nodded. "Brok Silversmith? I believe my mother was distantly related to his father."

Torin shook his head. "Is this really the time to discuss family histories?"

Bari nodded. "Right then. What is the quickest way up to the sun-realm?"

Drombir chuckled and held a finger high above his head. "Up of course. This way. And, by the Mastersmith, let go of my collar, you hulking beast. Surely you are all faster than me, battered and bruised. Besides, is it not in my own interest to get you to the surface and out of my hideout as soon as possible?" Grimsa grunted and let go of the *nidavel*. Drombir straightened his shirt and grabbed one of the dark blue cloaks sealed that lay on the bench.

"A weapon," said Bryn, "Before we leave, you owe me a weapon. I traded my horse for a *nidavellish* treasure and by the gods I will get one. You swindled me before, but now you'll make good on your promise." Torin and Grimsa nodded and crossed their arms.

Drombir looked as if he might protest but, as he saw little hope of sympathy from around the room, he relented. "Fine. I don't have any blades at the moment but take this instead." He waddled up to the hot hearth and, from the mantle, pulled down a long, curved bow with a braided leather grip strung with silver thread. "This bow is called *Haukur*. It once belonged to a great captain of the Myrkheim city guard."

Bryn gleamed as he slung the bow over his shoulder. "And what does it do?"

"What do you mean?"

"Isn't it enchanted?"

Drombir rolled his eyes and huffed. "Not every item to come out of a *nidavel* forge is enchanted." Bryn frowned.

"There might be more weapons laying around this ash-filled hovel," Grimsa said, "Perhaps we should search a moment?"

Wyla stomped her foot. "We've wasted enough time in this damp hole. Gatewatch needs to know that Ur-Gezbrukter is on the move." The others nodded and so they all followed Drombir out the door without another word.

They continued up the small tunnel rather than turn back down toward the main tunnelway. The air was now less musty and dry in Torin's nostrils; it was warmer and more humid. Above their heads there was a steady rumble, a river perhaps. The deep sound soothed his aching head and made him sleepy. At first, he suspected some sort of magic but then realized that perhaps it was simply the battle with the *skrimsli*, the night-long march, and his empty stomach. Any time his eyes got heavy and his head dropped down, a sharp tingle of pain from his side woke him up again.

Then the tunnel became so narrow that Torin had to crouch down. Grimsa protested with curses and groans but it was the quickest way out and there was little to argue about. Inga also struggled to crawl with her broken arm, so their progress was slow. Nevertheless, they pushed on, driven by the hope of escape from those miserable caves.

The roar above them became louder and louder until it was almost deafening in Torin's ears. He wondered if a river could make such a noise and, if it was a river, what might happen if the water broke through the roof of the tunnel and flooded it. He felt his heart skip a beat, but he pressed on, inch by inch, ever upward through the caves.

At last the company stopped. Sweat dripped down Torin's back and arms and stung the burn on his side. The stuffiness of the warm humid air and the tight walls seemed to nearly suffocate him, and he drew deep breaths in large gulps. He heard a groan and a grunt ahead of him, Drombir, by the sound. Then he felt something waft over his face that he had not felt for a very long time—cool, fresh air.

15

◇ FAMILIAR PLACES ◇

FRESH AIR rushed in through the tunnel and filled the cramped spaces between the companions. Erik shrieked with joy when he felt the cool breeze and Torin gave a deep sigh. One by one, each of the company emerged from the small tunnel into the realm of air and sky.

Torin took his first, shaky step out of the caves and stretched out his stiff back. Though his eyes were braced for rays of sunlight he saw none. It was night. The breeze brushed past his sweat-drenched shirt and chilled the itch on his legs underneath the *skrimsli* blood stains. As he craned his head back slowly, some of the knotted muscles in his shoulders came loose. There above him he saw a thousand stars that glimmered like crystals against the black dome of the night sky.

Bari rubbed his eyes and leaned back. "By the Mastersmith! What a sight."

Grimsa also leaned his head back and stared up at the shimmering stars. "By sweet Fyr and all the gods, some part of me thought I might never see those glittering beauties again."

The soft sounds of the night, grass that rustled and the trickle of creeks, were nearly drowned out by that thundering roar they had heard inside the tunnel. Torin turned and saw that it was not a river that made the noise but a waterfall that towered high above their heads. A warm vapour floated off the column of frothy water and dampened their cheeks and eyelashes.

Wyla made a strange sound, a sort of shocked gasp. She pointed up at the falls and called out to the others. "Wait, I know this place. This is Frostridge Falls!"

Torin's eyes opened wide as he looked up and recognized the craggy outcrop of rock near the top. "By the gods, I think you're right."

Before Torin had finished the last word, Wyla pounced on top of Drombir and, once again, began to throttle him with both hands. "You greasy rat! So, it was your troupe that left us stranded on the top of that cliff. This is all your fault! You'll pay for this, you wretched cave-dwelling cretin!"

Torin and Grimsa yanked Wyla off the flailing *nidavel*. Drombir dashed back toward the door but slipped on the slimy rocks. Bryn caught him before he managed to escape down the dark tunnel.

Wyla kicked and twisted. "Let me at him! If anyone has the right to beat that bushy-faced bandit, it's me."

"I'm not sure beating him would do much good," said Bari, "It would do nothing but inflame his companions to seek revenge. I can think of another way of causing him nearly as much trouble as he has caused us."

Drombir's eyes opened wide as Bari approached him. The young *nidavel* pulled a knife from its sheath on his belt and sharpened it with a whetstone from his pocket.

"Kinsman," Drombir said, "my dear kinsman, what do you mean to do?"

"You are no kinsman of mine," said Bari, "you are a thief and liar."

Bari knelt beside him and flicked his knife back and forth across the old bandit's face. Drombir screamed like a madman.

Torin leaned over to see what Bari was up to but couldn't move much because Wyla still kicked with fury. When the young *nidavel* stood up, Torin expected to see blood on the blade but there was nothing on the knife but a few tufts of curly grey hair.

There on the ground, eyes wide with shock, was a nearly hairless Drombir. His great bulbous head and his tiny pointed chin had only little bits of stubble left on them. The *nidavel* groped his naked head and squeaked like a mouse.

Bryn and Bari were the first ones to burst out into laughter, but the others soon followed. Even Wyla, who a moment earlier had fought to pommel the *nidavel*, now doubled over in uproarious wheezes of laughter, barely able to breathe.

Drombir's face went red as an autumn apple and, with another squeal of horror, he dove across the rocks and down into the dark depths of the mountain tunnel.

"By the gods," Bryn said, "I don't think I've ever seen such a sight in my life."

Bari giggled and wiped a tear from his eye. "Like I said, that will be about as much mischief to him as he caused you and your company. No *nidavel* would dare show their face like that and I would reckon it will be a few months before he has enough hair to present himself anywhere."

Bryn made his way around the falls, down the slippery rocks and on to the wild grasses. He looked up to the top of the moonlit cascade of white-frothed water. "It really is Frostridge." Then he turned and gazed far down the shadowed valley. "I can see the glow of torches down in Gatewatch from here."

Erik clapped and nearly fell right over. "Thank the gods, we are almost home!"

Each one helped the other down the slimy rock slope and onto the dirt path that had led them to Frostridge days ago. Torin thought of how they scaled the wall, of the trolls and the *nidavel* and the *skrimsli*. It was a wonder they had all made it back to this place alive. Now thoughts of a hearty meal and of soft straw beds in the rafters of Fjellhall filled every corner of his mind.

The path wound its way over the tapestry of tiny creeks and lush mounds that filled the lower part of the valley. All along, the company could see the distant glow of hearth fires burning in Gatewatch and the silent trails of smoke that rose up like white beacons. Still the sky was clear as crystal and the moon hung over the valley just above the pale peaks at the top of Shadowstone Pass. The chirp of small insects played percussively alongside the trickle of creeks and the rush of wind over the wild grasses.

Grimsa stopped and sniffed the night air. "Is my mind playing tricks on me or is that the smell of a roast over the fire in Fjellhall?"

Torin laughed. "It may be a trick, or it may be that your nose is more finely tuned than mine to the smell of food."

"Or," Bryn said, "that you are standing so close to Grimsa that all you can smell is his reek."

Bari sniffed the air and shook his head. "I don't smell anything like cooking, but I am most interested to see what you *madur* eat. And what is this place, Fjellhall? Is it the hall of the king in Gatewatch?"

Grimsa licked his lips. "Not the king but the queen."

"The Queen?"

Wyla shook her head and laughed. "No, she is not the queen. Keymaster Signy of Fjellhall is the Master of Brews. Her staff runs the kitchen and the guest quarters at the largest mead hall in Gatewatch."

Torin chuckled. "While Grimsa might swear allegiance to the Greyraven with his lips, his stomach is more likely to side with her."

Bari frowned. "You *madur* are strange creatures."

Wyla shook her head and sighed. "As strange to you as you are to us."

Despite their thick *nidavellish* cloaks, the night air was cold, and a chill crept under their skin. Each one dreamed of sitting next to a roaring fire with a cup of hot stew to warm their bellies. Torin, as always, let his mind drift back to Ten-Tree Hall. As a boy he would wander the woods until the sun had set, then, when night had settled, he would sneak back into the hall and warm himself by the dim embers of the great hearth. Sometimes his father would scold him for being out late, but more often his father would call for mulled wine hot from the cauldron and tell stories in the dying glow of the embers. Now the thought of mulled wine, the sweet sticky fruit juices and the rich spices, made his mouth water. He knew that if he were to arrive home that night, he would be the one with a story to tell. One day, he told himself, he would return to Ten-Tree Hall and recount their adventure to his father and all those he grew up with. He tucked that thought away in his mind and kept walking with a grin on his face.

The smoke that rose from the homely hearths of Gatewatch drew closer and closer until, at last, they reached the East Gate. Torin chuckled as he recalled their first encounter with Gavring, the relief and the joy of arrival after a long and arduous journey. Though it had taken a fortnight to travel from Ten-Tree Hall to Gatewatch, it seemed to him that the journey of the last few days was far longer.

Wyla pounded her fist on the gate and tilted her head back as she called out. "Hail, Master of the East Gate."

There was a shuffle from within the gatehouse and then the clomp of heavy steps up stairs. A dark figure appeared far above them. "Wyla, is that you?"

"Yes."

"Thank the gods! And Master Torin, Master Bryn, Master Grimsa, and the others?"

"We are all here," said Grimsa, "and we are very hungry. Let us in right away before we starve to death out here!"

Gavring stumbled down the gatehouse stairwell with thunderous steps and yanked the winch wheel to open the gate. As the iron-strapped timbers rose, Torin saw the great man's hulking form in the moonlight. For a brief second, he thought that Gavring looked like a troll, his wild hair like the leaves and twigs he had seen on Cragh and Bhog. Torin shook the thought from his head and stepped forward to greet their friend.

"By my oath to the Gatewatch, I thought I would never see you lot again," Gavring said. "Where did you go? Patrols combed the whole valley all the way up to Shadowstone Pass." Wyla and the three companions embraced Gavring one by one.

"The answer to that question requires some time as there is much to tell," said Wyla.

Grimsa nodded. "And I believe it may also require a cup of ale and a bowl of stew."

Gavring laughed. "Of course. And I'll be glad to hear it. But I won't be the first. Captain Calder has ordered that if you return you are to be taken to him straight away."

Bari stepped forward and gave a slow bow. "Greetings, Gatekeeper Gavring, I am Bari, nephew to Brok the Silversmith of Myrkheim, the city of the Mastersmith."

Gavring's eyes opened wide and his mouth dropped open. "Now I am even more curious to hear what you lot have been up to. I would be glad to welcome you, Master Bari, especially if you are friends of these companions, but there are no *nidavel* allowed in the city without an escort by order of Captain Calder."

"We can serve as escort," Torin said, "he'll be with us anyways."

"Besides," said Bryn, "who from the garrison will be glad to wake up at this time of night?"

Gavring tugged at his beard for a moment then shrugged. "Well, I guess that will have to do for tonight as it is indeed late. But any trouble that arises from his being here will fall on your heads."

Bari's face flushed red. "I assure you, Gatemaster, I shall be no trouble to you or anyone else here in Gatewatch."

"I'll be off duty shortly," Gavring said, "the second watch is almost due to relieve me. After you report to Captain Calder, I assume you will be headed to Fjellhall?"

Wyla's eyes darkened. "We have foul news, Gavring. I will report to my father right away. I will meet the rest of you at Fjellhall once I have warned him."

Gavring's eyebrows popped up. "Warned him?"

"You'll know soon, Gavring," said Wyla, "but I know my father well and he will be angry if we tell anyone before him." With that she left, her quick steps silent on the stony street, and disappeared down a darkened alleyway.

Gavring stroked his beard then turned to Torin, Bryn, and Grimsa. "You three looked like trouble from the first." He saw Inga's broken arm tied up in a sling and shook his head. "That needs fixing too. Now go, quickly, to Fjellhall and clean up so I can hear exactly what kind of trouble you have stirred up."

As for that, they needed no encouragement. It was as if the trials of the past few days had been forgotten while they raced through the streets of Gatewatch. Familiar smells, like pine-scented smoke and fresh-cut cedar, filled Torin's nostrils as they drew closer to the towering hall. In the moonlight it cast an enormous shadow over the street, which swallowed the company as they stepped into it. Only the dim light of fading embers in the hearth guided them through the darkness to the threshold of the ancient hall.

Bryn slowly opened the door. In the doorway slept one of Signy's hall hands, a young man with a roundish face and wide shoulders. Torin recognized him from the trial in Stonering Keep. He woke with a start when Grimsa poked him then gasped and sputtered as he stood up. "Who would, who-who would enter Fjellhall?"

Grimsa stepped forward and smiled, his white teeth lit with an eerie glow. "We are the company of Torin Ten-Trees." The hall hand looked up and stumbled back as Grimsa took a step forward. Then he saw Bari, who smiled and gave a bow, and the young man's face went pale, as if the *nidavel* were some sort of haunted spirit.

"That's a, you're a, a *nidavel?*"

Bari rolled his eyes and bounced on his heels. "Yes, I am Bari, nephew to Brok the Silversmith. Though I suspect that doesn't mean much to you."

The hall hand began to gather his wits and bowed in return. "Greetings, Master Bari."

Torin lifted his shirt and exposed the wound on his side, horribly burned and scabbed. "I need someone to take a look at this."

The hall hand went whiter than before and perhaps a bit green. When he took a step back his torso swayed, and he nearly fell right over.

Torin sighed. "I reckon that person is not going to be you."

The racket at the door had roused a few of the other hall hands. One of the older ones stepped forward as the pale-faced door keeper edged away. He was slim and fair-featured with a familiar face. Torin recognized him as well; it was the hall hand that had shown them to the baths their very first day in Gatewatch.

"Asleif," said Torin, "gods keep you."

Asleif's sleepy eyes popped wide open. "Torin Ten-Trees? By sly Odd and all the gods, we had all given you and your party up for dead."

"Not dead yet," Grimsa said. "But we are hungry." Asleif nodded and hurried away.

A moment later Keymaster Signy appeared from the far end of the hall with Asleif at her heels. Her silver-white hair was in long braids which were twisted together and fell over her shoulder. Her blue-grey eyes cut through the dark like twinkling stars. Wrapped around her shoulders was a thick cloak of tan fur which draped all the way down to the floor. From across the room, Torin watched her march right up to him with a scowl on her face.

"Trolls blood, Torin Ten-Trees! This is the second time you've come trouncing into my hall looking like a vagabond and smelling worse. And I warned you about that Wyla girl before the testing, didn't I?"

Signy narrowed her eyes and pursed her lips as she raised herself up on her toes toward Torin's face. For a moment Torin thought she was going to smack him. She glanced side to side, perhaps looking for Wyla, then she sat back on her heels. Her face relaxed into a pleasant smile and she sighed. "But it is good to have you back at home, safe again." She looked at the others. "And you, Bryn. And you, Grimsa."

Grimsa blushed. "Keymaster Signy, through all our trials the thought of your hall was the beacon of hope that gave me the strength and the will to press onwards."

The others laughed and Signy chuckled. "Yes, the thought of food or ale is the great motivator for you Jarnskalds, isn't it?" Then she saw Inga's arm tied up in a sling. "Well, we will have to do something about that too, won't we?" Last her eyes fell on Bari. "And who is this we have here?"

"This," Bryn said, "is Bari, nephew of the Silversmith Brok."

Signy tilted her head. "Brok? Who is Brok?"

Bari stepped forward and gave another slow bow. "Keymaster Signy, I have heard many tales of your skill as a brewer and of the greatness of your hall. My Uncle Brok is a fine crafter of silver in Myrkheim, the city of the Mastersmith below the mountains."

Signy's eyes lit up. "Myrkheim? Then you really did travel a long way. Well, Master Bari, you are most welcome in my hall and, when the time of your return comes, send greetings to your esteemed uncle from me."

Bari grinned ear to ear and nodded. "Thank you, gracious Keymaster, I will do that. I will long remember your kindness. As a token of appreciation please, take this." He presented a silver ring, bright with fine strands of woven silver, which glittered in the dim light of the hall. Signy thanked him with a smile and a nod. She allowed him to slip it on her finger then stepped back and held it up to the light.

"A beautiful ring," she said. "Thank you."

Keymaster Signy then glanced down at their muddy, ragged boots and tightened her lips. "Now, not one of you is taking a step further into this hall with those filthy boots. Get on to the baths and my staff will have something for you to eat when you are in a more presentable state. Then we will get the full story tomorrow morning. Asleif, see them to the baths." He already had a stack of fresh tunics tucked under his arm and motioned for them to follow him out the door.

The night was pleasant, and the stars still shone high above them. The silver moon had reached its zenith and now floated high above the craggy mountain ridges. Its light flooded the street with a pale white light which, now that Torin thought of it, seemed brighter than the blue glow of the tunnels and perhaps even Myrkheim itself. In his heart he yearned for the sun, to feel the warmth of that fiery globe. Of course, he would have to wait for sunrise which, if he wasn't so drowsy, he might have waited up for.

Down the crooked alleyways and up the narrow streets they followed Asleif until they arrived at the arched stone door to the baths. Each one in the party was glad then that it was not a cold night and, with great relief, rid themselves of their itchy, blood-soaked garments.

Erik wrinkled his nose and frowned when he looked toward the entrance to the baths. "Are we really going down another tunnel?" he said, "I think I've had enough of those wretched holes."

"This one is bigger," Inga said, "so Grimsa won't get stuck."

Asleif picked up Torin's shirt and held it as far away as he could. "I'm not sure this rag can be salvaged." It had been soaked through with sweat, blood, and grime in the tunnels and the hole from the *skrimsli* spear-blade was larger than the neck opening.

Torin chuckled at the sight of his ragged tunic. "Perhaps not. But do try to save the cloaks if you can. They were a gift from Bari's uncle and, if not soaked in *skrimsli* blood, might be fine garments."

"*Skrimsli*? Those awful creatures from the caves? I've heard that they never ventured out above ground."

Bryn shrugged. "I can't say if they venture out or not, but they crowd the tunnels like swarms of rats. We were attacked twice by those foul monsters."

"In the tunnels? You mean you were in the *nidavellish* tunnels? Under the ground?"

Grimsa grunted. "Yes, there is quite a tale, but I think it shall be told tomorrow. My stomach is grumbling and the only thing between me and a meal is a quick bath, so let's get it over with."

Asleif nodded, his mouth open, and disappeared behind them as the company descended the steps.

Torin thought it strange to have so much room above his head and on either side of him. However, unlike the dry, level passages of the *nidavel* tunnels, the floor was slick and covered with moss and lichens. Each step he took carefully, so not to slip down the stairs. The embers of dying torches glowed just enough to keep the passage lit.

Bari nearly fell over when his foot slipped over a slick bit of moss. "What wretched workmanship! These steps are all uneven and the passage reels and twists like a drunkard. It is as if whoever crafted these steps simply chose a natural uncut hole in the mountain and carved steps into it."

"I think that was likely the case," said Bryn, "we *madur* are less skilled in stone craft that you *nidavel*."

"Stone craft? By the Mastersmith, I cannot call this craft at all. Perhaps, when this business with the trolls is over, I can persuade some masons from Myrkheim to help you poor creatures straighten out this pitiful tunnel."

While Bari seemed entirely serious, the others laughed. The thought of a troupe of *nidavel* coming to Gatewatch was almost as ridiculous as they, the company of *madur*, had seemed in Myrkheim.

"I will look forward to that day," said Torin.

When they reached the baths, they washed quickly as no one had much in mind but something to eat and a dry place to sleep. Wherever the *skrimsli* blood stained his clothing, Torin now had blotchy red rashes. The dirt and grime on his skin came off in layers as he scrubbed, and it took some time to get the crusted blood out of his hair. Though the hot water soothed his aching joints, his back and legs were still stiff. Purple and green bruises covered his knees and the burned scab over his ribs stung like a hundred little thorns poking into his skin. Soon everyone was washed and eager to return to Fjellhall.

After they stepped out of the bath, each shook themselves dry and pulled on a clean tunic. When his head slipped through the neck hole, Torin was surprised to see Asleif in the tunnelway that led back to the surface.

"It is a bit late for a swim, isn't it?"

Asleif frowned and looked down. "I am sorry, Master Ten-Trees, but I am here to deliver some bad news."

Grimsa shifted his tight-fitting tunic. "Bad news?"

Bryn chuckled. "Has Keymaster Signy run out of ale?"

Before Asleif could respond, a few cloaked figures stepped into the room from the tunnelway. The largest of them pulled back her grey hood to reveal a flushed face and long braids of yellow hair.

"So, there you are," the bulky figure said. Torin recognized her as she stepped forward. It was Almveig, the troll slayer whom Captain Calder had put in charge of their company back in Stonering Keep. "You all have some explaining to do."

"It is quite a tale," said Bryn, "but perhaps it would be told better over a cup of soup and a pint of ale than down in this muggy tunnel?"

She smiled with a wicked crook in her brow. "I am glad you are ready to entertain. Captain Calder is waiting to hear your tale, though I would not hold out for either soup or ale. He is known for many things, but not for his patience or his hospitality."

Bryn looked at Torin with a frown. Grimsa gulped and stroked his beard at a nervous pace. Behind Almveig, four more cloaked figures stood silently with their arms crossed and their faces grim.

Almveig stepped forward with her hands on her hips and leaned in toward the companions. "Torin Ten-Trees, Bryn of clan Foxfoot, Grimsa Jarnskald, Asa and Inga Grettir's-Daughter, and Erik Common-son, you are under arrest by decree of Captain Calder." She saw Bari and her eyes popped wide open. "And you too, whoever you are."

Bryn's eyes popped wide open and he stepped back. "Under arrest? For what?"

Almveig crossed her arms and leveled her gaze. "For desertion. You were ordered to present yourself at the gates of Stonering Keep the morning after the testing. That was five days ago."

Asa stomped her foot and threw up her hands. "We did not desert. For five days we have been trying to return."

Almveig chuckled. "I hope for your sake you can convince Captain Calder of that."

"This is ridiculous," Grimsa said. "But I'm sure we can sort it all out in the morning."

"Not in the morning," said Almveig, "now. Captain Calder is waiting. Do I have to drag you over to the barracks or are you done whining?"

From his belly, Torin felt a flicker of anger flare up. "Whining? You have no idea what we have gone through to get here."

Almveig's eyes widened and she drew her lips tight. "What you have gone through? If we are speaking of grievances, I think mine outweighs yours."

"What do you mean by that?"

Her face flushed red and she drew in a deep breath before she spoke. "Three days ago, I led my new company on their first patrol. By the Vimur River, we were ambushed. Six trolls fell on our company all at once. They did not quarrel or argue among themselves but worked together to force us into the river. I had never seen anything like it before."

Now the room was deadly quiet. The companions and the Greycloaks listened with wide eyes. Only the soft rush of water deep down in the cavern disturbed the silence.

Almveig narrowed her eyes and swallowed before she continued. "Alvid and Buri tried to slip past the trolls but they were crushed, stomped flat by the largest of them. The sound of their bones cracking still rings in my ears. The rest of us defended ourselves as best we could on the slippery river rock. A few of the others fell before we were waist deep in the icy water of the Vimur. My foot slipped and the river carried me downstream. Some of the others could not swim." A hot tear raced down Almveig's flushed cheek. "I only managed to drag Elsa back to the shore. All the others drowned in the Vimur." She grit her teeth and sneered. "And now I see all of you here are still breathing, so yes, my grievances do outweigh yours."

Torin looked at the rest of his company, exhausted and hungry, then shook his head as Almveig turned to leave. With slow, heavy steps he followed her out of the baths. The rest of the company came along one by one. The Greycloaks, stone-faced and wordless, followed the company up the crooked stairs.

16

◇ LUCK TURNS ◇

WHEN THEY REACHED THE SURFACE, the first hints of sunlight tugged at the horizon. They lit the sky with a faint pink colour that faded into speckled stars far overhead. From up the valley, a cool breeze wafted through the crooked streets and over the thatched roofs of the stone buildings. The wispy remnants of smoke that rose from the stone hearth chimneys wavered in the wind and drifted off toward the wilds over Stonering Keep.

As he felt the hard, stone street under his feet, Torin wondered what he would have done if they had been with Almveig and the rest of her company. Could they have overcome the trolls? Would they have been pushed into the river? Which of them would have survived, if any? He glanced over to Bryn and Grimsa, to Asa and Inga, and to Erik and Bari. He thought now that perhaps their unwanted diversion over Frostridge, through Fanghall, and into Myrkheim was a great bit of luck.

Almveig led them through the silent streets, past Stonering Keep, and up to the north wall of the city under the shadow of Ironspine Ridge. Wooden barracks and stables stretched out from the rock face. Their construction was crude compared to the rest of the buildings in the city, probably raised by conscripts rather than carpenters. What they lacked in craft they made up for in hardiness. Some of the timbers had barely been cleaned of their branches; the strong, round trunks were like iron columns of cured wood. It seemed there was no shortage of trees when they had been built and so the stacked timber walls were all of thick, uncut cedar slabs. At the base of the wall, all manner of supplies were piled haphazardly: crates of vegetables, stacks of furs, racks of iron tools. The whole place smelled of cedar, horses, leather, iron, and sweat.

Almveig approached a small wooden door in the wall and pounded it with her fist. "Almveig Jorun's-daughter, here with the deserters."

Bryn threw up his hands. "We are not deserters. If you would only listen to us, then we could explain."

Almveig turned and with a quick swing of her fist, hit Bryn square on the jaw. His head jerked to one side and he toppled over onto the cobblestone street. His forehead hit the ground with a resonant knock.

Torin blinked, his jaw open and his eyes wide, then rushed over to Bryn's crumpled form. "Bryn?"

Almveig sneered at the unconscious figure before her then shook her fist and spat. "You lot have given me enough trouble. Any other complaints?"

Grimsa shrugged and nodded. His face was flushed red and his jaw was clenched tight. He took a step forward and pointed his finger straight at Almveig's face. "Yes, I have many. But you are the first among them all."

In the moment Grimsa spoke, Torin was still crouched over Bryn. Behind him he heard the shuffle of feet followed by a tremendous crash that shattered the quiet dawn. He swung his head around and saw that Grimsa and Almveig had toppled over into a pile of vegetable crates. Now each wrestled viciously amid the broken wooden boxes to get the other in a hold.

As one of the Greycloaks figures rushed toward him, Torin managed to jump out of the way. As he whirled around, another one of the Greycloaks caught him by the shoulder. With a jerk to the side, he wrenched himself loose then shifted that momentum into a blow. It landed squarely in the middle of the man's chest. With a groan the Greycloak's hood fell over his face and he stumbled backward a few steps.

Inga cried out as one of the guards grabbed her by her broken arm. Asa and Erik both rushed toward Inga to free her. Grimsa wrestled with Almveig, and Bryn, still dazed, lay still on the ground.

The first Greycloak that had swiped at Torin now charged again with heavy steps. From a crouched position, Torin launched himself at the assailant and knocked him off balance. The figure reeled and fell straight into a stack of small barrels against the wall, which toppled and rolled away in every direction.

As Torin adjusted his stance to defend himself against the others, the door to the barracks burst open. A dozen grizzled Gatewatch veterans poured out and joined the brawl. Torin dodged a fist, then felt a kick against his shin which sent him over backwards. His hand caught the cold stone before he fell over onto the ground, but then the wind was knocked from his chest with a kick to the ribs. He gasped and clutched his side where the spearwound was, as calloused hands seized his shoulders and dragged him into an upright position. Just when he thought he had caught a breath, another blow came from the fray of fists and feet and angry faces. Then Torin hunched over and drew a raspy wheeze through his tight chest. A foot planted in the middle of his back sent him to the ground with a crash, his chin bashed against the rough rock. Torin's head throbbed and his lungs screamed silently for air.

A gruff voice rang out over the din. "Enough!"

The foot that had pressed Torin to the ground released him. He raised himself up onto his elbows for a moment to catch a breath then, despite the fire in his legs and the pulsing pain in his side, he forced himself to stand.

Above the crowd of Greycloaks and battered companions stood Captain Calder. From the top of the steps, he peered down at the company with icy grey eyes, one as sharp as steel and the other dull like slate. In the cold morning air, wisps of fog poured out from his nostrils in slow, steady breaths, and his wide chest, wrapped up in a bear cloak, rose and fell in time.

Calder pointed his gnarled finger at Torin. "You. With me. Throw the rest in the stocks."

Whether the fight had gone out of the company or they were too far outnumbered, there was little resistance then. Two burly Greycloaks pulled Grimsa up by the arms and dragged him into the barracks. The women that grabbed Asa and Inga were not gentle, and Erik whimpered when a stocky young Greycloak shoved him toward the door. Bari shook his head and went along without protesting. A broad woman slung Bryn, still limp, over her shoulder and disappeared into the smoky doorway.

Captain Calder kept his gaze fixed on Torin for a moment longer, then turned and stepped inside. In the tussle, Torin's wound had broken open again. He felt pain flare up in his side where the spear-wound, blistered and scabbed, still leaked a bit of blood. With a clenched jaw, Torin cast a narrow-eyed glance at Almveig. Then he followed Calder over the threshold and into the barracks.

The others turned down a set of stairs into the lower rooms, but Calder continued down the roughhewn corridor to a small hall. The central hearth was not lit, but small fires burned in ash pans around the edge of the room. Tattered banners, wax candle mounts, and rusted iron weapons hung on the coarse walls of stone. A single row of benches lined the perimeter, interrupted only by a large wooden chair worn smooth with use. Across the seat and the arms were furs of various kinds. The seatback was carved with runes, some which looked *nidavellish* and others which looked like some foreign or forgotten language. Around the edge, all manner of monsters, trolls and wolves and bears, were crudely etched.

Captain Calder stood in front of the chair and muttered some words which, it seemed, were not meant for Torin to hear. As he turned and sat down, his shift in weight made the boards beneath his feet creak. Again, he stared at Torin with an empty, distant expression. Then he motioned to the bench on the side of the room. With cautious steps, Torin kept his shoulders square to the old man and shuffled over. He glanced back at the door and was relieved, if only slightly, to see no one had followed them. He settled into the bench and met Calder's wordless stare.

Calder lifted his snow-grey eyebrows high up, exhaled, and relaxed into his chair. "First, understand this Ten-Trees: if you utter a single lie in my presence, I will have you hanged from the West Gate tower overlooking the wilds. I will call on rats to nibble your feet and ravens to peck your eyes out before I cut your rotting corpse down and throw it to a pack of squealing boars."

Torin did not flinch or break his gaze, but felt his stomach start to knot up inside him. He wondered where Wyla was and what conversation she had with the gruff man before him. Calder nodded and took Torin's silence as a statement of understanding.

"So, now you'll tell me where you have been the past week and what you have been up to when you should have been here."

Torin cleared his throat. "After the trial in Stonering Keep, we climbed up to Frostridge Falls through a *nidavel* tunnel. Someone, or something, closed up the passage while we were up on the ridge."

"Someone or something? I don't suppose you could be more specific?"

"I don't know for sure."

"Well, then give me your best guess."

"There was a company of *nidavel* led by one named Drombir. They swindled us out of our horses when we first went up Shadowstone Pass on our way to Gatewatch. I think it was one of them."

Torin waited a moment but Calder did not respond, so he continued. "We tried to return to Gatewatch by climbing over the ridge and around the mountain. It was dark and the forest fog grew thick. We got lost and ended up in a troll cave."

"A troll cave? And these trolls, they didn't kill you?"

"No. Well, one of them wanted to eat us but the other insisted that they keep us for a gathering of trolls. They called it a *Trollting*. The others were to be some sort of trophy."

Calder leaned forward on his knees. "The others? Not you?"

"Not me," said Torin. "The others ate food off the troll's table when it seemed the trolls were gone. It put them in a deep sleep. That's how they were captured in the first place. I didn't eat anything and so I didn't fall under whatever magic they had cast upon the table."

Calder pulled a thin smile across his face and nodded. "So, tell me of this *Trollting*. I, who have served the Gatewatch for more than thirty years, have never heard of such a thing. What reason would trolls have for gathering together in one place?"

Torin leaned in toward Calder and lowered his voice. "Didn't Wyla tell you? They gathered to greet the Troll-King. Ur-Gezbrukter, son of Gezbrukter, who has returned to claim his father's domain."

Calder sighed and shook his head. "Wyla was full of the same nonsense." He stood up with a grimace and started to walk out of the room.

Torin jumped up and stepped toward him. "Captain Calder, wait. We are telling the truth. You must prepare Gatewatch for his attack."

Calder whipped around and stepped up so close that Torin stumbled back a step. "I must do nothing. But I will deal with your fanciful stories and your company's desertion." Two burly grey-cloaked figures stepped into the room and seized Torin by the arms. "Take this whelp down to the stocks with the rest of his company."

Torin dragged his feet and shouted after Calder. "There is more! We were given a secret weapon, a way to defeat the Troll-King. We brought it with us."

Calder stopped and sighed. Then he turned back toward Torin and shrugged. "Well, Wyla left that flourish out of her tale. Now I am keen to know, what is the weapon and where did you find it? A magic sword dug up from a barrow? An enchanted hammer stolen from a *jotur* while he slept?"

"Neither. We have a chunk of Sunblaze the size of my fist."

At this Calder's stiff shoulders relaxed and he stroked his beard. "Sunblaze? Now that is interesting. Where is it?"

"It is tucked inside my cloak in Fjellhall. It is locked up in a copper box."

Calder stood in thought for a moment longer, then pointed his finger at Torin. "I would be far more willing to believe your story if I saw that Sunblaze with my own eyes. I will have two members of my company go to retrieve it. But woe to you if they do not find it there."

Torin nodded and relief flooded his body. Calder, no doubt, would see the Sunblaze and, with any luck, might believe that the Troll-King was on his way to Gatewatch. With this hope, he did not struggle as the guards dragged him through the narrow hallway and down the stairs to the prisoner's den. The others sat in stocks, neck and wrists bound by a weighted wooden panel.

Though there was a swollen bruise on his face where his head had struck the ground, Bryn had come around and now greeted

Torin. "Looks like we are all back in binds, Torin, though better to be a prisoner in Gatewatch that in Fanghall with the trolls."

Grimsa grunted and spat. "I never thought I would receive a heartier welcome from a *nidavel* under the ground than here in Gatewatch. But here I am, wishing I was back in Myrkheim feasting with Master Brok and listening to your stories, Bari."

Bari sighed and shook his head. "In all my travels I have never been treated in such a way."

There was a young woman in a green cloak, one of the new recruits, stationed by the door who pretended not to listen. She had been assigned to keep watch over the company. Torin saw her nervous eyes grow wide and dart back and forth between the speakers as they talked.

"Agreed," said Torin, "I don't think I'll have to wager my head in a duel of riddles with Captain Calder, though he seems rather keen to hang me anyways."

The two Greycloaks who had escorted him down shoved his neck and wrists into place and closed the wooden panel over his head. The rusted hinge squealed closed and the latch snapped shut. They had no mind to listen to the company's stories and left without so much as a word.

Asa coughed and then craned her neck over toward the others. "What did Captain Calder want?"

"After threatening to hang me, all he wanted was to hear the story of what happened."

"And?"

"I told him, but he didn't like the tale. I don't think he believes us."

Bryn frowned and adjusted his position. "What about the gifts from the Mastersmith? Isn't that evidence enough?"

"I told him about the chunk of Sunblaze back at Fjellhall. Once he sees that I think he might believe us."

A snore came from across the room. It was Erik. He lay limp in the stocks that held his neck and wrists and, with his mouth lolled open to one side, had managed to fall asleep.

"By the gods," said Grimsa, "how are we going to sleep with him snoring like that?"

Bryn groaned and stretched out his legs. "How are we supposed to sleep at all in these stocks? I wonder how Erik managed it."

"Let him sleep," said Torin, "we won't be in here for long. In fact, I'll bet they have already found the Sunblaze and are on their way back to straighten things out."

So they waited. The woman assigned to guard them did not utter a word, though they pestered her with questions about why they were bound and for how long and what sort of food they might get hold of while locked up. Then, as the minutes rolled into hours, drowsiness took each one in turn, until only Torin and Bryn remained awake.

Thin beams of sunlight peeked through the roughhewn timber walls. On the floor they lit swirls of dust which occasionally whirled up in little clouds and then settled again. Torin wished then that he could see the bright blue sky and feel the warmth of the sun on his skin. For days his eyes had seen little more than the dim glow of the blue minerals that lined the *nidavellish* tunnels. Now, back above the earth, he and his company were confined once again to this cramped dim-lit space.

Bryn shifted again and sighed. "Where do you think Wyla is?"

"I am not sure. She wasn't with Calder when he questioned me, but he seemed to be comparing our stories quite closely."

"Surely the Sunblaze will be evidence enough that we really went to Myrkheim. And what about the Troll-King? He is gathering his forces to attack Gatewatch as we speak. Instead of preparing, they are wasting time trying to turn us into criminals."

Torin felt a knot tighten in his stomach as he realized this false accusation would be reported and, in time, would reach his father. He imagined the old man, now grey-haired and round-bellied, hunched over his high seat in Ten-Tree Hall. He would not shout out in anger, but he would brood, and, in time, it would eat away at him like one hundred tiny termites in a cedar plank. His only son and heir branded a coward and a traitor. Torin shook the thought from his head. "We cannot allow that to happen."

Footsteps came from down the hall outside the crude prison. Torin and Bryn looked at each other, hope lit in their faces, and they smiled. The latch to the door rattled as someone on the other side began to open it. The others woke with the racket.

Their faces fell when the door creaked open. It was Wyla dragged along by two Greycloak guards. She squirmed from side to side, but the man and woman who held her arms had a steel-strong grip on her. "Let go of me you troll-faced maggots! I am telling the truth and you all know it. We need to prepare! The Troll-King is coming! I have seen him with my own eyes!"

Torin saw that Wyla's nose was bloody and her right eye swollen. A surge of rage flared up in his chest and he shook the stocks that shackled him. The chains jangled and the wood creaked, but it did not break. "Wyla! What happened?"

Wyla's red eyes met Torin's and she sniffed. "My father," she said. She shook her head and kicked one of the guards in the ankle. "Let me go, you cellar rat!" Her bared teeth almost caught the shoulder of the woman who gripped her left arm.

The Greycloaks did not flinch at her words but they also avoided her swollen gaze. The older guard looked down at the cellar floor. "Calder's orders." Without another word they dragged her to one of the empty stocks. The younger woman in the green cloak assigned to watch the prisoners closed the latch, as the others held Wyla's wrists and neck in place. She shrieked and kicked but could not work herself free.

After the latch clicked closed, Wyla fought for another moment then went limp. Her legs shook and her hair fell over her face like long moss in the wild forest. Torin saw her shoulders heave and heard a soft sob come from under her mess of hair. A wave of rage swelled again in his chest and he cursed the stocks that held him back.

Bryn's face was red and his eyes bleary as he looked over at Wyla, bruised and bound. He shook the stocks and kicked the wall behind him. "By thunderous Orr and all the gods, Calder will pay for this."

The Greycloaks who had dragged Wyla in chuckled at Bryn's bold comment and moved toward Torin. "You're next, Ten-Trees."

Wyla's head shot up, at least as far up as it could in the stocks, her face a mess of sweat, tears, blood, and hair. "Don't you touch him, you pig-faced, worm-fingered monsters!"

The Greycloak turned to face Wyla with a cold, flat stare. "Calder's orders."

When the latch came off, Torin tried to tug himself free of their calloused hands but he was too tired and weak to break loose. Their fingers were like iron binds and dug deep into his arm so that he could feel the pressure on his bones. With a heave, they hauled him toward the door.

Bryn called out and kicked against the wall behind him. Grimsa roared and tried to lift his stocks right out of the ground but nothing would budge. Wyla screamed again and the others looked up, pale-faced.

"Bryn, Grimsa," said Torin, "Wyla!"

But it was too late. The guard had closed the door behind them, and now Torin stumbled up the steps and out of the barracks.

The yellow sunlight hit Torin's face like the crash of a cymbal. It had been days since he had been exposed to its brightness and it burned in his eyes like fire. Slowly the intensity cooled such that he could squint, and the stone street at his feet came into view. A few moments later, he managed to raise his head to see the houses and shops of Gatewatch whisk by as they dragged him onwards.

Torin had guessed their destination; the Greycloaks were headed for Stonering Keep. They passed through the rough wooden doors into the crude stone courtyard. The stain of blood from the slain bear at their trial still lingered near the town gate. Captain Calder stood at the center of the keep with half a dozen Greycloaks. Torin's throat was already dry and it itched even more as he recalled Calder's threat to hang him. The grim company did not greet them but remained silent at their approach.

"I have to guess," Torin said, "that your Greycloaks did not find the Sunblaze, because you are still treating me and my companions like outlaws."

Calder sneered and spat. "Not outlaws. Deserters. And you are incorrect. My men found the case of Sunblaze exactly where you had described it would be."

Torin felt his legs threaten to shake. His stomach rolled inside his ribcage like a starving mutt and his head throbbed with every beat of his heart. "Then how else am I to convince you of our innocence? That we should be preparing for Ur-Gezbrukter's attack?"

At this Calder chuckled and shook his head. "Let me worry about this so-called Troll-King, Ten-Trees. We were just discussing your company's sentence."

Torin saw now that one of the hooded figures beside Calder was Almveig. He looked closer and saw Gavring also.

"Send them to the smithies to sweep floors," Almveig said, "or out to the fields to dig for potatoes. They will never be worthy of the Greycloaks."

"I'd give them lashes," said another, "then put them back on patrol."

Gavring frowned, his great bushy eyebrows furled. "I for one believe their story. How else would they have come upon so much Sunblaze?"

"They could have found it," Almveig said, "while they were poking their heads into *nidavel* holes up the valley."

Calder looked at Gavring then sighed and stroked his beard. "Alright then. This is my decision. Public stocks for the lot of them until sundown and then kitchen duties for two weeks. After that I will reconsider their bid for patrol." The others nodded and the Greycloaks escorting Torin dragged him back to the public stocks along the main street in Gatewatch.

17

◇ THE DRUMS OF WAR ◇

THAT EVENING a storm blew over Gatewatch. Torin watched darkening clouds gather and billow up into black towers that churned and swelled. In the air hung the smell of the storm, sharp in the nose, which grew stronger with every gust of wind. Far to the west, over the wilds, the sun dropped below the horizon and lit the edges of sky around the storm clouds in red and orange and purple. Soon the storm hovered directly overhead, its huge shadow like a giant raven over the whole settlement. A crack of lightning split the clouds like a canvas sack, and a roll of thunder shook the city as the downpour began. The thick droplets of rainwater fell on the back of Torin's head as he stood, hunched over, in the public stocks at the center of town.

As soon as it started to rain, Wyla laughed. Torin craned his neck toward her and saw white teeth in the glowing darkness, her bruised face and strands of wet black hair lit only by the frequent flashes of lightning. There were purple bruises around her wrists, but she stretched her hands out and up to the open sky.

"By the gods," said Wyla, "I love a storm."

Torin's hair fell over his face and the water droplets trickled into his eyes. He realized then that he was thirsty and, though it felt foolish to drink rainwater, he swallowed whatever he could catch on his tongue. He thought of how long a night spent soaked in the stocks would be and cursed their luck again. Calder, Almveig, and the others now feasted in Fjellhall without them. The thought of a warm hearth, fur-covered benches, and a cup of steaming cider made Torin's body ache.

A flicker of movement caught Torin's eye through the rain. He peered through the shadowy drizzle and saw a cloaked figure obscured by a pile of wood. The figure dashed out of hiding and scuttled closer to them. It ducked behind an empty cart and, after it was sure there was no one else about, ran right up to Torin.

Torin squinted in the darkness but could not make out the face. "Who is there?"

Two thin white hands pulled up the hood. It was Asleif, from Fjellhall. "It seems your tale was not so well received." He took hold of the stocks and unhooked the latch. Torin's arms and neck fell free and he collapsed onto the slick, wet rocks. The young man's eyes darted back and forth, as he crouched down.

"Keymaster Signy sent me. Some Greycloaks are speaking of strange movements along the edge of the wild wood. She thinks the Troll-King may strike sooner than anyone expects, but Calder won't listen."

Torin shook out his wrists and sighed. "At last. Someone with some sense."

A horse whinnied a little way off and Asleif jumped. "I must go. They will notice my absence before too long and I can't risk being seen."

Torin nodded and smiled through the trickles of rainwater that ran down his face. "Thank you Asleif! And thank Keymaster Signy on our behalf." Asleif gave a nervous smile, then bowed quickly and dashed off into the grey drizzle.

Torin went to work releasing the others. Each stock was secured by a latch which swung down on a hinge. While this latch was positioned so that it was impossible to reach while locked up, it was easily unlocked by a pair of free hands. In a moment, all the others were free. Each one shook out their sore wrists and stiff neck.

"Bless the Mastersmith," said Bari, "by the look on that Grey-cloak's face, I thought they might be sending us all straight to the gallows."

"They may yet," Torin said, "unless we can convince them of the truth."

Bryn shook his head and strands of wet hair flopped from side to side. "I fear it may be revealed too late. How long has it been since the *Trollting*? Ur-Gezbrukter has had days to gather his army."

"Keymaster Signy believes us. Gavring might believe us too," said Grimsa, "though his gate is on the wrong side of the city."

Then the rain fell harder, so they shuffled away from the empty stocks and huddled together under the awning of a small house. Torin still felt droplets hit his knees and feet but the rain no longer pelted his face where he stood. He was careful to stay out of sight from the window. Through the warped glass came a soft yellow light which flickered and dimmed. Perhaps there was a stew on the fire or mulled wine bubbling over the flames. He thought then of a warm, dry bed and tried to stop the shiver which shook his limbs.

A low ring hit his ears, so low its frequencies rattled in his chest. At first, Torin thought it might be a tremor in the earth but then it struck again, a bold brassy bass note.

"Wyla," said Torin, "what is that noise?"

The whites of her eyes cut through the dusky dark. "It is the alarm bell. I have only heard it ring once in my life before this."

Erik's eyes opened wide and his face went pale. "Can't you see? They know we escaped," he said, "Run!"

Just as Erik turned to run, Wyla grabbed him by the collar and yanked him back. "They would not ring the alarm for us. The bell rang twelve years ago, when I was just a child, because of a fire that ravaged a quarter of the city. Some great threat has come upon us and I don't see smoke."

Torin cast his eyes toward Stonering Keep and narrowed his gaze. "Then let's make for the West Gate and welcome Ur-Gez-brukter with steel."

"Steel, yes," said Grimsa, "but where will we find weapons?"

Wyla frowned. "There are long-axes in the armory as well as fine-strung bows and dry cloaks. It is usually under guard, but with the alarm ringing we may be able to sneak in."

A smile broke over Bryn's face and he clapped his hands. "Then, by the gods, let's slay some trolls!"

Wyla led the company down back alleyways and side streets to avoid the Greycloaks that rushed toward Stonering Keep. With quick steps they slipped through the door of the armory, which had been left unlocked, perhaps because of the alarm, and rummaged through its stores. Though most of the weapons had already been taken, they found enough long-axes to outfit the whole company, each with a thin, sharp blade on one side of the axe-head and a pointed pick to pierce troll hide on the other. There were also a few daggers, long and thin, like needles, which were more suited to Bari's size, and a longbow made of thick yew, which Asa claimed. Inga would have preferred a bow, but because her left arm was still in a sling, she took an axe instead.

In the corner, stacked in a neat pile, were the grey cloaks of the Gatewatch rangers, folded and wrapped in twine. Erik watched Wyla snap the twine rope and distribute the cloaks. "Are we allowed to wear those? Don't we need to earn them?"

Torin laughed as he slung the cloak over his shoulder. "If we haven't earned them yet, then we will today."

Bryn tested the leather grip of the axe in his hand and gave it a swing. "How many times did we dream of bearing a long-axe as a Greycloaks when we were children? Now here we are, though I wish it was a less desperate hour."

Grimsa chuckled as he felt the cold steel edge of the axe blade with his thumb. "Yes, this is exactly what I always hoped for, a chance to test my strength against the troll horde."

Wyla smiled. "For once I have to agree with Grimsa. Today those who doubted us will see our courage and our quality first-hand. For now, cover your head with your hood so that we are not recognized in the street, but once the fighting begins, let them see exactly who we are."

Out from the armory and through Gatewatch they hurried toward the western wall. The rain dwindled and the gloomy shadows of dusk fell across the city. The streets were empty and silent except for the ring of the bell and the distant din of gathering warriors. A strange mix of sensations sloshed together in Torin's chest: excitement then fear, pride then panic, courage then cowardice. With every step he took, his feet felt lighter, like a hawk that skims just above the ground, and each pound of his heartbeat in his ears was like the strike of a war drum.

They passed the empty stocks. It seemed no one was concerned with the escaped company now that the bell was ringing. Still, each one pulled his or her hood down a bit further and shuffled along the other side of the street. Wyla led them toward the southern edge of the western wall. In no time at all they reached one of the crumbled towers that made up the rugged defenses.

Bari frowned and tilted his head. "What use will this wall be against the troll horde? It looks ready to fall by its own weight."

Grimsa smiled and squeezed the grip of his axe. "It is not a wall that keeps our land safe from trolls, but the steel and blood of those who defend it."

Wyla sighed as she looked up at the decrepit pile of stones. "You sound like my father. He always said that if we repaired the wall, the warriors of Gatewatch would grow soft sitting behind their shield of stone. Now, we will see if steel and blood are enough to stay the horde."

Torin heard the doubt in her voice. It echoed alongside the doubts that rang inside his own head. Memories of Ur-Gezbrukter on his throne in Fanghall, the dream of Ten-Tree Hall burning, and the deathly valley full of wispy Watchers, all threatened to quench the flame of courage that burned in his chest. He stepped toward the others and raised his axe. "Long live Beoric's kin! Long live the Gatewatch!"

The others raised their axes and cheered, with their white teeth barely visible in the grey dimness that had followed the storm. In through a crumbled door and then up a set slick spiral steps, they clambered onto the wall.

The wall was only about one and a half times as high as Torin and it was wide enough for only two or three people to stand in the best of sections. However, it stretched across the whole valley, all the way from Frostridge on the south edge of the city to Ironspine, the jagged ridge to the north. Eight small towers, just like the ones they had climbed up in, had been built into the rugged wall, four on either side. In the middle stood Stonering Keep which bulged out into the expanse of wild grass and low shrubs that led into the western wilds down valley. Up close, the keep had seemed formidable, but under the shadow of Frostridge and before the vast expanse of wilderness beyond, it looked like little more than a village gatehouse.

A blaze of fire came from the center of Stonering Keep. Greycloaks hurried back and forth from the storerooms for wood to feed the fire. Soon that column of flame lit the courtyard, its smoke sent off in a slow drift down the valley by the growing wind. Torin saw runners, their faces lit by the fire, light torches and carry them down the wall. Inside each of the eight watchtowers another fire was lit, a chain of red ember beacons whose light filled the valley.

The last to be lit was the torch in the southernmost tower where the company was gathered. The runner from Stonering, breathless and sweaty, extended his hand and offered them the torch.

"Take it," he said, "light the tower."

Bryn snatched the torch and clambered up the side of the tower. One rock slipped loose under his foot, but he recovered and then disappeared over the top of the tower wall.

Torin lowered his hood and stepped toward the runner. "What news? Why the alarm?"

The runner leaned over and fell against the wall so that he could sit and recover. His heavy frame looked ill-fit for sprinting, and he wheezed with every breath. "A rider," he said, "a rider returned from the wilds."

Wyla crossed her arms, careful to keep her hood on. "That does not sound like cause for alarm."

The Greycloak lifted his face, flushed and sweaty, and took a deep breath. "He came back without a head. Cut clean off at the neck."

Torin's heart kicked in his chest like a spooked horse and he felt blood surge to his face. Grimsa growled and Inga gasped. "Gods help us."

"Then another," said the runner, "she had no head and no arms." He swallowed deep and then coughed. "The last horse had no rider at all, just a blood-soaked cloak tied to its saddle. Trolls are cruel, but never have I seen such bold treachery. Something has changed. Perhaps those untested whelps were right about this so-called Troll-King after all."

Torin heard a thump behind him. His hand went to his axe, but before he drew it, he saw what had caused the sound. Erik had fainted, collapsed into a pile beneath a crumpled grey cloak. He lay still for a moment, then jerked awake. Asa helped him up onto his unsteady feet.

Torin extended his hand toward the runner. "What is your name?"

The runner clasped his forearm and nodded. "My name is Stein." With a heave the runner stood up on his feet. "And yours?"

Torin pulled back his hood. "I am Torin Ten-Trees, son of Jarl Einar of Ten-Tree Hall."

Stein's eyes grew wide. "You were all locked up!"

Wyla pulled her hood back as well. She let her long, black braids fall down her shoulders on either side and planted herself firmly beside Torin. Grimsa did the same.

"By the gods," said Stein, "I am not sure how you lot got loose. Captain Calder would not be glad to hear of it, but I suppose we need every blade now." Then the Greycloak saw Bari and took a quick step back.

Bari gave a short bow. "I suppose I should introduce myself as well. I am Bari Wordsmith, nephew to the great Silversmith Brok in the house of Mastersmith Ognir."

"I did not know that Gatewatch was recruiting *nidavel* now."

"We'll need all the help we can get," said Torin, "besides, Bari is one of the most celebrated figures in Myrkheim."

There was a crackle high above them, followed by a lone cheer. Bryn peered down at the company from high up in the tower. "Finally, the fire is lit. The rain had doused the wood, so it took a while to start."

"Thank you," Stein said, "I am getting too old and fat to be clambering up towers."

Wyla stepped toward Stein and narrowed her gaze. "What will you report when you return to my father at Stonering?"

"If he asks, I will say an able company has taken up the defense of the southernmost tower. I reckon we may be far fewer after the night has passed."

Wyla's face softened and she slapped the man on his shoulder. "Good luck, Stein. Gods keep you."

Stein turned away and hobbled back down the wall toward Stonering Keep. The flare of the beacons atop the towers lit his path all the way down.

Wyla turned to the company, her face dark and grim. "No troll passes by this tower. With blood and steel, we will defend it, to glory or death!"

"To glory or death!"

The companions did their best to repair the wall in front of the tower. With stones and shattered beams, they raised some of the most crumbled sections. Another bow and a half-filled quiver of arrows had been left at the top of the tower. Bryn climbed up again and claimed it, though he said he wished he had *Haukur* instead, the bow that Drombir had given him. Asa followed him up. Together they cut small strips of cloth from their waxed grey cloaks and wrapped the tips of their arrows. From the beacon, they could set them ablaze before firing them at the trolls. The others, down on the wall, sharpened their weapons with a whetstone that Bari had in his pocket. All was quiet as night fell over the valley and the clouds above cleared away.

From somewhere far off, down the winding valley among craggy trees, came the sound of a drumbeat. The thud was deep and richly resonant. Torin peered into the dark gloom that hung between the low shrubs and knotted branches but did not see anything stir.

Then the drumbeat sounded again, this time in a steady rhythm. Battle cries went up from warriors all along the wall and war horns rang from Stonering Keep. Near the West Gate, Torin saw tiny flickers of flame as two or three dozen archers lit their arrows from the beacon fire. The call to fire rang out across the valley and a volley of arrows was loosed. In graceful arcs they soared upward, so high that they glowed against the sky like blazing stars.

As the smoldering arrows began to fall, they lit the valley with a dull red light. That is when Torin saw them, a host of grisly shadows on the move. Across the whole valley, groups of trolls bounded forward like wild beasts, some on two legs and some on four. The arrows overshot their targets and fell into the swampy marsh behind the quickly advancing line.

Now the trolls were within the light of the watchtower torches, their empty yellow eyes wide with rage. Three of them rushed toward Torin and his companions at the southern watchtower. Their craggy limbs, still covered in moss and mud and twigs, shook like trees in a gale. One of the creatures opened its gaping mouth and cried, an awful screeching grind like twisted metal and falling rocks. It pulled ahead of the other two with terrible speed.

Bryn and Asa each loosed a fiery arrow from the top of the watchtower. One sunk into the closest troll's leg and the other into its wide snarling mouth. The creature howled and thrashed as it snapped off the arrow shafts. Then it threw its gnarled hands up over the wall and began to climb.

The company roared and assailed the gruesome fingers of the troll with their axes, as if the knotted knuckles were the roots of a mighty tree. Where Torin struck, the hand pulled away, but a finger stayed, a great knobby stub which toppled over the wall and down onto Torin's foot. Still it twitched and clawed with its one misshapen nail. A shudder ran through Torin's whole body as he kicked it away.

The other two trolls reached the wall and ripped apart the hasty repairs that had been made to the weaker sections. With every swipe, enormous handfuls of stone and splintered wood were pulled down. Torin knew the wall could not last.

Wyla cupped her hands and shouted up at the watchtower. "Arrows! Fire on the first troll! Torin, go with Grimsa and stop that troll up the wall. I'll go deal with the other one. Quick! The wall won't last for long!"

Torin and Grimsa rushed over the uneven stones to where the barricades had been nearly levelled. With a grunt, Grimsa stepped toward the clawed troll hand and sunk his axe into its wrist. The hand pulled away with a jerk and the troll screeched, the awful twisted sound ringing over the din. Along with the writhing fingers, a large chunk of stone came away. Grimsa, who had struck from the edge of the debris, lost his footing as the wall crumbled. Down over the rubble and stones he rolled, off the wall and onto the far side. Torin looked over the edge and saw Grimsa face down on the ground near the troll. The monster roared and lifted its fist high in the air.

"Grimsa!"

Just as Grimsa rolled over, the troll's bloody fist fell with a crash. The impact shook the wall under Torin's feet, and he nearly lost his balance. His heart stuttered when it seemed as if his Grimsa had been crushed, but then he saw the large man scrambling away from the clenched troll fist on all fours.

Torin looked at his axe, then gripped it firmly with both hands. The troll stood only a few paces away from the wall and had turned to strike at Grimsa again. As it lifted its fist a second time, Torin leapt right off the top of the wall. With his own raised axe high over his head, he brought it down mid-air with all the force that his weight and his arm could muster.

The axe blade split the troll's skull from behind. Torin hung from the axe handle, firmly fixed in the monster's head, as his feet flailed in the air. A black ooze trickled down the shaft and he swayed back and forth with each waver of the troll's body. Then, with a great thump, the troll crashed down on its side. The force of the fall flung Torin down the marshy hill in a frenzied tumble.

When Torin came to a stop, he felt numb for a moment as both the stars above him and the ground below him spun. With a heave he righted himself. In the red blaze of the tower's torch light, he saw Grimsa run toward him, axe in hand. Near the wall, crumpled over on its side, the troll lay dead.

Grimsa yanked Torin up to his feet with his free hand. "Torin Ten-Trees, you damn fool." The huge man wrapped Torin in an embrace and squeezed nearly all the air out of him. He let go and slapped Torin on the back. "By the gods, you saved my life and you killed a troll. Now I owe you two drinks!" From further up the wall, some Greycloaks saw the dead troll and cheered.

Torin, still wide-eyed and dizzy, steadied himself on Grimsa's arm. "There are more of those monsters to slay before the night is up. Where is my axe?"

Grimsa pointed back toward the troll. "Right where you left it."

Through the moonlit shadows they slipped up the slope toward the wall and the dead troll. With a few heaves Torin managed to yank the axe free of the skull. He wiped as much of the black ooze off the blade onto the tall grass as he could. The troll's tongue lolled out to the side and its teeth still grimaced. Worst of all were the eyes which still seemed to glow with a sickly yellow light. Torin shook his head then followed Grimsa up the crumbled section of wall.

The first troll that had reached the wall and lost a finger to Torin's axe now flailed and writhed with a dozen fiery arrows sunk into its slimy skin. The stench of the burnt troll flesh nearly knocked the breath out of Torin's chest. Bryn and Asa kept up the barrage.

Wyla, Erik, Inga, and Bari were in more desperate circumstances. The third and largest of the trolls hurled boulders at the wall to knock it down and stood far out of axe range. Torin saw one stone fly right over Wyla's head and smash into the tower. She cursed as she dove out of the way then sprang back to her feet.

Torin looked up at the tower and shouted to Bryn and Asa. "The big one! Shoot at the big one!"

Bryn had already cocked an arrow and drawn his bowstring tight. He spun his torso toward the rock-hurling troll and let it loose. The shaft struck the beast in the side as it bent over to pick up another rock. With a roar of anger, it stood straight up and whipped its head back in pain. The troll's gnarled fingers tore out the arrow and black blood oozed down from the wound. It fixed its yellow eyes on the archers up in the tower and bellowed. Another arrow, loosed from Asa's bow, struck it in the ribs and sent it into a frenzied rage.

The troll barrelled straight at the tower with clenched fists raised high above its head. Erik and Inga leapt out of its path right before the creature leapt up onto the wall and smashed its base. The rattle and grind of stones deafened Torin's ears as the tower began to topple backwards into the city.

Bryn gripped his bow and leapt off the tower as the stones fell away beneath his feet. He tumbled down onto the wall and rolled onto his side. Asa had made for the edge but tripped and fell out of sight. Inga screamed as Asa disappeared among the rubble and the dust and the smoky embers of the tower's torch.

The troll lay still, belly down, on the wall. Its massive knuckles were raw and bloodied. When it began to pull itself up, Wyla climbed its clumps of tangled, moss-strewn hair to its head. It roared and tried to grab her but could not; Inga and Bari hacked at the troll's arms from one side, Torin and Grimsa from the other. With her free hand, Wyla gripped her axe and hacked its neck again and again until a fountain of black blood spurted out. After another minute, the troll ceased to flail and went limp where it lay on the wall.

The remaining troll screeched when it saw the larger troll dead and fled as fast as it could back down the valley and into the wilds. Even from two hundred paces, the smoldering arrows in its hide still glowed. Wyla shouted and held her axe up as she watched the creature flee far into the darkness.

18

◇ BLOOD & STEEL ◇

THE LAST SCATTERED EMBERS of the tower torch had smoldered and died. Now nothing but the moon and the stars lit the southernmost section of the wall. Grimsa helped Bryn up while Erik and Inga went to search for Asa among the rubble, the dust, and the smoke.

"Asa! Asa!"

A sputter and a cough came from somewhere among the dust and stones and shattered wooden beams. Inga caught a glimpse of her sister and ran to her side.

"Asa! By the gods, your leg." She whipped her head back toward the others and shouted to them. "Quick, she's trapped! Come help me lift this beam off her."

Asa grimaced and groaned. "How bad is it?"

As Torin clambered over the rocks toward her, he saw that her left leg had been crushed from the knee down under a heavy, splintered beam. It took three companions on each side to lift it, and they could hoist it only a little ways. When they heaved it up, Inga dragged her sister away from the debris.

Asa screamed when she saw her leg, a shrill ring that drowned out the battle that still raged further down the wall. Her face went pale and she drew in only short, panicked breaths. The weight of the beam had twisted her foot to the side most unnaturally and the bone had broken somewhere between her knee and her heel. She grabbed Inga by the waist and clutched her sister's cloak with a white knuckled grip. Inga embraced Asa with her good arm and wailed at the sight of her sister in such pain.

Torin felt sick to his stomach. The fury that burned his gut was of such magnitude that he thought it might sear him right in half. His hands quavered but there was nothing he could do other than look on the sight with clenched fists and bleary eyes.

From one of the houses nearby came an old man and an old woman. Their eyes were wide with fear as they approached the company. The white-haired couple peered over the others and saw Asa there on the ground.

"We saw what happened," the man said. "Is she still alive?"

The old woman sighed. "Thank the gods, she is."

Though his hands and knees trembled, the old man knelt beside Inga. "My name is Ivard and this is my wife Angrid. We have fletched arrows for the Greycloaks for many years but have never born an axe or a sword. Our arms are too frail now to pull even a bowstring. We do not know how to fight. and if the trolls breach the wall. we are doomed. It is a shame to feel so useless at a time like this. But there is one thing we can do. We can help your companion."

Angrid nodded and laid her hand on her husband's shoulder. "We have a bed of straw that she can lay on. and strong spirits to ease the pain."

The rest of the company looked to Inga, her tear streaked face covered in dust and bits of soot. She looked down at her sister for a moment more. then wiped her eyes with the sleeve of her cloak and sniffed. "I will stay with my sister." She motioned toward Asa's shattered leg with a limp gesture. "Though when the time comes, I don't know if I will be able to do it." Asa's eyes widened and she shook. At the sight, Inga's face broke again, and she wept bitterly.

Erik knelt beside Inga, his face hard with grief. "I will stay along with Inga and do what needs to be done, when the time comes." He looked up at the others. "I know I am not destined to be a great warrior like all of you. If it weren't for Wyla I would have run away at the testing in Stonering Keep. All along, I tried to convince myself that I was bold enough to be worthy of this company. But I could hardly believe my eyes when you slayed that towering troll. I was still quivering behind a chunk of the wall, barely able to breathe, much less move. No, there is too much fear in me and not enough courage in the face of those monsters. But I can face other trials: trials of grief." He turned to Inga and she nodded, her eyes shut tight and head bowed.

Torin gripped Erik's shoulder. "I for one am proud to have taken the blood oath with you."

Wyla nodded. "An oath is an oath, as good today as it was back at Frostridge."

"Go," said Inga, "Erik and I will take care of Asa." She looked down at her sister and clenched her jaw and fists. "And by the gods, spill as much troll blood as the earth will drink." Torin, Bryn, Grimsa, Wyla, and Bari thanked Ivard and Angrid with a nod, then embraced Inga and Erik before they turned back toward the wall.

Down towards Stonering Keep, Torin saw that Greycloaks still struggled against the gnarled fingers and knotted fists of the troll horde.

"They need help," said Grimsa, "what are we waiting for?"

Torin peered out into the darkened wilds. "We can't leave this section of wall unguarded."

"There are no trolls in sight this far up the valley," said Wyla, "but there are plenty down near Stonering Keep, and my axe-blade is thirsty."

Bari squinted, then tugged on Torin's cloak. "Look! Up the valley, back toward the Shadowstone Pass, a small cluster of torches is approaching the other side of East Gate. Who could that be?"

Bryn peered up where the *nidavel* had pointed and gasped. "Bari is right, there is a mob of torches headed toward the East Gate."

"Perhaps King Araldof Greyraven sent reinforcements?"

"Unlikely," said Wyla. "How could they arrive so soon?" Then her eyes widened. "Gavring will be the only one on guard. All the other Greycloaks are here at the western wall."

Torin frowned and looked back toward Stonering Keep. "Bryn, you are the quickest of us all. Run to the East Gate and find out who or what that is. Come back to the wall if they are friendly, though I suspect they are not." Bryn nodded and dashed down the wall and into the dark, crooked streets.

Wyla pushed past Torin. "Well, I'm not sitting guard while a battle rages down valley."

Grimsa followed her with his eyes, then nodded and turned to Torin. "I am of the same mind."

Torin shook his head and sighed. The shadows across the wilds seemed empty but his conscience urged him to stay. "Has any good ever come of following Wyla when she storms ahead?"

Grimsa scratched his beard. "Good? Perhaps not. But it seems that's how all our best adventures begin." With that Torin, Grimsa, and Bari ran after Wyla down toward the battle.

The thrust of the troll's attack was focused on the West Gate at Stonering Keep. As they came further down the wall, they saw how desperate the situation had become. The gate itself, made of thick-woven iron bars, had been pried off and bent into twisted scraps. About half a dozen trolls had broken into Stonering Keep and were caught up in a skirmish with a host of Greycloaks in the torchlight.

Wyla had just reached the next battered signal tower ahead of them when a horn blast rang out over the field. Far down valley, a dark figure atop a mighty horse emerged from the wild shadowed trees. He was the source of the sound and as he raised the horn to blow it a second time, they could see the curved instrument glow with blue light. As Torin and Grimsa caught up with Wyla, the smaller band of trolls that had been attacking the signal tower retreated and raced back toward at the West Gate.

Wyla pointed her axe out over the field. "Ur-Gezbrukter!"

One of the grey-cloaks from that tower steadied herself, hands on her knees, and breathed heavy. "What did you say?"

"Ur-Gezbrukter," said Wyla, "the Troll-King. He has come to reclaim his father's realm."

Another of the Greycloaks there at the signal tower recognized Wyla and the other companions from Stonering Keep. "Wait. You are Wyla Calders-daughter! And these are your companions. So, you were telling the truth after all?"

"Of course, I was," Wyla said, "Look with your own two eyes stone-brain. Just like I said, the heir of the ancient Troll-King Gezbrukter, the *jotur*, Ur-Gezbrukter, has come to avenge his father's death at the hands of Beoric. Will you all believe me now?"

When the horn rang a third time, it rumbled the wall itself with its powerful tone. The figure on horseback shed his cloak and was suddenly illuminated. A silver coat of mail shone like the moon overhead and a silver helm with gold wings flickered with yellow fire. The tinge of blue on the distant figure's skin and the white braids of his beard confirmed it could be none other than Ur-Gezbrukter himself. He drew a mighty sword which erupted into flame, its steel edge orange with heat, and charged ahead toward the breach in Stonering Keep.

Wyla raced down the wall without a word and the others followed. The muscles in Torin's legs burned, but the terrible sight of the Troll-King on horseback spurred him forward. Bari fell behind, his short legs too slow to keep up. In a few minutes, they had reached the chaos in the keep.

The courtyard reeked of singed flesh and troll stench. A handful of dead trolls lay among the fallen Greycloaks. Many warriors had been smashed or thrown or stomped by the monstrous creatures, and the sight of their still, broken bodies, filled Torin with rage.

At the center of the keep, Captain Calder roared and lifted his gruesome axe high above his head. Through the darkness, Torin saw the old man's good eye, icy grey and filled with fire. Calder skirted aside when a troll tried to stomp him flat, then struck it at the knee. The troll shrieked in pain and toppled over. No sooner had it hit the ground than he struck again. His silver-grey hair whipped back and forth with each frenzied stroke. Then he dropped his axe and lifted the troll's awful severed head as high as he could. The black ooze of blood dripped down over his face and grey braided hair. He roared again and the other Greycloaks cheered, their courage rekindled.

Torin looked at Wyla and saw tears gather at the corners of her eyes, some twisted expression of fear and pride on her face. She gripped her axe and set her eyes on the closest troll. Torin saw what was in her mind.

He stepped up beside Wyla. "For Asa!"

Grimsa nodded and joined them. "For Asa!"

All three of them sprinted forward and launched off the crumbled ledge, axes raised high overhead. Torin felt weightless as he hung in the air. Nothing but the sound of his heart pounded in his ears. In his mind, he imagined a silver raven, grey feathers fluttering, as the wind whipped past his reddened cheeks.

Then his axe sunk into the troll's shoulder and his chest struck the troll's leathery hide. He tried to hold on as he had done before, but the blow had knocked his breath from his chest, and he tumbled to the ground. On all fours, he gasped for air.

Wyla had also fallen off, but Grimsa still gripped his axe shaft and would not let go. The troll wailed and waddled back and forth as it tried to shake the great man loose. When one of Grimsa's hands came off the axe, Torin's heart skipped, but Grimsa caught a great knotted tuft of troll hair as he swung back up toward its head. Now firmly fixed, he kicked against the troll's back and dislodged his axe with his free hand. The enchanted arm-ring gifted to Grimsa by the Mastersmith glimmered in the fire light as the great man swung the axe toward its open mouth.

The blade connected at the jaw with a crack, and black blood spurted high up into the air. Grimsa fell off the troll and hit the ground in a clumsy, rolling tumble. The creature tottered and fell with a crash which was met with a cheer from the host of Greycloaks around the keep. Torin and Wyla ran to Grimsa and helped him to his feet as the other Greycloaks rushed forward toward the few trolls that remained.

Grimsa leapt up, his eyes wide, and a grin spread across his bearded face. "By the gods, I did it!"

Torin embraced his giant friend and slapped him on the back. "You are a real troll-slayer now!" Grimsa roared and raised his fists, which made Wyla double over in laughter. She jumped on both of them and knocked them over. Torin saw her smile at Grimsa, then at him, and for the first time saw a look of pure joy in Wyla's face.

Wyla fought to catch her breath. "Damn you both, Torin Ten-Trees and Grimsa Jarnskald," she said, "you two are the most reckless men I've ever known and by the gods I am proud to call you shield brothers."

"And you," said Grimsa, "are without a doubt the wildest woman I've ever met."

Now the four trolls that remained inside the courtyard began to lose ground against the slick axes and fiery arrows of the Greycloaks. Step by step they backed toward the twisted remains of the West Gate. Just when it looked as if they might turn and run, the low-toned horn rang out and nearly deafened everyone in the keep.

A flash of blue light illuminated the hole in the wall where the West Gate had been. With a crash, the hooves of *Sterkur*, Ur-Gezbrukter's giant golden-maned horse, leapt over the rubble and into the bloody courtyard with the Troll-King on its back. Ur-Gezbrukter raised his blazing sword toward the sky and blew his horn again. Many Greycloaks toppled over as the blast of sound hit their eardrums. The *jotur's* silver chainmail shone like the blaze of stars and the wings of his helm were beacons of golden-flamed light.

"Hear me, lowly *madur*, you maggots and usurpers! I am Ur-Gezbrukter, rightful heir to this land and king of trolls. Tonight, the blood of my father Gezbrukter, which has gone unavenged for one hundred years, will be reckoned for. The streets of Gatewatch, this wretched hovel, will run with blood."

Calder stepped into the light of the fiery sword and held his axe high. Dried troll's blood, black and crusted, covered most of his face and his braided beard. "By thunderous Orr and all the gods, I curse you troll-wight! No fiend has passed through Gatewatch in over one hundred years and none shall while I still breathe!" He shook his axe and snarled, his white teeth like those of a wild wolf. About a dozen other Greycloaks rallied to his side and steeled themselves.

Ur-Gezbrukter laughed and dug his heels into *Sterkur's* hindquarters. The great horse reared back and then charged forwards. It trampled straight over Calder with its heavy hooves, then leapt up and bore its master over the inner wall into the unguarded city. Those warriors who had rallied around their captain froze with terror as the *jotur* disappeared behind the wall.

Before anyone could collect their wits, two more trolls stumbled over the remains of the West Gate and into the courtyard. Torin saw one of the Greycloaks, eyes red and bleary, seize Calder's axe and bite down on the steel shaft above the grip. His whole body shook, and his face and ears went as red as mulled wine. Others around him bit their own axes and trembled with maddened fury, faces crimson and eyes bulged. The Greycloak who had taken up Calder's axe ripped off his shirt and cloak with his bare hands, his mouth and beard frothed with spit, and hurled them away. Then, bare-chested, he gripped his captain's axe and charged toward the trolls. The others whooped and howled as they followed him into the fray.

Wyla ran to where her father lay, still as a stone. Torin and Grimsa retrieved their axes and chased after her. A few steps from Calder's crushed body, she wailed and collapsed. Her hair fell over her face and her shoulders heaved. She reached out a trembling hand and rested it on her father's crumpled chest. A trickle of crimson blood came from his mouth and mixed with the black troll blood on his cheek. One slate-grey eye stared up toward the stars. Torin and Grimsa knelt beside her and hung their heads. Torin, bleary-eyed, lifted his heavy hand and placed it on her back as she wept.

Torin looked down at the fallen captain and saw that Calder's left hand was tucked inside his cloak. It was positioned unnaturally, as if Calder had moved it after he had been trampled. Just visible beneath the blood-soaked furs, his rigid fingers clutched a copper box.

Torin snatched up the box and opened it. "The Sunblaze!"

Wyla and Grimsa looked up, each with reddened eyes and flushed cheeks. The warm glow of the precious metal lit their faces. It was not just a flicker of light, Torin thought, it was a flicker of hope.

"Use it!" said Wyla. "Tear these cursed trolls from the land of the living."

Only one of the three silver-gold leaves remained. Torin wiped his fingers on his cloak to dry them and then plucked it, careful not to let any drop of blood or bead of sweat touch it. With his free hand, he closed the box and tucked it back into his cloak.

Three more trolls had shoved through the West Gate and now swiped their talon-sharp claws at the Greycloak defenders on top of the wall and on the ground. Their roars were like the click and grind of sliding stones, and every stomp of their feet made the ground rumble. The bare-chested warrior who had charged ahead with Calder's axe lay in a pool of his own blood at the center of the courtyard. The axe, snapped in two, lay beside him.

Torin dashed toward the fallen warrior with the sliver of Sunblaze held aloft. The largest troll saw him approach and fixed its massive yellow eyes on him. In a twisted sort of smile, it pulled back its lips, then lifted its shaggy, moss-covered arm to strike him. Torin dropped the last Sunblaze leaf into the ruby red pool of the warrior's blood, then dove away from the deadly claws.

When Torin tumbled to a stop a moment later, nothing had happened. But then, just as he looked up to see the troll raise its arm again, there was a crack like lightning. A blaze of white light streaked straight up about ten spear lengths, like a flaming star, and flooded the courtyard with its brightness.

Everything went quiet. Torin thought perhaps he had been deafened, or even killed, by the blast. As the smoke blew away in wispy whirls, he saw the troll towering over him, arm raised, ready to strike. But it didn't. It stood perfectly still, with a foul sneer etched on its face. Torin hopped up, ready to dodge another blow, but the troll did not flinch. With his mouth wide open, he walked right up to the troll and touched its trunk-sized leg. It was cold to the touch and hard as stone.

A great cheer went up from the embattled Greycloaks that remained in Stonering Keep. Some were so stunned they could do nothing but stare at the rigid statues. A few of the bolder souls dared to walk straight up to the rock giants and spit on them. A tattered Greyraven banner that had fallen to the ground was hoisted up over one of the larger trolls. Then the whole company raised their axes and spears and bows high overhead and cheered.

Amidst the cheers, Torin saw Bari scramble down the wall and hurry over to where he stood at the center of the courtyard. "Torin! Wyla! Grimsa! The East Gate is under attack. Gavring and Bryn cannot hold out much longer!"

Torin could barely hear Bari above the shouts of the Greycloaks, so he leaned down and bent his ear toward the winded *nidavel*. "The East Gate? Attacked by Ur-Gezbrukter?"

"Bryn found me on the wall when I had fallen behind you. He says a band of *skrimsli* found a way into the valley east of Gatewatch and fell upon the East Gate. No doubt it was by Ur-Gezbrukter's command, though I have never heard of *skrimsli* venturing above ground. Bryn hurried back to help Gavring."

"What of the Troll-King?"

"That," said Bari, "is a stranger matter still. I saw him leap over the wall at Stonering Keep on his golden steed, and I worried he might set the whole city on fire all by himself. Instead he dashed straight through and disappeared over a broken section of the wall on the eastern side. Last I saw, he was galloping up the valley, though where he means to go, I don't know."

Torin then thought of Shadowstone Pass and the field of grisly statues, of Drombir's cup and the array of constellations, of the two pale peaks in the moonlight and the empty stare of the Watchers. "Gods help us. If he reaches Shadowstone Pass, we are doomed."

Just then Grimsa and Wyla ran up to Torin and tackled him in an embrace.

"Thank the gods for the Mastersmith and his precious Sunblaze," said Grimsa.

"There is no time to celebrate. A band of *skrimsli* is attacking the East Gate."

Wyla's eyes shot open. "By the gods, let's go."

"Wait," said Torin, "that's not all. The Troll-King galloped through the city and is headed toward Shadowstone Pass." They looked up the starlit valley to the snowy peaks at its end.

Grimsa's face went pale and he swallowed. "The Watchers."

Torin nodded. "We must find horses and chase him down. We will never make it in time on foot."

Wyla gritted her teeth and cursed. "I know where we can get horses. But what about the East Gate?"

Bari pulled a ring from his cloak and Torin recognized it as *Havaerari*, the ring given to him by the Mastersmith himself. "I'll spread the message here." A small tear glimmered in the corners of the *nidavel's* small brown eyes. "May the Mastersmith's gift keep you alive, Torin Ten-Trees, Wyla Calders-daughter, and Grimsa Jarnskald. Use it well!"

Grimsa picked Bari up and squeezed him until he wheezed. "You are the only damn *nidavel* I've ever liked. If we come back alive, I'll expect to hear a few more of your tales."

Once Bari had recovered, he nodded and grinned. "Of course, Grimsa."

As Torin and Grimsa chased Wyla up over the wall and back into the city, they could hear Bari's voice boom over the roar of the Greycloaks. "Listen, warriors of Gatewatch! A great victory has been won over the trolls here at the West Gate. But do not rest yet! A horde of *skrimsli*, foul cave-dwelling creatures, now pound their spears on the East Gate. Quick, to Gatemaster Gavring!" The boom and echo of Bari's voice faded in Torin's ears as they raced through the streets toward the barracks.

When they arrived at the stables, Wyla tore a torch off the wall and held it up to light the dim stalls. They were empty save for a few frightened mounts near the back. Torin approached a black-maned horse with nut-brown hair. Its dark eyes were wide with fear but, when he caught the loose reigns, it whinnied and settled down. He stroked its neck until the terror had faded from its eyes.

"That's a good horse," Wyla said, "her name is Kvolda."

Torin repeated the name and stroked Kvolda's side. Wyla mounted a sleek tan-coloured horse. It had a dark mane with a brilliant stripe of white that ran straight down the middle. "This is Morgunn. She is small but also quick and sure-footed."

Grimsa grunted and crossed his arms. "Do you have anything larger than these ponies? I think I might snap the spines of these twiggy little steeds."

Wyla shrugged. "There is always Bollo."

"Bollo?"

"The mill horse. He turns the grindstones. He's twice the size of these mounts but he's stubborn as a donkey."

Torin hopped up onto Kvolda and smirked. "Stubborn as a donkey? Well, then he and Grimsa should get along just fine."

Grimsa chuckled and rubbed his hands together. "Finally, a steed of quality! And we'll see how stubborn that stallion is."

Wyla had not exaggerated. Bollo's shoulders stood taller than Torin's head and was nearly as long as Kvolda and Morgunn together. Its coat was dark, except around its hooves which were covered in shaggy white hair. Grimsa grabbed hold of the reigns and Bollo jerked back. Perhaps the horse had expected him to let go, but Grimsa clutched the reigns with white knuckles and did not budge an inch. It twisted its head to the side and glared at Grimsa straight in the eye. Grimsa narrowed his gaze and growled back. For a moment each held strong. Then Bollo's eyes closed and the great horse shook its mane. With a long whinny it bowed its giant head.

"Troll's blood," said Wyla, "Bollo has never bowed to anyone before."

"A stubborn horse indeed," said Grimsa, "though not quite as stubborn as me!"

When the three companions had readied their mounts, they made for the East Gate. The clang and clash of iron and steel filled their ears as they rounded Fjellhall and galloped down the cobbled stone. At last they saw Gavring and Bryn atop the gatehouse, bows in hand.

Wyla yanked her reigns to halt Morgunn, then cupped her hands around her mouth and shouted up to the gate tower. "Bryn! Gavring! We need the gate opened!"

Bryn heard Wyla's voice and tugged on Gavring's cloak. Torin could see Bryn's mouth move in the gatehouse torch light as he spoke, as well as Gavring's red-faced reaction. Then the great red-haired man looked down and saw the three companions on horseback. He gulped hard and then raced down the rickety steps to the ground where the gate winch was located.

Gavring shouted down at the company from the top of the tower. "You can't mean to go after the Troll-King by yourself? We'll quash these *skrimsli* then we'll go together as a host."

Torin grabbed his reigns and called out to the gatemaster. "We have to go now, Gavring. We think he means to resurrect Gezbrukter's ancient horde at Shadowstone Pass."

"Resurrect them? How?"

"No time to explain, just let us through!"

"That's nonsense! Just the four of you chasing him is a race to your own end."

"If Ur-Gezbrukter is able to resurrect the ancient horde, we are all doomed."

There was a great sadness in Gavring's eyes then. He looked first at Torin, then at Wyla. His shoulders fell and his eyes drooped closed. Then he nodded and turned toward the great winch.

"Greycloaks," said Gavring, "Riders are ready to pursue the Troll-King. Prepare to defend the East Gate!"

Bryn fired one last arrow off the top of the tower then scrambled down the stairway. Torin could see the feet and the spears of the *skrimsli* huddled right outside the entrance. Gavring spun the winch as fast as he could, and the gate rose quickly.

Gavring did not take his hand off the winch but called back to Wyla. "Take my bow," he said, "you'll need it more than me. Besides, my axe is hungry to drink the blood of these foul monsters. Now go! Go!"

Wyla kicked her heels into her steed and veered toward Gavring. He threw the bow to her as she galloped by. Bryn hopped up onto Bollo behind Grimsa just as he and Torin each spurred their mounts and snapped the reigns.

All three horses trampled straight over the *skrimsli* horde as they raced out onto the road that led up to Shadowstone Pass. Behind the company, the East Gate fell shut and with a thud and a crunch. Torin drew in the crisp night air that rushed by his face as the smell of blood and fire faded. Though his eyes watered in the wind, he set his gaze up toward the two pale peaks that loomed high over the valley.

19

◇ BETWEEN PALE PEAKS ◇

MORGUNN, KVOLDA, AND BOLLO galloped up the valley slope. Their heavy hoofbeats tore out clumps of muddy grass from the ground, which was still wet from the evening storm. The companions heard nothing but the rush of wind in their ears, as their hair and their hoods whipped like ragged flags. Soon, Gatewatch shrunk into a smoky glow far behind them.

Away from the light of the torches, Torin's eyes adjusted to the darkness of the shadowed valley. The path was narrow but sure, and the horses found the well-worn groove in the earth by feel. They passed Frostridge Falls where steam rose up toward the silver moon. Still higher in the valley, the raindrops that had clung to the long grass had crystallized as ice, and now shook and shimmered as the horses thundered past. Above the mountain ridges on either side stretched a tapestry of constellations that glimmered with soft white light.

Yet the two steel-grey peaks, each capped in white snow and light green ice, were still far ahead. Shadowstone Pass, its black rock field a pit of darkness in the pale light, lay between them like a gaping throat; the field of beastly figures, sun-stricken trolls, were the small jagged teeth.

"Look," said Bryn, "up there!"

Torin squinted and saw a small figure, alight with gold and silver, at the foot of the Shadowstone Pass.

"Damn our luck! He has already made it. Faster!" He snapped the reigns and stood up in the saddle as Kvolda's hooves pounded the earth at a greater pace.

When they approached the base of the mountain, a swell of dark clouds had gathered between the peaks high above them. The clouds turned slowly and pulsed with an unnatural rhythm. Between the folds of churning cloud, thunder rolled and small spears of lightning flashed blue over the valley. With every rumble, Torin's stomach turned as he thought of the Watchers rising from the field of ash and bone. When he thought he might vomit, he gripped the reins tighter, breathed deeply through his nose, and kept his eyes fixed on the glowing figure far above him.

Wyla was the first to start up the switchbacks on the scree slope. They made slow progress as the horses slowed to a trot and sometimes slipped on the loose rock. As they climbed, Torin recalled the ember eyes of the ghostly host and his own tumble down the slope.

Then, from high above them, a blinding bolt of lightning shot straight over their heads and into the knotted wood below. The next instant, a crack of thunder followed and boomed so loud that it made Torin's ears ring. Morgunn, Kvolda, and Bollo reared and whinnied in fear.

Kvolda lost her footing and slipped. Torin squeezed his legs around her sides and clenched the reigns with both hands to stay in the saddle. As the horse panicked, she tried to back up but bumped into Bollo. Spooked by the collision, Kvolda then threw her head back and tried to turn around. Of course, the path was too narrow for this and so she started to slip down the scree slope. Torin leapt off her back but was caught in the slide of scree and tumbled down the hill toward the dark forest below.

Round and round Torin tumbled until at last he settled in a pile of loose rock and swirling dust. Through the shadows, about fifty paces away, he saw Kvolda get up and bolt away. As the sound of her hoofbeats disappeared in the distance, he cursed and rolled onto his back.

He wished then that he had never come to Gatewatch, never climbed over Frostridge, and never journeyed to Myrkheim. What did he know of trolls or of *jotur*? Why was it that he and his companions were the ones to face Ur-Gezbrukter? As he lay still, limbs loose, he closed his eyes and wished another bolt would strike him dead.

Another lightning bolt did strike a tree, not twenty paces from where he lay. It shattered the air with its whip-like crack. In the silence that followed, Torin heard the crackle as the branches burned. His fingers felt the heat from the strike still warm in the ground. With wide eyes he sat up and looked at the smoke that rose from the charred stump. It had been an oak tree, just like the ones that surrounded Ten-Tree Hall. Tears of anger filled his eyes as he remembered his dream of his father's hall, its timbers aflame with Watchers all around and Ur-Gezbrukter gloating over it all.

Then, in the orange-yellow glow of the flames, something glinted. Torin wiped his bleary eyes, leaned forward, and squinted. Though his body ached with bruises, he forced himself to stand and slowly stepped toward the ashen stump. The glint flashed again.

"By the gods, could it be?"

There, in the charred crook of the fiery stump, lay the spearhead *Skrar* which he had received from Drombir in exchange for his horse. When they first travelled to Gatewatch, that terrible night at Shadowstone Pass, he recalled now that he had stowed it away in the crook of an oak tree. Now it glowed in the light of the fire, an iridescent silver-white amid the flicker of orange and yellow flames.

Torin took his axe and knocked *Skrar* out of the fiery stump. He let it cool on the ground a moment before he picked it up and wiped off the black charcoal with his cloak. The pain in his limbs and the fear in his heart melted away as he looked upon the rune-carved spearhead. In his mind, he saw *Skrar* fly through the air and pierce the Troll-King right through the heart. He smiled and thought this, perhaps, was a weapon worthy of such an enemy. A sapling nearby provided the shaft. In a few quick strokes of his axe he had it cut down to size and cleared of twigs and branches. *Skrar* fit tightly on the end of the stripped sapling and, though the wood was still green, it held firm.

Behind him he heard the pounding of hoof beats. He hoped it was Kvolda but instead, he saw Wyla ride Morgunn toward him at great speed. When she saw Torin and the mighty spear, her eyes opened wide.

"By the gods, where did you get that?"

"It is the *nidavel* treasure I chose from Drombir's company when we first travelled up to Shadowstone Pass. It is called *Skrar*, or Screamer, and I hid it in an oak tree for fear of its magic. I meant to retrieve it some time later, perhaps once I had a means to sell it. But as I lay here, that very tree was struck by a bolt of lightning."

Wyla's eyes widened and she extended her hand to him. "Surely it is a sign."

"If it is, let's not waste it," said Torin. He took Wyla's outstretched arm and hopped up onto Morgunn behind her. He held *Skrar* in one hand and linked his other arm around Wyla's waist as she yanked the reins back. Her hair smelled of smoke and her cloak held the scent of trolls' blood. Torin breathed deeply through his nose and thought to himself that it was a magnificent smell. Despite their differences, he wished then that they had more time to spend together. Then he thought of the Troll-King high above in Shadowstone Pass and he shook his head. He knew what they had to do.

Morgunn was slow as she bore them both along the steep mountain path, but it seemed Bollo was slower. Up and up they went until they found Bryn and Grimsa dismounted from their giant steed. Bollo had laid down against the gravel slope. It was clear he would go no further. Torin and Wyla dismounted about twenty paces down the trail. Morgunn was nearly ready to collapse as well.

When Grimsa saw the spear, *Skrar*, in Torin's hands, he clapped and laughed. "Ha! How strange. Yet again I am glad of our encounter with that scheming *nidavel*. I think he has helped us far more than he meant to! Now hurry up, before Ur-Gezbrukter wakes a second army of trolls."

The four companions climbed the last part of the trail on foot. After a few more switchbacks on the scree slope, the trail levelled off and straightened out toward the black-stone rubble field where dark clouds swirled and pulsed. This blocked the pale light of the stars, so that each had to fumble along the path at times when shadows fell over the trail. Crackles of thunder and flashes of blue lightning lit the path every few seconds, then all fell back into darkness.

At last they reached the top. They snuck off the path to a spot behind some jagged boulders. In turn, each one dared to peer out and survey the ashen rubble. Not too far overhead, the clouds swirled around the center of the field but there was no sign of the Watchers, at least not yet.

Ur-Gezbrukter, still mounted on *Sterkur,* stood in the middle of the field. As a gust of icy-cold air blew past the companions, Torin thought that the clouds seemed to be gathering closer and closer to the *jotur.*

Grimsa's face was white and his voice trembled. "What now?"

"There is no cover between here and where he stands," said Bryn, "and even if we could sneak up close enough, he would tower above us on his horse."

"The spear," said Wyla, "that would reach."

Torin nodded and tested *Skrar* in his hand.

Ur-Gezbrukter then drew his sword. A dozen sparks of lightning from the clouds arced toward it as the *jotur* raised it high above his head. With a loud bellow he called out over the empty field. "*Drjupa!*"

As if some barrier that had held the storm above him burst, the swirl of black cloud dropped down in a twisted funnel to where his sword blade was and broke over the ground. Like the spread of black blood in water, it crept into the spaces and the gaps between the broken rubble and shattered bones. Still it pulsed and sparked. Then the sky was clear of the dark clouds and the ground was covered in a black fog which undulated unnaturally.

Once the last of the storm cloud had settled, Ur-Gezbrukter spread his arms and shouted. "Rise, ancient souls! Hear my words! I am Ur-Gezbrukter, son of Gezbrukter, and rightful heir to his domain. Long you have slept. Now wake. Wake!"

A ripple ran through the fog, and dark figures rose slowly out of the shadowy mist that clung to the ground. Embers kindled and crackled as each Watcher took its grisly form. Torin felt his arms shake and his teeth rattle. A chorus of wretched cracks, creaks, and grinds filled his ears. The other companions peered out from behind the stone too and saw a sight like they never had before. Stones shook themselves loose and collected into piles underneath each of the ember-eyed Watchers. Then, as if moved by invisible hands, they stacked themselves and filled the foggy forms. Humped shoulders, enormous arms, and uneven heads emerged as the rubble stuck closer together. Then the field was filled with still, silent statues: an army of stone trolls made of black ashen rock.

Less than twenty paces away, Torin thought he heard movement. If his mind had not betrayed him to fear, then he had actually seen one of the statues move its fingers. A moment later, the arm extended and its shoulders flexed. Then the whole statue shook, and small flakes of stone fell off to reveal a bulky body. There it stood, a colossal troll, the biggest Torin had ever seen. Another troll nearby broke out of its rocky shell and roared. All at once, the crack of crumbling rock rang out from every direction and echoed off the peaks. Shadowstone Pass came alive with the sounds of a troll army awakened.

Torin could no longer see Ur-Gezbrukter but could heard him shout. "Awake! Awake! Rise up and take back the kingdom that was wrenched from my father's grip!"

Bryn, his face pale and sweaty, grabbed Torin's shoulder. "We are too late! The trolls will capture us if we show ourselves now."

"Curse our luck," said Wyla, "What about the Sunblaze?"

Torin nodded and shook his shoulders. "Yes, but we need liquid of some sort." His heart sunk in his chest as he realized there was no water to be found in a field of rubble and dry bones. His heartbeat pounded against his temples and he felt dizzy. He thought again of the berserk warrior back at Stonering Keep, laid low in a pool of his own blood. That had been enough. He felt his heart pump hard in his chest, then felt sick deep down in his stomach.

Bryn grabbed his shoulder and shook him from his morbid stupor. "The peaks! The peaks have snow!"

Wyla shook her head. "We'll never make it in time. Besides, it is a treacherous climb up to where the snow is. It is more likely that we would fall to our death before we reached the snowcap."

Bryn breathed quickly and waved his hands. "No, it could work. We don't have to climb. We've got two bows. We could skewer the Sunblaze with an arrow and then fire it into the peak."

Torin's heart skipped a beat and then he nodded. "Yes, that could work."

His hands shook terribly as he pulled the Sunblaze from his cloak. He let it fall from its box onto the ground. The roar of the trolls rose like the howl of wind so that he could not hear the others speak. With the blade of his axe, he pressed into the soft metal. When a drip of sweat from his forehead nearly landed on the Sunblaze his heart skipped. He took great care then to keep his beaded brow back from the silver-gold apple.

The Sunblaze split into two neat halves as the axe sliced through it. Wyla and Bryn each took an arrow and pressed the sharpened arrowhead into the soft metal. Torin watched Bryn pick up his arrow and test it. The metal was light and so the shaft of the arrow did not droop or curve.

Torin peered over the rock again at the host of trolls. At that moment, their attention was directed at Ur-Gezbrukter, but there were so many of them. He shuddered to think what might happen if Bryn or Wyla were seen. Then, as a quick wind cleared the thick fog, his plan became clear.

"I will distract the Troll-King while you two sneak around," Torin said, "Ur-Gezbrukter will recognize me from Fanghall. Make sure you are in range of the snow on the peak and do not fail. My life depends on it."

Bryn swallowed hard, and Wyla looked back at Torin with tear-filled eyes.

"I swore an oath," said Bryn. His voice faltered but he cleared his throat and shook his head. "Right where that foul monster king stands now. I swore to protect Gatewatch and I swore a pact of brotherhood with you. I will not let you down." Torin gripped Bryn's shoulder and Bryn nodded.

Grimsa grunted and huffed. "And I suppose I am to just sit here?"

Torin chuckled and shook his head. "No, my friend. If, by luck, the Sunblaze works, we still must face Ur-Gezbrukter." Torin gripped the shaft of *Skrar* then extended it toward Grimsa. "I will keep the Troll-King occupied until the Sunblaze has struck the peaks. Stay hidden until he is in range, then hurl *Skrar*. We'll only have one chance and your arm is stronger than mine, more than twice as strong with that enchanted arm ring from the Mastersmith."

Grimsa flexed his arm and nodded. Before he took the spear, he embraced Torin with both arms. Then he took *Skrar* and narrowed his eyes. "Long live the Gatewatch."

"If the Sunblaze does not work, I will keep Ur-Gezbrukter occupied as long as I can. But you three must race back to Gatewatch to warn them." The others nodded with grim expressions.

Lastly, Torin turned to Wyla. Her grey eyes were like the reflection of the moon in rippling water. A tear broke free and raced down her cheek as she looked back at him. After a moment, she lurched forward, grabbed the back of his neck with both hands, and kissed him hard.

"Damn you, Torin Ten-Trees."

Torin sat dazed for a moment as the taste of her lips lingered. Before he could reply, she had snatched up Gavring's bow and the Sunblaze arrow. Without another word, she wiped her eyes on her sleeve then slipped off into the shadowy field toward the southern peak.

Bryn and Grimsa smirked at each other. Then Grimsa slapped Torin on the arm and chuckled. "That's strange. I thought she loathed the very sight of you."

"I think she still does," said Bryn.

For a moment Grimsa watched Torin stare off into the darkness where Wyla had disappeared, then the big man snickered. "Look here! The great Torin Ten-Trees, struck dumb by a sweet little kiss."

Bryn chuckled. "You know if Wyla heard you say that she would knock you flat."

Grimsa put his finger to his lips and grinned. "That will be our secret."

Torin shook his head and sighed. "Alright, enough of your tittering. You two are worse than tavern maids!" He gripped them both by their shoulders. "Gods protect us now. Long live the Gatewatch." Bryn and Grimsa nodded then set to work.

Bryn made for the north peak, careful to stay low and take cover behind whatever rubble remained strewn across the field. Grimsa stayed hidden behind the boulder, and Torin, without an axe or a shield, crept toward the horde of trolls.

Though his view was obscured by the crowd of beastly forms, he could hear Ur-Gezbrukter's voice booming across the valley. "Long you slumbered! Greatly you suffered! Accept my claim to this land and I will lead you to victory over these usurping *madur*. Name me king!"

Torin stood up and cupped both hands around his mouth. "I shall name you, but not as king. I name you Maggot-Beard! I name you Stench-Bringer and Dull-Wit!"

At this, the curious murmurs ceased and the grisly crowd searched for the source of the sound. Torin took another step forward and kept calling out as loud as he could. "I name you Slow-Wit and Fat-Nose!"

The crowd of trolls parted where Torin stood, so that he could see Ur-Gezbrukter at the middle of the host. The *jotur's* eyes were flames of fury against his blue-white cheeks and his nostrils flared wide above the white braids of his beard. He yanked the reigns and *Sterkur* reared back. Its golden mane flashed under the star lit sky as the Troll-King lifted his gleaming sword.

Ur-Gezbrukter pointed his blade toward Torin. "Gatar Mind-Thorn, I shall now silence your stuttering head by cutting it off. That will give me great pleasure. But before I do, take stock of this host: the mighty horde of my father, Gezbrukter. I shall take even greater pleasure in the knowledge of your suffering at the final doom of Gatewatch. You would have been wise to stay hidden away in Myrkheim."

Torin's heart lurched at the mention of Myrkheim. How the Troll-King had learned of that disturbed him, but he kept his expression calm. "I think it is you, not me, who will soon find his plans torn to pieces as in the teeth of wild wolves."

Ur-Gezbrukter laughed and the host there with him began to chuckle in snorts and grunts. "As in the teeth of wolves? Look at you. You approach me without a sword or a shield, without an axe or a spear, with nothing but empty words. You are a goat and a fool."

"If I am a fool then what does that make you? Or have you forgotten so soon that I bested you in a game of riddles?"

Again Ur-Gezbrukter's eyes flared and his voice fell low. "I remember well that you fled the contest like a weasel. And where were you when my horde stormed the wall of Gatewatch? The defenses are broken. Were you too cowardly to stand against me there? Now your plight is hopeless."

Torin's knees shook so hard that his voice nearly trembled though he fought hard to keep it steady. "You underestimate me, Ur-Gezbrukter, son of Gezbrukter, and not for the first time. I demand that you lay down your sword and surrender. I will not ask again."

At this a great roar rang through Shadowstone Pass. The gravel-grind of the troll's gargled chuckles sounded like a rockslide down the side of the mountain. The Troll-King laughed so hard he nearly fell from his horse. "Do you mean to slay me with mirth?"

Sweat trickled down Torin's back and his spine tingled with nervous energy. He wondered how close Bryn and Wyla were to the peaks, or if they had already fired the Sunblaze arrows and failed. "Very well then. You have left me no choice but to destroy you."

"Bring him to me," Ur-Gezbrukter said, "let me see the fear in his eyes before I cut them out of his head."

Two trolls stepped forward to grab Torin, but he ducked out of the way. The larger troll swiped again and knocked Torin back so that he stumbled and tripped on the rocks. He barely had time to scramble to his feet before the other troll loomed over him. With a heavy thud, its foot came down where he had been just a moment ago. Though he was not crushed, the edge of his cloak was caught underneath its gnarled toe. The troll scooped him up in its leathery fingers and broken-nail claws. The cloak tore under its foot as the troll lifted him up.

Though Torin thrashed and kicked, he could not free himself. The more he struggled, the tighter the troll gripped him, so that for a moment he thought he might suffocate. In its unshakeable grip he was taken back toward the horde and to Ur-Gezbrukter who sat atop his horse. When Torin saw the gleam on the Troll-King's blade not fifty paces away, his heart threw itself against his ribs, his mind raced, and his whole body began to sweat as if he had been thrown into a furnace.

Then, like a flash of lighting, the entire pass was lit with blinding bright white light. Half a second later, an explosion, the sound of shattered rock and ice, smashed against Torin's ear drums. While the sound still rang in his ears, a second flash lit the pass and again he was blinded and deafened. Unable to see or hear, he thrashed and wiggled against the rock-hard grip of the troll who had caught him. Despite the muscled fingers that clutched him, Torin managed to slip out of his cloak and down onto the ground.

He dashed away as quick as he could but stumbled and fell. When he sprang to his feet again, he noticed the eerie silence. Nothing but the soft whistle of wind ran over Shadowstone Pass. The grunts and the shuffle of feet had ceased. His eyes grew wide as he took in the scene: an army of trolls frozen as if by some strange magic. With a wince, he stretched his hand forward so that he could feel the troll that had caught him. It was still warm to the touch, but was, undoubtedly, just lifeless rock. Torin could then hear nothing but his heartbeat pounding hard in his ears.

There came a wretched cry from somewhere deep in the labyrinth of stone trolls. It was a wail and a roar, both hoarse and fierce as it echoed off the twin peaks. Torin ducked and hid himself behind one of the statues. There was still the Troll-King to slay.

He heard the *jotur* dismount from his horse. No doubt the field of trolls would be too treacherous for his horse to cross quickly. Ur-Gezbrukter's breath was heavy and his voice hoarse. "Damn the Mastersmith, that scheming maggot! And damn you, Mind-Thorn, you slime-tongue rat! I'll not rest until I have your head!"

Then all went quiet again. Neither the sound of the giant's steps nor the sound of his breathing could be heard. Despite his efforts to control it, Torin's own breath grew short and he gripped his chest as if his heart might spring out. In quick bursts, he sprinted from statue to statue, back to where Grimsa waited with *Skrar*. He cursed himself for having left his axe behind. Again, he dashed out into the open and dove behind the feet of a stone troll. Another twenty paces and he would be back to where he had left Grimsa. He drew a deep breath and sprinted with all the speed at which his feet would carry him.

Grimsa and Wyla were huddled against the rock, their backs pressed up against the flat stone. Torin snatched up his axe and slipped in beside them.

Grimsa leaned over, a great grin spread over his face. "It worked! And here I was ready to meet the gods."

"We may yet," said Wyla.

Some distance away they heard the shuffle of feet, then a shrill cry. "Run, Torin!" Torin's heart dropped in his chest and he gasped. It was Bryn that had called out.

Somewhere within the field of statues. Ur-Gezbrukter grunted and spat. "You are not the rat I was after."

"Quickly! He caught me! Run!"

The *jotur* laughed in a deep, wicked tone. "Torin? So that is your true name, Mind-Thorn. Come face me, Torin, or your companion dies."

Both Wyla and Grimsa reached out to hold Torin back, but he was too quick. He sprang to his feet, gripped his axe with both hands, and called out with all the grit he could muster. "Here I am, Troll-Prince. My axe thirsts for your blood!"

Wyla hopped up to her feet and Grimsa rolled on his side to push himself up. Torin motioned for them to stay. "Wait until that monster has shown himself, then spring up once he is distracted." His companions nodded.

He planted his feet on the frozen ground and wringed the axe-grip with white knuckles. With some effort, he managed to slow his breath, but his heart still raced. Below his shaking ribs, his stomach threatened to upheave itself. Still, he stood firm.

The Troll-King stepped out from the field of stone statues, which was like a forest of silent shadows. His golden helm was gone, and silver hair tumbled down off his head in every direction. Through a few loose strands, his eyes burned into Torin with fury, his white teeth clenched tight and his bluish cheeks flushed almost purple. The *jotur* had thrown off his chain mail as well so that his bare, heaving chest glistened in the moonlight. In one hand, his sword was raised high, and in the other was Bryn, who he dragged by the hair.

Torin planted his feet and waved his axe. "You do not seem so confident without a horde of trolls to fight your battles, so release him and fight me."

Ur-Gezbrukter smiled then yanked Bryn up by the hair so that his feet dangled off the ground. Then he drew back his sword and ran it straight through Bryn's chest.

Torin had seen the whites of Bryn's eyes as the *jotur* had lifted him up, heard him cry out. But when the cold steel blade burst out from his chest, Bryn went stiff in all his limbs and was suddenly silent. His mouth and eyes were stretched wide open. Then he coughed, and crimson blood spilled out of his mouth and down over his chin. The *jotur* pulled his sword back and tossed Bryn aside.

Inside Torin's chest, an explosion of boiling blood shot through his neck straight to his head. All around him the edge of the world darkened until Ur-Gezbrukter was all that he saw in his narrow field of view. Then the white starlight was tinged with red, as all but the terrible face of the Troll-King blurred. Torin's ears and forehead blazed with heat and his body shook at the spine like the tremor of an earthquake. From his mouth came a noise like he had never heard before, as if it came from something, or somewhere else. It tore at his eardrums and rattled in shaky echoes off the two towering peaks.

He did not feel his feet touch the ground as he rushed forward. He did not feel the weight of the axe in his hand. It was no longer an axe but a part of him, like the talon of an eagle or the claw of a bear. When the Troll-King's sword flashed, his axe swung up to meet it. The clang of steel on steel rattled his arm like a hammer to his bones but he felt no pain. He struck again and again, but Ur-Gezbrukter met every savage strike with his smoking sword. Everything was a blood-red blur of rage, each strike more ferocious and desperate.

Then Torin's foot slipped and the Troll-King knocked him back onto the ground. As he fell, he swung his axe around and caught the *jotur* in the thigh. Ur-Gezbrukter roared as a trickle of blood ran down over his knee. Before Torin could jump up again, the giant stomped on his wrist and pinned his axe-wielding hand to the ground.

"Now," Ur-Gezbrukter said, "you die."

As the giant drew his sword back, a shrill shriek split the air. Torin saw Ur-Gezbrukter's angry narrow eyes shoot wide open only an instant before a spear dove into his chest. The *jotur* stumbled backwards and dropped his sword. Both of his blood-stained, pale-blue hands gripped the spear's shaft. With a gasp, he tugged at *Skrar*, buried in his heart, but it would not budge.

Torin scrambled over to the *jotur's* sword and heaved it up with both hands. With a grunt he swung and thrust it into Ur-Gez-brukter's stomach. The giant fell back with a crash, his hands still wrapped around the spear-shaft in his chest. Torin was nearly kicked flat by the Troll-King's flailing feet but managed to brace himself against the blows.

Ur-Gezbrukter gasped and sat up, his lap full of red blood. Torin could see his pupils, wide black disks of despair, and the whites of his eyes which pulsed with swollen, red vessels. As if a surge of lightning had filled his arms and back, Torin drew out the sword from the *jotur's* stomach with a heave and swung it with every ounce of might within him. It caught Ur-Gezbrukter at the neck and swung straight through. The *jotur's* head rolled off his massive shoulders and fell to the ground behind him with a thud.

Torin dropped the sword and fell over onto his side. His whole body throbbed as sweat poured down his face and his lungs rasped for air. The stars spun above him, but he forced himself to stand. Crackles of pain shot through his wrists as he struggled to get up, and his wound from the underground tunnels burned like fire. He tossed his head from side to side in search of Bryn. There he lay, not ten paces away. Torin stumbled forward and collapsed next to his fallen friend.

"Bryn!"

Bryn's gaze was fixed straight up at the sky. His mouth, ringed with blood, did not move; neither did his chest, which was damp and warm with red liquid. Torin's eyes brimmed with tears and his hands trembled as he stretched them out. He laid them both on Bryn's lifeless chest and let his forehead fall onto the bloody cloak.

Jabs of pain, like the thrust of a knife with every breath, filled his chest and he wept.

He heard Grimsa roar and fall beside him. The huge man pushed Torin aside and started to shake Bryn by the shoulders. Then he sat up and gripped the front of his own cloak. With an awful cry he tore it right down the middle, then crumpled over in great heaving sobs.

Torin lay on his side for a moment, numb and cold. He felt a hand on his tear-streaked face and opened his eyes. Wyla knelt beside him and held his trembling hand. He gripped it hard and emptied his body of every tear it had to give.

20

◇ THE BURNING PYRE ◇

FOR A LONG TIME, Torin, Wyla, and Grimsa, sat still under the silent stars. The frigid wind chilled Torin's hands and feet, but at that moment the numbness was a relief. Grief ravaged his heart like a blazing flame as the image of Ur-Gezbrukter's sword through Bryn's chest flashed over and over again in his mind. And like fire, it would die down only to flare up again as Torin willed himself to look over at Bryn's lifeless form. Wyla looked down at him too, her face torn with grief. Her mouth opened as if to speak but no words came.

Grimsa was still wild with sorrow. He beat the ground next to Bryn's body with his fists and tore whatever shred of his shirt he could manage to grab hold of. Torin saw that the great man's hands were bleeding, cut on the rock. He heaved himself up and grabbed one of Grimsa's arms as it swung. Wyla grabbed the other one and both had to grip as tight as they could to hold him back. Still Grimsa rocked and wailed.

"Grimsa, stop!" said Torin. "He's gone."

For a moment the great man froze; a mass of hair, shredded cloth and dirt-stained tears. Then he slumped his head and leaned forward slowly until his forehead rested on Bryn's chest.

Soon exhaustion took them, and each rolled back onto the ground. Through his bleary view of the sky, Torin tried to recall what the stars had looked like the night they had first come over Shadowstone Pass. He thought of the firemead Bryn had saved for them and the toast of brotherhood they had made with Drombir's cup. Further back, his mind wandered to Ten-Tree Hall and all the trouble they had got in together as boys. Bryn's laugh echoed in his memory like the flicker of a candle, beautiful but too painful to touch.

Grimsa sniffed and wiped his eyes with his great hairy arm. "They will take him, won't they?"

Wyla sat up and smiled through the lines of grief that crossed her face. "The gods must have seen it. Bryn fired first. It was his arrow that rained bright light and crumbled rock down on the horde. I almost lost my balance with the rumble. Then I fired my arrow and the sky lit up again. Surely the gods will welcome him into their halls."

Torin kept his eyes on the stars. "I wish he were here with us instead. If only they would send him back."

Grimsa's brow crumpled with pain and he squeezed his eyes shut. "I should have thrown *Skrar* earlier. I hesitated because I thought I might hit Bryn, but I should have thrown it anyways. There was a chance."

Wyla touched Grimsa's shoulder. "It was Ur-Gezbrukter that did this, not you. You fulfilled your duty as a friend. You avenged Bryn." Her voice trembled and she drew in a quick breath. "And you avenged my father too."

Grimsa shrugged then shook his head. "Vengeance is not like they make it out to be in the songs and the old tales. They say it is as sweet as mead, but it is a bitter, bitter root."

As Grimsa spoke, they heard the sound of footsteps. Torin thought at first that perhaps one of the horses had lost its way and returned but in the grey shadows he saw a large figure coming toward them.

"Torin! Wyla! Bryn! Grimsa!"

It was Gavring. When he reached the top of the pass, he stopped and gasped. He raised his axe with both hands and widened his stance as if to fight but nothing stirred. Over the field of moonlit statues, he gazed with wide eyes, the stony trolls so nearly life-like in their frozen forms. Then his shoulders went slack and he let his axe down slowly.

"Gavring," said Torin, "over here!"

The Gatemaster jumped at the sound, then saw Torin wave. "By the gods, you're alive!" With a few great bounds he ran over to where they stood.

Gavring saw Bryn's body on the ground and his face fell. Then he stretched his huge hairy arms wide and pulled all three companions in toward him. "May he laugh with Odd, drink with Orr, and kiss the sweet lips of Fyr."

Gavring squeezed the three companions again then released them. When he looked up, he saw Ur-Gezbrukter, headless, a few paces away. "What is this? The Troll-King dead? You three have much to tell! When that great light came from Shadowstone Pass, the *skrimsli* fled as quickly as they had come. I feared it was the Troll-King's magic. Any who were brave enough came with me to face the Troll-King; the rest are standing guard at the East Gate."

"It was the cloud and the thunder, not the light, that was the work of the Troll-King," Torin said. "He woke the Watchers with whatever dark magic brought them back to life. When we arrived, Gezbrukter's ancient horde stood here in Shadowstone Pass, just as we are standing here now. They heard Ur-Gezbrukter speak and began to gather around him."

"Torin tried to distract them," said Grimsa, "and nearly got himself stomped flat by one of the biggest trolls in the horde. He goaded Ur-Gezbrukter just long enough so that Bryn and Wyla could get within arrow's range of the peaks."

Gavring eyes were wide as Torin continued. "We had taken the Sunblaze from Captain Calder after he fell at Stonering Keep. We split it in half and gave some to Bryn and Wyla. Each shot some up at the peak on the end of an arrow. That flash of light was the Sunblaze as it struck the snow."

"And it did this to the trolls?"

Torin nodded. "Just like in the old stories."

"It was Bryn who fired first," said Wyla, "and I fired mine soon after. The Troll-King moaned and howled bloody vengeance, so we ran to where Grimsa was." Wyla breathed deep and motioned toward Bryn's body. "Bryn didn't make it."

Grimsa's eyes swelled again with tears. "That wretched Troll-King lifted him up by his hair and ran him through with his terrible golden sword, the bastard."

Torin looked down at Bryn again. "I charged ahead with my axe, but it was too late. Ur-Gezbrukter would have killed me too if Grimsa had not thrown the spear."

Gatemaster Gavring furrowed his brow and looked again on the dead *jotur*. He scratched his beard and shook his head. "My ears do not believe it, but my eyes cannot argue with the truth. The Troll-King is dead!"

About a dozen more Greycloaks stumbled up the path, breathless but determined. Each had been ready to fight, just like Gavring, but now stood in awe of the silent valley. With them was Bari, doggedly determined to keep up with the grizzled warriors. Gavring waved them over to where the others were. Torin, Wyla, and Grimsa each wiped their faces and straightened themselves to greet them.

"The Troll-King is dead," said Gavring, "Come! See for yourself!"

Bari's face lit with a wide grin when he saw Torin, Wyla, and Grimsa at a distance. "Thank the Mastersmith! You're alive!"

The Greycloaks cheered and waved their arms at the sight of Ur-Gezbrukter. Two of them raised up his severed head. Some threw down their weapons and laughed while others stared, mouths wide open, at the stone troll statues. One dared to reach out her hand timidly to touch the stone teeth on one of the snarling faces. After a moment, Gavring called them all back over to where Bryn lay.

"Warriors of Gatewatch," he said, "Look! We have almost lasted the night. The horizon glows orange with the coming of the sun. Soon it will be day, though I admit just a short while ago I thought I might never see its light again. And we might not have if we had met this horde of trolls full of life and blood." He looked down at Bryn's body and shook his head. "This young man, still a newcomer to us, turned these trolls to stone. He and Wyla Calders-daughter fired arrows laced with Sunblaze up at the snowy peaks. That Sunblaze, given to them by the *nidavellish* Mastersmith, caused the unnatural light that we saw from Gatewatch." He waved his hand toward the three companions. "These three here have accomplished this heroic deed and we will celebrate with mead and feasting in Fjellhall. But Bryn of clan Foxfoot will taste neither food nor drink in this world again." Gavring saluted Bryn, his axe pressed hard against his chest. One by one, other Greycloaks came to honor him where he lay.

Last to step up was Bari, his hands clasped behind his back and his head bowed. Tears glimmered at the edge of his eyes and his lip quivered, but he managed to speak. "This verse I dedicate to Bryn of clan Foxfoot, friend of the *nidavel* and beloved companion of he who was named Gatar Mind-Thorn by the Troll-King himself."

Bryn, fair friend, has fallen
By cruel and foul blade
Our hearts are torn in two
With tears we shed our pain

Now the sun glows softly
Now the stars are dimmed
No hope have we to see
His bright eyes e'er again

As Bari spoke, the first rays of sunlight lit the horizon with fiery reds and purples. The troll statues cast long shadows over the company. But soon the sun's rays reached over the stone monsters and fell on those gathered around Bryn. There was warmth in the light, and the sky shifted from orange to the bright blue of day.

Gavring walked over to where Ur-Gezbrukter lay. He stared at the *jotur's* massive limbs, now sprawled lifeless on the ground. "What of the great horse?"

The Greycloaks found *Sterkur* among the field of stone-still figures. Its eyes were wide and wild. When it saw them approach, it whinnied and shook its head violently. Ur-Gezbrukter's spear and shield, which had been mounted on the saddle, dislodged and fell to the ground with a clang. There also was the Troll-King's golden helm and silver shirt of mail which had been cast aside on the rocky ground. *Sterkur*, spooked by the Greycloaks, raced over the rubble and galloped away toward Gatewatch.

Gavring lifted the mighty shield in one hand and the silver spear in the other. The shield he laid, face down, beside Bryn and the spear he slipped through the shield grip. He yanked *Skrar* out of Ur-Gezbrukter's chest and ran it through the grip as he had done with the *jotur's* spear. Then he turned the shield over and pulled the spears apart at an angle so that the shafts stuck out from under the gleaming metal. With great care, he scooped

Bryn's body up in his enormous hands and laid him on top of the shield. "Who will bear Bryn back in honor?"

All the Greycloaks there volunteered, but Torin and Grimsa elbowed their way forward. Each grabbed one of the shafts near Bryn's head, just below the spear blades. Wyla had taken hold of the other end of *Skrar* and Bari had snatched the end of Ur-Gez-brukter's spear. Together they lifted Bryn up, the spears lashed to the shield through the grip underneath. Bari rested the shaft on his shoulder while the others held it at their sides. Then, with heavy steps, they started back toward Gatewatch. Gavring picked up the coat of mail, the golden helm, and Ur-Gezbrukter's sev-ered head, then followed close behind them. The other Greycloaks trailed along in somber procession.

They carried him down the loose switchbacks to the path that wound through the green valley. The grass was lush with dew and glinted in the golden morning light. Little was said among the four companions as they carried their fallen friend. Torin's wrists ached until they burned, but the pain was a welcome distraction. On and on they went, past the forest and the falls, until Gate-watch came into view. When they reached the East Gate, the sun was already high up in the sky.

Slain *skrimsli* littered the area surrounding the entrance to the city, and barricades had been raised where the creatures had top-pled sections of the wall. Black, billowing smoke rose in several leaning columns and all was silent.

Gavring stepped forward and raised up Ur-Gezbrukter's head. "The Troll-King is dead! Long live the Gatewatch!"

All along the wall, heads peered out from behind barricades. One of the Greycloaks stood up, her arm raised to block the sun-light. "By the gods, it's true!"

A great cheer went up all along the barricaded wall. As the gate winch turned, its creaks and grinds welcomed them into the city. Gavring held the head of the Troll-King high for all to see.

Behind him, the companions bore Bryn through the city, past Fjellhall, toward Stonering Keep. The warriors along the wall followed them into the cluttered courtyard.

The crowd of warriors and townsfolk followed them into the circular courtyard. The corpses of the slain trolls had turned to stone in the morning light, strange dark statues in Stonering Keep. Among the slain Greycloaks, at the very center, lay Captain Calder. He had been covered from the chest down with one of the Greyraven banners that had fallen from the wall, his pale face still set in a grim scowl.

Torin, Grimsa, Wyla, and Bari set Bryn down beside Calder. Gavring looked down at them and hung his head. He lifted Ur-Gezbrukter's head and gave it to Torin. It was so heavy that Torin nearly dropped it, but he was able to secure his grip before it fell.

Gavring lifted the golden sword up and spoke to the silent crowd. "This man is Torin Ten-Trees, son of Jarl Einar Ten-Trees. With this sword he cut the head from Ur-Gezbrukter, the twisted heir of our ancestor Beoric's ancient enemy, the Troll-King Gezbrukter."

Torin looked at Grimsa and hoisted the head toward him. Grimsa caught it as Torin spoke. "I struck the head off the Troll-King, but it was Grimsa, son of Gungnir Jarnskald, that struck the death blow. With a great spear he pierced the heart of the Troll-King as the fiend raised his sword to kill me. For this, I name him Grim-Spear."

Grimsa looked down at the head in his arms and smiled. Then he turned so that all could see him. "My father will be proud to hear of this, but I am not the one to keep Ur-Gezbrukter's head." He turned to Wyla and tossed the gory trophy to her. She stooped and caught it as it fell into her arms. "It was Wyla Calders-daughter who led us to Frostridge Falls. I wanted to stay here in Gatewatch and feast in Fjellhall before our testing, but if we had, the Troll-

King would have taken the city. We would have never learned of the *Trollting*, or known of the return of Gezbrukter's heir, or met the Mastersmith. She was the one who fired the Sunblaze arrow into the mountain. It is she that deserves this honor, not me. So, I now name her Wyla White-Blaze."

At this a great roar of cheers and shouts came from all gathered there: nearly every person in Gatewatch. Wyla tried not to smile but could not help it. She hoisted Ur-Gezbrukter's head high up so all could see. "Long live the Gatewatch! Long live the Grey-raven!" Torin, Grimsa, Bari, and Gavring clapped and cheered.

When the noise had died down, Wyla laid Ur-Gezbrukter's head at her father's feet. Her lips moved but Torin could not hear what she said as she spoke to her father's still body. Then she knelt beside her father and hung her head.

Gavring called out with a great booming voice. "Greycloaks! Kin of the Greyraven! Tonight we will feast in Fjellhall to celebrate our victory over the trolls, but for now we must tend to the dead. If your kinsman or friend fell in the fight, prepare a pyre for them in the valley outside the East Gate. Lay them on the pyre and we will say our final farewell tonight. If you did not lose a dear one, then take to these stone trolls with picks and hammers. We will break these statues to pieces, and with them rebuild this broken wall. For over one hundred years the wall has stood, and look, it still stands! Long live the Gatewatch!" Once again, cheers erupted, and all went to work either seeing to the dead or attacking the stone statues with vigour.

Grimsa and Bari picked up Bryn on the shield and carried him back through town. Torin moved close to where Wyla knelt and placed his hand on her shoulder. Her back went stiff for a moment, then she leaned into him and rested her head against him. "I am so tired."

"So am I," said Torin. "I wish I could fall asleep and then wake to find all this was a dream."

A swarm of people came with hammers and picks to smash apart the stone trolls. Others came with long planks to carry the dead out of Gatewatch to the green hills up valley. Some laughed and others cheered whenever a chunk of troll crashed to the ground.

"Torin! Wyla!"

They turned their heads toward the sound of the voices and saw Eric, Asa, and Inga. The group made its way through the courtyard slowly, Asa's one arm over Inga's shoulder and the other over Eric's. She limped forward with awkward steps. Where the beam had crushed her leg, now there was just a stump wrapped in ragged, bloody cloth.

"By the gods, you're alive!" said Asa.

"We heard you chased after Ur-Gezbrukter," said Inga, "We thought we would never see you again!"

Erik nodded. "You must have a great tale to tell!"

Asa nodded. "How did you do it?"

Torin and Wyla stared at Asa's missing leg though they did not mean to. Asa glanced down at it for a moment then straightened herself and up and looked them with a stern face. "The trolls, they took this from me. But we succeeded, didn't we? We fulfilled our oaths."

"We did," said Torin. He swallowed and then looked down at the ground. "Bryn did not make it."

Asa and Erik stared, blank-faced. Inga shook her head.

"Not Bryn!" said Erik. "How?"

"He fired the Sunblaze up at the peak, just like we planned," said Wyla, "But the Troll-King ran him through with his sword before we could land a blow."

Then they embraced each other, one by one. There was joy in their reunion but sorrow in their loss, so few words were spoken.

Greycloaks bore Calder's body through the city and the company followed them up past Fjellhall and out the East Gate. There they had built a great pyre of stacked timber and hoisted Calder's body up on top of it. Torin looked out over the valley and saw dozens of wooden pyres which cast long shadows over the green hills in the late afternoon light. Upon each pyre a body had been laid; those who knew the one laid upon it set down wildflowers and long grass at its base. Grimsa and Bari had prepared Bryn's pyre not too far from where the rest of the company stood. His body had been wrapped in a grey cloak, and the bow given to him by Drombir was placed on his lifeless chest. Grimsa and Bari greeted Asa, Inga, and Erik, while Torin and Wyla lingered behind.

Torin looked at where Bryn was laid and then to where Calder's body rested. "Where will you stand when the fires are lit?"

Wyla looked down at the ground, a frown across her face. "Duty says I should stand by my father, but I think he despised me no matter how hard I tried to please him. Bryn was more like a brother to me. I will stand at his pyre when the fires are lit."

Torin nodded. "He would be glad to have you there."

They stood in silence for a moment more, then Wyla sighed. "That kiss up at Shadowstone, I didn't mean anything by it. I just thought I was going to lose you."

Torin smirked as he shrugged his shoulders. "Don't worry. Nobody else but Grimsa knows it happened. Besides, he will probably drink enough tonight to forget most of what happened today."

Wyla grinned, then looked up valley toward the peaks. Her smile faded. "I still can't believe he is gone."

The two peaks shone like crystal beacons in the fading light. Torin squinted and raised his hand to block the reflected sun.

"You know, I was ready to give up on finding you in the tunnels," Torin said. "Bryn was the one who insisted we keep up the search."

Wyla widened her eyes and punched Torin's shoulder. "Really? Well, perhaps I should have kissed him instead."

Torin shook his head and chuckled. "I think Bryn would have liked that."

Wyla smiled back at Torin and together they walked toward Bryn's pyre.

From the East Gate came a procession led by Keymaster Signy, who bore a bright burning torch. In the flicker of its light, Torin could see swirls of red paint on her forehead and beneath her eyes. A long braid of white hair hung down over one shoulder and the keys at her waist jingled with every slow step. She wore a long black dress which flowed loosely around her wrists and ankles like smoke. Many attendants followed her with unlit torches in hand.

The sun fell toward the horizon and the sky glowed red and orange. All was quiet in the valley as Keymaster Signy raised her torch and pointed it up toward Shadowstone Pass. The attendants gathered around her to light their own torches before they spread out to light the raised pyres scattered across the valley.

The twilight was dim now and only the torches provided enough light to see clearly. As the attendant approached Bryn's pyre, Torin recognized him as Asleif from Fjellhall. The pale-haired youth nodded at Torin and the rest of the company but did not speak a word. In the solemn silence, Asleif looked at Bryn for some time then hung his head.

Keymaster Signy stood beside Calder's giant pyre and now raised her torch high. One of the Greycloaks blew a curved horn, sounding a long and mournful note. Then all the torches were lowered to the pyre where the flames licked the dry long grass and the wildflowers. Torin heard a crackle as the fire of Asleif's torch first caught the brush, then spread quickly to the rest of the pyre.

One last time he looked at Bryn's face. Then he let his eyes drop to the flames and, in the rhythmic flicker, replayed every memory he could of his childhood friend. Torin recalled the first day his father had welcomed Bryn to Ten-Tree Hall as a foster-son. They had both seen only ten winters by then and when the snow fell again, they were closer than kin. Year after year, hour after hour, he had spent so much time with Bryn that it was hard to imagine a future without him.

Wyla woke Torin from his trance with a tug at his sleeve. "Look," she said.

Torin looked over the valley and saw dozens of pyres, orange-yellow flames that filled the valley with small spheres of warm light. All around the fires were the tiny shadows cast by those gathered round it, like the long, thin strokes of a brush wet with paint. The rising columns of smoke tilted up valley, as if they meant to carry the ashes of the dead back home.

As Torin's eyes followed the smoke-trails, he saw the most magnificent sight. Ripples of blue-green light cut the night sky in half, a heavenly trail ablaze with luminescent flame. Bari's eyes were fixed on the sky, and he stood, speechless, underneath the trails of blue-green light. After a few moments of awe, he turned to the rest of the company. "By the Mastersmith, what is that?"

"Those," said Grimsa, "Are the shimmering lights. They say that when the gods travel between worlds, they walk on a flaming rainbow road." Moisture had gathered in the corners of Grimsa's eyes as he spoke, and it glinted in the shimmering light. "That can only mean that the gods have come for Bryn and the others, and that he will soon be feasting with all his ancestors."

While they stood below the dancing lights, the fires burned bright. The flames consumed the pyres like a thousand hungry tongues. Then, one by one, each fire died down to heaps of ember and ash and bone. Again, the mournful sound of the horn rang out over the valley and the dim shadows around the fires began to move back toward Gatewatch. The company lingered long after the last party had departed for the feast at Fjellhall.

Though night had fallen and the fires had died, the twinkle of the stars and the blaze of the shimmering lights kept the valley softly lit. Across the valley, Torin saw the white froth of Frostridge

Falls burst over the top of the ridge and settle slowly at its steamy base.

Torin looked over at Wyla and smiled. "It's a beautiful sight, no doubt, but I bet the view would be even better from the top of Frostridge Falls."

Grimsa's eyes shot open and he stomped his foot. In an instant his face had gone as red as a hot iron and he threw his hands up in the air. "By the gods, not again! Skipping out on a feast at Fjellhall to clamber up that damned ridge is what got us in all this trouble in the first place."

Asa and Inga laughed out loud and Erik shook his head. Bari looped his thumbs through his belt and leaned back in a deep chuckle which made his beard wiggle. Wyla leaned on Torin and together they laughed deep in their bellies.

Grimsa looked around blankly for a moment, the crimson in his ears fading, then grinned a wicked smile and punched Torin in the shoulder. "Damn you, Torin Ten-Trees. I'm hungry! If Bryn is in the halls of the gods, he's got plenty to eat, so let's get to the feast." With that, the company walked back toward Gatewatch until they had reached the East Gate. Through the empty streets they laughed until they reached the stone steps that led up to the entrance of the great hall.

Torin threw open the doors of Fjellhall and let the warm air, rich with sweet and savoury smells, rush past him. Fjellhall was resplendent with green and silver banners which hung proudly on the high walls. Wreaths of wildflowers were strung up between the mighty wooden pillars and many juicy roasts smoked and sizzled over the roaring fire that ran down the middle of the hall. Grimsa and Wyla followed him with Bari, Asa, Inga, and Erik not far behind. All the way down, the twin tables had been laid full of dark-grained bread and head-sized wheels of white cheese. Along the center, on a fine-threaded green cloth, sat elaborate copper candlesticks topped with red wax candles that lit the feast with small yellow flames. Dried fruits and luscious berries filled shiny copper bowls while small oak barrels dripped with golden mead and brown ale.

When the doors slammed shut behind the company, the whole hall, full of Greycloaks, townsfolk, elders, and children, went silent. For a moment, all was still, save the for flicker of the hearth and the candle flames. Then, at the far end of the hall, Gavring stood from his place at the end of the bench and raised his mead horn. "Attendants, get this company food and drink! Clear a space here on the bench for our friends. Torin, Grimsa, Wyla, all of you, come over and sit with me."

All eyes followed the company to where they sat. Each of them was given not one but two horns full of sweet golden apple mead. Then Gavring raised his horn and all present raised their drinks along with him.

"To Torin Ten-Trees, Wyla White-Blaze, and Grim-Spear," said Gavring. The echo of his voice boomed through the lofty rafters.

"And to Bryn Foxfoot," said Torin.

Wyla nodded and sighed. "And to my father, Captain Calder."

"To those fallen," said Asa.

Inga nodded. "And to those still with us."

Lastly, Keymaster Signy stepped up onto the table and raised her mead horn. "Long live the Gatewatch!" All there toasted and cheered, a deafening roar of pride and mirth and sorrow. And so, the great feast began.

◇ ACKNOWLEDGEMENTS ◇

If you ever tell someone you'd like to write a book about trolls, and they look you in the eye to say it's a great idea, then marry them. I did. This book would surely have died a slow, torturous death in the recesses of my hard drive if not for Melinda's unwavering support, her keen editorial eye, and her persistent curiosity about 'what happens next'.

Some people skydive. Others jump onto angry bulls and try to ride them. Still others publish works of fiction by new Canadian authors. And so, I am extraordinarily grateful to two such people, Lewis Slawsky and Alex Wall from Crowsnest Books, who gave me a shot at doing what I have always wanted to do.

My (yet to be realized) international acclaim was probably not what inspired you to pick up this book; more likely, the cover caught your eye. For that I am indebted to the incomparable Helena Rosova who designed and painted the cover art by hand. Her distinctive artistic style, inspired by her studies of ancient Scandinavian artifacts, is an incredible addition to the aesthetic appeal of this book.

Just as humans are not born adults, books do fall out of the author's imagination as polished products. They begin in infancy as little more than an idea then grow and mature into their final forms. The first draft is, of course, its stage of puberty. Thank you to everyone who read through the first draft of The Gatewatch and saw its potential, specifically Lionel Chambers, Matthew Aasberg, and Kairi Gillingham.

To the community of Viking history enthusiasts, podcasters, and authors: your support and encouragement was only outmatched by your constant reassurance that I am not the only one in the universe obsessed with the Norse Myths. Especially to my earliest supporters in the Viking community, namely Siobhán Clark, Steven T. Dunn, and Ian Stuart Sharpe, *tusen takk*.

◇APPENDIX—THE LAY OF BEORIC◇

I. BEORIC LEAVES THE GRIM ISLES

It has been told of old
   Our fathers on Grim Isles
   Sailed stern ships with firm grip
   Salted water fearing
But one son named Beoric
   Bore little love for fish
   He scorned the barren sea
   And sought to twist his fate
So, sun-starved winter done,
   To his kinsfolk spoke he,
   "Why dredge this dreary sea
   While realms do empty lay?"
Laughter rocking rafters
   Rang long through drafty hall
   "Tell! Where lay these fair lands?"
   His father loud did mock
"There west where wicked kings
   Will glad make you their thrall?
   The sun-scored southland sands
   Or east o'er endless seas?"
Forth Beoric burst, "Nay, North!
   Bear witness to this oath:
   North shall I set my sail
   So come doom or glory!"

Some thought his words well-wrought
　　With Beoric oath did take
　　Then each their ship equipped
　　Eager for voyage North
Six were Beoric's brothers
　　Three did sail beside him
　　Three did grieve them leaving
　　Their father cursed him thus:
"So go then! Greet thy doom!
　　'Neath waves great fiends await.
　　Or meet on Northern shore
　　Some other loathsome fate."
Many men then trembled
　　His mother wailed and cried
　　But father bore for him
　　Not pity, fear, or pride

II. BEORIC SLAYS KOLKRABBA

Through great gales North they sailed
　　Oar and rudder thrashing
　　Rolling waves wide riding
　　Til, for rest, took shelter
But none there knew what lurked
　　Neath those writhing waters
　　Foul ancient foe below
　　Cruel Kolkrabba found them
Beast o'erturned brother's stern
　　Her slick arms Beoric saw
　　With white rage he did fight
　　Empty waves long slashing
Grey waves then went silent
　　Loud wailing Beoric cursed
　　Bent on violent vengeance
　　Against the vile sea-beast

So quick they took thick rope
  Prows then lashed together
  Tightening formed round ring
  To keep ships from rolling
Then longest hook he took
  Ram's head on it skewered
  Down ship-ring's center dipped
  All waited, weapons drawn
Long laid strong Kolkrabba
  Far below them lingering
  But hook sunk deep did keep
  That devil in their grip
"Haul heavy!" Beoric called
  Well hard his whole crew pulled
  Til tentacles slick spilled
  Upon their tethered decks
Hewing, black blood spewing
  Each boat's crew hacked slick arms
  Til Beoric killed the beast
  Upon his blood-soaked deck
Harbour guard hard vanquished
  Safe haven there they won
  On that beast they did feast
  And mourned their fallen kin

III. THE WOMAN IN THE WOOD

So landed Beoric's band
  Fair timber halls they built
  Those dark woods held good game
  Thin backs and arms grew thick
But night would bring wild things
  Which walked the woods and bogs
  Worse than the cursed wolves
  Trolls most foul and wicked

Yet heart did bid him dare
    Ever deeper wandering
    Strange words he heard and songs
    Full of grief and sorrow
"My sister were you mad
    To make so cruel a trade?
    To tear me from fair woods?
    Beast-bride of me you've made!"
On her silver streaming
    Moonlight saw her suffer
    So also Beoric saw
    Sitting, hiding, listening
"Hail pale stranger," said she,
    "Long I saw you coming.
    Now tell well—what are you:
    Wicked foe or hero?"
Beoric grunted bluntly,
    "Bear your own keen judgement:
    My crew slew Kolkrabba
    And many crafty trolls."
"Fortune fair this moon bears
    For sister mine conspires
    To dread Troll-King wed me
    So she might take these woods."
Grave word he gave and blade
    There onward her to guard
    So, like a spell, love fell
    Binding burning spirits
With Beoric she went quick
    Through dark and guarded woods
    Out of her sister's grip
    And on to Beoric's hall

IV. BEORIC AND FYRA

Wide-eyed many met her
   Fyra, foreign maiden
   Red hair like flaring fire
   Eyes green as frigid seas
Beoric's brother wondered
   "Who is this you have brought?
   Dark things I fear cling close
   To her tattered cloak-edge."
His words Beoric heard not
   For by her beauty snared
   His heart and mind were blind
   To his kin strong grumbling
Addressing all she called
   "Tell! Why this harsh abuse?
   Have I to one done harm
   Or spoke ill in this hall?"
"Betrayed by my sister,
   Lysa, bitter schemer,
   Heartless she would wed me
   To tyrant of these woods."
Those there rose up at once
   Their anger like red iron
   "What king could claim this wood
   Won with our crimson blood?"
"No word here heard," she asked,
   "Of horde-lord Gezbrukter?
   Waits he high in Gatewatch
   His promised bride to wed."
Then their thoughts were darkened
   Fear made their anger thick
   Beoric bore thoughts of war
   With boldness there he spoke

"This long have we held strong
　　Against the restless horde.
　　Let fear not steer us now,
　　Nay, let's slay this troll lord!"
Stern words stirred great courage
　　So gathered kin for war
　　Most of that mighty host
　　Would soon be seen no more

V. THE BATTLE OF GATEWATCH

Over rivers raging
　　Through rugged forest trod
　　Mighty host most valiant
　　All, for war, made ready
To Gatewatch through the pass
　　There in between pale peaks
　　Arrived to drive at last
　　All threat of trolls from home
Sunset done, dusk settled
　　Dark shapes stirred, rocks shifted
　　In gloom loomed figures great
　　Long grey silence breaking
Horrid Troll-King howling
　　All his dread host calling
　　Trolls like thunder rolling
　　Grim-faced rushed to maul them
Beoric he stood bravely
　　Gathering scattered brothers
　　Shield sisters yielding
　　Soon all round him rallied
Slashing, Bashing, Breaking
　　Battered white bone shattered
　　Screaming, red blood streaming
　　All night sharp steel edge sang

Dawn drew near to breaking
   Troll-King desperate fighting
   Saw first light bright shining
   All trolls turned to hard stone
Eyes by red rays blinded
   Troll-King reeling stumbled
   Quick leapt Beoric boldly
   Bearing wrathful death strokes
This he then swore sternly
   No troll shall thereafter
   Between pale peaks be seen
   If kin of his prove brave
Funeral pyres blazed with fire
   Burning fierce 'til nightfall
   Long did songs of sorrow
   Echo under starlight

VI. THE DEATH OF BEORIC

All back at Beoric's hall
   Awed by his daring deed
   There hailing him as king
   Thick bear cloak on him laid
So there Beoric the Bear
   Took Fyra as his bride
   Then watches three he set
   To honor those who died
Gatewatch in mountains grey
   Stagwatch the wood did guard
   Seawatch to brave salt waves
   All the realm strong keeping
And so that land secured
   For some time was held tame
   In such rich soil toiling
   Sons and daughters prospered

But one bitter winter
　　In Beoric's well-lit hall
　　A stranger came to stay
　　Black hair neath silver cloak
"So this is he," she said,
　　"Sly Kolkrabba's slayer,
　　Great Gezbrukter's killer.
　　With this glass I praise thee!"
Holding golden goblet
　　Ruby liquid glimmered
　　Up to lips cup lifted
　　Red stains lingered after
But Beoric was not quick
　　To sip her bitter wine
　　So said she, "Drink with me
　　Or say you are coward."
That draught brought Beoric's death
　　Loud bellowing he fell
　　Fast fleeing, cloak she shed
　　Lysa, Fyra's sister
Long sang they mourning songs
　　With grief and wrath so wild
　　Yet all had this small hope
　　Fyra held Beoric's child

◇ AUTHOR BIO ◇

JOSHUA GILLINGHAM is a Canadian author from the scenic city of Nanaimo, BC. There he enjoys life with his adventurous spouse and their two very unadventurous cats. The Gatewatch, his debut novel, was born of his unremitted fascination with Norse Myths and Icelandic Sagas. Joshua's lyrical maritime ballad *The Queen of the Rose Marie* was selected for the Short Story Dispenser Project hosted by Short Édition and his award-winning essay *Becoming a Resilient Writer* has been featured in WordWorks Magazine by the Federation of BC Writers. When he is not hunched over his laptop, sipping coffee, and tapping frantically at the keyboard, Joshua performs Irish and Maritime music with The Ugly Mugs and designs Viking-themed board games for Little Hammer Games.

Find more at www.joshuagillingham.ca
or on Twitter – @JoshMGillingham

◇ BOOK CLUB QUESTIONS ◇

1. What was your overall impression of The Gatewatch? How did it make you feel?

2. What was your favorite quote or scene?

3. If you could sit down and sip a cup of mead with one character from the book, then who would it be?

4. Which character did you relate to most throughout the story and why?

5. Which character did you find most annoying or irritating?

6. How did the ending sit with you? What sort of feeling were you left with as you read the last line?

7. What would you have challenged Wyla to in Chapter 4: Mead & Mayhem?

8. Did you solve any of Torin's riddles in before you read the answers during Chapter 9: A Duel of Riddles? If so, which ones?

9. What were your feelings about the *nidavel* after Chapter 11: Secrets at Supper? Would you have trusted the *nidavel* if you were Torin?

10. Would you have gone after Wyla when she ran off in Chapter 13: Scorched Beards? Why or why not?

11. If you could ask Joshua Gillingham a question about The Gatewatch then what would it be?

◇ BOOK CLUB CHALLENGES ◇

1. Find a Norwegian or Icelandic recipe online and make it for your book club meeting.

2. Have each of your members write their own verse in the form described in the Preface.

3. Have each of your members write their own riddle. Bonus points if it rhymes!

SNEAK PEEK — THE EVERSPRING (SEQUEL TO THE GATEWATCH)

◇ CHAPTER 1: AN OATH FULFILLED ◇

A GRIM FIGURE sat alone at the end of a long wooden bench in an empty hall lit by nothing but crackling embers. The scent of burning cedar was sharp in his nose and smoke stung his eyes. The light of the fire barely reached the rafters that towered high over his head. There, in dim flickering shadows, the great wooden beams hovered over him like a row of enormous black ravens.

He sighed and swirled what little mead was left in his drinking horn. Some of the sweet frothy liquid sloshed over the rim and ran into his beard as he tilted the cup back to slurp the last mouthful. With a frown, he eyed the empty horn for a moment then tossed it over his shoulder. He wiped his face on the sleeve of his tunic as it skittered across the stone floor. Over the past winter his beard had grown long and now it nearly touched his chest. He stroked it slowly and let his gaze settle again on the dying fire.

At the far end of the hall the doors flew open. The embers lit up all along the hearth just as the lone figure felt a brisk rush of fresh air blow past his face. A large man stumbled into the room and braced himself against the other end of the long table. Through the darkness, he could see the figure blink and squint into the shadows.

A gruff voice called out. "Torin? By the gods, drinking without me?"

Torin dropped his head down to the table and let his arms sprawl out across the rough cedar planks. "Go away, Grimsa."

Torin heard the creak of the iron door hinges again as another entered the hall.

"Is anyone here, Grimsa?"

Torin recognized the voice. It was Signa, Keymaster Signy's daughter. Signy held the key to that mighty hall in which Torin sat, and indeed it was rare to find that she was not there. However, tonight was the spring solstice and, like nearly every other soul in Gatewatch, she would be out in Stonering Keep enjoying herself at the festival.

"Look who I found!" said Grimsa. "Torin Ten-Trees drinking all by himself in Fjellhall."

Signa peered into the darkness. "Torin? What are you doing here?"

Torin lifted his head off the table and winced at the sharp daylight coming in through the door. "What does it look like? Drinking. What are you two doing here?"

Grimsa had stepped closer and now Torin saw a blush rush over the huge man's face. Signa grinned and grabbed Grimsa's arm. "Just a bit of privacy. The rest is none of your business. Did you know that Grimsa is going to ask my mother tonight at the festival?" Signa held up her left hand so that it caught a streak of sunlight. On her finger glimmered a ring, polished silver inset with sparkling emeralds. "Green emeralds," she said, "My favorite color. It reminds me of glittering dew on fresh spring grass."

Grimsa blushed a darker hue of red, nearly purple, and smiled ear to ear. Torin had wondered if Grimsa would work up the courage to ask Keymaster Signy for her daughter's hand in marriage by the Spring Festival. Apparently, he had.

The next day, after the festival, all the Gatewatch recruits that had arrived two years earlier, including Torin and Grimsa, would be released from their oath of duty. Most recruits returned home to the life and family they had known before. A select few would be offered Greycloaks which meant a permanent place among the veteran troll hunters of Gatewatch. Grimsa had always been keen on achieving the latter, even more now that his engagement might rest on it.

Signa hopped up on the bench and kissed Grimsa. "Well, so much for privacy. I'll see you two at the festival." With that, she danced out of the hall, twirling to the beat of a tune inside her head.

Torin pushed himself up off the bench and grinned. "That's quite a ring. She seems happy. So do you."

Grimsa cleared his throat, his ears still as red as wild cherries. "A few months back I sent word to Bari to bring it all the way from Myrkheim."

"Bari's here?"

"He just arrived. I didn't know he would bring it himself!"

Torin nodded and smiled. In his mind, he could still see Myrkheim, the underground dwelling of the dwarves, or *nidavel* as they called themselves. The colossal underground city, with its strange hexagonal columns locked together like a puzzle, was still as clear in his mind as the day he had first seen it. That was a long time ago, nearly two years now. He thought of the mysterious Mastersmith, and Bari's Uncle Brok who had hosted them. Then the smile fell from Torin's face and his eyes softened. "So, you are going to stay?"

Grimsa shuffled his feet and stared at the long bed of embers in the hearth that ran down the middle of the hall. "What would I do if I went back? Start a farm? Become a trader? I don't have the head for that sort of thing. But I can slay trolls. And Signa is here." Grimsa let a quiet moment pass then shifted his weight and crossed his arms. "You?"

Torin shook his head and sighed. "I don't know. I guess that's why I'm drinking here in Fjellhall by myself instead of with everyone else at the Spring Festival."

Grimsa scooped up two horns from the floor and trudged over to where Torin sat. He tilted the nearly empty mead barrel at the end of the table to fill them both and sat down. The bench creaked as Grimsa let his weight rest on it. He passed one of the horns to Torin then sipped his own.

Torin stared down into the mead horn and frowned. "What if I stayed? What if I didn't go back to Ten-Tree Hall and instead lived the rest of my life here with you and Signa, with Wyla and Gavring, with Keymaster Signy and all the others?"

Grimsa shrugged. "You could. Besides, your father could remarry. He could have another child."

Torin shook his head. "No, he is old. And he won't remarry. He told me once that he never will."

"Couldn't his nephew, your cousin, Varik, take his seat in Ten-Tree Hall?"

"It would break my father's heart. Besides, Varik is a spineless, conniving weasel. The hall would go to ruin."

"What does Wyla think?"

Torin took a big swig of mead then wiped the froth off on his shoulder. "I'm not sure. She's not speaking to me right now."

Grimsa chuckled as he stood to refill his horn with the last bit of mead in the barrel. "Is she still sore about losing that game of King's Table last week?"

"No, no, it's not that. It's because I haven't decided whether or not to stay." Torin sighed and his shoulders drooped down. "She said that if I am leaving, she doesn't have another word to say to me anyways."

Grimsa sat down again and slammed the table with the palm of his free hand. "Well, damn the rest of them. What do you want to do?"

Torin swirled his mead a moment more before he answered. "I'd like to dig up Ten-Tree Hall plank by plank and move it up here to Gatewatch."

The huge man grinned wide. "Imagine that. You could rebuild it up valley, maybe right beside Frostridge Falls. What a view you would have."

Torin and Grimsa lingered a moment more over the mead, then toasted the Gatewatch with their last swigs. In some ways Torin felt as if he had just arrived; in other ways he felt he had always been a troll hunter patrolling the wild woods beyond the rugged town of Gatewatch. Outside the hall they heard voices and the shuffle of feet as more of the townsfolk made their way to Stonering Keep for the festival. Torin looked at Grimsa and the hulking man gave one firm nod. Together they walked out of the hall toward the Spring Festival, arms over each other's shoulders, partly as a sign of brotherhood, but mostly for balance.